D0711901

The Messiah Secret

"An entertaining hunt-and-chase thriller that races from the English countryside to a hidden valley in the Middle East . . . appealing and clever protagonists coupled with intriguing history." —*Publishers Weekly*

"A superbly crafted novel which follows in the footsteps of *The Da Vinci Code*. . . . However, *The Messiah Secret* stands alone among its contemporaries for one simple reason. It breaks new ground . . . a tightly worded, sharply written thriller." —CrimeSquad.com

"Exciting and gripping . . . [Becker's] intelligent mixture of fact with fiction really . . . gets your adrenaline racing." —Euro Crime

THE LOST TESTAMENT

JAMES BECKER

A SIGNET BOOK

SIGNET
Published by the Penguin Group
Penguin Group (USA) LLC, 375 Hudson Street,
New York, New York 10014

USA | Canada | UK | Ireland | Australia | New Zealand | India | South Africa | China
penguin.com
A Penguin Random House Company

Published by Signet, an imprint of New American Library, a division of Penguin
Group (USA) LLC. Previously published in a Transworld Publishers edition.
For further information contact Transworld Publishers, a division of Penguin
Random House, Ltd., 61–63 Uxbridge Road, London W5 5SA England.

First Signet Printing, December 2013

Ⓟ REGISTERED TRADEMARK—MARCA REGISTRADA

ISBN 978-0-451-46645-7

Printed in the United States of America
10 9 8 7 6 5 4 3 2 1

To Sally, as always

ACKNOWLEDGMENTS

Any novel is a collaborative effort, and I've been very fortunate to have, in Katy Loftus, a keen and enthusiastic—but above all very competent and personable—young editor who has done so much to shape this book. For her, and for the rest of the highly motivated team at Transworld out in darkest Ealing, I'm very grateful. Let's have lunch again, and soon. And I obviously can't forget my wonderful agent and good friend, Luigi Bonomi, who has always done his best to consistently and brilliantly shape my career as an author. To him, and Ajda and Alison and everyone else at LBA, my heartfelt thanks. Onwards and upwards!

This book is a work of fiction, but several of the incidents described are founded on real events, including the robbery that acts as the catalyst for the story. The criminal organization described is also real, and the revelation at the end has its basis in the historical record.

PROLOGUE

Byzantium

AD 325

"Bring him forward."

Two trusted soldiers from the emperor's personal body-guard saluted their master, then turned and strode out of the temporary council chamber, each step they took accompanied by the metallic clattering of their armor and weapons.

Moments later, the two soldiers reappeared, a nervous-looking civilian now walking between them. They continued to the very end of the chamber, where Flavius Valerius Aurelius Constantinus Augustus, accepted only the previous September as the fifty-seventh emperor of the entire Roman Empire, sat flanked by a coterie of advisors.

"So, Flavius, what did you discover?" the emperor asked.

The civilian looked even more nervous at that moment, and Constantine had a sudden realization that he wasn't simply overawed by being in the presence of the most powerful man in the world. Flavius had been in his employ for years, and had spoken with him countless times. There had to be something else that was disturbing him, and if Flavius was worried, then that was a real cause for concern.

Before the man could speak, Constantine raised his hand, demanding silence, then glanced at his advisors.

"This is a private matter," he said. "Kindly leave us."

Without a word, the half a dozen or so officials standing on both sides of the throne filed out of the chamber, followed by the servants and other retainers stationed elsewhere in the room. Constantine then instructed the two soldiers to retire to the opposite end of the chamber, out of earshot, but ordered the guard commander, the officer in charge of his personal bodyguard, to remain close beside him. Constantine was far too cautious a man to allow himself to be left entirely alone with anyone, no matter how apparently trustworthy and loyal, and Marcellus had proved his loyalty beyond doubt on numerous occasions.

"It is not as we had hoped, Our Lord," Flavius began. "I have seen the original document, and the claims made in it are powerful and very damaging."

Constantine gestured, and the guard commander stepped forward, took the document Flavius was offering and handed it to his master. The emperor unrolled the parchment and read the Latin text written on it. Then he read it again.

Constantine was not a scholar, but he had no doubt of the authenticity of what he was holding. The report he had just read was, he was quite certain, both authentic and accurate. And that posed a major problem for him, and for his empire.

"Where did you find this?" he asked.

"It was in Rome," the man replied. "I walked into the archives and searched through the documentation relating to Cohors I Sagittariorum until I found it. Then I brought it to you."

For perhaps two minutes the emperor remained silent, staring at the parchment in his hand, reading and rereading the words, his acute political mind pondering the direct implications of the document, and how best to use it to his own advantage. From the first, he'd realized that the matter he'd sent Flavius to investigate posed an indirect—but still a potent—threat to him, and would call his leadership and political judgment into serious question if it ever came to light. But it was also clear that without the document he had just been handed there was no direct proof of certain statements made by a notorious troublemaker almost one and a half centuries earlier. He held the key to the matter—held the single surviving item of undeniable proof without which the story was nothing more than an unsupported allegation in his own hands. And the only other person who knew anything about it was Flavius himself.

In fact, Constantine suddenly realized, the document was less of a threat to him than a potent weapon he could use to his own advantage. He was starting to distrust the ambitions of the leader of an emerging religious movement that was beginning to spread its influence across the empire. But he could bring that group to heel anytime he chose, simply by threatening to reveal what this document stated.

And that left only one other matter to be taken care of; and the emperor had made his preparations for this step as well.

Constantine gestured to the guard commander, who took a couple of steps forward and then stood waiting, his right hand resting on the hilt of his *gladius*. Behind Flavius, the two other soldiers of the bodyguard strode swiftly into position, standing a few feet behind the civilian.

"I thank you for your diligent efforts on my behalf, Flavius, in this matter as in many others over the years," Constantine said, "and I apologize for the necessity of what I now have to do."

"I don't understand." Flavius stared at the emperor, the truth dawning and a look of fear spreading across his face.

With another gesture, the two soldiers stepped forward, seized Flavius by the arms and held him firmly in place.

"I dare not risk anything of this matter becoming known. I know you would not willingly divulge what you have learned, but I cannot take any chances. I'm sorry, but this has to end now, my old friend. I bid you farewell."

"No, no, Our Lord, I beg of you. Please, not this."

Constantine ignored Flavius's agonized pleas and turned to the guard commander.

"One blow, so he doesn't suffer."

Marcellus nodded, drew his sword and stepped directly in front of Flavius.

"Keep a firm grip on his arms," he ordered, as the doomed man struggled ineffectually in the steady grasp of the two soldiers.

The guard commander drew back his right arm and with a single and massively powerful blow drove his sword right through Flavius's body, the pommel slamming into the man's ribs as the point of the blade burst out of his back in a spray of blood.

For a second or two, Flavius just stared ahead, his eyes wide, his mouth open in a soundless scream of unbearable agony. Then a gout of blood poured out of his mouth and his head fell forward.

Marcellus let go of his weapon and stepped back.

"Drop him there," he ordered, and the two soldiers lowered the limp body of the dead man to the stone floor of the chamber.

Then Marcellus took a dagger from inside his tunic and handed it to one of the soldiers.

"Cut me," he ordered, "in my left shoulder. Twice. Not too deep."

Obediently, the soldier ran the lethally sharp blade across Marcellus's left upper arm, making two cuts that immediately started to bleed copiously. The man didn't even flinch.

"Now drop the dagger beside him," he went on, and then turned around to face Constantine.

"As you ordered, Our Lord," he said.

"Excellent," the emperor purred. "Now summon help."

When the other soldiers and advisors ran back into the council chamber, the scene spoke for itself. The treacherous Flavius, so long a trusted emissary of the emperor, had suddenly changed his allegiance and drawn a dagger to make a cowardly attack upon the ruler of the empire. An attack barely foiled by the selfless heroism of Marcellus, himself badly injured in the assault.

As the bloody body of the "traitor" was dragged out of the room, and Constantine was congratulated on his lucky escape from death, nobody thought to ask what had become of the parchment Flavius had been carrying when he had entered the chamber.

That was the first time in over three hundred years that blood had been spilled because of that single sheet of parchment, but it was destined not to be the last.

1

"Stop! I heard something."

Instantly both figures froze into immobility beside the wall. They could almost have been twins, though they were unrelated, both slimly built men of a little below average height, wearing black close-fitting clothing and dark-colored climbing shoes. Even their hair was black, and they had the typically swarthy complexion of people who live around the Mediterranean.

Neither man had begun his working life as a professional thief. They had both worked as members of an acrobatic troupe in a traveling circus, honing their climbing skills to a high degree of perfection. But after retiring they'd quickly acquired a reputation in certain circles in Italy: these men could be relied upon to get into the most heavily protected of buildings, complete the job they had been hired to do, and keep their mouths shut afterward.

And that was precisely why they were then in the midst

of Vatican City, carrying out perhaps the most dangerous commission they had ever been given.

For a minute, the men remained immobile, two dark and silent shadows against the light-colored stone of the wall, listening intently. Then Stefan took a half step closer to his companion and murmured in his ear.

"What did you hear?"

"It sounded like a stone falling, something like that. Are you sure there are only two guards on duty tonight?"

"That's what we've been told: one two-man patrol, nothing more; and they should be a long way from where we are right now. I've checked the patrol route, and the gardens are not a high priority."

"I hope you're right. I suppose we'll find out soon enough. Let's go."

Dragan grinned at him, his teeth a white slash in the darkness. Then he opened the black fabric rucksack at his feet, extracted a metal grappling hook, the points and shaft coated in thick rubber to muffle any noise, and seized the rope about two feet from the end where it was attached to the hook. He whirled the hook in a circle half a dozen times, then released it. Both men watched critically as the hook sailed up into the air and then vanished over the top of the wall. There was a muffled clunk as the hook came to rest somewhere out of sight.

Cautiously, Dragan reeled it in, pulling the rope toward him and down the wall hand over fist. Suddenly the rope went taut, and he took a step backward and peered up toward the top of the wall.

"I think I can see it," he whispered. "Just check it out, will you?"

Stefan reached into his pocket and took out a small but powerful torch, black tape placed in a crisscross pattern over the lens to cut down the amount of light that would be emitted. When he switched it on the narrow beam clearly showed two of the four hooks jutting out over the top of the wall.

"That looks secure to me," he said quietly. "Do you want to go first?"

"Yes."

Dragan picked up his rucksack, closed the flap and slung it over his shoulders. Then he seized the rope with both hands and climbed up it with as little difficulty as if he'd been ascending a flight of stairs. At the top of the wall, he paused for a moment to check the positioning of the grappling hook, then gestured for his companion to join him.

Moments later, both men were in position, sitting astride the wall as they repositioned the hook so that they could descend into the gardens that stretched out before them. Once they were down at ground level again, this time on the inside, Dragan flicked the rope expertly to dislodge it. The rope represented their escape route, and they dared not leave it in position in case the roving patrol passed by the wall and noticed it dangling there. As soon as the hook fell to the ground, he picked it up, coiled the rope and replaced it in his rucksack.

"That was the easy bit," he said. "Now we have to do a bit of proper climbing."

Neither man had set foot inside the Vatican before, but they moved with unerring certainty. Both of them had spent the previous two weeks studying detailed plans of the Holy See, and they now knew their way around with as much familiarity as if they'd been regular visitors.

Their objective was the Apostolic Library, located off the Belvedere Courtyard underneath the Apostolic Palace, the Pope's official residence. The library had been founded in 1420 by Pope Nicholas V with an initial endowment of some nine thousand books, but was later incorporated into the Vatican Museum and by 1965 it contained more than a quarter of a million volumes.

The two men couldn't enter the building at ground level—that would be impossible to do undetected—so they would be taking a very different route to get inside. The Stradone dei Giardini runs along the side of the Belvedere Courtyard, between the line of linked buildings and the gardens to the west, and that would be where they would make their entrance. A couple of minutes later the two men stopped near the Fountain of the Sacrament to make absolutely sure they were unobserved before they crossed over to the side of the building.

"I don't see or hear anything."

"Neither do I. Let's go."

The two dark shapes, deeper black shadows in the blackness of the night, flitted silently across the roadway, then crouched down beside the wall of the building, again checking in all directions. The next few minutes would be the most crucial of the entire operation, and if they were spotted neither man was in any doubt about what would happen to them.

"Still clear," Stefan said.

Dragan nodded, and then both men took a step back and stared upward at the vertical wall that formed one side of the building. Ten feet away from where they were standing, a water pipe ran all the way down the wall from the gutters at the edge of the roof high above them. The pipe was in excellent condition—the Vatican, as one of the richest organizations in the world, didn't stint on the maintenance costs of its buildings—and within seconds the dark shape of one of the two men, a coil of rope looped around his shoulders, was already a dozen feet off the ground and climbing swiftly up toward the roof.

They didn't need to climb all the way up. Near the top of the building, a balcony beckoned, though it was a few meters from where the water pipe ran down the wall. But just below the balcony was a narrow ledge, barely wide enough for a human foot, and that would provide the means of access they needed.

When he got almost opposite the balcony, about thirty feet above the ground, Dragan stopped to catch his breath—he wasn't as young, or as fit, as he used to be—locking his hands around the back of the water pipe while his climbing shoes rested on one of the junctions. Then he stretched out his right foot, the thin sole allowing him to test his foothold on the ledge before he trusted it with his full weight.

It felt solid, and after a couple of seconds he released his grip on the pipe and flattened himself against the wall as he began edging his way along the ledge. When he neared the balcony, he reached up, stretching as high as he could go, until his hand closed around the carved stone that formed the top of the wall around it. He took a firm grip, then pulled himself up and onto the balcony itself.

Moments later, he lowered the climbing rope he'd been carrying and waited while his companion attached their two rucksacks to the end of it. Then he hauled them up to the balcony and waited a couple of minutes for Stefan to follow in his footsteps and climb up the pipe.

At the back of the balcony was a set of double doors flanked by two windows, all of which were locked, a fact that surprised neither man. They had expected no less, but glass is fragile, and once they were satisfied that the roving patrol they'd been told about was nowhere in sight, the curved end of a crowbar swiftly disposed of one of the panes of glass in the door, and within a minute both men were standing inside the building, the door closed again behind them.

"This way."

They walked cautiously out of the chamber accessed by the balcony and stood for a moment in the passageway outside, where a single dim light was burning. It provided just enough illumination for them both to study the plan they had been given. Then they moved on, heading for one very specific part of the building.

"The Sistine Hall," Dragan murmured a few minutes later, pointing at the sign beside the doorway. "That's it."

None of the interior doors in the building appeared to be locked, the staff presumably believing that the external doors offered sufficient deterrent to thieves, and as soon as both men were inside the room, they split up and began their search.

By any standards, they were surrounded by treasures: glass cases containing ancient manuscripts and other relics, intermittently illuminated by the narrow beams of their torches. In one case lay an enormously valuable fifth-century New Testament written in Greek. In another, documents signed by Martin Luther. In yet others were a collection of love letters sent by King Henry VIII to Anne Boleyn, an essay written by Galileo to the Cardinal who later became Pope Urban VIII, a letter from the painter Raphaello, and another letter, this one sent by Michelangelo to the Superintendent of St. Peter's. But they barely glanced at any of these priceless exhibits. They were looking for two very specific objects, and in a couple of minutes they had found them both.

"Over here."

The two men stood side by side looking down at one particular case.

"That's it?" Stefan said, comparing what was written

on the sheet of paper in his hand with what they were looking at inside the glass case.

"Yes," his companion agreed. "In fact, that's both of them."

The glass on the locked display case wasn't armored in any way and offered no more resistance to the crowbar than the pane of glass on the balcony door.

"These other old books and stuff have got to be worth something."

"More than you or I could ever earn in a dozen life-times," Dragan said, "but you know the way we work. We do what we're paid to do and nothing else." He opened up the neck of his rucksack while his companion lifted out the two objects they had been told to steal, and laid them carefully inside it.

As they walked down the corridor between the Hall and the Borgia Apartment the younger thief grabbed the other's sleeve and gestured toward a glass case.

"Look at this," he whispered. "It's gold, a crown of gold."

"Yes, but—"

Before he could finish his sentence, Stefan had already lifted his crowbar and cracked the glass that covered the ancient relic.

"What are you doing?"

"Look, I know what you said, and you're right. But this is gold. We can have it melted down, so it'll be un-traceable. We're only ever going to get an opportunity like this once."

Without waiting for a reply, Stefan plucked the gold crown out of the shattered display case and placed it in his rucksack. Almost as an afterthought, he also picked up a small and highly decorated copper and enamel box and took that as well.

*   *   *

"Put those on now, and don't take them off until I tell you."

The order was unsurprising. They had encountered their employer only twice before, and each time they had been blindfolded and driven some way outside Rome to a large and clearly expensive villa, and the entire time they'd been in the building the man himself had been out of sight behind a screen, so they had no idea who he was, except that he probably wasn't Italian, because his instructions had been relayed through an interpreter.

This time, the journey to the villa took about forty minutes and, after removing their hoods, they were led through to the same room they had been in previously. There, an arrangement of screens had been placed at one end, and a table positioned more or less in the center of the room, the man they believed to be an interpreter standing beside it.

"Do you have them?" the man asked.

By way of answer, Stefan opened his rucksack, lifted out the two objects they had been told to steal and placed them on the table.

The interpreter smiled for the first time since they had seen him.

"Excellent," he purred. "You have done well. Now leave the room while my employer inspects these two relics."

Stefan reached out his hand to pick up the rucksack, but the interpreter shook his head.

"You can leave that here. My employer will not take long."

The two men glanced at each other, then shrugged and left the room as they'd been told. They had no option but to comply: the presence of two tall and heavily built men standing by the door ensured that. They were ushered into a small anteroom by one of these two guards, who then took up a position in the open doorway.

But the interpreter had been right. Less than ten minutes after they'd been told to leave, the two men were called back inside the room. The scene appeared to be exactly as it had been when they'd left, albeit with three small changes: in addition to the two literary manuscripts they'd been told to steal, the golden crown and the enamel box were also placed on the table—their rucksacks had clearly been searched—as well as a single piece of brown parchment.

The interpreter stared at the two men in a disapproving fashion.

"The instructions we gave you, the most specific instructions issued by my employer, were extremely simple. He wished you to steal these two manuscripts"—he pointed at the two leather-bound objects on the table— "the work of the Italian poets Petrarch and Torquato Tasso, and nothing else. Yet you apparently saw fit to take this crown and box of mementos too. Why was that?"

For a moment, neither man replied. Then Dragan took a half step forward and pointed at the crown.

"It was my decision," he said. "It was obvious that the theft would be discovered almost immediately, and I thought it might help to muddy the waters slightly if we picked up another couple of items from the library while we were there, to disguise the real objective of the robbery."

That was nothing like what had actually happened, but as a spur-of-the-moment improvization, he thought it was quite inventive, and almost believable.

The interpreter stared across the table, his eyes moving from one man to the other; then he nodded, turned and disappeared behind the screens at the far end of the room.

The sound of muffled voices could be heard. After about half a minute, he returned.

"We applaud your quick thinking, though my employer does not believe you for a moment. You took the other two objects, intending to keep them for yourselves. However, that is not important because you did recover what you were paid to find. Now we have one other question for you." The interpreter pointed at the single sheet of parchment lying by itself on the table. "What is that?" he asked.

The two men stared at the object.

"I've no idea," Dragan replied. "I've never seen it before. We picked up the two sets of manuscripts from the display case and took nothing else from that room."

"That was at the back of the Tasso collection, but it is obviously not a part of it."

Dragan shrugged. "Sorry. I've no idea."

"Very well. You have already received half of the agreed fee, and later today we will pay you the remainder, once you have completed one further task for us."

"That was not a part of our arrangement," Dragan replied. "We were to carry out the theft, deliver the goods to you and then we were to be paid."

"But you've already broken your part of the agreement by stealing these two other items. My employer is a fair man, and he has agreed you may retain the enamel box and the additional sheet of parchment and try to sell them if you wish. Call it a bonus. And the additional task we want you to perform is very, very simple, but we will be watching you to make sure that you complete it exactly as we order. You are to take the crown and the two manuscripts, place them in a secure metal container we will provide and then throw them away at the precise time and place that we tell you."

"What? I don't understand."

"You don't need to. You just need to do what we ask."

Five days later, the man who had organized and paid for the apparently pointless burglary in the Vatican left Italy in his chauffeur-driven car. Hidden in a secret pocket in one of his sets of matching suitcases were the two original manuscripts, handwritten by Petrarch and Tasso, which he would store securely in his extensive collection of ancient relics as soon as he got back home.

In the meantime, from what he'd been able to gather from the newspaper reports in Italy, Vatican officials appeared quite satisfied that the first-class forgeries he'd commissioned the previous year were actually the real thing, dumped by amateur burglars who got cold feet. All in all, and despite the somewhat unexpected greed of the two burglars he'd employed, it had been one of his most successful collecting expeditions.

2

Vatican City, Rome

14 April 2010

Adolfo Gianni was dying, and he knew it.

The doctor's diagnosis of terminal cancer of the lungs had not been entirely unexpected. He'd been coughing for years, and recently his chronic shortage of breath had got significantly worse. He'd put it down to old age, to the body simply getting less able to cope with the rigors of day-to-day life, but when he'd noticed blood on his handkerchief after one particularly violent bout of coughing, he'd guessed the worst.

He remembered the consultation a few days later very clearly. When he'd heard the diagnosis, he'd immediately remarked to the doctor that it was extremely unfair.

"I've never smoked a cigarette in my life," Gianni had said, his voice resigned and flat, "or even associated with people who enjoy an addiction to tobacco."

"That's probably the commonest cause of lung cancer," the doctor had replied, "but there could be a number of other reasons for the disease taking hold. Several chemicals and foods have been identified as possible carcinogens, and some recent research has even suggested that burnt diesel fuel could also be a cause. And Rome traffic has always been heavy. Your illness may simply be a product of your environment, nothing more."

"What about treatment?" Gianni had asked.

The suddenly grave expression on the doctor's face would, the old cleric knew, remain etched on his memory until the very end, which he guessed would be rather sooner than he had hoped.

"I am terribly sorry to have to tell you that there really is almost nothing we can do for you. You are not in the best of health generally, quite apart from the cancer, and at your age I don't believe that an operation would be possible or advisable. And," the doctor had continued, "even if such a surgical procedure could be performed, I have little hope that doing so would achieve very much. As far as I can tell, the cancer is simply too far advanced for that. We can, of course, control the pain you will soon start to experience but, to be perfectly frank with you, that is about all we can do."

For a few moments Gianni hadn't responded, his brain reluctantly processing the quietly clinical death sentence that had just been pronounced. And then he had asked the inevitable question.

"How long have I got left?"

Again the doctor's face had clouded.

"I can only give you my best guess. Perhaps six months, perhaps less. Perhaps a lot less. It will all depend upon how aggressive the cancer is, on how quickly it invades all the tissues of your lungs. The truth is that I really don't know, and I'm certain that no doctor would be able to give you a definitive answer. But at least I'm sure that you will have ample time to make your peace with God."

Gianni had smiled slightly at that.

"I made my peace with God a very long time ago," he had replied, "though I still have one more task I must complete before the end."

Actually, the doctor had been somewhat optimistic. Within six weeks Gianni had been forced to take to his bed in his tiny room in Vatican City, a bed that he knew he would never again leave.

And now, as he slipped in and out of consciousness while the opiates did their work and eased the burning in his chest, reducing it to a dull but persistent ache, he guessed that the end was near. But he still had one more duty to discharge before he finally stood before his maker.

Adolfo Gianni waved away the nun who had been adjusting the flow of painkilling drugs through the intravenous line attached to his left arm, and gestured feebly to the other man, a slim and dark-haired young priest wearing rimless spectacles, who was standing uncomfortably against the wall of the room, mounting the death watch.

"Yes, Father," the man murmured, stepping forward immediately and looking down at the frail, thin-faced man, his head outlined by a virtual halo of white hair, who lay on the bed, his body markedly and almost daily diminished by the disease which was steadily killing him. "Do you wish me to administer the *viaticum* now?"

Despite the pain in his chest, a clutching tightness that made breathing difficult and any kind of strenuous movement completely impossible, Gianni summoned a weak smile from somewhere.

"Not quite yet, Francis. I can delay the last rites for a little while longer, I believe. No, I must see Father Morini."

3

Until his terminal illness had forced him to cease work within the Vatican, Adolfo Gianni had been the Prefect in charge of the Secret Archives, and of the staff of priests appointed to work there. The archives weren't a collection of dusty books and manuscripts ranged on shelves in a darkened room, but were bright and busy most of the time, people coming and going throughout the hours of daylight, and often late into the evening as well.

When it became clear that Father Gianni would not be able to continue with his work, another very senior cleric, Father Antonio Morini, had been appointed in his place, and had been spending most of his time in the archive ever since, improving his knowledge of the way the system worked and familiarizing himself with his new employment. Francis Gregory knew exactly where he would find his new superior.

He knocked twice on the Prefect's door, waited a few seconds, then opened it and stepped into the office.

The man sitting behind the desk was heavily built, his broad shoulders straining at the fabric of his habit, with a ruddy, round face, topped by a thatch of graying hair.

He looked more like a farmer than a senior Vatican official.

Morini looked up as the young man entered his office and gave him a slight sad smile.

"Has he finally slipped away?" he asked.

Gregory shook his head.

"Not yet, Father, but I think the end is very near. I offered him the *viaticum*, but he declined, at least for the moment. Instead, he asked me—in fact, he told me—to summon you to his bedside."

"Perhaps he wants me to personally administer the last rites to him?" Morini wondered.

Again Gregory shook his head.

"Possibly, but I think it's something else, something that he wants to talk to you about."

Morini nodded, glanced at the papers covering the desk in front of him, and then stood up.

"I could do without the interruption, but of course in these sad circumstances I will speak with Father Gianni if that is his wish."

Morini closed and then locked the door of his office—some of the documents he had been studying were fairly sensitive and, even within the Vatican, curious eyes were to be discouraged—and the two clerics strode away down the corridor.

A few minutes later, Gregory opened the door to Gianni's room and stood to one side as Father Morini stepped into the chamber. The dying cleric's eyes were closed and he did not appear to have moved, but Gregory noticed that there were flecks of blood around his mouth that had not been there before. The medically trained nun was still in attendance, and as they entered she was again altering the dosage of the opiates the old man was receiving. Seeing Morini, she dipped her head in respectful salute and retreated to sit on a chair in one corner.

Morini crossed the short distance to the head of the single bed and looked down. He reached out and took hold of Gianni's right hand and applied gentle pressure.

The dying man opened his eyes and looked up, summoning a weak smile.

"Thank you for coming, Antonio," he said.

Then he glanced around the room and noticed the two other people in attendance there. He gestured to Morini to bend forward slightly and murmured into his ear.

"You must be my confessor, Antonio, and what I have to tell you is for your ears alone," he muttered. "Please ask the others to leave the room."

Morini nodded. Like every other Roman Catholic priest, he fully appreciated the sanctity of the confessional.

"The Father would like me to take his confession," he said, turning to Gregory. "Can you and the Sister please give us a few minutes alone?"

When the door closed behind Gregory and the nun, Morini again turned to face the old man, and knelt down beside the bed so that his head was as close as possible to Gianni's.

"We are quite alone now, my old friend—just you and me and the heavenly Father. I will gladly hear your confession and grant absolution."

Gianni nodded, the movement of his head barely perceptible.

But what he said next was not at all what Morini had expected.

Gianni clutched the younger man's hand with a grip that was surprisingly firm and began to speak in a low and weak voice.

"I am not confessing my sins, Antonio. I attended to that matter regarding my departure from this world some two weeks ago. I didn't believe I could commit any important sins just by lying here, except perhaps being guilty of sloth."

Morini smiled at the feeble joke.

"So how can I help you?" he asked.

"What I have to tell you is a confession of sorts, I suppose, but it is far from personal, and involves my professional position here in the Vatican hierarchy, a position that you now occupy. I have some important information to impart to you, and you must solemnly swear never to share what I have to say with anyone else, inside or outside the Vatican."

Gianni sank backward onto his pillow. The effort of speaking at all was clearly taking its toll on his ravaged body.

Morini stared at him, wondering if the opiates—or even the disease itself—had deranged the old man, if he was hearing drug- or pain-induced ramblings with no basis whatsoever in fact. But Gianni neither looked nor sounded as if that were the case. His voice was weak and slightly slurred, but his eyes were bright with intelligence.

"What information?"

"First you must swear never to reveal what I'm about to tell you."

Morini shook his head in slight irritation, then did as the old man asked.

"I swear by Almighty God that I will tell no one anything I learn in this room. I would never breach the secrets of the confessional under any circumstances, and I will accord whatever you tell me here exactly the same status."

"Good. How long have you been here, in the holy city?"

Morini looked slightly taken aback at the question.

"Just under twenty years," he replied. "Why?"

"I arrived here in the mid-seventies, and I became Prefect at the end of the nineties. Even now I still remember having an interview, a very similar interview to this one, in fact, with my predecessor. Who also, if I recall correctly, had contracted a form of cancer. Perhaps the disease is one of the risks of this particular job."

Gianni paused for breath, and perhaps to order his thoughts before he continued.

"I have a good idea what you're thinking at this precise moment, because when I was in your position I, too, wondered if my predecessor as Prefect was deluded or suffering from some kind of mental instability in addition to his other infirmities. But he wasn't, and neither am I.

"I'm quite sure, Antonio, that you know most of the history of the Vatican and of the Church that we both serve, but there is one incident that took place almost half a century ago that only received a limited amount of publicity at the time, and that has been virtually forgotten about today. You've probably never even heard of it, but it was perhaps the most dangerous event ever to take place here in the Holy See."

"Dangerous? Dangerous to whom?"

The old man's grip tightened on Morini's hand.

"To everyone. To the very foundations of our Church, and to the faith espoused by countless millions of followers of our true religion around the world."

Morini felt a sudden chill run through his body. Whatever he'd been expecting, that wasn't it.

"You'd better tell me exactly what you mean," he said.

What the old man had to say didn't take long. But the implications of what he said were shattering.

4

"Dear God," Morini murmured when Gianni finished speaking. "Dear God, save us all."

And then Morini fell silent, as his mind processed the information he had just been given. Finally, he began questioning the dying man.

"But why did they put it there? Why didn't they lock it away somewhere in the archives? Or even destroy it?"

Gianni shook his head. "I don't know. I suppose the fear was that wherever it was hidden in the archives there was always a chance that some researcher might stumble over it one day. Destroying it was not really an option. You know as well as I do that the Vatican hardly ever destroys anything. I suppose putting it inside another exhibit in a glass case, in a part of the Holy See to which public access was never granted, and choosing a display case that would never be opened except under the tightest supervision and only then by senior Vatican officials, was seen as the safest alternative."

"Which we now know wasn't safe at all," Morini retorted. Then he asked the obvious question. "Does anybody else know about this?"

"The Prefect of the *Archivum Secretum Vaticanum* at the time we are talking about obviously knew what had happened, and he conveyed that information to the Holy Father. In return, he was ordered to reveal the facts to nobody except his immediate successor in charge of the archive. I was the third Prefect to bear the weight of this information and this responsibility, and you are now the fourth."

"And His Holiness? Does he know about this?"

Gianni nodded slightly.

"Since that date, every pope has been made aware of it, and keeping each pontiff informed is one of your duties. If our present Holy Father should succumb while you are in the post, you will be required to explain the situation to the new occupant of the throne of St. Peter. It is likely that you will be summoned to a private audience with His Holiness over the next few weeks to discuss this, once I am no longer here. But nobody else, nobody at all, inside or outside the Vatican, must ever learn what you now know."

Morini nodded, his mind still reeling.

Then Gianni's grip tightened on the younger man's arm.

"But you do understand, Antonio?" he asked, his voice beseeching. "You do understand what must be done, what the Holy Father has instructed is to be carried out if the unthinkable happens?"

Morini nodded again.

"You need have no concerns about that, my old friend. I know where my duty lies, and the importance of the Mother Church. You can rest assured that I will take whatever steps are necessary to ensure that it will never, ever, see the light of day."

"And the other measures that I explained to you?" Gianni insisted.

"They are unpleasant," Morini said, choosing his words carefully, "but in the circumstances I am certain that they would be entirely justified. Those, too, I will arrange to carry out if it ever becomes necessary to do so."

5

London

Present day

"I don't know what it is about that woman," Angela Lewis said, "but I find her incredibly irritating."

She and her former husband, Chris Bronson, were relaxing in the lounge of her flat in Ealing, watching the large LED television that she'd purchased the previous day and that Bronson had then spent hours installing after they'd got it back to the flat. For the last thirty minutes they'd been watching a popular antiques program.

"I know exactly what you mean," Bronson replied. "She's always got this smug-git expression on her face and you can just tell that she thinks she's absolutely wonderful. It's a pity, because apart from her I really enjoy the show. But I suppose for you this antique stuff all feels a bit amateur?"

"Not exactly. The world of antiques is simply enormous, and there's no such thing as an expert on everything. I know my way around ceramics, obviously, because that's what I do all the time, but every time I watch this"—she raised one elegant bare leg from the footstool and pointed it at the television screen—"I learn something new, something outside my particular specialization."

"And I suppose like everybody else you keep hoping that some hideous vase or something you pick up for a few pence at a car-boot sale actually turns out to be some long-lost priceless relic from the Ming Dynasty so that you can retire on the proceeds," Bronson suggested.

Angela glanced at him, a smile playing over her lips.

"There are a couple of problems with that scenario," she said. "First, the chances of a Ming vase—or any other really valuable antique—turning up at a boot sale are vanishingly small. And second, I've never been to a car-boot sale, and I've no intention of going, so if your idea of a dirty weekend is tramping around a muddy field in the rain wearing Wellington boots and looking at stalls covered in overpriced twentieth-century souvenirs from Brighton and Blackpool, you'll be going by yourself."

"Actually," Bronson said, "my idea of a dirty weekend is a lot less like that and rather more like the one we've just spent."

"Installing television sets?" Angela laughed.

"I was thinking more about what we got up to *after* I'd lugged the box up the stairs and got the thing working."

"Well, I thought you deserved a lie-down after all your efforts. That's the only reason *that* happened."

"Of course, of course. In fact, I feel as if I could do with another lie-down right now. Unless you've got any better ideas, that is."

Angela stood up from the sofa and looked at Bronson, running a hand through her shoulder-length blond hair. Yet again he was struck by her resemblance to a mid-thirties Michelle Pfeiffer, especially her mouth, though her eyes were green rather than blue. Bronson still entertained occasional fantasies about seeing her in a Catwoman outfit, but the time had never seemed quite right to suggest it.

"We'll have to eat something at some point, I suppose," Angela said, "but right now I'm not really that hungry. Maybe if I took a bit of exercise, that would give me more of an appetite."

Then she turned round and walked over toward the hallway that led to the bedroom, her hips swinging under her short skirt.

"That works for me," Bronson said, standing up quickly to follow her.

Forty minutes later, having comprehensively unmade the bed and done their best to exhaust each other, Bronson and Angela lay side by side, propped up on pillows and each sipping from a glass of red wine.

Angela seemed somewhat distracted, which was unlike her.

"Is everything OK? Are you busy at the museum at the moment?"

Angela shook her head. "Not really. Well, in a way, yes. I mean, there's nothing much of any interest going on there at the moment, but we're actually pretty busy. To be perfectly honest, I'll be quite glad when the next two weeks are over."

"Why?"

"You know I enjoy my work, but about ten days ago I had another two boxes of potsherds delivered to me, and for whatever reason the powers that be have decided that they needed results quickly. I presume there's some exhibition coming up and they want to put some of the reassembled vessels on display. The trouble is that all the shards of pottery seem to be about the same size and almost exactly the same color, so trying to achieve anything meaningful is a bit like doing a jigsaw puzzle when you have no idea what the finished picture is supposed to look like."

"That must be incredibly frustrating," Bronson said.

"It is. It's frustrating and boring and important and urgent all at the same time, which is a pretty unpleasant combination. I'm not looking forward to tomorrow morning at all. Which is why I want to make the most of today," she added, snuggling up close to him.

6

Cairo

The present Khan el-Khalili souk dates from 1380, but it had been known as a Turkish bazaar for decades before that date. The name itself is something of a misnomer, because *khan* translates as a "caravanserai," rather than a bazaar or market, and is a reference to the stopping place for traders and their camel trains that grew up on that site in the fourteenth century. In those days, Cairo was one of the most important merchant towns anywhere on the old Silk Road, and the Khan el-Khalili area was where most of the trading in the city took place.

In the latter part of that century, the Sultan Barquq began his madrassa in Bayn al-Qasrayn, sparking a re-building program, one phase of which resulted in the establishment of the souk. It's changed very little over the centuries. It's still Cairo's main souk, a maze of narrow streets, twisting alleyways, tiny shops, street traders, medieval arches and bizarre architecture, mosques and madrassas. The sights, sounds and smells—especially the smells of the spices—would be familiar to anyone who had ever visited a Middle Eastern bazaar: in fact today it is visited by almost as many tourists as locals. Visitors walk in a daze, staring about them at the astonishing range of goods for sale, at the antiques and antiquities, carpets and *kilims*, lamps, gold, silver, jewelry, alabaster ornaments, pottery, shisha pipes, cloth and textiles, clothing and anything and everything else.

On a particularly stuffy day, while pale and sweating visitors ambled through the streets and alleys of the souk, a local dealer slipped silently and efficiently through the crowds. He dealt in antiques and collectables—a term that covered almost everything—and knew that many of the objects he saw on the stalls, being touted to passing tourists as genuine ancient relics, were probably significantly younger than he was, and in some cases might have been made as recently as the previous day.

Anum Husani visited the souk almost daily, trying to seek out the genuine goods, the occasional real bargains, and any attractive items of whatever age that he could sell through his shop. He knew most of the stallholders, and was in his turn known by them. He knew what he was looking for, and was used to getting what he wanted at a price he felt was fair, even if the negotiations involved prolonged haggling and more than one visit to the seller.

As was indicated by his first name, Anum Husani was the fifth child in his family. The son of comparatively wealthy parents, he had been born and brought up in the city. His second name—which followed tradition in that it was his father's first name—meant "handsome," which proved the optimism of his parents, if nothing else, because his face was dominated by a large, curved and bladelike nose, and under his scrubby beard his cheeks were marked by a rash of old acne scars. His eyes were perhaps his best feature, their piercing blue hinting at an interesting genetic mix somewhere among his forebears, and clear intelligence shining from them.

As was his habit, Husani paused for a few minutes at one of the many tiny cafés deep inside the souk and drank thick black coffee from a cup little bigger than a thimble. He was about to continue his searching when a trader he recognized approached him, smiled a welcome and then sat down.

They exchanged greetings and discussed friends, family and acquaintances for some minutes, before the trader finally worked his way round to the matter he wanted to talk about.

"I have something that might interest you," Mahmoud began.

"I'm interested in lots of things," Husani replied vaguely, gesturing at a number of items he had already purchased at various stalls in the souk. A few old pottery vessels and a couple of pieces of jewelry lay on the small circular table in front of him. "What have you got?"

"You've heard about the building work going on over at al-Jizah?" the trader asked.

Husani shook his head.

"They were demolishing a couple of buildings," Mahmoud explained, "and a large battered metal case turned up in the rubble. Nobody had seen the object before the demolition started, and I think it's possible that it might have been hidden under the floorboards of one of the rooms, or possibly secreted within a wall."

Mahmoud paused for a moment and looked keenly at his companion.

Husani's interest and attention were obvious, and he gestured for the trader to continue his story.

"One of the workmen forced it open, obviously hoping that there was something of value inside it, but all it contained were papers, so he tossed it away. Another one of the men working there is known to me and thought I might be interested in the case itself, even if there was nothing worth selling inside it, so he picked it up and brought it to me."

Husani shook his head and picked up one of the pieces of jewelry he had purchased that morning, his attention already wandering.

"I have no particular interest in metal cases, my friend," he pointed out.

Mahmoud nodded.

"I know that," he replied, "and in fact I have already sold it to a tourist, who of course paid far more than it was really worth. But I also examined the papers that were inside it, and I think you might like to see those."

Husani shook his head again.

"I mostly deal in relics and artifacts," he said, dropping the necklace on the table and lifting up an old pottery lamp, "things like this. Documents, even very old documents, have little value for me. They are usually difficult to sell, and are also quite fragile."

"But you have sold parchments and scrolls in the past?"

"Parchments only occasionally, but scrolls, yes, because they are decorative and the tourists like them, even the modern fakes. But you said the box contained papers. Did you mean that they were scrolls?"

"Not scrolls, no, but there was one piece of thick paper that looks very old, and I didn't recognize the writing on it. That is the object I thought you might be interested in seeing."

Husani nodded slowly. Mahmoud was a competent market trader, but a generally unsophisticated and uneducated man, and what he was describing as "thick paper" might be parchment or vellum, either of which could suggest considerable age. On the other hand, it could also be simply a sheet of thin cardboard. But whatever it was, Husani guessed it was probably worth his while to take a look.

"Is it at your stall?"

"Yes. My cousin Rashid is there now, if you would like to see it."

"Very well, my friend," Husani said, careful not to appear too enthusiastic because that would encourage Mahmoud to raise the asking price of the object. "There are a few other dealers who have offered me relics, and I need to see them now, but I will be at your stall within the hour."

Husani arrived at Mahmoud's small establishment just over forty minutes later, having found nothing of real interest in the other stalls.

Mahmoud opened a battered leather suitcase and removed a pile of yellowing paper.

"That," he said, as Husani looked at the bundle of pages, "is exactly the way the papers appeared when I opened the metal case. The unusual one is right in the middle."

Husani picked up the top sheet and studied it for a few moments. It appeared to be part of some kind of contract or agreement—the numbers on the left-hand side of the indented paragraphs suggested that very clearly—and he thought the language was Spanish, or perhaps Italian. What struck him as odd was that the first paragraph was numbered "17A," which suggested that there must be at least two or three other pages that would presumably contain the earlier sections of the document, but none of the pages immediately underneath appeared to be in any way related to the sheet he held in his hand. Some of the sheets were unusual sizes, and the color of the typewritten text varied from blue to black.

Those pages that had dates on them suggested that the papers had all been acquired at more or less the same time, because they were all from roughly the same period, the early to mid-1960s. But, glancing at the text on each one as he did so, Husani guessed that the typewritten sheets had probably been selected at random. They looked like nothing more than a miscellaneous collection of discarded business documents.

And that gave him pause for thought. There were two fairly obvious reasons why somebody should have decided to stuff the metal case with such pages. They might be there to protect something, the pages acting as nothing more important than packing material, or perhaps they might be a kind of basic disguise—something to show an inquisitive customs officer if he insisted on the case being opened and checked. Or maybe, he decided, the pages could be performing both functions, acting as a protection and a disguise.

"This is exactly how you found them?" Husani asked.

Mahmoud nodded. "Exactly. I lifted the bundle of papers out of the case and examined the sheets just as you are doing now, but I didn't change the order of the pages, in case that was important for some reason."

He paused for a moment and glanced shrewdly at Husani.

"So is it important, my friend?"

"At this moment, I have no idea."

Husani ran his fingers down the side of the bundle of papers until he felt something thicker and stiffer approximately in the middle of the pile. He took hold of the stack of pages that overlaid it, and lifted them all to one side.

The object was not particularly impressive. It looked like a sheet of brownish cardboard, but as soon as Husani touched it he realized that it was actually parchment, and it looked old. There were words written on it, the letters barely visible and extremely difficult to make out. He picked up the parchment by its edges and held it up to the dim light streaming through a section of the roof of the souk, angling it to try to make out what was written on it.

At first, he could only pick out the occasional letter, but then he saw one word fairly clearly, and a tingle—like a shot of electricity—passed through his body. Beyond a shadow of a doubt, what he was looking at was written in Latin.

7

Most of the forged scrolls and parchments Husani had handled in the past were clearly of recent origin, the ink black and the writing easy to read. The text he was looking at now was barely legible at all, and Husani had not the slightest doubt that it really was old. He'd never heard of a forger successfully fading ink on parchment to this extent and with this degree and feeling of authenticity. What's more, assuming everything Mahmoud had told him was the truth, and the dates on the papers were accurate, the object had been locked away in a steel box since about 1965, almost half a century earlier, and that more or less ruled out the chance of it having been manufactured as a fake antique. If somebody had made it, they would also have sold it, not hidden it away. Nothing else made sense.

So it was old. The next question was did it have any value and, if so, what was it worth? And if it was valuable, just how little could he persuade the rascally Mahmoud Kassim, well-known in the souk for always demanding the highest possible price for anything he had on offer, to sell it for?

With an expression of uninterest on his face, Husani put the parchment to one side and then examined the sheets of paper that had been underneath it. It was immediately clear to him that these pages, too, were just as uninformative as those he'd already looked at. The only common factor seemed to be that they had been typed at about the same time, in the mid-1960s, as the other sheets. Other than that there was nothing to link them, and none appeared to be of the slightest interest. At the bottom of the pile there were a few sheets of newspaper, one of which he examined. It was clearly Italian in origin—the name of the paper made that clear—and also dated from 1965.

Husani still had no idea what the significance was of the piece of parchment, or what the Latin text on it was describing, but the way it had been hidden, or protected, in the center of a stack of paper, locked inside a metal box and then secreted away somewhere in a house, suggested that it was important in some way. He needed to buy it as cheaply as he could and then try to find out exactly what it was.

Mahmoud was still looking at him, an eager expression on his face.

"Do you know what it is, that thick paper?" he asked.

Husani had found from his previous dealings with Mahmoud that the man often knew far more than he was prepared to admit at first, and it was a mistake to try to deceive him on such matters. A little truth often went a long way in his negotiations.

"It seems to be a sheet of parchment," Husani began, and Mahmoud immediately nodded.

"That was what I thought, too."

Husani nodded. He'd guessed as much. Mahmoud would certainly have done some investigating himself before offering the object for sale to anybody. And the trader's next words confirmed his suspicions.

"I've had a look at the writing on it," Mahmoud said, "and I think I've been able to make out a couple of words, or most of the letters, anyway. It looks like Latin."

"What were the words?" Husani asked.

"I think one was a place-name and the other possibly the name of a man, but the ink is faded so badly that I can't be absolutely certain. I ran some searches on the Internet on what I think they were, just in case they were of some significance, but I didn't find out anything particularly interesting—not to say they won't yield something of importance if an expert were to look at it."

Husani looked away from Mahmoud's face and down at the parchment.

"From what you've said, you probably know more about this than I do. I'm fairly certain that it's a piece of parchment, but that's about all I can tell you about it. Like you, I can see the writing on it, and I can make out a few of the letters, but it's so indistinct that it might be impossible to ever decipher the whole thing. The only other point is that it looks to me as if the parchment is quite old, but other than that, I really have no idea what it is."

Mahmoud's expression changed, a frown replacing his earlier eager smile.

"So do you think it has any value?" he asked.

Husani replaced the parchment on the lower stack of papers, added the remainder and put the entire pile back into the old leather case before he replied.

"Possibly," he said, "but I doubt if it's worth very much. Pieces of old parchment are not exactly rare, and I have several for sale in my shop right now, all in much better condition than this. At best, I think this is nothing more than a curio, something I might be able to sell to a tourist just because it is so obviously old, and not because it has any other importance."

"Then I could sell it myself," Mahmoud suggested, clearly expecting Husani to disagree.

"You could indeed, and if that's what you want to do, I wish you luck," Husani replied, deciding at that moment to call Mahmoud's bluff. He closed the catches on the suitcase and turned as if to leave the storeroom.

"On the other hand," Mahmoud went on, "it's not the usual kind of item that I would sell. Would you make me an offer for it? I'll include the suitcase and the papers as a part of the deal."

Husani turned back to look at the trader.

"You know as well as I do that the papers are completely valueless, and the case is so old and battered that most people would just throw it away, not try to sell it. I'm not sure that it's even worth my while bothering about the parchment," he finished. Then he suggested a figure that was little more than the old leather suitcase was worth by itself.

Mahmoud reeled backward somewhat theatrically, clearly appalled at the sum offered, and proposed a figure more than ten times higher. And then the haggling, the part of the transaction that in truth both men enjoyed more than any other, began.

8

Many people think Vatican City is living in the past. The fact that the official language is still Latin—a dead language that is spoken by no other nation anywhere else in the world—the medieval weapons carried by the Swiss Guard, the burning of incense, using different colored smoke to signal the choosing of a new pontiff, and the ancient robes worn by the senior clergy who attend the Pope, all hark back to the Middle Ages. What they don't realize is that these facts deliberately conspire to suggest that both the Vatican and the papacy are essentially medieval in nature, an anachronism.

In fact, nothing could be further from the truth. Behind the chanting and the piety and the centuries of tradition and custom, the papacy of the twenty-first century is every bit as modern as any multinational corporation or Western government, and with good reason. The Catholic Church has had more than its fair share of problems over the last century. Some were self-inflicted, like the assistance given at the end of the Second World War to wanted Nazis to escape from the ruins of Germany and establish themselves in new lives and with new identities elsewhere in the world. The whole question of resistance to birth control also showed that the Vatican, and most especially the then Pope, was completely out of touch with reality, by promoting unlimited expansion of the human race at a time when the world was already grossly over-populated.

Perhaps most worrying of all for the Vatican were the fundamental criticisms of religion itself, whether from academic sources or from popular books—especially criticisms of Christianity and Roman Catholicism. The basis of the problem was that science had now been able to explain virtually everything from the creation of the universe itself right through to identifying the most fundamental particles, the very building blocks of every kind of matter.

In Australia, just to look at a single nation that particularly concerned the Church, belief in Christianity fell from over 95 percent of the population to just over 60 percent in the twentieth century alone, and the fastest growing "religion" on that continent was, in fact, atheism.

And while Christianity, though still the world's largest religion, was in possibly terminal decline, other religions that shared no part of the Christian ideal, such as Islam, were beginning to grow.

The portents for the future were not good, and successive occupants of the Throne of St. Peter had been made very aware that the last thing the Church needed was any other damage to the core beliefs of Christianity. And it was the growth of the single largest communication medium in history, the Internet, that had provided them with the tools they needed to detect any such undesirable ripples of doubt.

At the end of the twentieth century, the governments of Western Europe and America had created a global monitoring system known as Echelon, a way of eavesdropping on telephone conversations, faxes and electronic mail transmissions from almost anywhere in the world. The purpose of Echelon was entirely laudable: the detection of potential terrorist activity before it could be turned into a devastating reality. To achieve this, the security services of the world employed a program known as the Echelon Dictionary, a vast list of words that the monitoring system was created to detect, and that it was hoped would lead to the surveillance, and if necessary the arrest and imprisonment, of potential suicide bombers and members of terrorist groups.

The Vatican, for all its enormous wealth and influence, possessed neither the resources nor the legal authority to create such a global monitoring system. But some years earlier, as the first handful of computers began to be connected to the fledgling network that would soon begin to grow exponentially into the Internet, a group of far-sighted and technologically literate priests working at the Vatican had seen the potential of the new information resource and also realized that it could be a useful—perhaps even an essential—tool to help guarantee the future of the Church.

Like every large organization, there were a fair number of skeletons in the Vatican's closets, documents and objects which, if they ever saw the light of day, would cripple—or at least very severely damage—the Church's credibility. And it made sense that anyone who discovered even a hint about any such dark secret would very probably use an online search engine to research the topic. A kind of early-warning system was needed.

So the Vatican approached the emerging companies operating the search engines and explained the concerns the Church had. And, because almost all of the owners of these companies were American, a nation with far more than its fair share of fundamentalist Christians, getting agreement to install monitoring software had proved to be surprisingly easy.

The result was a loose and informal arrangement with the providers of all of the major search engines on the Internet. Somewhat like the Echelon Dictionary, the Vatican's monitoring system—known to the handful of indoctrinated senior clerics in the Holy See as "Codex S," a nod to perhaps the most important single extant book in the Christian world, the fourth-century *Codex Sinaiticus*, a Bible handwritten in Greek—was programmed to detect certain words being entered into the search engines, particularly when two or more of those words were entered together. The date and time would be noted, and the search term recorded, the information then being fed back to the Vatican.

As a further refinement, when any such search term was entered, the monitoring software would also locate the precise Internet address of the initiating computer. Every computer that accesses the Internet is allocated either a permanent or a temporary address—this is essential to ensure that responses go to the right place—and also geographically locates that computer. So by this fairly simple method, the Vatican was informed every time any search that might be considered dangerous to it was entered on any computer in the world, as long as one of the principal search engines had been used.

Early that morning, in a large open-plan office in a building in a part of the Vatican to which the public, and almost all of the staff of the Holy See, never had access under any circumstances, a speaker system attached to a desktop computer emitted five short beeps, indicating a hit from the monitoring system. The room was unmanned for most of the time, but a log was maintained at each of the workstations and these were combined into a master electronic document that was inspected at least once a day.

Late that evening, a senior member of the Vatican staff inspected the log and immediately saw the two words that had triggered the response by the monitoring system. His orders were clear, and he followed them straightaway. He printed a hard copy of the entry and then ran a simple program that identified the precise geographical location of the computer from which the search had been generated, translating the Internet address into a street address.

Then he left the room, secured the door behind him, and made his way quickly through the corridors and passages of the building to the Secret Archives. There, he went straight to the office occupied by the Prefect in charge, Father Antonio Morini, and placed on his desk a sealed envelope containing the printouts.

9

That evening, Husani fired up his home computer and began to do his own research. Within a very short time, it was clear to him that almost all of the papers in the case were in Italian.

He identified an online translation service, and converted some of the words into Arabic. That didn't help much, except to confirm what he had first suspected: the pages must have been randomly chosen, and what was typed on them was of absolutely no importance. Most of the phrases he translated had very obviously been taken from various sorts of business correspondence, letters, draft contracts, price lists of goods and the like.

But at least Husani could now discount the papers and get to the item that excited him. He turned his attention to the parchment, placing it on the table in front of him and angling a couple of bright desk lights toward it so that its surface was clearly visible.

In the much better lighting then available to him, he found that a few more of the letters and words were visible. And it was possible, he knew from talking to other traders who tended to specialize more in this kind of relic, that other examination techniques, such as bathing the object in infrared and ultraviolet light, could sometimes reveal text that remained invisible to the naked eye.

Husani knew that whatever value the object had must be determined by the text that would be revealed: it was the information that was important, not the parchment itself. The message, not the medium.

He took a few clean sheets of paper, a pencil and an eraser, positioned his desktop magnifying glass on its mount over the first line of words on the parchment and began to carefully copy out every single letter that was clear enough for him to identify. Where he could see that a letter existed but was unable to determine what it was, he marked the paper with an underscore because that, he hoped, would help him when it came to trying to translate the Latin. And the writing, he was still quite certain, *was* Latin.

He worked his way down the sheet of parchment, filling in those letters he could easily identify, then started again from the top and repeated the process, this time concentrating on the gaps in the text. Then he did the entire process once more, just to make absolutely sure that he hadn't missed anything. Only after he had completed this did he begin looking at the words and letters he had written out, to see if he could make sense of any of it.

At first glance, he wasn't hopeful.

He had managed to transcribe only a dozen or so words at different points in the text, and for three of those he wasn't entirely certain that all the letters were correct. All the other words he had tried to decipher had at least two illegible letters, and in some cases all he had been able to ascertain was the approximate number of letters in the word, and nothing more.

It was, he supposed, a start, and he decided he would begin working with what he had. Using his pencil again, he circled the handful of words on the paper that he was reasonably certain he had transcribed correctly, then turned back to his computer and opened up a Latin dictionary.

Ten minutes later, he looked down at the result. No two of the words were consecutive, and they had appeared at widely separated points on the sheet of parchment, so he wasn't expecting to make much sense out of them. At best, he hoped that the translations from the Latin would give him an indication of the subject matter of the text.

Altogether, there were nine words in addition to the two words that Mahmoud had already partially deciphered and that he had believed were parts of proper names. None of them appeared to be particularly helpful. In the order in which they appeared on the parchment, the translated meanings were: "down," "along," "fighting," "battle," "soldiers," "street," "house," "ran" and "cloak." And there was another word that he couldn't make any sense of because it didn't appear in the dictionary—could that be another proper noun, perhaps the name of a town or other location?

It looked to him as if it was a description of a skirmish, possibly between a Roman legion and some unspecified enemy, but exactly who that enemy might have been, and where and when the conflict had taken place—because he had never heard of any town or country that sounded like the proper name he thought he'd discovered—he had absolutely no idea.

But Husani believed that it was worth pursuing. If the skirmish was important enough, then commercial organizations such as museums and even the history departments of universities might be interested in acquiring it, as well as the antiquarians and collectors of relics around the world who were his usual big-spending customers.

Clearly, what he needed to do was get far more of the text deciphered. And he had a good idea how that could be done, and exactly who could help him.

10

Father Antonio Morini stared at the sheets of paper on the desk in front of him and clasped his hands together almost as if he was in prayer. The conclusion seemed utterly inescapable. The nightmare that he'd hoped he would never experience while he was in the Holy See had materialized. Somehow, the relic that he had hoped—had, in fact, come to believe—had been either destroyed or lost forever, had apparently reappeared, and in Cairo, of all places.

He stood up abruptly from his desk and walked across to a small wall safe located in one corner of his office. Unusually, the safe had both a numeric keypad and a physical keyhole. Morini loosened the neck of his habit and pulled out a long chain at the end of which was a slim silver key. He inserted the key in the lock and turned it once clockwise, then entered a six-digit code that he personally altered at the end of every week, and turned the key clockwise a second time. Then he removed the key, grasped the handle on the left side of the door, rotated that a quarter of a turn and pulled open the door.

Inside the safe, hidden beneath a pile of folders, was a slim and sealed red file, devoid of any name or other identifying features apart from the single Latin inscription *A cruce salus*, which translated as "From the cross comes salvation." Before he had listened to his dying predecessor, Morini would have had no difficulty asserting that that statement was the absolute truth. But with his new-found knowledge, it seemed to him more like a cruel joke.

He took out the file and carried it back to his desk, where he cut through the tapes around the heavy seal, the impressed image on the wax causing him to cross himself as he recognized it.

The *Annulus Piscatoris*, the Ring of the Fisherman, was an important part of the regalia of every pope, a new version of the ring being cast for each incumbent, and was kissed as a mark of respect by visiting dignitaries. In the past it had also been used as a signet to authenticate documents signed by the occupant of the Throne of St. Peter, but that practice had stopped in 1842. Its use was clearly a measure of the importance of the documents contained within the file.

Morini extracted the contents, a mere half a dozen sheets of paper, five of them providing information and a series of instructions, and the other one a very short list, bearing only three names, together with brief information about those individuals and their international telephone numbers. He placed the last sheet to one side and then began to read the secret protocols that had been entrusted to him alone.

The document began by stating that the protocols had been formulated by the reigning pope just under half a century earlier, and had been approved by every pontiff since then, including the present occupant of the Throne of St. Peter. Even so, Morini was scarcely able to believe what he was reading. Several times, in his office in the

Secret Archives, he stood up and walked around his desk as he struggled to reconcile the implications of the orders he was reading with what his conscience was telling him.

But in the end, and despite his personal misgivings, he knew absolutely where his duty had to lie.

11

Propaganda Due, better known by the abbreviated name of "P2," had been founded as a private Masonic lodge in Italy in 1877, its membership principally drawn from the Italian government, but it had later expanded to include the heads of all the country's intelligence services, Cabinet ministers, prominent public figures, senior clergyman and, inevitably, senior members of the Mafia.

For decades, P2 had avoided the limelight, not least because the Catholic Church had officially banned Masonic membership for all priests, but in the late 1960s a massive financial and political scandal broke when it was revealed that the head of the Vatican Bank, Archbishop Paul Marcinkus, had joined the organization. And not only that, but Marcinkus, along with the P2 lodge treasurer Michele Sindona and his protégé Roberto Calvi, had created hundreds of fictitious accounts in the Vatican Bank as a convenient device to allow the Mafia to launder drug money. Even worse, in an extremely ill-advised move in 1969 a large portfolio of the Holy See's investments had been handed to Sindona to manage, with the result that the Vatican lost the equivalent of almost a quarter of a billion dollars over the next six years.

That brought matters to a head, and on 27 September 1978 Pope John Paul I announced his intention to immediately remove Archbishop Marcinkus and three other P2 members from the Vatican Bank, in a belated attempt to, as it were, cleanse the Augean Stables. The following morning, the Pope was found dead in his bed.

As is the invariable custom in the Vatican, no autopsy was performed on this apparently fit and comparatively young Pope—he was only sixty-five—who had reigned for a mere thirty-three days. It is, of course, entirely possible that his announcement about Marcinkus and his death less than twenty-four hours later were entirely unconnected, but very few people inside or outside the Vatican really believed that the pontiff had actually died of natural causes.

The death of John Paul I might have stopped the immediate dismissal of the archbishop, but the bastions around P2 were already beginning to crumble, with Sindona being arrested in 1980 and Italy's largest bank, the Banco Ambrosiano, which had been headed by Roberto Calvi, collapsing two years later. There was a sudden spate of unexplained deaths of men who were involved in either P2 or banking operations connected to it, including Calvi himself, whose body was found dangling from a rope underneath Blackfriars Bridge in London.

And, just as nobody believed that Pope John Paul I had died peacefully in his sleep, nobody believed that Calvi had committed suicide, especially when it was learned that his secretary had also killed herself on the very same day by jumping out of the window of her office in the Banco Ambrosiano building in Italy. Eventually

Calvi's "suicide" verdict was overturned and changed to "cause of death unknown," which was almost as inaccurate: it was quite certain that he had died of asphyxiation due to the rope around his neck. What wasn't known was precisely how he came to be hanging from the end of that rope, but most people presumed that P2 had struck once again with lethal force.

In the aftermath of this scandal, which had not only reverberated within the Vatican but also swept through the Italian government and the world of international banking, P2 seemed to quietly fade away. But, as with so many organizations in Italy, this was not exactly the case. The Masonic charter had been withdrawn from the P2 lodge in 1972, but in reality membership of the brotherhood had only ever been a convenience, and the powerful members of the lodge, drawn by now from most of the nations of Europe, knew they could function perfectly happily outside Masonry, just as they had functioned for so many years outside the law.

So officially P2 had ceased to exist; in reality it remained as a shadowy entity, answerable to no one but still inextricably linked with both the Vatican and the Catholic Church in a relationship that was virtually symbiotic. The Church benefited financially from some of P2's quasi-legal business ventures, while the Vatican ensured that the lodge received an important measure of protection from exposure in the media and elsewhere. And so P2 remained, as it had been almost from its inception, the Vatican's first and most powerful ally.

And it was the head of this organization that Morini must contact—the instructions in the file were clear and unequivocal. Only they could resolve the problem that he and the Church now faced.

He read the final paragraph of the instructions once

more, then noted down the person's name and telephone number, and the code word the document listed. Finally he closed the file and locked it away again in the safe.

Then he left his office, returned to his room in the Holy See, changed into civilian clothes and walked out into the streets of Rome. That, too, had been specified in the protocols, which had clearly been reviewed on an occasional basis by both his predecessor and the Holy Father himself to take account of changes in technology. Under no circumstances was he ever to use either his personal mobile telephone or any of the landline phones within the Vatican City. His contact with the three widely dispersed members of P2 was to be by public telephone—and he was never to use the same one twice—or by an anonymous pay-as-you-go mobile phone, which he was also never to use within the Holy See.

12

The calm male voice on the end of the line said the single English word "Yes?" in a neutral tone before lapsing into silence.

"The code word is 'Angharad,'" Morini said, replying in the same language. "I will call you back in ten minutes."

"No," the voice said, suddenly louder and instantly commanding. "Remain where you are and I will call you. Five minutes."

Before Morini could reply, the line went dead. For a few seconds the priest just stood there, looking at the telephone handset he was holding; then he replaced it and stepped away from the booth. There were no seats anywhere nearby, but there was a low wall a few yards away, near enough to the booth that he'd certainly hear the phone when it rang, but not so close that he would appear to any passersby to be waiting for a call.

About two minutes after he'd ended the call, a middle-aged woman with badly dyed blond hair partially obscuring her face, and wearing old jeans and a shapeless jumper, despite the heat of the day, walked up to the phone booth, slid coins into the slot and embarked on what looked like a lengthy and somewhat acrimonious call. She wasn't shouting, but it was the next best thing.

Morini glanced at his watch, counting the seconds, but he knew there was almost nothing he could do about it. The last thing he wanted to do was attract attention to himself, and if he did anything to cut short the woman's call, that would certainly result in some kind of a scene.

Five minutes came, then six. When his watch showed that seven minutes had elapsed since he'd ended his call, and despite his misgivings, Morini decided he had to do something. He got up and walked across to the phone booth, stopped right beside it and fixed his gaze on the woman using the phone. After a few seconds she became aware of his presence and turned to stare at him, an irritated expression on her face. Embarrassed but determined, Morini stared back at her, pointed at the telephone in her hand, and then tapped the face of his watch for emphasis. The woman turned her back on him, but Morini simply walked around to the other side of the booth and repeated his actions.

A few seconds later the woman angrily slammed the phone down on its rest and stepped out of the booth. Morini moved to one side to allow her to pass, and received a mouthful of invective for his trouble, the insults liberally laced with a scattering of descriptive words that the priest had not heard in a very long time.

But Morini didn't care because as the woman walked away, simmering anger evident in her every stride, the telephone began to ring, and he immediately snatched up the handset.

"Hullo?"

"This is the fifth time I have tried to call you back," the cold voice at the other end of the line snapped. "What happened?"

"This is a public phone box," Morini began, "and a woman stopped here to make a call."

"The next time you use a public telephone to call me—if there *is* a next time—you will remain in the booth until I call you back. Is that perfectly clear? My time is too important to waste."

"I understand."

"I hope you do. Now, I know who you are, or at least the position you hold and the organization you represent. And if your documentation is current, you will know my name—or one of the names that I use—and the group that I control." The man's voice dropped to little more than a whisper, and his tone seemed to exude a cold menace that Morini found instantly alarming. "I hope for your sake that you have not contacted me for some trivial problem. What has happened? And before you speak, be aware that it is possible that this call may be monitored, so choose your words with care."

Morini had anticipated that he would need to explain the circumstances to the man, and had prepared a simple overview. He talked for less than ninety seconds, taking care to mention no names or any other definitive information.

Almost as soon as he'd finished, the other man replied.

"I hope that you and your masters realize that this is an entirely self-inflicted problem," he said. "If there was anyone in your organization with a functioning brain, they would have made sure that the relic was destroyed centuries ago. Instead, you not only kept hold of it, but you failed to keep it in a secure location, which is why you're now in this mess."

"I'm sure that the people responsible believed they were doing the right thing," Morini couldn't help but plead.

"They were wrong," the man replied flatly. "Now, I hope you have an untraceable mobile phone because you must send me a text message giving me all the information I need to resolve this situation. I want names, addresses—IP addresses as well as geographical locations—a full description and photograph of the relic, and any other information that you have about it and what happened to it. You already have my number, and as soon as you send me the text I will have your mobile number as well. From now on, we will mainly communicate using mobiles rather than landlines. When I reply I will send you a list of times when you are to be available to take my calls. At those times you must be outside your place of work—your entire place of work, I mean."

"That may not be possible," Morini objected. "I have duties that I need—"

"You will adhere to the schedule. Your duties are of secondary importance to resolving this situation. You will also need to advise your masters that this may end up being a costly operation, and I do not anticipate any disputes over my expenses. One last question."

"Yes?"

"Which languages do you speak?"

For a moment or two, Morini didn't reply, because he couldn't see the relevance of the question.

"English," he said finally, "and Italian, obviously. I'm reasonably fluent in French as well. Why do you ask?"

"Because you will be relaying my instructions to the contractors who will be carrying out the work."

"That was not my understanding," Morini replied, in surprise. "I believed that your organization would take over and resolve this problem. You must have people who can speak as many languages as I can."

"I do, but they will not be employed for this job. Either you translate my instructions as I have ordered or I'll take no further part in this situation and you can solve the problem yourself, using whatever resources you have. I will not allow the Vatican to deny their involvement if this matter ever makes the news. We won't be your scapegoat anymore."

"But I have no resources," Morini protested. "You know that."

"Then it should not be a difficult decision for you."

"I really don't like this."

"I'm not asking you to like it. I'm just telling you to do it. I expect to receive your detailed text message within the next fifteen minutes."

The line went dead, and Morini stepped out of the telephone booth with a feeling of relief, and a hint of apprehension.

He had all the information to hand, some in his head, other pieces of data—such as the IP address of the Egyptian market trader in Cairo—written down on a folded piece of paper tucked inside his wallet. He walked a few yards down the road to one of the cafés that dot the streets of Rome, sat down and ordered a drink, and then quickly composed a message that included all the information that the Englishman had demanded. He read it through twice to make sure that he'd covered all the details, then pressed the button that would send the text into the ether.

Rather sooner than he'd expected, his phone beeped to signal the arrival of not one, but two text messages. The first one listed the times of day when Morini was to be available on his mobile phone and outside the physical limits of the Vatican City. When he saw these, Morini knew it was going to be difficult for him, but it was at least possible. The second message was longer. It contained a name and a telephone number in Cairo and then a very detailed list of orders, which Morini was to pass to this man.

When he read through this section of the message—and began to understand the implications of the instructions he was about to give—Morini's resolve began to waver. The cold and clinical directions sent by the Englishman admitted of only one possible result. Morini knew, without the slightest hint of a doubt, that if—when—he contacted the P2 representative in Cairo, within a matter of days, or possibly even hours, a human being, a man he'd never met, was going to die.

For several minutes, Morini walked the streets of Rome, lost in thought and struggling to reconcile what he knew had to be done with what his conscience was screaming at him. Eventually, he stopped on the corner of a narrow alleyway where a wood and metal seat was positioned, and sat down with a deep sigh. He clasped his hands in front of him and bowed his head in prayer.

But whatever help or inspiration he was seeking didn't materialize, and after a short time he stood up again, a sick feeling in the pit of his stomach, and took his mobile out of his pocket. He knew he really had no choice. No choice at all.

He made sure he could not be overheard, and then dialed the number he had been given for a man named Jalal Khusad in Cairo.

For a few seconds after he'd ended the call Morini didn't move, just bowed his head in prayer again, his lips moving silently.

13

"Can you do it, Ali?" Anum Husani asked.

He was sitting with a man in a small café near the center of the city. Ali Mohammed was a slightly overweight man with a round face and delicate, almost effeminate, features and wearing a crisp white suit. He wasn't Husani's only contact on the museum circuit in Cairo, but in this case he was the most useful, because he had access to sophisticated testing and investigation equipment in the section of the museum where he worked.

Ali Mohammed took a small sip of the thick, almost black liquid from the tiny cup in front of him. He replaced the cup on the table, looked up at Husani and shook his head.

"It might not be as simple or as definitive as you seem to think, Anum. I know you believe that I can just switch on some machine, stick a sample in it somewhere and wait for it to tell me everything there is to know about it, but it really isn't like that. You've told me you've bought a piece of parchment with some writing on it. A few of the words are legible but the vast majority are not. I do have equipment in the laboratory which can read letters which have faded badly, but it all depends on how and why they've faded—whether it's just because of the age of the piece, or if there's some other reason, like water damage or bleaching by the sun."

Mohammed drained the last of his coffee with a single swallow, grimaced as he tasted a few of the grains on his tongue, and took a sip of water to clear his palate.

"It's quite possible," he went on, "that I'll be able to read everything on the parchment as clearly as if it had been written yesterday. It's also possible that I won't be able to decipher any more of the text than you have already read. That's what you have to understand. I can make no promises at all. Now, do you still want me to go ahead?"

Husani nodded. Every time he had approached Mohammed with requests of this sort, to ask the man to unofficially use some of his laboratory equipment to help date a relic or elucidate some ancient writing, he had had to sit through a similar kind of explanation. He almost knew the words by heart.

But he didn't mind, because although Mohammed always appeared somewhat reluctant, the man had invariably agreed to carry out every investigation he had requested, and in almost every case he had achieved entirely satisfactory results. In return, Husani had paid him a cash sum that wasn't so large it would embarrass the scientist, but certainly big enough to ensure that Mohammed was always pleased to see him.

"Ali, my friend, of course I want you to go ahead. And if you find that you can't help me at all, I'm still very grateful that you're prepared to even try."

Husani reached down to the beige canvas messenger bag that was resting against one of the legs of the table at which they were sitting.

"You've got it with you?" Mohammed sounded surprised.

"Of course I have. It's only a single sheet of parchment, and weighs almost nothing. I thought that if you decided you were able to look at it, I could hand it over to you straightaway."

He lifted the flap on the bag and removed a piece of thin cardboard folded in half and secured with a couple of large elastic bands to make a rudimentary folder. He slipped off the bands holding it closed and gently spread apart the two sides.

"This is it," he said, unnecessarily.

Mohammed didn't touch the parchment, but simply bent forward to look at it closely. Fresh parchment is almost white in color, but it tans with age, eventually turning a dark brown. Unfortunately, many of the early inks shared a similar characteristic, turning from deep black into a brownish color over the years, making some ancient writings almost entirely illegible without the use of specialized techniques.

"I can see a few letters," he remarked. "What have you managed to decipher so far?"

"A handful of words, no more, and not enough to show what the text is about, except that it appears to describe some kind of military action. I think it's probably something to do with the Roman Empire, because it's written in Latin."

Mohammed nodded slowly.

"I might be able to do something with this," he said. "As far as I can tell, the parchment itself isn't damaged, and that suggests that the ink has simply faded because of the passage of time. How soon do you need the results?"

Husani smiled.

"The same as always, my friend. Yesterday or, if you

can't do that, as soon as possible. This relic will earn me no money at all while it's in your laboratory."

"Very well. I shall try my best, although I am not promising anything."

"Excellent. Thank you, my friend."

"It might also be worth getting an accurate estimate of the age of the parchment using radiocarbon dating. I can't do that at the museum, because we don't have the expertise or the equipment, but I could send it out to an external laboratory."

"I thought that method of testing destroyed the specimen?" Husani asked.

Mohammed shook his head, then nodded.

"It does, but these days, with modern techniques, the laboratories need only a tiny sliver of material to work with. So do you want me to try to get a date for the parchment? I could take a very small clipping from the edge. It would hardly be noticeable, and if you can show independent proof of age, that would probably help you when you come to sell it."

"Yes, it's a good idea. Just make sure that the piece you cut off is as small as possible. Let's meet back here tomorrow at five."

Minutes later, the two men stood up, exchanged a few last words and then separated, Mohammed walking back to the museum where he worked, while Husani headed in the direction of his home.

From that moment on, both men's lives were to be changed forever.

14

Before Ali Mohammed began carrying out tests on the parchment, he examined it closely under the bright lights on his workbench. He didn't know how much of the text Husani had been able to read with the naked eye, but there were certainly several words that could fairly clearly be seen. It was also obvious to him that the text was indeed written in Latin, as Husani had indicated at their meeting.

What's more, two words in the text stood out, because they both appeared to be proper names, and he decided he would quickly check to see if they were significant in the context of Roman history.

The bulk of the data in the Cairo Museum computer system was concerned, predictably enough, with the history of Egypt and the surrounding area, and apart from a single reference to a known place name in ancient Judea, his search proved fruitless.

Many museums around the world are linked on a kind of academic Intranet—a restricted-access wide-area network, to allow scientists and academics in one country to directly research the work of other professionals studying the same field but in different countries—and he did a general search of this resource as well, but with exactly the same result.

Almost as an afterthought, he wrote a brief e-mail requesting specialist assistance, looking up the name of the recipient from his extensive database of contacts around the world, and marked the message as high priority before sending it.

15

The instructions he had been given were clear and unambiguous, and the timescale extremely restricted. Nevertheless, the contractor—the name he was using for this particular job was simply "Abdul"—did not act immediately. That would be the mark of an amateur, and he had always prided himself on his consummate professionalism.

So before he did anything at all, he found a quiet corner on the road a little before noon, a position that gave him a clear view of the house. He placed his begging bowl, with a few coins inside it, on the ground in front of him and sat down cross-legged, his back against the wall behind him. With his ragged brown cloak wrapped around him to conceal his muscular body, the tattered hood covering his head and leaving his face invisible in the shadow, he looked just like any one of the thousands of beggars on Cairo's streets. He made certain that his hands remained out of sight, because everyone in his trade knew that hands were the one thing you couldn't disguise.

He remained in that position, almost motionless, for over three hours, watching the house with a virtually unblinking gaze. He had no photograph to guide him as yet, only a somewhat contradictory description supplied by his current employer, and this address.

When a middle-aged man who roughly matched the description he had received eventually arrived at the house, Abdul still did nothing. He now knew that the information he had been given was correct: the man returned to his home for lunch on most days, rather than visiting a restaurant somewhere in the city. And now he also knew his face.

For about another hour and a quarter Abdul remained sitting against the wall on the opposite side of the street and then, with a look into his begging bowl—a glance that revealed there were a few more coins in it than he had started with—he stood up, wrapped his cloak more tightly around him, picked up his stick and hobbled slowly away, heading in the direction from which the target had approached the house.

Abdul was an expert in surveillance tactics and techniques, and knew that even the most unobservant target might notice a beggar suddenly standing up and following him down the street. So after walking a short distance from the house, he turned into a side street and continued along it a little way before stepping into an alley. He checked all around him to ensure that nobody was in sight, and then with one swift movement dropped the beggar's cloak to the floor, revealing a somewhat creased and faded white linen suit underneath, the kind of garb worn by many low-level Cairo businessmen. The well-worn suit was a couple of sizes too large for him, deliberately chosen to hide his powerful build. His face was tanned under a thatch of black hair, with regular and unremarkable features. It was a difficult face to memorize, and was one of his most important assets, more or less essential in his line of work.

He had discarded his limp along with the cloak, and, seconds later, strode briskly back to the street, where he stopped and looked in both directions, to check that the target hadn't left the house in the brief period while he was switching identities.

Abdul walked slowly down the street, intently studying a paper he had taken out of his pocket and unfolded, a bit of supporting camouflage for the image he was trying to create. He should, he hoped, look like a businessman lost in thought as he studied a contract or a list of goods. Occasionally, he stopped for a few moments to apparently study the paper even more intently before walking on.

If his guess was right, the target should be emerging from his house fairly soon to return to his stall in the souk, and would overtake him on the street, which was just what Abdul wanted.

He paused again, as if in indecision, and looked back along the street, back toward the target's house. Even as he did so, he saw the main door swing open and a figure emerge. He was too far away to confirm the man's identity, but Abdul had little doubt about who it was. His timing had been almost perfect.

16

Less than five minutes later, after Abdul had turned back toward the center of Cairo, the paper now tucked away again in his pocket, the target overtook him. Abdul let him get about fifty yards ahead before he began to increase his pace, slowly picking up speed until he was matching the other man. As if linked by an invisible tether, the two men weaved their way through the gathering crowds around the souk.

The moment the target entered the market, Abdul moved closer, now shielded from detection by the mass of people thronging the alleys, because it was vital that he didn't lose sight of his target. In fact, the task proved easier than he had expected, because he had only gone quite a short distance inside the souk before the target stopped beside a stall and then walked around to the back of it.

Of course, Abdul knew he might just be a friend of the stallholder, and might have dropped in for a chat or something, so he strode on past and then stopped, apparently looking down at a collection of beaten brass trinkets on another stall.

Moments later, he relaxed. The target had taken a set

of keys from his pocket, unlocked a storeroom situated behind the stall and disappeared inside it. When he re-emerged, he took up station behind the stall itself, dismissing the man who had previously been manning it.

Abdul had successfully identified the stall operated by his target, and more importantly the storeroom behind the stall, where he presumed the man would keep some of his more valuable items under lock and key. But there was nothing more he could do for the moment, because of the crowds milling around in the souk.

However, being aware that the easiest option was always the best, he walked up and took a careful look at the goods being offered by his target, just in case the item he'd been told to recover was actually on sale in the stall. The most cursory glance showed that the man had nothing resembling the relic for sale.

After a moment, Abdul decided that asking a few questions was a viable option, so he picked up a curved and ornamented dagger and looked at it closely.

Clearly scenting a sale, the target—he knew the man's name was Mahmoud Kassim—immediately stepped close to Abdul and pointed at the knife he was holding.

"You have a good eye, my friend," he began, opening his sales pitch. "That, as I'm sure you already know, is a genuine Persian dagger, at least two hundred years old, and in almost perfect condition." He nodded approvingly as Abdul slid the blade out of the sheath and studied the metal. "Very few knives of this sort ever come onto the market, and those that do are almost always very well used and often incomplete, perhaps missing the sheath or some of the decoration. That dagger would be an excellent investment for you."

Abdul looked at him with a slight smile, slid the knife back into the sheath and tossed it back onto the stall.

"You needn't bother trying to deceive me," he said, "because I'm in the trade. You and I both know that this so-called Persian dagger was made in the backstreets of Cairo about a month ago, and is almost worthless. But even if it was the real thing, I wouldn't be interested in it. I only deal in old documents, parchments and scrolls and relics of that sort."

Having planted the seed, Abdul fell silent, hoping that Mahmoud would mention the ancient parchment he had been told the trader possessed. But the Egyptian's response disappointed him.

"You should have said you were a dealer, and then I wouldn't have wasted my time with you. I don't deal with scrolls or any other objects like that. I'm sorry."

Abdul nodded.

"Can you recommend any other traders in the souk who might have such relics for sale?"

Mahmoud shook his head, the scowl still on his face.

"If you are a specialist in that field, you are most unlikely to find anything here to interest you. Much like my Persian knife, most of the scrolls for sale in this market are aimed at tourists, and are produced to order by a handful of people who make a living by manufacturing these objects. I don't think you'll find a genuine antique scroll for sale anywhere here."

"And no pieces of parchment either?"

Again, Mahmoud shook his head.

"Not in this souk, no. Not as far as I know."

As Abdul strode away, he was beginning to wonder if his employer hadn't made a serious mistake. He knew the way that the Egyptian mind worked—being a member of that nation, he could consider himself something of an expert on the subject—and he was absolutely certain that if Mahmoud Kassim actually had the relic in his possession, he would definitely have offered it to him for sale, and that meant one of two things.

Either his employer, the man whose contract he had accepted very late the previous evening, had got it wrong, and the relic was actually in the possession of some other trader in the area, or for whatever reason the target had decided to keep the parchment for himself, and it was no longer for sale.

Before he did anything else, Abdul decided that he would contact his employer and raise his concerns.

He walked some distance away from the souk before finding a quiet spot and taking out his mobile phone. There were no numbers stored in the memory. All of the telephone numbers Abdul used were held either in his head or on his computer in a hidden and encrypted directory that could only be accessed by the application of a twelve-digit key, a key he changed every month. In this case, he had committed the man's number to memory, and dialed it.

His call was answered almost immediately.

"Do you have it?"

Neither man would mention any names or anything else that could possibly incriminate them. Calls from one mobile to another were fairly secure, but it simply wasn't worth taking a chance.

"No," Abdul replied. "I have spoken to the man and he says he does not have it. By his manner, I don't think he was lying—unless he is a much more sophisticated man than I think. How certain is your information?"

"An intercept was performed yesterday. We know that it must be in his possession."

Abdul thought for a moment before replying.

"Actually," he said, "all that information proves is that he has come across it. It doesn't prove that he still has it."

"Perhaps. But he is the only lead we have, so you are to continue as we discussed. It is essential that we find and recover the object."

"And the man?" Abdul wanted to be absolutely clear of the course of action he was to follow.

"He is expendable. All other considerations are secondary to the object's recovery."

17

"I'll be quite glad when I've finished this," Angela Lewis remarked, to nobody in particular.

"I thought you liked being busy," the man standing almost opposite her on the other side of the long workbench said.

Angela put down the magnifying glass she had been using to examine the badly crazed surface of a potsherd and rubbed her eyes.

"I do, Charles," she replied, "but at the moment there's just so much work piling up here that I simply can't see the end of it. And, of course, with summer leave now virtually upon us, there isn't anybody else I can ask to come and give me a hand. I'd love to be able to get out of here and look at something else for a few days."

She gestured to the two large open cardboard boxes sitting close to her on the workbench. Her job as a ceramics conservator had always fascinated and infuriated her in almost equal measure. There were few feelings to compare with the profound sense of satisfaction she always found when she was able to reassemble a pot or a jar from a collection of shattered fragments. But every time she was presented with a new task, the feeling of frustration mounted.

Charles Westman grinned in acknowledgment at her words. His particular specialty was ancient weaponry, which only rarely involved the reassembly of anything. In fact, he was only in the laboratory to check that a Saxon sword that had recently been found in a field in East Anglia was being properly cleaned before preservation work started on the metal.

"I thought you'd have had enough of gallivanting around the world tracking down ancient relics with that ex-husband of yours."

"I don't think I'm away from the museum as much as you are, Charles. This is really only a part-time job for you, isn't it?"

Westman nodded.

"I'm fortunate in that respect, yes, my dear. I don't actually have to work, but the job here is still useful for all sorts of reasons. But I think Chris Bronson—that is his name, isn't it?—is a bad influence on you. Whenever he comes into the picture, things always seem to take a turn for the worse and you end up running for your life. Surely a bit of normality is a welcome change?"

Angela bridled slightly.

"That's as may be," she replied, "but one thing you can say about Chris is that time spent with him is never boring. Life-threatening, yes, occasionally, but boring, never. And this"—she pointed again at the boxes of potsherds awaiting her attention—"is very definitely boring."

Westman smiled at her. When Angela was in this kind of mood, he knew exactly which buttons to press to get a rise from her.

"But you have to look on the bright side," he said. "Just think how pleased the museum will be when you've assembled another anonymous pot which they can put on a display alongside dozens of other anonymous pots. Every time you walk past it you'll get a warm fuzzy feeling of tremendous satisfaction."

Angela lowered the fragments of pottery to the workbench and glared at him.

"If this relic wasn't almost two thousand years old, and I hadn't signed for the blasted thing, I'd be very much inclined to throw it at you," she snapped.

Westman's smile grew broader.

"Just winding you up, my dear, doing my bit to keep up your spirits. In fact, I really think you could do with a break before you start throwing things around and hurting people. Now, I've got nothing much to do for a while, so do you fancy a cup of coffee?"

"Canteen or proper coffee out in the streets somewhere?"

Westman looked slightly insulted.

"Proper, obviously. What kind of a man you take me for?"

Angela snapped off the desk lights, stood up and eased her aching back.

"You really don't want me to answer that, do you, Charles? I've known you for too long," she teased, wondering, and not for the first time, about Westman's personal circumstances.

He was unlike most of her other colleagues at the museum, who tended to be casually and comfortably scruffy. Westman was about six feet tall and slightly overweight, carrying just a few extra pounds, but always clean-shaven and immaculately dressed in a three-piece suit, a silk handkerchief in his breast pocket and his shoes buffed to a high shine. He wasn't handsome in the conventional sense, his nose a little too big and slightly crooked, but with friendly gray eyes and a ready smile, and he had always been pleasant company.

In fact, Angela had a sneaking suspicion that he fancied her, which presumably meant he wasn't gay as she'd first suspected, but he'd never made any overt move that could confirm this.

She took a last glance at the pottery crowded together on her workbench and shook her head.

"At times like this," she said, "I almost wish I'd become a palaeontologist. At least they get to spend some of their time out in the field."

Charles Westman shuddered elaborately.

"Far too crude, my dear, all those bones and teeth and fossilized poo. And sunburn—if you're lucky—and too much dirt under your fingernails. No, not really your style at all, I think."

Just after they'd left the laboratory, Angela's laptop computer emitted a musical tone. She'd received an e-mail.

18

The souk never really closed, but as the heat of the afternoon sun diminished slightly and the shadows around the stalls deepened and lengthened, most of the tourists and serious buyers began to leave. And by the middle of the evening most of the stallholders and traders had followed their example, locking away their goods in their storerooms or chests or other secure locations, and leaving the area to enjoy their evening meal.

So when Abdul returned, a couple of hours before midnight, the souk was virtually deserted. Just a handful of traders were still in evidence as they locked up their shops or tried to interest any remaining tourists in some last-minute bargains. He ignored all their blandishments and strode swiftly along the narrow alleyways until he reached Mahmoud's stall.

It was, as he had expected, deserted, the storeroom door closed and locked. But that wouldn't be a problem. When he'd been talking to the Egyptian trader earlier that day, Abdul had glanced at the keyhole on the storeroom door and the bunch of keys that Mahmoud had placed casually on the stall itself. The ability to get inside a locked room was more or less one of the qualifications of his profession, and he knew this one wouldn't be difficult. He knelt down in front of the door, virtually invisible to anyone passing unless they looked over the top of the stall, and removed an L-shaped lock pick, a tool known as a twirl, from his pocket. Then he set to work.

His expert probing fingers quickly identified the mortise lock as having only three levers—barely adequate for an interior door in a house, and certainly not sufficient for a storeroom that quite probably held valuable artifacts. One after the other, the levers fell prey to his twirl, and in a little over a minute he was able to stand up, glance around to ensure that he was still unobserved, then open the door and step inside.

He pulled the door to behind him and checked that the storeroom had no windows through which torch light could be seen. But the space was in total darkness.

Abdul took a slim pencil torch from his pocket and switched it on. He first looked all round to ensure that there were no signs of an alarm system, though the quality of the door and its lock suggested to him that this was unlikely. Satisfied, he then began searching the contents of the storeroom.

The search wasn't easy because, although he knew exactly what he was looking for, he had no idea what it would be stored in. Some objects he knew he could ignore. His employer had explained that the parchment would be fairly fragile and certainly would not be rolled and placed inside a jar or anything of that sort. So Abdul could not even look at the contents of two of the shelves, because they only held pottery vessels of different sizes. But that still left a large number of boxes whose dimensions were large enough to contain the relic. Checking each of those took him a considerable length of time. In fact, it took him so long that he had to change the batteries on his torch halfway through.

He finally gave up just after midnight, stood for a few moments in the open space in the center of the cramped and crowded storeroom and shone his torch methodically at everything in it. Then he nodded in satisfaction. He had checked every possible hiding place and container that was big enough to take the parchment, and his conclusion was obvious. If—and Abdul still wondered just how big an "if" this was—the trader Mahmoud had the parchment, he hadn't secreted it in either his storeroom or the stall itself, which was completely empty.

The only other place left to look was the target's house, so that's where he was going to go next.

19

Minutes later, Abdul was standing in a doorway across the road from Mahmoud's house, carrying out a final reconnoitre. No lights were burning, and he could hear no sound emanating from the building.

He checked carefully up and down the street, then crossed the road and walked silently down the alley that ran along one side of the property, continuing his surveillance. Again he noted nothing to alarm him, and so with one swift movement he vaulted over the low wall at the back of the house, to land in Mahmoud's tiny rear courtyard.

As he had expected, both the back door and the two windows that looked onto the courtyard were closed and locked. Using his torch, he examined the lock on the door, and then the catches on the windows. Immediately, he ruled out the windows. There were no external keyholes, and the only way in using that route would be to break the glass, which would be fairly noisy.

The lock on the door was far less of a problem. Abdul didn't bother with a lock pick this time, just took an object shaped rather like a small pistol from his pocket, stuck the end of it in the keyhole, applied a gentle turning force to the tool and then pulled the trigger half a dozen times. The professional-quality gun pick did its job efficiently. After a second or two he was able to turn the tool in a complete circle, and was rewarded by a click as the dead-lock retracted.

He reached into his pocket, pulled out a pair of latex surgical gloves and carefully slid them onto his hands. They were longer than normal, the cuffs extending about halfway up his forearms, and were another essential tool of his often messy trade. Then, cautiously, he opened the door just wide enough to allow him to slide his body through the gap, and pushed the door closed behind him.

There were, Abdul knew, two possible approaches to locating the missing relic. First, he could wander about the house, looking in every room and hoping to see it lying on a table or a desk somewhere, or perhaps spot whatever box or protective sleeve Mahmoud had placed it inside. But that could take all night and there was absolutely no guarantee that the search would be successful. If Mahmoud knew that the parchment was valuable, he might well have locked it away in a safe or strongbox somewhere.

The second approach was what might be termed the direct option. Instead of trying to find the parchment, Abdul would find Mahmoud himself and make him a hand over the relic. And that option appealed to him far more.

His footsteps barely audible, he moved from room to room on the ground floor, thoroughly checking each one in turn to ensure that nobody was in them. Then he found his way to the wooden staircase that ran through the center of the house and made his way up it as quietly as he could, keeping close to the wall on the right-hand side, where he hoped the treads would creak as little as possible. Every two or three steps he paused and just listened, but heard nothing.

On the landing, he saw four doors. Two were closed and the other two were standing open. He inspected the open ones first, finding that one was just a small storeroom, and the other a bathroom. Then he stepped across to the first of the two closed doors and pressed his ear against the wood, listening intently. There was no sound from inside the room that he could detect, so he grasped the handle and turned it cautiously, easing the door open as soundlessly as he could.

The room was apparently a spare bedroom, equipped with two single beds, neither of them made, just two wooden frames and mattresses visible in the pale moonlight filtering through the thin curtain at the window.

That was good news. Abdul was a professional and always tried to avoid causing collateral damage. If there had been a couple of children sleeping there, he would probably have had to kill them as well. As it was, he assumed that Mahmoud either lived alone or at worst had a wife sleeping beside him.

Abdul eased his way out the empty bedroom and stepped across the landing to the other closed door. Again he listened, and this time he could detect a faint sound, a rhythmic gentle snoring that was clearly audible even through the thickness of the closed bedroom door. That was all he needed to know.

There was a small automatic pistol tucked away in Abdul's pocket, but he really didn't want to have to use that weapon because of the noise that it would make. His knives would be just as effective and completely silent. And, in reality, he much preferred the personal contact a knife offered.

He seized the door handle and began to turn it very gently. It was possible that Mahmoud had bolted or locked the door on the inside, and it would not have surprised him if the door hadn't budged. But in fact, it swung open easily on its hinges, and he immediately stepped into the bedroom.

This was by far the biggest room on the upper floor of the house, large enough to accommodate a substantial double bed, a couple of freestanding wardrobes and three chests of drawers. On one side of the room was another door standing ajar, and through the opening Abdul could see the white gleam of sanitary fittings. Clearly the room possessed an en suite. Abdul smiled slightly to himself. When he'd met Kassim briefly in the souk, the trader hadn't struck him as a man used to such comparatively luxurious surroundings.

His heart rate increased just slightly. It was now time to get the information, and the relic, which he had been paid to do. The time for stealth was over.

20

The assassin strode across the room, stopped beside the bed and snapped on the bedside light. He wasn't sure whether it was the sudden brightness flooding through the room or the noise of his footsteps, but as he took his final pace, Mahmoud woke up with a jerk and a snort.

Instantly, Abdul drew his knife from the leather sheath attached to the waistband of his trousers and held the blade six inches in front of Mahmoud's face.

The trader's eyes widened as he looked at the cold steel blade glinting in the light, and then focused his eyes beyond the weapon at Abdul's face staring down at him.

"You're the dealer," he stuttered. "You came to my stall, looking for parchment."

Abdul nodded.

"You have a good memory," he said, "and I'm still looking for a sheet of parchment. One parchment in particular. One that I know you have."

Mahmoud shook his head slightly, panic growing in his eyes.

"I told you. I don't have any parchments for sale."

"My information is different. I know that you spent

some time searching the Internet for some very specific words, words that could only have come from one source. And you know what that source is as well as I do."

Mahmoud's expression changed as realization dawned.

"Oh, that parchment. But I don't have it anymore. I sold it on, sold it to another trader. But it was almost illegible," he protested. "Hardly any of the words on it could be read. Why is it so important to you?"

"It's not important to me at all," Abdul replied, the point of his knife moving down Mahmoud's face until it rested lightly and threateningly on the thin skin of his neck below his chin. "But it is very important to the man who's paying me."

For a couple of seconds, Abdul considered his next course of action. Mahmoud could well be lying to him, he knew, and the parchment might be concealed somewhere inside the house, in a safe or elsewhere, or the man might genuinely have disposed of it. Before he left that room, he needed to be absolutely certain of the truth. And he was very good at uncovering the truth.

"Are you right-handed or left-handed?" he asked.

"What?"

"It doesn't really matter, I suppose," Abdul replied.

Then, in a blur of action so fast that Mahmoud had absolutely no time to react, Abdul seized the man's right arm, wrenched it over so that his wrist was resting on the table beside the bed, and slammed his knife straight through the back of Mahmoud's hand, pinning it to the wood.

The Egyptian's howl of pain filled the room as blood welled from the penetrating wound, pooled on the table and began to drip onto the wooden floor below. Abdul pressed the bedsheet over the trader's mouth, muffling the sound. Kassim jerked in the bed, perhaps trying to sit up, or to reach for the wound with his left hand, but before he could do anything at all, Abdul had produced a second knife and held it firmly against his throat.

"Quiet," the intruder ordered. "That just shows how important it is for you to tell me the truth. Make me believe that you're holding nothing back, and I might just walk away from here. If you lie, you'll die. It's as simple as that."

He moved the second blade slightly away from Mahmoud's throat until the point rested on the tender area below the man's left shoulder blade. He changed his grip on the knife very slightly, then slowly began pushing it into Mahmoud's flesh, the honed and polished double-edged blade easily penetrating about an inch into the man's body.

Again, Mahmoud howled in muffled agony, his scream barely audible behind the makeshift gag Abdul was applying. His body twitched under the assault and sweat sprang to his brow as the pain increased.

Abdul knew the signs, knew that the man under his knife would do almost anything to make him stop. Now he could find the truth.

"The first question is easy," he said, moving the sheet away from Kassim's mouth, "because the answer is either yes or no. Do you still have that parchment?"

Mahmoud shook his head desperately from side to side.

"I told you. I sold it to another dealer."

"So that would be 'no,' then?"

"No. I mean, yes. I don't have it. I don't have it any longer."

Abdul nodded.

"So who did you sell it to?"

For additional emphasis, he turned the knife slightly in

the wound on Mahmoud's shoulder, eliciting another anguished cry of pain, quickly muffled.

"Another dealer," he almost shouted. "His name is Anum Husani. He deals in old manuscripts and other relics, and he has a shop in Cairo."

Abdul nodded again, then gave the knife another twist, the point scraping along Mahmoud's collarbone.

"The address would be helpful," he said, his sentence almost drowned out by the other man's muffled scream.

His voice quivering and laced with agony, Mahmoud stammered out the address of Husani's shop, an address that Abdul immediately filed away in his memory.

After a further prod from the knife blade, Mahmoud followed that with a physical description of Husani. But when Abdul asked for the man's home address, his victim was unable to help, and even twisting the blade in a fresh wound didn't produce the information he wanted.

"You're absolutely certain?" he asked, altering his grip on the handle of the knife very slightly, and feeling Mahmoud's body tensing in pointless anticipation of the pain to come.

"Yes, yes. He has it. I sold it to him, but I don't know where he lives. Please, no more."

"I do have some good news for you," Abdul said after a moment, withdrawing the knife from the man's shoulder and wiping the blood from the blade on the sheet. "I believe you. I think you're telling me the truth."

He looked down at the man on the bed.

"But I also have some bad news for you," he added, and with another rapid movement he sliced the knife into the left-hand side of Mahmoud's throat and pulled it all the way across, the blade instantly severing the esophagus and the carotid artery. Blood spurted from the end of the artery, splashing onto the wall behind the head of the bed.

The man's body flailed on the bed as his left hand clutched desperately at his throat, but it only took seconds for the light in his eyes to fade away as his brain died.

"And that was the bad news," Abdul muttered, standing clear of the side of the bed and looking down at the corpse.

He wiped the blood off his knife on the sheet, then pulled the other blade out of Mahmoud's right hand, wiping that as well, but he didn't replace the knives in their respective sheaths. First, he needed to wash them properly. He stood up and checked that none of the blood he had spilled had got onto his clothing, but he could see no sign of it. The latex gloves were heavily stained, but he would dispose of them after he left the property. To avoid any of the blood being transferred from his gloves to his clothing, he first went into the attached bathroom and washed his gloved hands in the sink, drying the latex on a towel when he'd finished. Then he carefully washed both knives until not a trace of blood was left on them, dried them and put them away in their sheaths. He would bleach everything thoroughly later.

Five minutes later, he was outside the house, having relocked the rear door, and was making his way through the silent streets of the Cairo suburb.

21

That evening, Angela followed her usual routine once she got back to her apartment. She poured herself a large glass of wine, switched on the TV to inspect the day's news, and flopped down on the sofa, kicking off her shoes as she did so. Once she'd seen the headlines, she used the remote control to turn off the set, and then opened up her laptop.

She worked her way quickly through her work in-box, marking the vast majority of the e-mails not simply for deletion, but also to be bounced back to the sender—her way of trying to spam the spammers. As she glanced down the list of senders of the unread e-mails, one message stood out. She hadn't heard from that particular person for some months, and the area he worked in was of great interest to her.

She clicked it open, and read the fairly short message. The first couple of brief paragraphs were simply a polite catch-up, which her eyes skimmed over as she looked for the meat in the sandwich. Although she didn't know Ali Mohammed particularly well, she knew that he was not inclined to waste words, nor to contact her simply to ask what she was up to. He would have a very specific reason for sending her a message, and she was keen to find out what it was.

His question was in the final paragraph. A colleague had given him a sheet of parchment to work on. The relic appeared to be old, he explained somewhat unnecessarily, and the writing on it was largely invisible. He would be working on it to try to decipher exactly what the text said, and if it was interesting he would be happy to send her a photograph of the parchment and a copy of the text.

But in the meantime, there were a few words that could be read on the parchment and he thought the subject matter might prove of interest to her, in view of her previous experiences with relics from this period and location. The period, he went on to explain, was most likely late in the first century BC, perhaps a few years earlier, and the location was almost certainly Judea. Judea under the Romans, in fact, because the text on the parchment was clearly written in Latin, implying that it had been penned by an official in either the Roman government or the Roman army. And there were, he finished, two proper names that could be read, at least partially, and he would be interested to know if she had heard of them in any relevant context.

The first name, he explained, was "ippori" with two unreadable letters at the start of the word, which suggested it might be "Tzippori." Nothing else he could think of fitted. That had convinced him that the parchment referred to events in ancient Judea, because Tzippori, as he was sure Angela knew, was the old name for the town of Sepporis, which had been destroyed by the Romans in 4 BC, following the death of Herod. The second name was clearly Jewish in origin, but was also only partially readable, the letters that could be interpreted with certainty being *ef bar he*, the *bar* meaning "son of."

"*Ef bar he*," Angela muttered to herself, as she read the last paragraph again. It seemed to strike a chord somewhere in her memory, but for the moment she just couldn't pin it down.

She quickly typed a reply to Ali Mohammed, telling him that she would be interested in reading the complete text of the parchment if and when he was able to decipher it, and assuring him that she would investigate the information he had already given her. She sent the e-mail, closed the laptop and walked briskly to her kitchen. She pulled open the freezer and selected a frozen lasagne. When she was by herself, she never bothered cooking, relying mostly on ready meals of one sort or another.

She decided that she'd eat dinner, then spend some time researching the words Ali Mohammed had seen on the parchment.

But that plan was immediately shelved when Chris Bronson, her ex-husband and best friend, called and asked if she'd like to go out for a bite to eat.

It wasn't a difficult decision for her to make.

22

"You seem miles away tonight," Chris Bronson said, about three hours later, as he and Angela sat in a quiet corner of an Italian restaurant on the eastern outskirts of Ealing, two coffee cups on the table between them.

Angela was fiddling with the wrapped sugar cubes that had come with the coffee, piling them one on top of the other and then knocking over the small stack with a flick of her elegant forefinger. She paused in her repetitive construction and demolition operation and looked at him.

"Oh, it's nothing of any importance. I've had an e-mail from a man I've worked with in the past, out in Cairo. He's apparently been given an old piece of parchment to work on—he's an ancient document specialist—and he's asked me if a couple of the names in the text mean anything to me."

"And do they?"

Angela shook her head in mild irritation.

"That's the trouble. One of them is quite obvious—it's just the old name of a town in Judea—but the other one is only a partial name, just the middle section, and I'm quite sure I've seen or heard it before, but I just can't think where. It's not important, or at least I don't think it is, but it's just a kind of niggle, you know? Like an itch you can't scratch."

"I'm sure it'll come to you."

"It probably will," she replied, "and probably at about three in the morning."

Bronson nodded, then lifted his hands into the air and tried to get the waiter's attention. The waiter, who had studiously ignored them for most of the meal, finally noticed and disappeared behind the bar, eventually returning with the bill.

It had been raining earlier that evening, but when they stepped out of the restaurant onto the pavement, the slabs were already dry and, despite the illumination provided by the streetlamps, a few stars were clearly visible above them.

"I suppose you were expecting to stay the night?" Angela asked, as they walked the few hundred yards back from the restaurant to the apartment block where she lived.

Despite their divorce of a few years earlier, Bronson and Angela had remained good friends, sharing holidays and other exploits, occasionally even sharing a bed. Despite this, Angela still insisted she was not ready to have another go at their marriage—indeed at any marriage—though Bronson himself would like nothing better. While this arrangement occasionally caused heartache on both sides, it seemed to be the one that worked best for them both.

"I'd like to," he replied quietly. "I'm not working for the next few days," he added. "I just finished my part of a major investigation, so I'm due some leave."

"How nice. You can have a lie-in, then, while I brave the rigors of the District Line to central London," Angela said, rather waspishly for her. "Unlike you, I have a proper job to go to, with proper working hours, Monday to Friday, nine to five. That kind of thing."

"I think being a police officer does count as a 'proper job' these days," Bronson replied mildly. "But I'll get up at the same time as you do and then we can ride the Tube together. There's some stuff I need to do at my house tomorrow morning, so I can go on from there straight to Tunbridge Wells."

Angela nodded, but didn't reply.

"Is everything OK?" Bronson asked.

"Not entirely, no," she replied. "Perhaps next time you're pretending to be a gentleman you can escort me to a decent restaurant, one where the waitresses aren't all tarts."

"What?" Bronson felt entirely confused.

"I noticed you looking at that waitress, the one with the butt."

Bronson colored slightly.

"I like to look," he protested, "but I never touch. And so what if she's got a nice butt?"

"Well, when you're with me, Chris, I prefer it if you *don't* look, OK? It doesn't make me feel good about myself when the man I'm sharing a meal with spends most of his time looking at everyone but me."

Bronson was silent for a moment, conscious that he'd severely ruffled Angela's feathers, and without even being aware of it. No different to normal, then. And now she was looking at him with a peculiar intensity in her stare that was a good enough warning to concede the point.

"I'm really sorry," he said. "It won't happen again. I didn't even know I was doing it."

Angela dropped her gaze after a moment; then she shook her head.

"God," she muttered. "I'm sorry too. I'm a bit over-sensitive at the moment. Work is really boring, I can't find the answer to the question Ali Mohammed asked, and to see you drooling over that dyed-blond bimbo in a third-rate restaurant was almost the last straw."

She fell silent for a few seconds, then looked up at him.

"I will admit one thing, though."

"What?"

"She *had* got a nice butt. You were right about that."

"Yours is better," Bronson said immediately.

"Well, in that case . . ." Angela unlocked her door and led the way inside.

23

News, especially bad news, travels quickly in Cairo, and rumors of the torture and killing of a local trader were already sweeping through the souk.

Mahmoud Kassim had a cleaner-cum-housekeeper who visited his property every day, and her echoing screams when she walked into his bedroom had alerted almost everybody in the street. The Egyptian police were already investigating the murder, and had several firm leads, according to the gossip in the coffeehouses.

Abdul frankly doubted that, because he had been very careful to ensure he had left no physical traces of his presence anywhere in the property, apart from the dead body. But the uproar over the killing was unwelcome to him and to his employer.

"You should have disposed of the body, you fool."

Abdul was not used to being spoken to like that, and immediately his temper flared.

"I couldn't dispose of the body. Walking through the streets of Cairo carrying a corpse would have been far more dangerous than leaving him where he died. It's just unfortunate that this cleaning woman went into the house and found him so quickly."

"The word 'unfortunate' doesn't even begin to cover it. You do realize it's possible that this other dealer, this man Husani, will now be on his guard?"

Abdul shook his head and walked a little farther down the deserted alley, holding his mobile phone to his ear.

"Not necessarily. There is no obvious reason why he should assume that Mahmoud's death was anything to do with the object he bought from him."

The deep voice at the other end of the line gave a snort of disbelief.

"You'd better be right," he snapped. "You have not fulfilled this contract in a satisfactory manner to date. If you do not resolve this matter, and quickly, we may be forced to take further steps."

"Are you threatening me?" Abdul asked, his voice suddenly cold with barely suppressed anger.

"Yes, of course I am," the man replied simply. "You're not the only contractor in Cairo. Unless you deliver the parchment to me within the next twenty-four hours, we will terminate the contract and issue appropriate orders to another person. Orders that may indirectly include you. You have been warned."

Before Abdul could even begin to formulate a reply, the other man ended the call.

24

In a large and comfortable house on the southern outskirts of Cairo, Jalal Khusad, a heavily built and prosperous-looking middle-aged man, his face dominated by a large and very black beard, looked at his mobile phone with an irritated expression on his face. Then, with a gesture of disgust, he tossed the phone onto the tooled leather top of his mahogany desk.

Things were not going as he had planned. As a senior member of P2 in Egypt, he knew of the Englishman by reputation, and he didn't want to disappoint him. He couldn't afford to.

The matter had seemed simple enough and should not have been difficult to complete. All his contractor Abdul had been told to do was recover a single piece of parchment and eliminate whoever had possession of it. The assassin was well-known throughout Cairo and even elsewhere in Egypt for his success rate. How had he failed?

And now Khusad had to pass the information up the line. A call that he was dreading.

He opened a small notebook bound in red leather and opened it to a particular page. On it were a series of num-

bers. On first appearance they looked like rows of telephone numbers, but were simply a low-security way he had
devised of concealing the one genuine telephone number—a number that actually ran diagonally across the grid.

Below the grid were three time periods during which
the recipient would be available to take his call. Khusad
didn't know precisely who his contact was, but he knew
he was a senior person within the Vatican, and assumed
that he would have to leave the Holy See in order to use
his mobile phone without his conversation being overheard or his location identified. And, allowing for the
time difference between Cairo and Rome, the man
should be available right then.

Khusad ran one stubby finger down the list until he
came to the third number that, like all the others, began
with a zero. Then he dialed the digits that appeared in a
diagonal line running downward and to the right from
that initial number. He heard the ringing tone of the recipient's phone, and then his call was answered by a soft
and heavily accented voice.

"*Si.*"

Their rules for communication were simple and invio-
lable. Unless it was completely unavoidable, neither man
would use either his own name or the names of any of the
other people involved in the operation, mention any
dates or place-names, or refer to the relic directly. Both
parties doubted if any of their calls were monitored, but
it was never worth taking a chance.

"We don't yet have it," Khusad began, speaking in
French, "but we think we know where it is."

"That is not what I wanted to hear," the other man replied. "You told me that your agent, this man you had
hired, was acting immediately. And that he was competent."

Khusad had been expecting anger in response to his

call, but instead the voice in the earpiece sounded nervous and disturbed, almost frightened.

"His reputation suggested that he is normally very competent," the Egyptian replied, "and you will recall your instructions were to employ an outside contractor and not one of my own men to ensure complete deniability. In the event, I do not think a member of my organization would necessarily have fared any better. The man followed my instructions to the letter but in the interval between your orders being issued and him obtaining access to the premises, the goods had been passed on to a third party."

There was a brief silence while the recipient of the call digested this piece of information.

"So what of the original custodian? Is he aware of the significance and importance of the object?"

"As far as we have been able to discover, he had no idea what it was or why anyone would be interested in it," Khusad replied. "And now he has no knowledge of it whatsoever."

"You are quite certain of that?"

"He will not be telling anyone anything that he knew."

The man in Italy was silent for a moment, then spoke again.

"I suppose that has to be considered good news, in the circumstances. And now your agent will be approaching this third party you claim to have identified?"

"Exactly. I have told him we need to conclude this operation within twenty-four hours."

"You may need to retain this agent you have hired for rather longer than that. Our monitoring system here has detected another instance of the same search term being used, and we will expect you to take the same action with this individual as with the first custodian."

That was a piece of news Khusad had definitely not expected, or wanted, to hear.

"Perhaps this other search was initiated by the person who now has possession of the object," he suggested.

"Not necessarily. Do you know the occupation of the new custodian? And I need his name."

"I understand that he's just another market trader. His name is Anum Husani."

"Then you will definitely need to take additional action to ensure that this matter remains as confidential as we require. There is now at least one other person involved in this."

"How can you be certain of that?"

There was another pause before the reply came.

"Because the last search that our system detected originated from Cairo Museum. And we are also tracking an e-mail sent by that person. His name is Ali Mohammed."

25

Antonio Morini, sitting in civilian clothes at a table in a small café near the Tiber, ended the call and slipped the mobile phone back into the pocket of his light jacket. He had been worried about just how specific he should be in his responses, because the Englishman had emphasized so forcefully the need for security in all communications, and especially during telephone calls, to protect everyone involved. But he had come to the conclusion that he needed to risk spelling out the name of the man who'd originated the new search—indeed that he really had no other option. He had to ensure that the correct action would be taken.

The Italian priest was becoming more concerned with every hour that passed. What had seemed at first to be a simple and uncomplicated, albeit brutal, operation—to locate, seize and possibly destroy a piece of ancient parchment, and to ensure that the owner of the relic was in no position to tell anyone anything about it, ever—was beginning to assume unwelcome proportions.

He had prayed for guidance every night, and by summoning up every scrap of his faith he'd been able to rationalize the actions he'd been ordered to take, the instruction to eliminate the market trader in Cairo, telling himself that a dealer in relics was absolutely the last person who should have access to the parchment. If the man had realized what he held in his hands, and decided to sell it to the highest bidder or even went public with the contents, the consequences would have been catastrophic. It was a case of measuring the life of one unimportant but potentially dangerous individual against the spiritual well-being of tens of millions of worshippers around the world.

But now that man was dead, as the Englishman had instructed, and still the parchment hadn't been recovered. Worse than that, it appeared that another person, a second market trader, in fact, was in possession of the relic, and somehow he had managed to involve a scientist in a museum in Cairo. And that man had contacted a professional colleague about the parchment. Knowledge of the object was spreading uncomfortably fast.

Morini regretted the loss of even one life—as a priest all human life was sacred to him—but the situation he found himself in offered no relief. If he didn't relay the Englishman's orders, far more than just a couple of men would die, and he knew it. Feeling a dull ache of revulsion course through his body, he muttered another brief prayer, then took out his mobile again. He knew he had to pass on the latest developments to the Englishman. It would not, he anticipated, be a very enjoyable conversation.

He raised his hand and ordered another *caffè latte*. When the drink was on the table in front of him and he was satisfied that nobody was close enough to be able to overhear any part of his conversation, he dialed the number.

As before, the call was answered by a quiet English

voice that simply said "Yes?" and Morini glanced around him, checking his surroundings once more before he said anything. Then he briefly explained the new developments. When he'd finished, the man he'd called didn't respond for a few moments, and when he did Morini could hear the cold, suppressed anger in his voice, though his first words were a surprise.

"I apologize. With what you've told me, it's very clear that my agent in Cairo and the contractor he selected were inadequate, and I will take steps to remedy this, but only when the present operation has been concluded."

Morini felt a fresh pang of guilt, guessing that whatever penalties the Englishman intended to visit upon the two men in Egypt would almost certainly be painful and possibly fatal.

"So we have two further targets to take care of," the English voice continued, "and the precise location of the relic is still uncertain. It could be in the possession of the second custodian, or with the third, at the museum itself. In a few minutes I will send you a message with further orders. Anything else?"

"Yes," Morini replied. "There is one other matter, which concerns the scientist. He has supplied some details of the relic by e-mail to a professional colleague in England."

"What details?"

"According to the intercept program, only two or three words."

"It might only be two or three words, but that could be quite enough to be a real threat to you. I will make arrangements to attend to that person as well. As he's in England, there will be no need for you to get involved."

"It's a woman," Morini pointed out.

"Immaterial. When you reply to my text message, include everything you know about both the e-mail and the recipient."

For a couple of minutes after he had ended the call, Morini just sat at the table, the mobile phone still held in his right hand and his eyes staring vacantly in front of him.

He knew he was only acting as a conduit, relaying orders that had been formulated and decided upon by the Englishman who was in overall charge of the operation, as the protocols had stipulated. But he was still fighting a losing moral battle with his conscience. He knew with absolute certainty that the orders he had previously passed on to the man in Cairo had resulted in one death. But on the other side of the coin was the almost inevitable catastrophe of global proportions if the relic could not be recovered and its contents were made public. And that was a possibility that he simply could not tolerate.

Ever since Father Gianni's revelations, Morini had viewed everything about the Vatican and the Catholic Church in a very different light. But despite that, he still believed in the fundamental goodness of his religion, and knew that he would do whatever was necessary to protect it. The only thing he couldn't understand was why the damning—and damnable—parchment hadn't been destroyed centuries earlier.

The reality Morini personally was facing was that if the parchment were not recovered, he would be the one who would have to explain the sequence of events, and the inevitable consequences, to the Holy Father. And that was something he was desperate to avoid, at all costs.

The text message he'd been expecting arrived about five minutes later, and even before he read it, Morini had guessed the contents.

He read the text twice to ensure he hadn't missed anything, then finished his coffee, paid the bill and left the café. Five minutes later, from another pay phone he hadn't used before, his call to a mobile phone in Cairo was answered, and two minutes after that, he'd passed on the orders he had just been given.

Morini crossed himself as he ended the call, but in truth he was less concerned about the imminent deaths of two men in Egypt than he was about what the scientist had done. Ali Mohammed had e-mailed a woman in England, a woman—the software had informed him—who worked at the British Museum in London.

The leaks were getting worse and had now spread far beyond the borders of Egypt, and not for the first time he seriously doubted whether the contagion could be contained at all.

26

Abdul was intensely frustrated. He had the name of his quarry—Anum Husani—and the address of the man's shop, but he had no idea where the trader lived.

He leaned against a wall in a narrow alleyway, a few yards away from the entrance to the shop operated by his target, virtually invisible among the crowds of people strolling up and down. He had already walked into the shop to inspect some of the goods on offer, choosing a time when the trader apparently in charge of the establishment was busy with two other customers, and taking care to keep his face averted. All that had achieved was to confirm what he'd already guessed, that Husani wasn't on the premises. The description of the man he'd forced out of Mahmoud before he'd killed him was accurate enough for him to be certain of that.

He could wait for him, of course, but that would only work if the man was intending to visit the shop, and as it was already midmorning, that was looking increasingly unlikely. With the news of Mahmoud's death already coursing through the streets, and the only connection—as far as Abdul knew—between the two men being the ancient parchment, any prudent man would probably decide to lie low for a while. He needed to find out where his target lived, and as quickly as possible, before the trader ran for his life.

Abdul waited until Husani's shop was empty again, then strode forward briskly, pushed open the door and stepped inside.

"I have an urgent message for Anum Husani," he said, walking across the small shop to the counter at the back, behind which a swarthy and heavily built man, most of his face invisible behind a thick black beard, the hairs heavily curled with the apparent consistency of wire wool, was sitting and reading an Arabic-language newspaper.

"He's not here," the man replied, glancing up from his paper, "and he might not be here all day. Give it to me and I'll see he gets it as soon as he arrives."

"No," Abdul said. "I have to deliver it in person, and he must get it today."

The idea of such unseemly haste clearly puzzled the trader.

"But he isn't here, so you can't," he stated.

"Then I'll have to deliver it to his home address. Where does he live?"

The man put down his newspaper and looked at Abdul for a long moment; then he shrugged his shoulders, picked up a pencil and a small piece of paper from the counter in front of him, scribbled something on it and handed it to Abdul.

"He might not be there," he warned.

"Thank you," Abdul replied, glancing at what the man had written. Then he turned and left the shop.

He now had a good chance of concluding the contract that day—well within the tight timescale he had been given. And he hadn't even had to kill anyone to get this vital piece of information.

27

"You know Mahmoud Kassim?"

It wasn't so much a question as a statement of fact, because the market trader sitting opposite Anum Husani in the coffeehouse in central Cairo had been involved in at least one deal with both men in the past.

Husani nodded.

"Of course," he replied.

The other man glanced around him before he said anything else.

"Then you know that he's dead?" he said, leaning forward and lowering his voice.

"What?"

"Somebody broke into his house last night," the Arab trader explained, smacking his lips with something like relish. "I heard that he was so badly cut about with a knife that the police weren't even certain it was his body. Wounds everywhere, apparently, and his throat slashed open to the spine. The bedroom floor was covered in blood."

For a few moments, Husani said nothing as he processed what he had just been told. Even allowing for the normal exaggeration and dramatization that would have occurred as the startling news was passed from one person to another along the alleyways of the souk, the news chilled him.

Of course, Cairo had its fair share of violence, including not infrequent murders, but what had been done to the Arab trader sounded as if it was a far cry from the kind of casual brutality meted out on the streets between rival factions, or the depredations of even the most violent mugger. Those deaths, when they occurred, were usually quick, the fatal wound being administered by a single blow from a knife or, increasingly commonly, by a couple of shots from a pistol.

"What do the police think?" he asked. "Was he attacked by a gang of men, burglars? Or what?"

The trader shrugged his shoulders and took another sip of thick black coffee, then replaced the cup in the saucer.

"I only know what I've heard, what the story is on the streets, but it sounds as if a gang might have been involved. Anyway it wasn't just a killing, and he didn't die quickly. They cut him about first, maybe to try to make him talk, and then they slit his throat."

Husani nodded, and finished his own coffee, his mind whirling.

The introduction of torture added a new dimension to the killing, a dimension that was alarming on a number of levels.

Whoever had taken Mahmoud's life had clearly been after information of some sort and, presumably having obtained it, had then decided that the trader knew too much to be allowed to live. And the man was little more than a small-time market trader, successful in his own limited field, but most unlikely to possess any information of the slightest importance to almost anyone else. So his killer had to be after something very specific.

He was suddenly certain that Mahmoud hadn't just been the victim of an unusually aggressive and dangerous burglar. It was something much, much more than that.

Could the piece of ancient writing material be more significant than he had ever suspected? If so, it wasn't a big jump for him to guess that he was most probably the next name on the killer's list.

But there was, of course, another way of looking at it, an aspect that instantly appealed to his commercial instincts. If somebody was prepared to kill to possess the relic, then it obviously had to be of considerable value. The more Husani thought about it, the clearer his course of action became. Mahmoud would certainly have told his killer who had bought the parchment from him: anyone with a knife sticking into his body will tell the man holding it whatever he wants to hear. So the murderer would already be looking for him. If he was caught, he had no doubt he would suffer the same brutal treatment as Mahmoud Kassim, and whether or not he had the relic in his possession probably wouldn't make the slightest difference to his fate.

He had to act immediately.

Husani nodded to his companion, glanced at his watch and then stood up.

"I have to go," he said. "If you hear anything else about Mahmoud's death, please leave a message for me at my shop."

Almost before the other man had time to reply, Husani turned and in moments was lost to sight in the crowd of pedestrians on the street outside.

As he walked away, weaving around the tourists and shoppers and traders, Husani did his best to try to see if he was being followed, glancing back frequently and looking to both his left and his right. He saw nothing and as far as he could tell nobody was paying him the slightest attention, but that could just mean that he was being watched by a professional. Or that he wasn't under surveillance at all. He had no possible way of telling which.

He reached into his jacket pocket and took out his mobile phone. Keeping one eye on where he was walking to avoid colliding with other pedestrians, he opened up the contacts directory and used his thumb to scan swiftly down the list until he reached the entry for Ali Mohammed.

He heard the ringing tone in his earpiece, but after about twenty seconds the voice mail system kicked in. As soon as he heard that, Husani ended the call. He wasn't sure how security conscious Ali Mohammed was, but the last thing he wanted to do was leave a message on an electronic answering machine that could be played back at a later stage by somebody who might not have his best interests at heart.

Husani waited a few seconds, then pressed the redial button to make the call again. This time, the mobile was answered on the second ring.

"Ali?"

"I thought that might be you, Anum, calling a minute or so ago, but you rang off before I could reach the phone. I'm afraid you're a little too keen. I haven't had time to finish work on the parchment yet."

That wasn't exactly what Husani had been hoping to hear.

"Have you managed to do anything with it?"

"I've made some progress, yes, but I certainly haven't finished."

"Can you read any more of the text?" Husani asked.

"Yes, a bit, though it still needs a lot more work. I've used a couple of the latest techniques on—"

"Sorry, Ali, but I'm in a real hurry now," Husani interrupted. "Can you meet me at the usual café right away and bring with you the parchment and whatever you've managed to decipher?"

The confusion in Mohammed's voice was clear.

"But the devices and equipment I need are here in the laboratory. I won't be able to finish if you don't—"

Husani interrupted again.

"I'll explain everything when I see you. I'll be at the café in an hour. Please just get there as quickly as you can. And don't tell anyone anything about the parchment."

28

Ten minutes later, Husani closed the front door of his house, slid home the two interior bolts and stepped forward into the cool gloom of the property. He paused for a brief instant, listening intently, but he heard no sound inside the building, nothing to suggest that anyone else was there. His wife was spending a few days with some members of her vast extended family, up the Nile near Aswan, and wouldn't be back in Cairo for at least two weeks, and the children were with her. So at least they were safe.

Satisfied that he was alone, he ran across the hall to the room he called his study, a small and cramped windowless space at the back of the house, and opened his safe. There was a fat bundle of cash inside, secured with elastic bands and made up of multiple currencies including euros, American dollars and pounds sterling, as well as Egyptian pounds, all of which he'd acquired through his trading activities. He seized the money and his passport and tucked them into the inside pockets of his jacket.

Then he paused for a moment as he looked at the

third object in the safe, a small semiautomatic pistol. He'd owned the weapon—illegally, of course—for years, and occasionally took it out into the desert to a quiet area and fired a few rounds through it, just to make sure it still worked. Carrying it might just give him an edge over the man who'd killed Mahmoud Kassim, especially if the murderer only worked with a knife. On the other hand, he wouldn't be able to take it onto an aircraft with him.

He nodded to himself. It was an easy decision. If he came face-to-face with the killer somewhere on the streets of Cairo and didn't have the pistol in his pocket, he probably wouldn't even make it as far as the airport. He definitely needed the insurance policy that the weapon would provide. He took it out of the safe, extracted the magazine and loaded it from the box of .22 cartridges he also kept there, replaced the magazine in the butt of the weapon, racked back the slide to chamber a round and set the safety catch. Then he removed the magazine again and added one further cartridge to replace the one that was now in the breech, ready to be fired. There was no point in taking the box of cartridges because if he did meet the killer and fired every round at him, he certainly wouldn't have time to reload his weapon. If a full magazine didn't stop the man, Husani knew he'd be dead. He was also well aware that the .22 round was hardly classed as a man-stopper, but it was all he had. It would have to do.

He slid the pistol into the pocket of his trousers—he found Western-style clothing much more convenient than traditional Arab dress—locked the safe and left the room.

Then he ran up the stairs to the main bedroom, strode across to the shelves on the opposite side of the room and grabbed a selection of clothes, enough for about a week, plus his washing and shaving kit, and stuffed everything into a small leather suitcase. He closed it, set the catches, and headed back toward the stairs.

He'd only taken a couple of steps across the landing when he heard a knock at the front door of the house.

29

Treading as carefully and quietly as he could, Husani walked into the bedroom used by his two children and crossed to the window. He kept well back from the glass, positioning himself so that he could just see the lane that ran outside his house, and the area around the front door. He could see the figure of a man.

Husani edged closer to the window as the man outside repeated his knock. He couldn't make out the face of the figure standing in the road because of the hat he was wearing, the headgear completely obscuring his features.

It could be completely innocent, perhaps somebody wanting to buy or sell a relic, or even a messenger sent by the man who ran his shop, though in either case his assistant would surely have called his mobile to advise him. Husani didn't believe either scenario for a moment. A feeling of cold dread settled on him, and what happened next confirmed his fear.

The figure outside glanced in both directions along the street and then, with a click that was clearly audible to Husani in the room above, opened a switchblade knife and slid the point between the door and the jamb, obviously attempting to slip the lock. Husani thanked his lucky stars that he'd remembered to close both the bolts: unless the man kicked down the door, he wasn't going to be able to get inside the house that way. The downside was that the man outside would soon realize that somebody had to be in the property for the door to have been bolted on the inside.

He stepped back from the window, trying to decide what to do. There was a rear door to the house, but to reach it he would have to walk down the stairs that ran close to the front door, and if he did that the man outside would probably hear him, and perhaps guess where he was going.

Husani moved forward again to the window and peered down. As he did so, he saw the figure outside step back from the door and again glance all around him. This time he looked up as well, toward the windows on the first floor of the house that overlooked the street.

Immediately, Husani shrank back. He didn't think the man had seen him, but he couldn't be sure, and he muttered a curse under his breath. But he still needed to know what the man was doing, so after a few moments he edged cautiously forward again and looked down.

The man had gone. He wasn't in sight anywhere along the street. Husani looked in both directions, but the figure had vanished, and there hadn't been time for him to disappear around a corner or into an alley.

That could only mean one thing. He must have gone around to the back of the house, and Husani was very aware that the rear door offered nothing like the same level of security as the one that opened onto the street. He knew he had just seconds to act.

Heedless of the noise he was making, he ran out of the room and down the stairs, the pistol clutched in his right hand, the suitcase forgotten, abandoned on the landing. He ran across to the front door and wrenched back one of the bolts. Then he stopped. Suppose it was just a trick? Suppose the intruder had simply walked down the side of the house, and ducked out of sight, and was now waiting for Husani to obligingly open the street door so that he could push his way inside?

For a moment he stood there, his body quivering with fear and indecision. He left the second bolt in place and stepped to one side, to a small window that gave a partial view of the street, and looked out.

But almost at the same moment as he did so, he heard a splintering crash behind him, and knew in that instant that the man had broken open the rear door and was now inside the house.

The killer was right behind him

30

Angela Lewis often found that her subconscious mind was rather good at solving problems that her conscious mind for some reason had failed to cope with.

When she'd read Ali Mohammed's e-mail the previous day, she knew she'd seen or read the partial name *ef bar he* somewhere else but, like a library with no filing cards or index system, she simply couldn't retrieve it from her memory. Her searches on the Internet hadn't helped either. But almost as soon as she got up that morning, she had remembered exactly where to look.

While Bronson was still in the shower, tunelessly singing some awful pop song from the seventies, she opened up her laptop and carried out a couple of swift searches, both of which yielded somewhat sparse results. But at least she now had something to send out to Ali in Cairo, which might help him in his work. Her best guess at the significance of *ef bar he* was that it was the middle section of the Hebrew name *Yusef bar Heli*, and that alone made the parchment quite an important find. But it was the inclusion of the name of the Judean town of Tzippori—assuming Ali Mohammed had read the word correctly—

that suggested the relic could potentially be a discovery of great importance.

The only names that had been associated with that particular individual were purely apocryphal, with virtually nothing in the historical record to support any of them. However, it was widely believed that the individual had spent at least some time in Tzippori. Depending upon which source was consulted, the man had either been called *Yusef bar Heli*—or *Yusef ben Heli*, both *bar* and *ben* translating as "the son of"—or *Yusef bar Yacob* or *Yusef ben Yacob*. The man's father had most probably been named either Heli or Yacob—the historical record was unclear on that point—though his own name, Yusef, was fairly well established. If the parchment was contemporary with this man's life, and if the fragment of the name did in fact refer to this specific individual, historians might for the first time be able to establish something of the man's family tree. And if that proved to be possible, the ramifications could be simply astonishing.

If Angela was right, that single piece of parchment sitting in the Egyptian Museum in Cairo could be one of the most significant finds since the Nag Hammadi Codices or the Dead Sea Scrolls.

31

Almost sobbing in terror, Husani fumbled for the second bolt and pulled it back. He wrenched open the door, slamming it back against the frame and the wall beside it. He dashed into the street outside and started running for his life.

As he did so, he heard heavy footsteps behind him, pounding across the wooden floor of the house, and then the sudden crack of a pistol shot, the bullet crashing into the wall of the house on the opposite side of the road, a bare couple of meters behind him. Shards of stone flew around him as he ran, a couple nicking the skin of his face.

Husani was sufficiently familiar with pistols to realize he was still within accurate range of the killer's weapon, and the next shot, he knew, could bring him down. Without breaking his stride, he swung his right arm back toward his house, clicked off the safety catch on his own weapon and pulled the trigger three times in quick succession. He couldn't aim the pistol properly, but he didn't care about that. All he was trying to do was scare the other man enough to make his escape.

Another shot rang out, but the bullet missed him, again hitting the wall of a house on the street, and then a group of men stepped into view from a side alley, just a few meters in front of him. They'd obviously heard the sound of the shots and were peering about them cautiously, clearly wondering what was going on.

Instantly, Husani slid the pistol into his trouser pocket, out of view of the men, and dodged around them. As he did so, he risked a glance behind him. The man who'd shot at him was running down the street in pursuit, but was about fifty meters back. In that briefest of instants, Husani saw that his pursuer had also tucked his weapon out of sight.

The group of men had stopped in the street and were staring at the spectacle unfolding in front of them, as Husani fled down the street, the other man running hard after him.

Husani dodged right into an alleyway, then almost immediately left, down one that was even more narrow. These were his streets, a part of Cairo he knew well. What he didn't know was whether or not his pursuer was also a local, a man who might have an equally comprehensive knowledge of the area.

The alleyway was unusually quiet, with nobody in evidence, which wasn't what Husani had expected—or wanted. He knew that safety lay in numbers, in being able to lose himself in the crowds. There was another crack from behind him, as the killer risked one more shot at his prey, but as both the shooter and his target were running hard, accurate shooting was impossible. That, at least, was what Husani was hoping as he dodged and weaved his way down the narrow passage.

The alleyway ended at a blank wall, but a few meters before he reached it there was a narrow opening to the left, which Husani sped down, scattering a pile of cardboard boxes from one side of it as he did so, hoping that might delay his pursuer slightly. But still he could hear the pounding of footsteps behind him. And if anything they seemed to be getting closer.

At the end, a kind of safety beckoned, a crowd of people milling about in a small square. He burst out of the alley, immediately turned right and increased his speed, forcing his way through the crowd.

In a country where almost nobody moved quickly, a running man was bound to attract attention: two men doubly so. As Husani pushed his way through the melee, he registered the expressions on the faces of men he was passing, expressions that ran the gamut of emotions from shock to amusement.

On his left, Husani saw an old man pushing a handcart, loaded with sacks of some kind of produce. He reacted instinctively, spinning around behind the cart and tipping it over in one fluid moment.

The old man bellowed his rage, but Husani simply ran on, now with a couple of other men who'd seen the incident starting to chase him as well. That would have muddied the waters, he hoped, and the overturned cart might give him a few more seconds' breathing space. And he needed that, because now his breath was coming in short gasps. His lungs felt as if they were on fire and there was a sudden sharp, stabbing pain in his side from his exertions.

In amongst the agitated crowds, Husani dodged and dived, weaved and ducked, but his movements were slower and more labored than before, and he knew he'd have to stop soon or he'd just collapse. When he'd skirted around another large group of people, he halted abruptly and looked back. He was sure the man was back there somewhere, but at that moment he couldn't see him.

Husani seized the opportunity, and ran over to a small store on the right-hand side of the street. He stepped inside, closed the door behind him and retreated to the back wall, the proprietor looking at him curiously.

Husani glanced at him, and made the first excuse that came into his head.

"My wife's lover," he panted. "Chasing me. Trying to kill me."

The store owner nodded in sympathy, suggesting that perhaps he too had had experience of such matters.

"Use the back door," he said, and gestured behind the counter. "Through here."

Husani didn't hesitate.

"*Shokran*," he replied simply, "thank you." Then he stepped behind the counter and out into another narrow alleyway that ran behind the row of shops.

He looked both ways, but it was deserted. He turned and headed back the way he'd come, paralleling the street he'd run down, and walking quickly. Then he took the first cross-passage he came to, putting as much distance between himself and the killer as he could. Husani glanced back frequently, but saw no signs of pursuit, and after five more minutes he was convinced he'd made good his escape. He was now just one more middle-aged man wearing Western clothes in a city with a population of about twenty million people. Finding him now, Husani knew, would be significantly more difficult than tracking down a needle in a haystack.

At last he allowed himself to relax, and began walking a little more briskly. He didn't want to be late for his appointment with Ali Mohammed.

32

Husani sighed with relief, and for the first time since he'd sat down in the corner of the small café he released his grip on the butt of his pistol. Approaching the building was the familiar and somewhat rotund figure of Ali Mohammed, a battered brown leather briefcase tucked under one arm. Husani stepped to the door and waved to attract the man's attention. Moments later, the scientist stepped inside the café and sat down in the chair opposite Husani, a puzzled frown on his face.

"You have brought the parchment?" Husani asked, the tone of his voice betraying his concern.

Mohammed nodded and pointed at the briefcase, which he'd placed on the vacant chair beside him.

"Of course I have. It's in there, along with the photographs I've been taking to try to reveal more of the text, and a memory stick containing copies of the pictures. But why the sudden change of plan?"

For a moment, Husani toyed with the idea of explaining exactly what had happened to the previous owner of the piece of parchment, but decided that would be a bad idea, at least for the moment. He suspected that the scientist lived in a somewhat cloistered world, divorced from the harsh reality of life on the streets of Cairo, and the knowledge that a vicious killer was roaming the city looking for the relic tucked inside the briefcase beside him would comprehensively ruin not only his day but possibly the rest of his year.

It was better, he reasoned to himself, simply to make an excuse, even though he already knew that that would require him to sit through another lecture.

"I won't bother you with the details, Ali, but I have to go away unexpectedly, and I want to take the relic with me when I leave. That's why I'm in such a hurry."

A tall and excessively thin Arab, his face burned almost black by the sun and wearing a white *thawb*, the long tunic that is the traditional dress for Arab men, approached their table, a grubby white cloth held in his left hand. Husani and Mohammed both ordered coffee and glasses of water, Mohammed a small selection of sweet cakes, and the waiter retreated.

"So what have you found?"

"First, I need to explain a little about the parchment itself," Mohammed said.

Husani stifled his impatience. Although he knew that time was crucial, he also needed to hear everything that the scientist could tell him about the relic.

"You probably noticed," Mohammed began, "that the parchment is dark brown in color. That's an indication of its age, because when it's freshly prepared parchment is almost pure white. Unfortunately, simply looking at the color does not enable a researcher to estimate the likely age of the object, because the speed of the color change depends upon the conditions in which the parchment has been kept. The temperature, the humidity, amount of sunlight and so on. It will last longest if it is stored in a dark and very dry place and at a fairly constant temperature, although the temperature is not as important as the relative humidity.

"The color change of the parchment is one factor, and the ink is the second. Although the writing on the object now looks brownish in color, originally it would have been a deep black, and very easy to read against the white parchment. Because the writing is obviously Latin, it's reasonable to assume that the text was written by a Roman or perhaps by a scribe employed by the Romans, and so the ink used would most probably have been a form of *atramentum*."

Mohammed raised his hand to forestall Husani's obvious question.

"That isn't actually any one particular type of substance," he said. "The Latin word simply means a black-colored medium, so in Roman times an *atramentum* could be produced from cuttlefish ink, for example, or soot from a chimney or charcoal from a fire, the pigment then being mixed with water. Using soot or charcoal gave rise to a type of ink known as carbon black, for obvious reasons. Different sorts of *atramentum* could be used for other purposes, not just writing, such as dyeing leather or in painting, but the type used for writing became known as *atramentum librarium*."

"Presumably that was the origin of the English word 'library'?" Husani asked, pleased to have some faintly intelligent comment, however oblique, to add to the discussion.

"Yes, though indirectly. In Latin, *librarium* came to mean a 'chest of books or scrolls,' and the word was then absorbed into Old French in about the fourteenth century as *librairie*, meaning a 'collection of books.' "

"So is the type of ink important?" Husani asked, eager to get the explanation back on track.

Mohammed nodded decisively.

"Yes, because of how you should then treat the parchment or material. A later type of ink was known as iron gall ink, which was made from entirely different materials, and because the two inks have very different characteristics and origins, it's important to establish which type has been used, so that the correct conservation methods can be employed. I'm quite sure that in the case of this piece of parchment, because of its age and because of the use of Latin on it, that the writing was done with a form of *atramentum*, an ink made from some type of carbon.

"The other good thing about this parchment is that it looks as if it was only used once, which is actually slightly unusual. Preparing parchment from the skin of an animal, usually a sheep or a goat, was quite a long and complicated process, and it was very common in ancient times for a parchment to be used multiple times. When this was done, the parchment was known as a palimpsest."

"How did they rub out the original writing?" Husani asked.

"The method used is actually hinted at by the name, because it's derived from two Greek words that mean 'scraped again.' The parchment would be rubbed smooth to remove as much of the old ink as possible, and to prepare the surface to be written on again. And although this process appears to completely erase the original writing, at least to the naked eye, traces of it usually remain and can be seen when the relic is examined in a laboratory. The original letters can serve to partially obliterate the later writing."

"You mean that one set of words that you can't read can obscure another set that you also possibly can't read?"

Mohammed nodded.

"That's a somewhat crude way of putting it, but it's a

reasonably accurate statement. But in the case of your parchment, that's not a problem. The difficulty with this relic is much simpler. It's a matter of trying to decipher the faded and dark brown letters that have been written on a piece of parchment that has now aged to virtually the same color.

"Fortunately, we have a couple of tools that can help us in our quest. We've known for a long time that shining an ultraviolet light on the parchment and then photographing it with a high-resolution camera can reveal erased or hidden letters. The ultraviolet light makes the parchment fluoresce—it actually emits a bluish light—and that contrast enables us to make out the words. And particularly with inks derived from some form of carbon, we've found that photographing the relic using infrared light can also work well."

"And so that's what you did?" Husani asked, feeling some relief that the lecture appeared to be approaching its conclusion.

"That is indeed what I did," Mohammed confirmed. "I used both techniques, in fact, and both produced positive results. I won't get them out of the briefcase to show you, because the parchment is delicate and shouldn't be exposed to bright sunlight. And you really need to study the photographs using a magnifying glass to be able to decipher the text. I haven't tried to read it myself—I had only just completed taking the photographs when you rang, and I only had time to print copies of them before coming out to meet you—but quite clearly more of the words are visible in the pictures than we could see on the parchment itself, though by no means all of them. Hopefully you'll be able to decipher enough of it to work out what the text is describing."

Husani nodded his thanks and slid an envelope containing a number of banknotes across the table to the scientist.

"Thanks a lot, Ali," he said. "Can I take the briefcase as well?"

Mohammed nodded.

"I expected that you would want to do that, so I brought one of my old ones."

Husani took the briefcase from his companion and placed it on his lap. Then he made a decision, leaned forward and gestured for Mohammed to do the same.

"I suggest," he said, in a quiet but forceful voice, "that you forget all about me and this parchment. You may have heard about the murder of a market trader here in Cairo, a man named Mahmoud Kassim."

Mohammed nodded again. It seemed as if Husani had actually been one of the last people in the city to learn about the man's death.

"I bought the parchment from him, and I think it's most likely that he was tortured to make him reveal where it was. The man I believe killed him broke into my house less than an hour ago, and I only just managed to get away from him. That's why I'm leaving Cairo today, as soon as I can, and that's why you shouldn't tell a living soul that you've even seen the relic, and certainly don't admit to anyone that you did any work on it."

Beneath his tan, Mohammed had turned pale, and almost immediately glanced nervously around him, as if expecting to see knife-wielding murderers emerging from the crowd on all sides.

"I knew nothing of this when I handed you the relic," Husani insisted, "and I only heard about the killing this morning. I will tell nobody that you have had anything to do with it, but please be careful and watch your back for the next few days. I'm getting out of the city as quickly as I can."

Mohammed suddenly looked extremely uncomfortable, his glance sliding past his companion rather than looking him in the face, and Husani picked up on it immediately.

"What is it?" he demanded. "Who have you told?"

"It was just a professional inquiry," Mohammed stammered. "I sent an e-mail to somebody I know at the British Museum in London, just asking about the proper names I could read."

"Did you tell him what the relic was, that it was an ancient parchment?"

"It's a 'her,' actually, not a 'him,' and I did explain something about it. I don't think it's important, though, and when Angela replied, she said that the names didn't mean anything to her."

Husani nodded.

"If this woman contacts you again, I suggest you tell her nothing, just say the relic was removed by the owner or that you could read nothing else on it, something like that. The fewer people who know about this object the better, at least until I find out what's really going on."

"And how will you achieve that?" Mohammed asked.

"That should be easy," Husani replied. "It's not the parchment itself that is important. That's just an old piece of animal skin. It has to be what's written on it, and thanks to you I should now be able to read a lot more of it. Once I've managed to decipher and translate the text, I'll have a much better idea of why somebody decided poor Mohmoud had to die."

33

Before she continued with the jigsaw reassembly of what seemed like a million broken pottery vessels, Angela made herself a cup of coffee. She'd decided a while ago that the only way she could guarantee a decent cup, apart from visiting one of the cafés in and around Great Russell Street, was to have her own coffeemaker and buy her own beans.

The routine of grinding the beans in the small electrical gadget beside the filter machine and the pleasurable aroma the whole operation created were things she really looked forward to. The process helped her unwind each morning after the usually fraught journey on the packed Central and Northern lines from Ealing Broadway into central London.

As usual, she ground the beans—that day she had chosen a Blue Mountain roast—and started the water dripping through the loaded filter as soon as she'd closed her office door. Then she opened up her laptop and plugged it in. While she sipped her coffee, she wrote an e-mail to Ali Mohammed, explaining what she thought was the significance of the fragment of the Hebrew name, and asking him to confirm the provenance of the parchment he was working on. She also suggested that the British Museum would probably be interested in acquiring it, should it bear up to expert analysis.

Before she sent the message, she checked the local time in Cairo. Because of the two-hour difference, in Egypt it was just after eleven thirty, so Ali Mohammed should certainly be in his office by that time. She sent the e-mail, then savored the rest of her drink, made herself another cup, and walked out of her office and into the workroom where the boxes of potsherds awaited her attention.

Trying to assemble broken sections of pottery was both mentally and physically tiring. The edges of the fragments only rarely matched exactly because of other damage and there was, of course, never any guarantee that all the parts of a particular vessel were present in the box of bits, so a search for one missing piece could easily be a complete waste of time. She found that her eyes ached if she did the work for more than about two hours at a stretch, so at eleven thirty London time she abandoned her bench for a while and returned to her office, hoping that Ali would already have replied.

He had, but the contents of the message he'd sent were nothing like what she'd expected. The e-mail was short, but she read it twice, with increasing confusion and irritation.

Good morning, Angela,

    I am so sorry about the parchment. It was a mistake to have contacted you and the owner has now taken it away from me. Please do not concern yourself any more with the matter.

                                  Regards, Ali

What was going on? She looked again at the message she had sent to Cairo, to ensure that she had made her position clear, that she had emphasized the possible importance of the text on the piece of parchment. Had Ali conveyed any of that to the owner of the relic?

She certainly wasn't going to simply let it go.

She composed another message to the Egyptian, marked it high priority and sent it immediately. Then she made herself another cup of coffee and sat in her chair while she waited for him to reply.

It didn't take long.

> Hullo again, Angela,
>
> I will not get the chance to explain to the owner what you told me, because I had already returned the relic to him before I read your e-mail. But I doubt if it would have made any difference. There are other forces at work here, and already one man has been killed over this parchment. I am only telling you this so that you will appreciate the seriousness of the matter and please, I beg of you, do not pursue this any further. I have been sworn to secrecy, and I dare not continue this correspondence. Both the owner of the relic and I myself fear for our lives if our involvement becomes known.
>
> Ali

That was hardly the response Angela had been expecting.

She opened up her Web browser and typed "Cairo murder" in the search field. That produced over eighteen million results, but the news item she was looking for appeared right at the top of the list. There were five different reports from a selection of English-language newspapers, and she glanced at all of them before reading the longest and most comprehensive article in full, though the information supplied even by that report was noticeably sparse.

Brutal Slaying in Cairo Suburb

Yesterday police were called to a house on the outskirts of the city in response to an emergency call. A cleaner who worked at the property, owned by a dealer in antiquities named Mahmoud Kassim, had discovered the dead body of her employer when she arrived there that morning.

The property was immediately sealed off by the police while the scene was examined for clues to the perpetrator of the crime. In an initial statement, the chief investigating officer, Inspector Malanwi, explained that they had found one body in the property and that they were treating the death as suspicious.

In an exclusive interview for this newspaper, the cleaner, who wishes to remain anonymous, told our reporters that she had found the body of Mr. Kassim in the bedroom. The corpse was lying in the bed, and he had apparently been attacked during the night. The cleaner stated that he had the most appalling wounds, and she believed they had been inflicted with a knife.

Mr. Kassim was a well-known dealer in antiques and antiquities, and operated his business from a shop in the Khan el-Khalili souk.

That was little enough to go on, but if nothing else the

man's profession suggested that at least Angela was reading the right news item. She looked back at the other reports, but they added little fresh information.

As she read it again, she realized one other fact: Ali said that he'd returned the parchment to the owner on the day *after* the killing, so it can't have been this Mahmoud Kassim. The relic was still out there, somewhere.

There was one more thing she could do. She knew a bit about Ali Mohammed's work, and she could guess exactly how he'd handled the parchment when it had been given to him.

She thought carefully for a few minutes, then wrote another e-mail to the Egyptian scientist, read it through to ensure she'd got the right tone, and then sent it.

Five minutes after that, she was back among the potsherds, her actions mechanical and slow, her thoughts thousands of miles and two millennia away.

34

For the first time in his career, Abdul was beginning to doubt if he would be able to fulfill the contract he had accepted. What made it infinitely worse was that both of the targets he had needed to eliminate were amateurs— just two ordinary market traders. Finding and killing the first man hadn't been difficult, just rather messy. But the second target, Anum Husani, had simply slipped away from him.

With hindsight, he knew it was his own fault, because his tactics had been wrong. When he'd found that the street door of the house was bolted on the inside, he should have only *pretended* to go around the back of the property, and that would have forced Husani to open the front door to make his escape. But Abdul had thought he could break into the house from the rear so quickly that the other man wouldn't have time to get away. That had been a mistake.

The other fact Abdul hadn't bargained for was that the trader would be armed. That had been an extremely unpleasant surprise. From the sight of the weapon and the sound and impact of the shots against the walls of the houses in the street, Abdul guessed it was a very small-caliber pistol, probably a .22 or perhaps a .25, but even such a small bullet could maim or kill. It had thrown him off balance, and then the man had used his knowledge of the souk to make good his escape.

He had not the slightest idea where Husani was, whether he'd gone to ground somewhere in the city, at the house of a friend or acquaintance, perhaps, or was still out on the streets somewhere. Maybe he'd even taken a train or an aircraft out of Cairo and was already miles away. Abdul simply had no way of knowing, or of finding out.

Actually, that wasn't strictly true. He did have one lead he could follow: Ali Mohammed, the man who worked at the Cairo Museum, if the information Jalal Khusad had passed on to him was accurate.

So now Ali Mohammed was the next man on his list.

35

Abdul sat outside a small café on one side of Tahrir Square, near the center of the city on the east bank of the Nile and looked across at his next objective. Over a coffee and a sweet cake, he glanced through the guidebook he'd picked up and considered the potential problems the museum posed for him.

The Museum of Egyptian Antiquities, more commonly known as the Egyptian Museum or sometimes just the Cairo Museum, is the largest museum in Egypt and one of the most popular in the country. The guide claimed that it was visited by over one and half million tourists every year, as well as about half a million Egyptians, the main attraction being the Tutankhamun exhibition, especially the celebrated death mask of the boy-king, an image that has become virtually synonymous with the glory days of Ancient Egypt. This exquisitely fashioned solid gold mask, arguably the most beautiful ancient treasure ever recovered, weighs almost twenty-five pounds, and was placed on Tutankhamun's shoulders almost three and a half millennia ago, before his corpse was conveyed to its final resting place in the Valley of the Kings. The tomb had been discovered in 1922 by Howard Carter and the Earl of Carnarvon, and the array of treasures and artifacts, relics of incalculable value and outstanding historic importance, have since then resided in their new home on the upper floor of the Cairo Museum.

What Abdul didn't know, and didn't actually care about, was that the body of the boy-king himself was once again lying in the Valley of the Kings, in his burial chamber, having been taken back there in November 2007, exactly eighty-five years to the day after the discovery of his tomb. He was laid to rest there for the second time after his death in about 1323 BC, this time for eternity, but instead of the warm darkness of the original chamber in which he lay, surrounded by some three and a half thousand artifacts intended to assist him in the afterlife, his wrapped mummy is now on display in a climate-controlled glass box, a move intended to reduce the rate of decomposition of his body.

The guide also pointed out that it wasn't just Tutankhamun's treasures that made the museum a popular destination. The building also housed the mummies of eleven Egyptian kings and queens in a single hall, and there was a huge array of statues, jewels, coins, papyrus, sarcophagi, scarabs and a host of other relics covering the entire span of time from the predynastic and Old Kingdom periods right up to the Greek and Roman eras, a total of some 120,000 items, all contained within the museum's hundred-plus chambers, either on display or in storage.

Abdul closed the section of the guide he'd been reading and looked again at the museum. Getting inside the building wouldn't be a problem: he would simply have to buy a ticket at the door. Getting through the metal detectors could be a little more difficult.

But Abdul had a solution, intended for just such a situation. In fact, he had two solutions, one elegant, the other less so. A couple of years earlier, he had received a small package through the regular mail, sent from a mail-order firm in America to one of his post office boxes in Egypt. Inside the package were three knives of a most unusual type. They were almost entirely ceramic in construction, the only metal piece being the hinge pin on the clasp knife, but the other two knives, with fixed blades, contained no metal whatsoever. They were just as sharp and lethal as steel-bladed weapons, but were guaranteed to be invisible to metal detectors, and virtually undetectable by X-ray scanners as well. They were a gift to terrorists, and Abdul had been surprised just how easy it had been to purchase them.

Once inside the museum, he would have to get into the man's office or laboratory, which would presumably be in a part of the building to which the public had no access. But the more elegant option would ensure he could walk into the building carrying both his pistol and one of his knives, and be told exactly where Ali Mohammed worked.

And that was the option he was going to take, despite one obvious disadvantage. But he knew he could do something about that.

36

Ali Mohammed read the latest e-mail from Angela Lewis with growing concern. If she was right, and Mohammed suspected that she probably was, if only because of the events that had taken place in Cairo over the last couple of days, then the relic was too important to be forgotten about.

And that realization placed him in something of a quandary. Anum Husani had been adamant that he should just walk away, forget about the parchment altogether, for his own safety. But Mohammed was a scientist, and a part of his creed—part of the creed of every scientist, in theory if not always in practice—was the pursuit of knowledge. What Angela Lewis had suggested about the parchment was simply too compelling to ignore. He owed it to his own conscience, to the tenets of his profession, to investigate the truth of her suggestion.

What's more, he had the tools to do so. Although he'd given the photographs he'd taken of the parchment to Husani, the originals were stored on the hard disk of his laptop.

For another couple of minutes he sat at his desk, silently contemplating the situation; then he nodded to himself. Decision made. He selected all the photographs of the relic, and sent them to his laser printer. Studying the images of the parchment on his laptop wasn't really an option: he needed to have the pictures in his hands.

Printing the twenty or so pictures he'd taken would be a lengthy process, so he decided to reply to Angela's e-mail. When he'd finished the message, he paused, wondering if he was doing the right thing. Then, exhaling rapidly, he added a final short paragraph, and pressed Send.

But almost as soon as the e-mail vanished from his screen, Mohammed had an abrupt change of heart. He muttered to himself, typed rapidly, and sent another message. He knew he really had no choice.

37

Mohammed was just about to gather up the printouts when there was a knock on his door and one of the administrative staff peered in.

"Dr. Mohammed?"

"Yes. What is it?"

The admin officer appeared slightly perplexed by what he had to say.

"I have a police officer here who wishes to ask you some questions. Would you like me to witness the interview, or call anyone on your behalf?"

"What?" Mohammed realized the man appeared to think he was in some kind of trouble. "No, of course not. Send him in."

The man withdrew, and a moment later a smartly dressed man in a light-colored suit stepped into the office, smiling apologetically.

"I'm Inspector Dalani," he began, holding out a leather folder containing his identification, "and I think I may have given your staff member the wrong impression."

He glanced back at the door, which was just closing behind him.

"But I want to ask you some questions," Dalani continued, "and they relate to the murder of Mahmoud Kassim. May I sit down?"

Mohammed nodded.

"Of course," he replied, gesturing to a chair on the opposite side of his desk.

He stepped over to the printer, pulled out the sheets of paper and put them facedown on the end of his desk before he sat down again.

"Now, how can I help?" he asked, studying the man in front of him.

His visitor was apparently middle-aged and of average height and build, dark haired and with a tanned complexion and a thick black mustache: he looked remarkably similar to most Egyptian males. One slight incongruity was his face, which was rounder than Mohammed would have expected for a person of his build, but otherwise he was unremarkable. As he looked at him, the detective took off his jacket and hung it on the back of the chair, revealing his shoulder holster from which the butt of a pistol protruded. Then he rolled up his sleeves and sat down.

"It's really hot out there today," Dalani began. "Now, you've no doubt read about the brutal murder of Mr. Kassim in the newspapers?"

Mohammed nodded, but didn't interrupt.

"One thing that the newspapers have not reported, simply because we have not released the information to them, is that Mr. Kassim was tortured before he was killed. I think most of the news reports have suggested that he was hacked to death, but this is not in fact the case. The killer—and we believe there was only one man involved—used a knife to inflict enormous pain on the man before finally cutting his throat. I'm sorry if these details have alarmed you," he added, looking somewhat anxiously at Mohammed, who had noticeably blanched at the matter-of-fact tone and expressions Dalani had used to describe the slaying of the market trader.

"No, it's all right. I'm fine. Please continue. How can I help?"

Dalani nodded, took a small notebook out of his pocket and referred to what looked like a list written on one of the pages.

"It's fairly clear that Mr. Kassim was tortured to make him divulge information—that's the usual reason for torture, of course—and we think he was attacked because of a specific item he had come across in his dealings. We believe the killer was looking for a relic that Mr. Kassim had bought or had found—an ancient piece of parchment."

Mohammed nodded again. The Cairo police were obviously a lot better informed than either he or Husani had expected them to be. Dalani's next words confirmed that.

"We're quite certain the murderer didn't take the parchment from Mr. Kassim because, according to some of the people we've interviewed about this, he had already sold it to another dealer"—Dalani paused for a moment and glanced down at his notebook, to check the information—"a man named Anum Husani. So our concern in this matter is obvious. If the killer was prepared to slaughter Mahmoud Kassim just to obtain this ancient relic, then clearly he would have no hesitation in murdering Husani to achieve the same thing. We've had somewhat garbled accounts of shots being fired near Husani's house, and of a chase through the streets in that part of the city, but no reports of anyone being hurt. However, Mr. Husani seems to have completely vanished from sight, and that's where we think you can help us."

"Me?" Mohammed asked. "Why? And how?"

Again Dalani glanced at his notebook.

"We understand that you are acquainted with Anum Husani?"

Mohammed inclined his head.

"We aren't close friends, but I know him, yes."

"In a professional capacity?"

Yes, Mohammed thought to himself. They're *very* well informed.

"In a way, I suppose," he replied. "I'm an expert on ancient documents, and Husani sometimes deals in scrolls and codices and the like, so almost inevitably our paths have crossed. I don't work with him, because I'm employed by the museum, but I have sometimes advised him in a private capacity about relics he has come across in his trade."

Dalani smiled slightly.

"Good. So there are really only two questions I need to ask you. First, because it's imperative that we find Mr. Husani as quickly as possible so that we can protect him, do you have any idea where he is? And, second, did he consult you about this parchment he had obtained? Did he ask your opinion of it or show it to you or anything like that?"

Mohammed didn't reply for a moment, his thoughts spinning as he tried to decide how much he should admit to. But he could, at least, be truthful in his answer to the detective's first question.

"I've seen Anum Husani a couple of times in the last few days," he admitted, "but I have no idea where he is now. You've obviously tried his house and the shop he runs in the souk?"

"Yes, but he's not at either premises. Obviously we've stationed officers at both the locations in case he returns.

If he was hiding from this killer, have you any idea where else he might go?"

Again Mohammed could give a truthful answer.

"I'm sorry, but I've no idea. Because of his business he's acquainted with a lot of the other traders in the souk and elsewhere in Cairo, but I don't know of any that he works with very closely. I think his family live somewhere on the outskirts of the city—he's mentioned his brothers and parents to me a few times—but I don't know where. Presumably you could locate them easily enough?"

Dalani nodded.

"Other officers are already doing that," he said, "but I was more interested in any possible hiding places you might know of."

Again Mohammed decided he could give a truthful answer to this, or at least tell the detective a half-truth.

"As I said, I don't know Husani that well, but if he knew he was being chased by this killer, my guess is that he'd try to get out of Cairo as quickly as he could."

"Where to? Where would he go?"

Mohammed shrugged his shoulders and raised his arms, palms upward, a universal gesture.

"I have no idea. I don't think he has any friends or family outside the country he could visit. But as long as he has a passport he could probably go anywhere."

Dalani nodded slowly.

"That isn't what I wanted to hear, but what you say does make sense. Now, Dr. Mohammed, to the other matter. Did Husani talk to you about the parchment? Did he ask for your opinion, or for your help?"

Mohammed opened his mouth to reply, but before he could do so Dalani spoke again.

"Could I just say first that we already know—and I can't tell you exactly how because it's confidential—that he contacted you about this relic. So all I want to know is what help, if any, you were able to give him."

That information shocked Mohammed, and he was sure that his face showed his surprise. Despite Husani's earlier warning to him, there was, he realized, very little he could do now except tell this police officer the truth.

"Yes," he said. "You're right. Anum Husani did contact me about the parchment he had bought."

"And?" Dalani prompted him.

"It was very old and faded. Only a handful of the words on it—it was written in Latin—were legible. He asked me if I could use some of the equipment here at the museum to decipher the rest of the text, and I agreed to do what I could to help him. He let me have the parchment for a few hours, and I performed a number of operations on it. Noninvasive, of course."

Dalani leaned forward.

"And were your attempts successful?" he asked.

"I think so. I used a number of different techniques to enhance the writing, including bathing the parchment with infrared and ultraviolet illumination, and that certainly made more of the letters and words legible. But I haven't had time to study the results yet."

"Why is that?"

"Because I had an urgent call from Anum Husani asking me to return the relic to him, which I did immediately, of course."

"When?"

"Just this morning. I've only just printed the photographs I took while I had the parchment in my possession."

As he said this, Mohammed tapped the pile of pages beside him on the desk.

"May I see them?" Dalani asked.

"Of course."

Mohammed passed the pages across the desk to the detective, who flicked through them rapidly, glancing at each image for a few seconds.

"Are these the only copies?" he asked.

For the first time since the detective had walked into his office, Mohammed was slightly puzzled by the direction his questions were taking.

"No," he replied. "I gave one set to Husani, as he had asked me to do, because it was his parchment I was studying. And of course the originals are on my computer. I transferred them to the hard disk from the memory card in my camera."

"So that's three sets in all?" Dalani asked. "These, the copies Husani presumably has with him, and those on your computer. You mean your laptop, I assume?"

"Yes. I don't do private work on the museum's desktop computer, obviously."

"Just the three sets?" Dalani persisted.

"No. There is one other," Mohammed admitted, with a trace of embarrassment. "There were some aspects of the parchment, or rather the few words on it that could be read with the naked eye, that puzzled me, and I consulted a colleague about it."

"Are you talking about somebody here at the museum?"

Mohammed shook his head.

"No. A colleague in London, at the British Museum. She'd expressed her professional interest in the parchment and so I decided to send her copies of all the photographs I had taken of the relic. I sent the e-mail just a few minutes before you arrived, actually."

For a few seconds Dalani just stared at him across the

desk. Then he shook his head. When he spoke, his voice was harsher, but the tone almost sorrowful.

"Now that was a really stupid thing to do, Mohammed."

A prickle of unease swept through the scientist.

"What do you mean?"

Dalani smiled wolfishly at him.

"I'm talking about your stupidity in sending photographs of the parchment to London. And your stupidity in getting involved with Husani in the first place. Some lessons are only learned the hard way, as you're about to find out."

Dalani stood up, and in that instant Mohammed belatedly realized two things. First, there was no way that the Cairo police could possibly have known that Husani had contacted him about the relic. And second, he had no idea what a genuine Cairo detective's identification looked like.

But suddenly he knew exactly who the man sitting in front of him really was.

38

Desperately, Mohammed grabbed for the telephone, but the other man moved like a striking snake, leaping out of his chair and pinning his arm to the desk while with his other hand he pulled out a lethal-looking knife, the blade a strange shade of off-white.

Mohammed saw the knife and knew he had bare seconds to live. He opened his mouth to scream, but before he could utter a single sound the knife slammed into the left side of his torso, just below his ribs, and a surge of agony swept through him. He gasped for air and his world collapsed into waves of unbearable pain as his killer twisted the knife in the wound.

Mohammed fell backward, but his attacker followed him, leaping nimbly over the desk as the scientist crashed to the ground. He felt another searing pain as the knife was pulled out of his body, and stared up into the man's dark, almost black, eyes.

"Death improves a lot of people," the killer said, his tone light and conversational, "and I think you're one of them."

Less than a second later, the man slid the point of his

ceramic knife into the side of Mohammed's neck and drove it home, slicing through the arteries and esophagus. A huge gout of blood spurted out of the fatal wound.

As the light faded from Mohammed's eyes, the man stood up and inspected himself critically. There was a fair amount of blood on his right arm and hand—it was almost inevitable given what he had just done—but nothing anywhere on his clothing. That was why he'd removed his jacket and rolled up his sleeves as soon as he'd entered the office. He'd known from the start exactly the way the interview was going to end, and had made his preparations accordingly. And at least he hadn't had to torture or threaten the man to obtain the information he needed. His deception had worked perfectly. He'd extracted all the man's knowledge of the parchment, and he would take the photographs of the relic, and the laptop, with him when he left the office. Another loose end had been snipped off.

Somebody else would need to deal with the woman at the British Museum.

The only downside was that he still had no idea where he could find Anum Husani and the parchment.

There was a small sink in one corner of the room. Abdul stepped over to it, washed his hands and arms, and the ceramic knife, and dried both himself and the weapon thoroughly. Then he resheathed the knife, pulled on his jacket, and walked back behind the desk to look down at Mohammed.

Abdul bent down and seized the dead man's legs, moving the body slightly so that it was invisible from the doorway. Anyone looking into the office would probably just assume that the scientist was somewhere else in the building.

Then he extracted the data cards from three digital

cameras that were lined up on a shelf behind the desk, picked up Mohammed's laptop and charger and slipped everything into a computer bag he found leaning against the wall behind the desk. He slid the color photographs into a side pocket of the bag and left the office, pulling the door closed behind him.

Three minutes later, he walked out of the museum into Tahrir Square and strolled away. As soon as he found a quiet side street, he walked down it and, when he was sure he was unobserved, pulled off his jacket and reversed it, turning the white jacket into a dark blue one. He took a wide-brimmed floppy hat from his jacket pocket and put it on his head and then, after another glance around him, pulled off the fake mustache he had been wearing and removed the soft plastic cheek pieces he'd inserted inside his mouth to change the shape of his face.

When he walked out of the alleyway moments later, he looked different in almost every way.

39

When Angela checked her e-mails later that afternoon, she was surprised to see two from Ali Mohammed. She read the first message with a growing sense of disappointment. Yet again he told her that he felt any further investigation of the mysterious parchment was not a good idea because of the potential dangers that were very obviously linked to the relic, and he reaffirmed his belief that she should just forget all about it. In view of his previous message, that was not entirely unexpected, but still, her heart plummeted.

But when she opened the second message, which had been sent only a few minutes after the first, she discovered that for some reason he'd had an almost immediate change of heart. Angela couldn't suppress a small grin. He'd explained what little he knew about the finding of the relic, and had attached copies of all the photographs he had taken of the parchment, so that she could study it for herself. But he had again reinforced his warning not to publicize anything about it.

When she eagerly looked at the attached images on the screen of her laptop, she immediately came to the same conclusion Ali Mohammed had reached: she needed to print them. It would need many hours of work with a magnifying glass before she'd be able to read much of the text, and even with the photographs there were going to be a lot of words, and maybe whole sentences, that she still wouldn't be able to decipher. What she really needed was access to the parchment itself.

There was a color laser printer in her office, and a monochrome unit as well, and she decided that monochrome would probably be better, because it would perhaps be a little clearer. She selected the highest possible resolution, then busied herself making another pot of coffee while she waited for the laser to finish.

Then she took her cup over to her desk, with the stack of printed images and a powerful magnifying glass, and began to examine what she'd been sent.

Some of the photos looked a little odd, perhaps because they'd been taken by the Egyptian scientist using a special camera sensitive to either infrared or ultraviolet light, or maybe just by a normal camera while the parchment was being irradiated by one type of light source or another. But however Mohammed had done it, the images were reasonably good, some parts of the text showing up quite well. As far as she could tell from her quick survey, she might possibly be able to decipher perhaps a quarter of the writing. It was better than nothing.

She toyed with the idea of sending Ali an e-mail to thank him, but she decided a phone call would be more appropriate, and more personal.

She checked his e-mail on her laptop—he'd included his work number as part of the signature at the end of each message—and dialed the number in Cairo.

It rang several times before it was answered, and when it was, it was quickly apparent that the recipient wasn't Ali

Mohammed. She heard a couple of harsh Arabic phrases uttered by a male voice, and replied in slow and clear English.

"Good afternoon. I want to speak with Ali Mohammed, please."

Immediately the man switched to English, a language in which he was apparently fluent.

"Dr. Mohammed is unavailable at the moment. Who's calling?"

"My name is Angela Lewis. When will he be there, please?"

There was a slight pause before the man answered her question.

"What is your business with Dr. Mohammed?"

Angela hadn't expected the third-degree; she'd only rung up to thank the scientist for what he'd done. And something about the situation concerned her, so she decided that she wouldn't explain to this unidentified man exactly what she was calling about.

"I'm a colleague from London, but this was just a social call."

"From London?" the man queried.

"Yes. Look, it's not important. I'll ring him later."

And before the man could reply, she ended the call.

That, she thought, was rather peculiar. Presumably Ali had been in his office earlier in the day, because he'd sent her the two e-mails and the photographs, which he probably wouldn't have been able to do if he had been at home.

The other thing was the tone of the man's voice. It had sounded official, authoritative. Perhaps Ali was in trouble? Perhaps the owner of the parchment had found out that he'd been communicating with her about it and had complained to the authorities in the museum? That might explain both his unavailability and the attitude of the man who'd answered the phone. She'd leave it for a couple of days, she decided, and then call again. In the meantime, she'd just send a short e-mail to thank him for his help, but without mentioning either the parchment or the photographs.

Decision made, she again turned her attention to the photographs, and began transcribing some of the Latin words from the images onto a sheet of paper. She hadn't the time or the patience to do the whole thing in one go—all she really wanted to do at that stage was find out if her deduction about the partial name *ef bar he* was correct. If she could confirm that, it would be an important step forward.

She scanned the photographs until she found the group of letters she was looking for, and then nodded in satisfaction. The written name *was* what she had thought: *Yusef bar Heli* was written perfectly clearly, and that alone made the parchment valuable. Of course, she was very aware that Yusef wasn't that unusual a name in first-century Judea, but Heli was far less common, and the juxtaposition of the two names at least suggested that the parchment *did* refer to the man who was perhaps the most shadowy and least understood—yet at the same time enormously important—figure from that period.

40

Angela spent another ten minutes studying the pictures, picking out a number of other Latin words that she noted down, and did a quick and dirty translation of what she'd managed to read. Then she allowed herself another cup of coffee as a cheap and inadequate celebration, because it looked as if she'd been right. What she'd guessed about the parchment, what she'd deduced simply from the handful of words that could be seen by the naked eye, was now supported by her new and fuller translation of one particular section of the text. It almost certainly *did* refer to the Yusef bar Heli she had hoped it did, not some other man bearing the same name, and that meant the document was most likely of incalculable and international importance.

Of course, that conclusion assumed that the relic was genuine, and not some kind of elaborate forgery. To clarify that, she would need to see it for herself, along with experts in ancient documents who would be able to analyze the parchment. And, most probably, a small section of the relic would need to be sacrificed and sent for radiocarbon testing.

Angela was very familiar with the technique, which was simple enough in theory. All living things are made from carbon, the vast majority of it—approximately 99 percent—being carbon-12. There are two other isotopes, roughly one percent being stable carbon-13, and the remainder being trace quantities of the radioactive isotope carbon-14. Throughout their life, plants absorb carbon-14 through photosynthesis, and this is then passed up through the food chain to herbivorous animals and ultimately to predators, including human beings. On the death of any living thing, no more carbon-14 can be absorbed, obviously, and what is present in the body then begins to decay.

Carbon-14 decays into nitrogen-14, and has a half-life of roughly 5,700 years. By comparing the ratio of carbon-12 to carbon-14 left in an organic sample, the age of the plant or animal can be estimated with a fair degree of accuracy. The dating method can be used for samples up to about 60,000 years old, but is most accurate for material created in the last 26,000 years. It was radiocarbon dating that had conclusively proved that the Shroud of Turin was a medieval forgery, the material dating, with an accuracy of 95 percent, to between AD 1260 and 1390.

Radiocarbon dating of the parchment, Angela was certain, would be a quick, easy and conclusive way of establishing its age with a high degree of accuracy, and would go a long way toward confirming the authenticity of the text written on it.

But before that could be done, she had to get her hands on the relic, and at that moment she had no idea how she was going to achieve that. Her only real hope was that Ali Mohammed might have managed to convince the owner that it was valuable, and that he might either hand it over to a museum somewhere for analysis or, perhaps more likely, offer it for sale on the open market.

She thought for a few moments, and then sent out a brief and very general e-mail to all the museums in her database, couching her message in the vaguest of terms, but suggesting that the British Museum was interested in obtaining copies of early parchments, and especially those believed to date from around the first century AD, and originating in or near ancient Judea. That was all she could do officially, and without making it quite obvious what she was looking for.

Apart from that, and unless Ali Mohammed contacted her again, she was just going to have to keep her ear to the ground.

Before she left her office, she put the photographs in her laptop case along with her computer, then glanced at her watch. It was just before six, which meant she was in good time to meet Chris outside the museum.

41

When he rang his number late that evening, Abdul had expected that Jalal Khusad would be pleased to learn that he'd eliminated Ali Mohammed, but the man seemed to be more interested in the relic itself.

"I have the man's laptop, and the photographs he took of the object," Abdul said.

"Congratulations. So now you have a free computer. Shred the photographs or, better still, burn them. They're of no interest to me."

That wasn't the response Abdul had been expecting.

"But there might be useful information on the laptop. Maybe the target sent copies of the pictures to other people as well."

"I hope for your sake that he didn't. You told me he'd only been in contact with this woman in London."

"That was what he said," Abdul agreed, "but he could have been lying. Surely it's worth checking his e-mails, just to make sure."

"Yes, I suppose so. You're right. Check the hard drive yourself—I assume you're capable of that—and let me know if you find anything. When you're certain you've checked everything and identified everybody the man was in contact with over this matter, destroy the computer. I don't want any other images of the relic to survive."

Then another thought struck Khusad.

"What about the camera the man used to take the pictures?" he demanded. "Did you get that as well? Or take the data card out of it?"

"I covered that," Abdul replied. "There were three cameras in the man's office and I took the data cards out of all of them."

"So at least you got that bit right. I suppose that's something. But we must find this relic as quickly as possible, and the other man, the man in the middle of all this, still needs to be taken care of. And this time can you try to do it a bit more discreetly. I understand that the Cairo Museum is now swarming with police. That's the second time you've drawn attention to yourself."

"There wasn't any alternative. I couldn't afford to wait until he left work. And I can promise you that nobody would recognize me again. As for the relic and the man, find one and you find the other. The problem is that I have no idea where he might be. I think there's a good chance that he's probably left Cairo by now. He'll have taken a train or bus or a plane somewhere, and I don't have the resources to track him if he's done that."

"Then it's lucky that I have," Khusad replied. "And I have also obtained a photograph of the man, which I'll send to you."

"OK. There's also the matter of my fee."

There was a short silence before Khusad replied.

"Very well. I'll authorize another transfer to your offshore account for the work you've done so far, but I have been instructed to make no further payments to you until this matter is resolved. Keep your mobile switched on, and start looking for your target here in Cairo. As soon as we receive any indication of his whereabouts through his credit card usage or tracking him through his passport if he decides to travel, I'll contact you. In the meantime, assume he's still in the city somewhere."

Abdul pondered the situation. The resources and global reach that Khusad's organization could command were impressive. He knew that for a police force or anti-terrorist group or any other law enforcement operation, monitoring the use of either a credit card or a passport was comparatively straightforward, and a very basic procedure when trying to track a suspect. But he also knew that it was almost impossible for any private individual to achieve the same level of access. Who were these people?

42

About seventy yards down the street from the main entrance to an Ealing Broadway apartment block, a lone man sat in a nondescript saloon car, the radio playing softly in the background. His eyes were fixed on the front door of the block, and lying on the passenger seat beside him was a rather grainy photograph showing the face of an elegant-looking woman with long blond hair. The man had been stationed there for almost two hours, studying everyone who either went into or came out of the building, but so far he had seen nobody who resembled his target.

However, the picture he was using was a few years old, and was an enlargement of a much smaller image, which would make a positive identification even more difficult. The lighting around the entrance lobby of the apartment building was less than ideal, and he was so far away that using binoculars—he had a very compact but powerful set—was essential. And he knew that making a positive identification of any woman could be difficult because, unlike men, women often changed their style of hair and makeup, and that could change their appearance dramatically.

But despite all these factors, when two people approached the lobby of the building hand in hand, and the external security light flared into life, he identified the woman. He watched as she opened the door, inputting a series of numbers into the external security keypad, and held the binoculars to his eyes until she and her companion had vanished inside the building.

Only when they were no longer visible did he drop the binoculars onto the passenger seat of the car and pick up his mobile. He dialed a number from memory. In his business, he never used stored telephone numbers because if the phone was lost or stolen those numbers could compromise both him and the people he had called. His menu system was also set up so that the phone never kept a record of calls made and received. He made sure his own number was never disclosed to the people he called, and was changed on a weekly basis.

The call was answered on the fourth ring.

"Yes?" the quiet voice said.

"It's Jeff," the man replied. "I'm outside the building and she's just come back. But she's not alone. There's a man with her."

"Describe him."

"Big guy, dark hair. He's certainly over six feet tall and heavily built—muscle, not fat. He looks as if he could be quite handy in a scrap."

There was a short pause while the man at the other end of the line digested this piece of unwelcome information.

"That complicates things," he said. "I had hoped she would be alone tonight. Do nothing for the moment. Wait there and see if he leaves. If he does, you can carry on as planned."

The man in the car shrugged.

"You're paying the bill," he said, "so it's your call, but I can handle him, no problem. Get the job done in half an hour."

"Definitely not. You only go in if the man leaves the building. Understood?"

"Got it. So do you want me to stay here all night?"

"If this man hasn't come out again by, say, one in the morning, I think we can assume that he's staying the night. If he does that, you can try tomorrow night instead. And remember, this has to look like a burglary gone bad."

"I know what you want done and how to do it. Don't you worry."

43

Angela decided to ring Ali again at lunchtime. But this time there was no answer at all, and eventually the call went through to voice mail. She tried twice more over the next half hour, with the same result. There wasn't much else she could do.

Then a thought struck her. Egypt, she knew, was still quite volatile, with occasional riots and other forms of civil disturbance. Maybe something had happened in Cairo that could have prevented him getting to work that day. She hadn't been near a TV or radio since yesterday. She opened her Web browser and typed "Cairo news" into the search field.

The results were disappointing, or encouraging, depending on your point of view. As far as she could tell, there had been no riots or any other significant happenings in the city.

Then another result, toward the bottom of the screen, caught her eye. It was headlined "Savage Murder of Museum Worker," and the moment she saw that, she felt a sudden sense of foreboding. With trepidation, she clicked the headline and watched as the story loaded.

Savage Murder of Museum Worker

A manhunt is under way across Cairo today following the discovery of a murder victim at the Egyptian Museum. Police were called to the building after a member of the administrative staff found the body of Dr. Ali Mohammed, a specialist in ancient documents, lying in his office. It is understood that he had been killed with a knife. The reason he was murdered is uncertain and, although his personal laptop was missing, a police spokesman stated that robbery seemed an unlikely motive.

It has been established that Dr. Mohammed received a visitor that afternoon shortly before he was murdered, a man who claimed to be a police officer and who showed a form of identification to security staff at the museum to gain entrance. It is now known that this identification was a forgery, and a description of the alleged perpetrator has been circulated to all police stations and military units in and around the city. Members of the public are urged not to approach this man under any circumstances, but to call the police immediately.

A very poor-quality sketch of a man's face followed the article, and then a brief word-picture, which described the man as solidly built, a little under six feet tall, with a tanned complexion, thick black mustache and dark hair, and a round face. Which was little enough for any police officer to go on, Angela thought.

She read the report once more, and felt her anger at Ali's assailant growing more intense by the second. She hadn't known him well, but what she'd known about the Egyptian scientist she'd liked.

And then she had a realization. Ali had warned her not to get involved with the parchment, and had even hinted that his own life could be in danger because of it. And he had obviously—and very tragically—been absolutely right.

Suddenly, the parchment didn't seem so important anymore, not when two of the people known to have handled it had already been brutally murdered. Angela wondered if Ali's killing would mark the end of the matter, or if the man he had described as the "owner" was still out there somewhere, on the run from the killers and in desperate fear for his life.

She was about to return to her work when another thought struck her. She hadn't actually ever seen the parchment in the flesh, as it were, had never been closer than a couple of thousand miles to it as far as she knew, and had certainly never owned it. But she did have a number of high-quality images of it in her possession. Would that fact alone make her a target as well?

That thought was so stunning—and so alarming—that for a couple of minutes she simply sat still at her workbench, staring into space.

Then she shook her head. Surely, whoever had been responsible for killing the two men in Cairo wouldn't even know that she had been sent the images? But if they did, if they somehow found out what had happened, would they come after her?

44

Abdul had spent the day in the souk and the neighboring streets, his rationalization for choosing that area of the city for his search being that Husani might well go to ground in the part of Cairo that he knew best. He'd stopped briefly for lunch in a small café, choosing a seat outside so that he would have a clear view of all the passersby.

He paid the bill and started walking away from the café, but he'd only moved a few meters when his phone rang. Immediately, he stepped to one side, away from the press of humanity, and answered the call.

"Yes?"

"He's left Egypt," Khusad stated, without preamble.

"What? When? And where has he gone?"

"There is no need for you to know. Suffice to say, he's gone, and others will take it from here."

45

"So she still hasn't come back to the apartment? Why?"

"Listen, mate, I'm a hired gun, not a bloody mind reader. How the hell should I know where she is? If you want my guess, she's shacked up somewhere with that man I saw her with last night. You should have let me do her then. Him too."

In the study of a large semidetached house on the edge of Norwood, a middle-aged man with a round and almost cherubic pink face drummed his fingers in irritation. His plan had been thwarted the first night by the unexpected presence of Angela Lewis's male companion, and now tonight she hadn't returned home at all. There was also, he realized, the very real possibility that she wouldn't be there over the weekend either, possibly spending the time with him. That could mean that the earliest the contract could be completed would be Monday evening, and that might be far too late. And now his contractor was getting cheeky with him.

For several seconds he sat in silence, considering his options. Then he made his decision. The most vital thing, very obviously, was Lewis's death: the actual manner of it was of secondary importance.

"OK. Change of plan," he said.

"Good," the contractor replied.

"We know that the target is still going to work. Get to her that way, and make it look like an accident. If you pull it off, there's an extra grand in it for you."

"Where and when?"

"That's up to you, but no later than tomorrow night. You know where she works and what time she'll leave the building?"

"Yes to both. Just leave it to me," Jeff replied.

46

"I definitely think you did the right thing," Chris Bronson said.

They were sitting side by side on a somewhat tattered leather sofa in the lounge of Bronson's house in Royal Tunbridge Wells, an unremarkable crime thriller that contained a large number of technical errors being played out on the flat-screen television. Bronson had got so fed up with the program's obvious mistakes and clumsy dialogue that a few minutes earlier he'd muted the sound and they'd been half-watching it in silence ever since.

"As soon as I'd called you I felt so stupid," Angela replied. "I mean, how can a couple of murders in Egypt possibly be a problem to me here in southern England? How would the killer know anything about me?"

"Ah, well, that's the thing," Bronson replied, not sounding happy at all. "After you rang me, I popped into the station and sent a message to the Cairo police, asking for any information they could supply about the killing of Ali Mohammed. It's the kind of thing we do all the time with other police forces, though not usually with one as far away as Egypt. I just said that the crime might possibly have links to an ongoing investigation here in Britain. I asked if they had recovered the man's laptop and mobile phone."

Angela was staring at him with a peculiar intensity.

"And had they?" she asked.

"His mobile, yes, but there was no sign of his laptop in his office. One of the museum security staff recalled that the impostor, the fake police officer, had walked out of the building carrying a bag, quite possibly a laptop case. If Mohammed's computer was in the bag, it wouldn't take him more than a couple of minutes to discover that Mohammed had e-mailed the pictures to you."

"But do you really think that the man who's murdered those two people in Cairo would come after me in England? I mean, wouldn't an Arab assassin stand out a bit in London?"

Bronson smiled grimly at her.

"I don't know if you've noticed, but about the only language you don't hear spoken on the streets of central London these days is English. Arabic, French, Spanish, German, Italian, Russian and a whole flock Eastern European languages, yes, but English, no. I don't think an Egyptian killer would be any more noticeable than any other type of killer in this city. But, actually, I doubt very much if that man will be heading this way anytime soon, because he probably won't need to."

"What do you mean?"

"You've already told me that what's written on that parchment might have potentially significant connotations, and would certainly attract international attention if knowledge of it ever became public. And if—"

"I don't know that for certain, because there's still a lot of the text I can't even see, far less translate."

"OK, but you are quite certain it's an important find.

What's happened in Cairo is proof positive that some person or organization is actively looking for it, and eliminating anyone who knows too much about it. If they decided that you knew too much to be allowed to live, I imagine that some local contractor would be appointed to carry out the job here in Britain."

Angela shivered.

"A 'contractor'? You make hiring an assassin sound like arranging to have an extension built on your house."

There was no trace of humor in Bronson's expression or voice when he replied.

"That's the terminology that is used. A contract is offered, and the man who accepts it is, logically, the contractor. And the really sad part about it is that it can actually cost less, sometimes quite a lot less, to have somebody murdered than to build an extension. It all depends on the profile of the victim. Killing a politician or somebody who's nationally known will be expensive because it's risky. The assassin will possibly be going up against armed and trained bodyguards, and there are far more likely to be witnesses around if the victim has a face that everybody knows. But I'm afraid that you, my dear, are a nobody in this kind of context, and to arrange for your demise would cost no more than a few thousand pounds."

"That's absolutely disgusting! Are you actually saying that London is full of murderers for hire?"

"No, not really. Britain isn't anything like as bad as some other countries, but if you decide you do want somebody to vanish permanently, and you've got the money to pay for it, it's not that difficult to find somebody to do the job. I can't remember who said it—it might even have been Agatha Christie—but the reality is that the only reason anybody is alive today is because nobody wants them dead badly enough.

"People vanish from Britain's streets every single day. Usually, it's an entirely voluntary act, but there are lots of cases where the disappearance is involuntary and permanent. For children and young women, the obvious suspects are pedophiles and the kind of lowlifes who run prostitution rings, but when it's an adult male or female, and there are no apparent family problems, in many cases we suspect that they've been done away with, even if we never find the body."

"Is it that easy to get rid of a body?" Angela asked.

Bronson nodded.

"There are lots of places where you can hide a corpse so that it will probably never be found. A good deep grave in the middle of a wood isn't a bad choice, but that's quite hard work for the murderer. Easier options are under a new road or in a concrete bridge support. Or if the killing takes place near the coast you provide the corpse with a set of concrete boots or a length of heavy chain and then drop the body a few miles offshore. Human remains don't last very long in the sea. Or you can even bury it in a graveyard. Find a fresh grave where the coffin's only been in the ground a day or two."

Bronson leaned forward.

"But when it's a case of an assassin working for hire, it's different and they don't get rid of the body, because there's no point. They actually want the corpse to be found, because that proves that they've carried out the contract and then they can collect the fee. So when we find somebody shot or knifed to death with an absence of witnesses and the body left pretty much where it fell, we always cast a very wide net to try to find anyone who might have wanted that person out of the way."

Angela looked at him for a moment, then reached for her mug of coffee.

"You're not exactly filling me with confidence here, you know."

"Don't worry," Bronson said. "There is *one* difference."

"And what's that?"

"Here, they'll have to go through me first to get to you."

47

Anum Husani's route to the center of Spain had been somewhat tortuous.

Almost as soon as he'd walked away from the meeting with Ali Mohammed with the retrieved parchment and the photographs, he'd flagged down a cab and headed straight for the airport. He'd been careful—paranoid might be a better word—to check all around him before he even got in the vehicle, and had spent most of the journey peering out of the rear window, trying to see if the cab was being followed. Of course, in Cairo traffic that was an almost impossible task, but he'd done his best.

He'd paid off the driver at the airport, gone inside and found a vacant spot on one of the rows of back-to-back metal seats, and for almost an hour he'd just sat there, watching the crowds ebb back and forth in front of him, and trying to decide where to go. Again, nobody had appeared to be paying him the slightest attention. As far as he had been able to tell, he was safe.

His choices of destination had been fairly limited. At that time of day, late afternoon, most of the flights heading out of Cairo International Airport had been to places that he didn't want to go, like Dubai or Kuwait. He'd really wanted to get somewhere in Western Europe. Eventually, he'd bought a ticket for cash for the 18:00 Egypt Air flight down to Sharm el-Sheikh, the popular Red Sea holiday resort, got himself over to Terminal 3, lost himself in the crowds and had then boarded the flight without any problems. He had guessed there would be international flights out of Sharm that he could take, even if he had to wait until the following day.

Absolutely the last thing he'd done, before he walked through the security check and into the departures lounge, was lock his pistol in one of the small left-luggage containers. The weapon had very probably saved his life in his headlong flight from his house in Cairo, and he'd decided he didn't want to just throw it away.

The flight had taken almost exactly an hour, and as soon as he was on the ground, Husani had checked the departures board at Sharm. What he'd seen hadn't been quite what he'd expected. What he'd really wanted was somewhere like Paris or Madrid, but the only destinations on offer in Western Europe had been London, Manchester, Glasgow and Dublin. To be cooped up in an island like Britain wouldn't, he'd believed, give him the freedom of movement he might need.

But he'd recognized that he needed to keep moving, to get out of Egypt, and so eventually he'd taken the 21:15 flight to London's Gatwick Airport. The aircraft had been somewhat delayed on departure, not leaving until almost ten that evening, and hadn't arrived at Gatwick until just after two thirty on Thursday morning.

There had been no point in trying to find a hotel at

that hour, and there were no outbound flights either, so Husani had bought himself a selection of snacks and drinks from a machine, consumed his purchases and then tried his best to get some sleep, stretched out on another unyielding metal seat.

48

As Husani had blearily opened his eyes, his mind had already been working hard. He needed to travel farther, because once he revealed details of his find to the world, the spotlight would fall on him no matter where he went to ground. That was why he still wanted to get to Madrid.

And so, at a few minutes after ten that morning, he'd leaned back and tried to relax in his seat in the economy section of the Air Europa 737-800 for the two-hour flight to the capital of Spain.

Finding a hotel after he'd landed had been easy: he'd taken a cab ride to the center of Madrid and just picked one of the cheaper-looking ones at random. Then he'd taken a nap in his room before finally opening up the tattered briefcase that comprised all his luggage. He'd spent a few minutes looking at the photographs Ali had supplied for him, slightly disappointed that several sections of the text on the parchment were still illegible; then he'd locked away both the photographs and the relic in the room safe and ventured out onto the streets of Madrid to do some shopping.

He needed clothes and washing gear, obviously, plus a bag or suitcase of some sort to keep them in, but he also wanted to find a good-quality case with decent locks for the parchment. The clothing wasn't a problem, but tracking down a small and secure case was rather more difficult. Eventually he located something he thought was ideal in a specialist shop on the outskirts of the city center. It was a normal-looking small briefcase, but far heavier than its appearance suggested.

This was because both the base and the lid were lined with steel plates, each with a double layer of Kevlar for additional security. The case was, the shop assistant explained to him, virtually impossible to get into without a key. Levers and hammers would have almost no effect on it, and even high-speed drills would find it difficult to penetrate the multiple layers of protection. It would even deflect a bullet from a pistol, thanks to the Kevlar, he claimed.

It was a very expensive item, and would have made such a huge dent in Husani's remaining supply of euros that he took a chance and used his credit card to complete the purchase. He was going public quite soon with details of the relic, and so it really didn't matter if anyone knew he was now in Madrid.

The other expensive purchase was a netbook, also bought with the plastic card. He would need to use the Internet, and probably use it a lot, over the next day or so.

Weighed down with his new purchases, Husani returned to his hotel and locked the door behind him. Then he booted up the netbook, ran through the initiation sequence for the new machine, and started looking for an online Latin dictionary. Once he'd found one that seemed comprehensive enough, he started deciphering some of the sections of writing on the parchment.

By eight that evening, he'd translated about a quarter of the text that was legible, but what he'd read had only served to confuse him. It wasn't what he'd expected, though in truth he didn't really know *what* he'd expected. The sections he'd translated contained what sounded like legal arguments, none of which seemed either particularly interesting or revealing.

He locked the parchment, the photographs and his partial translation back in the safe, walked out of the hotel and found a quiet restaurant nearby, where he ate a simple meal, his thoughts distracted and confused.

When he returned to his room, he looked again at what he'd so far managed to decipher, conflicting emotions coursing through him. Nothing he'd read on the parchment seemed important enough to justify the extreme measures that had been taken back in Cairo. Was he missing something? There had to be some vitally important piece of information, some dark and dangerous secret, hidden away within the text. He just hadn't found it yet.

Perhaps, he mused, as he fell gratefully into bed, he would ask Ali Mohammed's advice about how best to proceed. With his greater experience he would be able to read more of the Latin and find out why the parchment was so important. And he was in the business, and might well be able to come up with a few suggestions about who might be worth approaching first with a view to selling the relic.

With that comforting thought occupying his mind, he quickly fell into an exhausted slumber.

49

That day, Angela was to realize just how important the relic was to the shadowy group of people pursuing it.

She arrived at work at the British Museum at her usual time, Bronson accompanying her as far as the entrance gate, before he headed back home. She had protested that it was unnecessary and stupid for him to come all the way up to London with her, but in truth she was actually very grateful.

Once inside the building, she felt quite safe and secure, and got on with her work in a fairly cheerful frame of mind. That lasted until just before eleven, when a member of the administration staff knocked on her door and stepped into her office holding a sheet of paper.

"Sorry to bother you, Angela," the girl said. "We don't quite know what to do with this e-mail."

Angela took it and read the brief message written in halting English. The text read:

I have what you want. Must talk with Angila friend of Ali. Only deal with Angila. Ali dead in Cairo.

She read the message twice, and nodded slowly.

"Does it mean anything to you?" the girl asked. "I only brought it to you because the sender mentions the name Angila, which is pretty close to Angela."

"Yes, yes, it does mean something," Angela replied, her heart starting to beat a little faster. "Can you do me a favor, please, June? Can you please copy the e-mail to my account here. I'd like to take a look at it myself, see what else I can find out about it from the header and the routing."

June smiled brightly.

"One of the IT guys did that already, actually. He can't be completely sure exactly where it was sent from, but he told me it was certainly somewhere in or near Madrid."

That was unexpected.

"Madrid?" Angela echoed. "I thought it must have come from Egypt. He was sure about that, was he?"

"Yes. But you can always give him a call if you want to ask him about it."

Angela shook her head.

"No, I'm sure he's right. It's just a bit unexpected, that's all. Anyway, I'd like to reply to this myself, so just forward it to my account, if you wouldn't mind."

Less than five minutes later, her laptop sounded a tone, and Angela opened up the e-mail. The routing indeed indicated Spain. And that, from her point of view, seemed like a much safer destination than Cairo, or anywhere else in Egypt.

She thought for a few moments about exactly what to say, then quickly wrote a short message.

Two minutes after that, she was knocking on the office door of her superior, a copy of the e-mail and the sheaf of photographs of the parchment clutched in her hand.

50

Chris Bronson was waiting outside the gates of the museum in Great Russell Street when Angela walked out just after five. She had a lot to do, and not a great deal of time to complete it.

They walked together westward along the street, heading for Tottenham Court Road, Bronson keeping a careful look out all around them as they did so. He didn't think Angela was in serious danger—at least, not yet—but he wasn't taking any chances.

Tucked into the rear waistband of his trousers was a loaded nine-millimeter Browning semiautomatic pistol, an entirely illegal weapon that he had acquired a long time ago. He was acutely aware that if he was caught with the pistol, he would face a prison sentence, notwithstanding the fact that he was a police officer authorized to carry a firearm on duty. But Angela's safety was far more important to him than any legal repercussions that might ensue. If she was attacked by anyone, he wanted to be quite certain he could protect her, and if it came to a firefight, he could always claim that he'd simply picked up the pistol in the confusion. He'd taken care that when he'd loaded weapon he'd cleaned each round and every part he'd touched in the past, and then used rubber gloves to charge the magazine and insert it in the butt. The only fingerprints of his that were on the Browning, he was quite certain, were on the outside of the weapon, and those he hoped he would be able to explain away.

As they walked, they talked.

"Are you really sure this is a good idea?" Bronson asked.

"Frankly, no, but I've talked to a couple of people at the museum, including my boss, and I've shown them the photographs of the parchment. They all agreed that it was of potentially international importance, and if the British Museum can possibly buy it, we intend to do just that. You won't believe the budget I've been given."

"So it'll just be your decision, then?"

Angela shook her head.

"No, not for a purchase of this importance. The museum's sending out an expert on ancient parchments and codices, and I'll meet him in Madrid. In fact, the only reason why I'm being sent out there at all is that the man who sent the e-mail—and I still don't know his name— said he would only deal with me. I suppose that was because I was a friend of Ali, so to some extent I'm a known quantity."

Bronson nodded.

"And you definitely want me to fly out there with you?"

"I told my boss I wasn't prepared to go unless you could come with me, just in case there's any trouble. One thing I know about you, that I've always known about you, is that you'd willingly take a bullet for me."

Bronson glanced at her and raised an eyebrow.

"I hope it doesn't come to that," he said mildly.

"And so do I."

They walked down the steps into the Tottenham Court Road Underground station. Bronson fed his one-day travel card into the slot on the turnstile while Angela slapped down her Oyster card on the one next door, and a couple of minutes later they were standing on the platform waiting for the next southbound train.

"So your plan is?" Bronson asked.

"First thing tomorrow morning we'll take a taxi to Gatwick and fly to Madrid. After that, I have no idea. Unless this anonymous man contacts me and tells me where and when to meet him, we'll just be taking a very short holiday in Spain."

"You still don't know who he is, then?"

"No. He gave no name in his e-mail, and his account was one of those anonymous Web-based ones, and his username was just a jumble of letters and numbers. When I replied, I gave him my e-mail address, obviously, my mobile phone number and also your mobile number, as a matter of fact."

"You were pretty sure I would come with you, then."

"I was absolutely certain about that," Angela said, grinning at him.

Bronson glanced up at the illuminated display board above the platform, which gave the times and destinations of the next trains to arrive. And then they both felt the telltale wind in their faces as the approaching Northern Line train pushed a mass of air through the tunnel toward them.

Most of the passengers standing waiting on the platform looked either at the display board or down the tunnel. Bronson did neither. He concentrated on the people themselves, on the waiting passengers.

Although the worst of the rush hour was over, the station was still crowded with people, many of whom had now moved slightly closer to the edge of the platform, in anticipation of the train's arrival, and to ensure that they would be at the front of the queue to get on board.

Angela traveled on the Underground every working day, and was well aware that, if the trains were crowded, waiting at the back of the platform would pretty much guarantee that she wouldn't get on the next train. She also took a couple of steps forward, so as to be nearer the train when it stopped.

As she did so, a man—heavily built and wearing a light-colored anorak, blue jeans and scuffed trainers—stepped into the space that had opened up between Bronson and Angela, and stood directly behind her.

Bronson grunted in irritation at the way the man had barged in, and stepped forward and slightly to his right, placing himself as close to Angela as he could get, which put him on the man's right-hand side.

It wasn't a shock of instant recognition, or anything like that, but there was something about the man that was familiar to Bronson in some way, though at that moment he couldn't place what it was.

The lights of the train were now shining on the tunnel walls, and the noise of its approach grew louder. It would arrive at the platform within a few seconds. And then, with a final rush of hot and fast-moving air, the train swept into the station, still traveling very quickly.

The man beside him shifted his position slightly as the train appeared and started to slow down. His head began moving rapidly from side to side as his gaze switched between the edge of the platform and the oncoming train.

And then things happened very quickly.

51

The man reached out and grabbed Angela's arms from behind, just above the elbow. She tried to turn toward him, but his grip was too strong, and although she opened her mouth, whatever she said was drowned out by the noise of the train. He started propelling her toward the edge of the platform and the certain death that waited just a few feet away.

And at that moment, Bronson realized why the man had seemed familiar. He'd definitely seen this person before—or somebody wearing precisely the same outfit—when they'd been walking down Great Russell Street away from the museum. And he'd just made his intentions lethally clear.

If nothing happened, in seconds there would be a scream and a tumble, and the smell of burning flesh as Angela's body made contact with the live rail and the lethal voltage running through it. And if that wasn't enough, the momentum and colossal weight of the oncoming train would be the ultimate guarantee that she would not survive.

As with so many things in life, timing is everything.

Bronson's movements were a blur. He took two quick steps forward, reached out with his left hand and seized the man's arm. He tugged as hard as he could, turning both the man himself and Angela slightly toward him. That moved her very slightly away from the danger area at the edge of the platform. But Bronson was only just getting started.

The moment the killer turned toward him, Bronson smashed his right fist directly into the man's cheek, knocking him backward. It wasn't a knockout blow, but it did its job, forcing the man to release his grip on Angela's arms. Knocked off balance, she stumbled and then fell clumsily to the ground. She was just clear of the platform's edge.

The killer regained his balance almost instantly and powered his right fist into Bronson's stomach. But he'd seen the blow coming, and managed to turn slightly sideways so that it missed his solar plexus, just catching the flesh below his ribs. It hurt, but it didn't incapacitate him. Bronson continued to turn, spinning on his heels, then threw a left jab, aiming for the right side of the man's rib cage.

The blow never connected, because his opponent swung his right arm down and backward, knocking Bronson's arm out of the way. Whoever the man was, he was used to street fighting.

And though Bronson, as a police officer, was trained in self-defense and unarmed combat, he wasn't sure how long he'd be able to last against this larger and clearly very competent opponent. He needed to finish this, and quickly.

Then the man reached toward one of the pockets on his anorak, and Bronson immediately guessed that he was going for an equalizer—a gun or a knife. He couldn't let that happen. Bronson took a step to one side, almost as if he was going to run away, then turned back and delivered a straight-leg kick to the side of the man's right knee.

The human leg is designed to bend at the knee, to allow for walking and running, but the joint is never intended to bend sideways. There was an audible crack as something broke, and the man tumbled sideways with a scream of pain.

By that time Angela had scrambled to her feet. She turned round and stared at Bronson, and at the fallen man lying on the platform just beside him. The crowd of commuters had parted almost immediately when the fight had started, and had formed a rough circle around the combatants. People getting off the train stared at Bronson with interest, but almost all of them then moved away, continuing toward their destinations as the new passengers started to board. Londoners were remarkably resilient in their outlook.

"Quick, get on the train," Bronson said urgently, scouring the platform for other threats. "Wait for me at Charing Cross. Stay where it's crowded."

Something about his voice told Angela that this was not the time to ask questions.

As she climbed into the train and stared back at him through the open doorway, he reached into his pocket, hauled out his warrant card and waved it at the handful of people who were still standing around and watching.

"This is a police matter," he said. "Go about your business."

He grabbed the man, who was now clutching his shattered knee with both hands, and unceremoniously pulled him back, away from the edge of the platform and to the back of it, where he propped him up against the wall.

Swiftly, Bronson checked the man's pockets, pulling out a cheap pay-as-you-go mobile phone and a slim wallet that contained just a single credit card in the name of "J. W. Williams" and about two hundred pounds in cash. He replaced the wallet but retained the phone. In the side pocket of the man's anorak he found a small semiautomatic pistol.

"You bastard," the man hissed, tears of pain running down his face. "You've bloody crippled me."

Bronson nodded. "That was the general idea," he said, standing up and examining the weapon he'd just found: a Heckler & Koch P7, an uncommon weapon to find anywhere outside Germany, where it was designed as a police pistol. The obvious identification feature was the grip catch on the front of the butt, which prevented the weapon from firing unless it was depressed. Bronson slipped the pistol into his jacket pocket, then turned his attention back to the man lying in front of him.

Now that the Underground train had departed, the platform was largely empty of people, though a few more passengers were beginning to arrive, part of the endless daily traffic through the London Tube system.

Bronson crouched down beside the man and stared at him.

"I don't know who you are," he began, "but I'm absolutely sure I know what you are, and what you intended to do. Who's paying you to kill the woman?"

"I've got no bloody idea what you're talking about. All I know is you attacked me on the platform. Completely unprovoked."

Bronson nodded, then casually rested his left hand on the man's thigh and pushed sharply downward.

The man's scream echoed around the confined space, and a couple of people turned toward Bronson and started heading in his direction. Again he waved his warrant card at them.

"I'm a police officer and the situation is under control," he called out. "This man is injured and I've already requested medical assistance."

Nobody apparently thought to ask how Bronson could have done that in the underground concrete cavern where no mobile phone could possibly work.

"If you get to a hospital within the next hour or so, you might walk again, but the longer you prat me about, the longer it's going to take. You've got two choices. The messy way is I do what I should do as a policeman."

"You're not a copper," the man snarled, interrupting him.

"I am, actually," Bronson said, "but that really doesn't matter. As I was saying, what I should do is scramble the paramedics, then arrest you for carrying a firearm, which will definitely put you in the slammer, and I'll testify at your trial that I saw you try to push a woman in front of a train, and that'll mean a charge of attempted murder, which should get you ten years at least. The trouble is, I'm in a hurry and that sounds to me like an awful lot of paperwork.

"The other option is you tell me what I want to know. As soon as you've done that, I'll call the medics and then I'll walk away with your gun in my pocket. You'll get treatment and won't be prosecuted, and you can continue with your sad career as long as your knee holds up. So I'll ask you again: who paid you to kill the woman? Or would you like me to lean on your leg again?"

The man shook his head, sweat springing to his forehead. He swung his right fist clumsily toward Bronson, who easily avoided the blow.

Bronson stretched his hand back down toward the man's knee.

"No, no, please don't. I'll tell you."

"I'm listening."

"I don't know his name. He called me a few days ago."

"Oh," Bronson said, "you advertise your services, do you? In the Yellow Pages, are you, under 'Killers for hire'? Something like that?"

The man shook his head.

"People know how and where to find me. Anyway, he called. Cash job. Five grand, two up front, two on completion, with an extra grand as a bonus. He gave me all the details—work address, home address and stuff—but he didn't tell me why he wanted her dead. They never do. I was supposed to do it in her flat, make it look like a burglary, an accidental death, if I could manage it, but yesterday he called me again, said he'd changed his mind and it had to be done immediately. That was the reason for the bonus."

Bronson nodded, even more grateful than before that Angela had decided to spend the previous night in his house instead of at Ealing.

"That's all I know. Now get me a bloody doctor."

"A deal's a deal," Bronson replied, standing up as the next Northern Line train pulled into the station. "I'll make the call as soon I get out of here."

52

Angela was waiting for Bronson in the open area of Charing Cross mainline station opposite platforms 5 and 6, from which trains down into the heart of Kent, to Orpington, Sevenoaks and Tunbridge Wells, normally departed.

"What the hell was all that about?" she demanded, as she walked up to him.

"That," Bronson replied, making sure nobody else could hear what he was saying, "was the long arm of whoever organized the killings in Cairo reaching out to you. He grabbed hold of you and was going to push you under the train. I could see what he intended to do, and so I stopped him."

Angela's face changed, her complexion turning paler as she absorbed this unwelcome news.

"I know he got hold of me, but I didn't know why. At first I thought it was you, just messing about. Are you sure?"

Bronson nodded.

"I had a chat with him after you'd gone. He told me he'd been offered five thousand pounds to make sure you didn't see tomorrow."

From somewhere, Angela summoned a weak smile.

"Only five thousand? So I'm not exactly in the big league, then." She paused for a moment, then asked: "Do you think he was the only one after me?"

"Probably. These people normally work alone. For the moment I think you're quite safe. And in any case, to-morrow we'll be in Spain."

He pulled out the mobile phone he'd taken from the man at the station and checked the log. As he'd expected, neither received nor called numbers were listed, the mark of a man who's either very careful or very paranoid. Or both. Bronson supposed that the techies might be able to find out more about where the phone had been and which numbers it had been in contact with, but they were all likely to be untraceable pay-as-you-go numbers—and in any case, they didn't have the time to find out.

He dialed triple nine and, when the operator asked him which service he required, he said, "Ambulance." When he was connected, he reported that he had seen a man collapse at the Tottenham Court Road Underground station. He thought he might be drunk.

53

"You can call our man in Cairo and tell him that the target's in Madrid," the Englishman said the moment Morini answered his call, "so they can stop looking for him anywhere in Egypt."

"How did you find out?" the Italian asked.

"He used a credit card to make a purchase at a shop in the city, and we traced him from that."

"That sounds as if it might have been a big mistake," Morini suggested.

"I'm not so sure. What he did might have been deliberate, or perhaps he decided that staying hidden didn't matter any longer. We think he could be intending to go public with the relic quite soon, in which case the whole world will know where he is. And what he's trying to sell."

"Then I hope you can locate him before that happens."

54

The Englishman had not been a popular choice within the ranks of P2 when he was selected as its new head, not the least because he wasn't Italian and didn't speak the language. But he'd taken the reins just over three years earlier when an internal revolt, a battle for control, had almost wrecked the lodge, a revolt that he had resolved in one short afternoon. He'd traveled out to Milan unannounced and personally executed the five ringleaders with his bare hands, using a baseball bat on four of the men and a knife on the last one, the man who'd started it. He had taken a long time to die and it had been very messy.

After that, nobody had ever questioned his competence or fitness for the job, and certainly not his ruthlessness.

Having completed the call to the cleric in Rome, the Englishman opened his small briefcase on the café table in front of him and took out the list of names and numbers, the annex to the document he had been instrumental in compiling. He needed to decide who would be the most appropriate person for him to activate in Spain's capital city.

What he required now was not just some hired thug who would be able to kill Anum Husani—that would be easy enough—but somebody who could first track down the man and recover the relic, and then eliminate Husani. And that, the Englishman knew, wouldn't be easy; not in a city of well over three million people, with more than double that number in the entire metropolitan area, and especially not when the only clues he had to go on were two credit card transactions that had taken place the previous day. Not to mention that Husani could have taken a flight out of Madrid by now, or possibly even out of Spain.

But, actually, he doubted that was the case. He believed that Husani had chosen Madrid deliberately. It was the third largest city in Western Europe, after London and Berlin, and had the largest metropolitan area after London and Paris. And because of Spain's Moorish heritage, people bearing an Arabic appearance were not an unusual sight there.

And there were probably other reasons as well. If he was trying to sell the parchment—and that was the only scenario that made any sense—then the most likely potential buyers would be the museums and well-heeled collectors of Western Europe.

What the Englishman was expecting, at almost any moment, was some kind of a news item or press release on the Internet that would alert potential purchasers to the existence of the relic. Tracing the origin of such a posting probably wouldn't help to track down Husani, because if he had any sense he would travel somewhere in the city that was well away from the hotel where he was staying and use a cybercafé there. And so far Husani had proved that he certainly wasn't stupid.

But if he were to sell the relic, his press release, or whatever medium he decided he was going to use to describe the parchment, would have to include some means of communicating with him—an e-mail address, a mobile phone number, or even a physical location, probably in a public place—and once that information was available, it would only be a matter of time before they found him.

55

The heat hit them as they stepped out of the terminal building in Madrid, a solid wall of warm and muggy air that seemed to suck sweat straight out of every pore on their bodies.

"God," Angela muttered. "Please tell me you got a car with air-conditioning."

"You're damn right I did. I've driven in Spain before, and you need air-con here even in the winter.

"There it is," Bronson added, as the lights on a light-blue León began to flash in response to him pressing the button on the car key.

They walked over to the car and placed their bags and laptops in the boot, before setting off through the Madrid streets.

The Spanish city looked very much like any other major city in Europe, a mixture of wide avenues and narrow streets, large and imposing public buildings and run-down apartment blocks. The worldwide economic recession had had a major effect upon the economy of Spain, and they were not surprised to see that quite a number of shops and other businesses were boarded up. But there were still a lot of cars on the road, most of them fairly new and many of them quite expensive makes. Clearly there were still some people in the country who were making money.

"Of course," Angela pointed out as they drove through the streets, "Spain has always had a very prosperous black economy. I think the Spanish regard income tax, and most other taxes, in fact, as an optional expense, and if there's any practical way of hiding funds from business transactions from the Hacienda—that's the Spanish taxman—then they would do it. They call it mattress money, because under the mattress is the one reasonably safe place where they can hide it."

"Then it's not too surprising that the Spanish economy is in such a deep hole at the moment, is it? I read one report that said about five million new homes had been built in Spain that nobody wanted, because the Spanish population is falling, not increasing, and it now probably stands at less than forty-five million. It's a bloody shambles!"

The hotel was located in a narrow side street close to a small square. It had its own dedicated parking area on the two underground levels beneath the building. Bronson drove down the ramp and easily found a vacant space; then he and Angela took the lift to the reception on the ground floor.

Their room was on the third floor, overlooking the street. It didn't take them long to put away the few clothes they'd brought with them, and as soon as they'd done that, Bronson suggested going downstairs for a drink.

"Bring your laptop," he said. "We can probably log in to the hotel Wi-Fi system in the bar, and then you can check your e-mails and see if that guy has come back to you. Here," he added, taking hold of her computer bag. "I'll carry it for you."

Angela looked at him suspiciously.

"You're being particularly nice to me at the moment. What do you want?"

"Only your body, much later, if you're willing to share it."

Angela looked at the large double bed that dominated the room.

"Well, we'll obviously be sleeping together because there's only one bed, but I haven't yet decided whether or not we'll be *sleeping* together. It all depends on how well you treat me and where we go out to eat tonight. And I don't want bloody paella."

56

Bronson ordered "*Dos cafés con leche*" from the slim, dark-haired young man standing behind the bar. He immediately replied in fluent English: "Two white coffees coming right up."

Bronson guessed he must look very English. Either that or the accent of his rudimentary Spanish had given him away.

"You've got Wi-Fi here?" Bronson asked the barman, abandoning all attempts at conversing in Spanish, as he placed two large cups on a machine.

The young man nodded, reached into a drawer and took out a piece of paper. He passed it over to Bronson and pointed at the letters and numbers printed on it.

Bronson passed the paper to Angela, then returned to the bar, where the barista was putting a couple of paper wraps of sugar on each saucer.

"Your English is very good," he said.

"It should be. My father's English but my mother is Spanish, so I grew up speaking both languages. Don't pay for this," he went on as Bronson pulled out his wallet. "I'll just stick it on your room bill. Much easier for all of us."

"Do you work here full-time?" he asked, then gave him the room number.

The young man shook his head.

"Not really. I'm trying to decide what to do with my life, and while I'm making up my mind my father thought working here would be a good idea. He owns the hotel, you see, so I'm just cheap labor, I suppose. Enjoy your coffee."

Bronson carried the cups over to the table where Angela was sitting, the laptop open in front of her.

"Anything from our mystery seller?" he asked.

"Nothing yet," she said, sounding downcast.

"I hope this doesn't mean we've wasted our time flying out here," Bronson said. "Or that your anonymous correspondent has met with some kind of an accident, like walking into the path of a bullet."

"Don't remind me," Angela said, with a slight shudder. "What did you do with that man's gun, by the way? Will you hand it in when we get back to Britain?"

"Probably not. I've never understood why New Labour thought it was such a brilliant plan to disarm all sections of the British population apart from the criminals. In my opinion, having the odd unlicensed weapon about the place is actually quite a good idea."

Angela looked worried. "But if you get caught with it, you'll be in a lot of trouble."

"You're quite right there, so I'll just have to make sure I don't get caught."

Before Angela could reply, her computer emitted a musical tone and she turned back to look at the screen.

"It's him," she said excitedly, and clicked the touch pad to open the message.

"What's he said?"

"He hasn't said anything, actually. The only thing that's in this e-mail is an address of a Web site."

She moved the mouse pointer over the underlined address and clicked the button. Her browser opened almost immediately, and a couple of seconds after that she and Bronson were both staring at the contents of the Web site.

Bronson was the first to speak.

"Well," he murmured, with a glance at Angela, "that's a bit of a bugger, isn't it?"

57

Bronson and Angela sat side by side and stared at the screen, their coffees forgotten beside them. What they were looking at wasn't, to be honest, much of a Web site. The home page had a simple title—"Ancient parchment for sale"—and contained a single color photograph of the relic itself. The second page contained slightly more in the way of illustrations, pictures that had clearly been cropped from those taken by Ali Mohammed. Each picture showed just a small section of the text that had been revealed by his sophisticated techniques.

The third page contained no pictures, and simply gave an e-mail address—the same address that Angela had already used in communicating with the hitherto unidentified owner of the parchment—and a name. The mysterious owner was at last revealed to be a man called Anum Husani.

"I don't understand," Angela said. "The only thing this tells us that we didn't know before is his name. I've already got copies of all these pictures, so why is he bothering to load them onto a Web site and then suggesting I view them?"

"Let's take another look at the e-mail."

Angela called it up again.

"That's what I thought he might have done," Bronson said, pointing at the top of the screen. "He didn't just send this e-mail to you. It looks as if he's sent it to every museum in America and Western Europe. He created the Web site just to show people what he's got for sale. He's obviously trying to generate a kind of auction for the relic. Is that likely to happen?"

Angela shook her head.

"That's difficult to say, because there are two things he hasn't mentioned. The first is what the text on the parchment actually says, so perhaps he doesn't know. I certainly don't, not fully. I doubt if any museum or collector would stump up much money without a full translation."

"And the other thing?" Bronson asked.

"In a word, provenance. A lot of museums won't touch any object if they can't establish full details of its history, because in the world of antiques and antiquities there are an awful lot of very accomplished counterfeiters. Some of them have managed to fool acknowledged experts in their fields, time and time again, like Tom Keating. He fooled almost everybody. He painted Old Masters, including Gainsborough, Renoir and Degas, as well as Samuel Palmer watercolors, and almost all of them were certified as genuine by art experts of the day."

"And nobody twigged?"

"No. Or, at least, not for a long time, and they really should have been picked up right from the start, because Keating always left a clue in his forgeries, something so blatant that any competent art examiner should have detected it immediately."

"What sort of clues?" Bronson asked.

"Oh, he was quite fond of writing a vulgar remark in white lead on the canvas before he started painting. Obviously it would be invisible once the work was finished, but it would show up immediately with an X-ray. Or he would use a type of material in the painting that would simply have been unavailable to the genuine artist."

"I remember him now," Bronson said. "I think I saw something about him on television."

Angela grinned at him.

"You certainly did. Once he confessed to what he'd done, he had his own television series teaching people—believe it or not—how to paint like the Old Masters. He was a likable old rogue."

"OK, this is all very interesting, but it doesn't get us anywhere." Bronson knew that Angela could go on forever about one of her favorite topics. "Did the guy from the Cairo Museum know the provenance—where the parchment came from?"

"If he did know, he didn't tell me."

"So it's possible that this relic was just found somewhere and has basically popped into existence now, and nobody has any idea where it's been for the last two thousand years, or however old it is."

"That's possible," Angela replied, "but I think—in fact, I'm certain—that somebody must have known exactly what the parchment is and where it's been. The Web site we're looking at is the only place where pictures of the relic have been posted, yet the first killing in Cairo happened almost a week ago."

"So somebody, somewhere, knew that the parchment had reappeared, and also how important it was," Bronson finished for her.

Angela nodded. "Exactly. And it looks to me as if this man Husani has realized that the best thing he can do to ensure his safety is to go public with details and photo-graphs of the relic."

"So do you think that now he's put the pictures of it onto the Internet he'll be safe? Because I don't. That Web site might be seen by a few dozen people at the most, and my guess is that whoever is after him will have enough clout to find out where he is and shut him up."

Angela nodded again. "That's why we have to find him first."

58

Father Antonio Morini was again wearing civilian clothes and walking steadily down a narrow street in Rome when he received a text on his cell phone from a British-registered mobile.

He continued walking as he took out his mobile and read the message, which was brief to the point of abruptness. It simply stated "On sale" and gave the address of a Web site he'd never heard of before, but he knew immediately what that had to mean. He turned around and immediately began retracing his steps, his stride noticeably brisker than before.

Back in his office in the Vatican, Morini sat down at the table and lifted the lid of his laptop to wake up the machine. As soon as all the programs were working again, he opened his browser and input the URL. Seconds later, he was staring at the images of the lost parchment.

This was immediate confirmation to him that the man Husani had obtained the genuine relic, but he still had no idea of the exact mechanism by which it had reappeared. The Vatican had for many years employed a policy of photographing books and manuscripts and other objects that were held in the Vatican Library or elsewhere in the Holy See, even objects it did not officially acknowledge that it owned. In an encrypted folder on his hard drive, Morini had copies of those original photographs of the relic. He was absolutely sure about what he was looking at.

Although it would take a lot of work before anybody would be able to read the entire text, Morini guessed that whoever possessed the parchment would eventually decipher it. And then they would fully understand why it was such a colossal threat to the credibility of the Vatican, of the Pope and indeed of the entire Roman Catholic religion.

He walked out of the Vatican again and as soon as he was out on the streets he made the call.

59

Within just a few minutes of looking at the images of the parchment on the Web site, Angela typed and sent a simple reply to Anum Husani, stating that she was in Madrid, was interested in buying the parchment for the British Museum, and asking him where and when he wanted to meet. She didn't mention the other museum official who would have to be there as well.

George Stebbins, a specialist in ancient manuscripts, and especially parchments, had also e-mailed her to say he'd just arrived in the city. He had been sent out by the British Museum to assess the relic and provide Angela with expert advice on its authenticity. Stebbins had checked into a hotel not too far away from the one where Angela and Bronson were staying, and suggested they meet that afternoon.

"Would he be a good judge of the provenance?" Chris asked.

"Not the provenance, because that's down to the seller, but he'll certainly be able to confirm its authenticity," Angela said. "He's one of the foremost experts in the field for this period. He'll be vital in getting the parchment authenticated."

"And have you had a chance to figure out any more of the text on the parchment?"

Angela shook her head. "When do you think I've had the time to do that? Plus I really need to see it before I can do more. The photographs Ali Mohammed took show far more of the writing than can be seen with the naked eye, but there are several parts of it that still aren't legible. I'm sure we've got enough sophisticated gear at the museum to read pretty much all of it, which is why we need to take possession of it."

Bronson looked slightly puzzled.

"But if you don't know exactly what the text on the parchment says, how do you know it's of any value at all? Surely you're not just going by that name you read on it? Yusef or whatever it was?"

Angela looked at him with an expression of mild irritation on her face.

"Actually," she replied, "I am, because that wasn't just a name. Yusef bar Heli wasn't just some man wandering about Judea two thousand years ago. He was a person that almost everybody in the world has heard of, but somebody about whom very little is actually known, because he was sidelined by his son. In modern English, we would translate Yusef as 'Joseph' and, according to those few accounts that have survived, a man called by that name married a woman called Mary, and they were the parents of a man who was much later known as Jesus Christ."

"You're kidding," Bronson said.

"I'm not. I still have no idea what the parchment is describing, but that name is clear enough to read, as is the name of the Judean town of Tzippori, and it is believed that Joseph spent at least some of his life in that area."

"But surely 'Yusef' was a very common name at that time?" Bronson argued. "And how do we know that Joseph's father was called 'Heli'?"

"We don't, but it's believed he was named either Heli or Yacob. As I said, very little is actually known about him. But the Tzippori reference, plus the fact that two men who had access to the parchment have been brutally murdered, suggests that the text probably does refer to this particular Joseph."

She looked down again at her computer screen, then back up at Bronson.

"I don't know what event or fact the text on the parchment is describing, but I'm as sure as I can be that there must be something, some groundbreaking secret, that the relic reveals. And if the parchment does reveal something about Joseph, the earthly father of Jesus, or even something about Jesus himself, then there's one very obvious candidate who would rather it were kept quiet."

"The Catholic Church again? Do you really think so?"

"I know it sounds crazy—but it's the only possibility I can think of. They have the reach and the motivation. If this parchment turns out to be a contemporary account of something that proves beyond doubt that, for example, Jesus wasn't crucified, then the entire basis of the Christian faith could be destroyed. This could go straight to the very heart of the religion."

60

George Stebbins arrived at their hotel in the middle of the afternoon. Angela made the introductions, and the document specialist joined her at their table while Bronson collected drinks from the bar.

"You know this might be a bit of a wild-goose chase, Angela?" Stebbins said, stirring a cube of sugar into his coffee. "It's not that difficult to fake a piece of text on a parchment."

He was in his late forties, comfortably plump and almost bald, not even enough hair on his head to attempt a comb-over. He apparently tried to make up for this with a bushy square-cut beard of a slightly reddish hue, which made his head, at least in Bronson's opinion, look like a large egg resting in a bird's nest.

"I realize that, but I have a feeling this is probably genuine. Most of the text only shows up when you bathe it in infrared or ultraviolet light, and I can't think of any way that could be faked. And, more worryingly, two people who are known to have seen and examined the parchment have been murdered, including one scientist that I knew personally."

"What? Murdered? Who was murdered?"

It was suddenly obvious that when Stebbins had been asked to travel out to Madrid to examine the parchment, he hadn't been given the whole story.

Angela took him through the whole sequence of events, from her first contact with Ali Mohammed to the present situation, including what had so nearly happened to her at the Tottenham Court Road Underground station, and that they were dependent on Anum Husani making contact in such a way that there would be no unwanted third parties at their meeting. When she'd finished, George Stebbins looked positively drained.

"I had no idea," he said. "All they told me was that an old piece of parchment had been found, which you were negotiating over, and the museum wanted me to come along as well just to confirm that it wasn't a recent forgery. Nobody told me people had been killed over it."

"Well, the good news," Bronson said, "is that those two deaths occurred in Cairo, and that's a hell of a long way from Madrid."

"But look what happened to Angela in London." Stebbins leaned forward, his hands gripping the table in anxiety. "What if they followed her here and are watching us now?"

"They might well be, but there's one important difference between here and both London and Cairo. In London, the man who tried to kill Angela followed her from the British Museum and one of the men who was murdered in Egypt was killed in his office at the Cairo Museum. I'm not sure about the other victim, but I'd be prepared to lay odds that he died either in his house or where he worked.

"The situation here is completely different. We can go and meet this man Anum Husani at any location of his

choosing, anywhere in the city, and there's nothing whatsoever to link either him or us with that meeting place. I
can't imagine they'll be able to intercept his e-mails, so
there shouldn't be any way they can find out where we
intend to meet."

Stebbins still didn't look entirely convinced, but nodded reluctant agreement.

"You might be right," he said. "So all we can do for
the moment, I suppose, is sit around and wait for this
Husani to send us details of the rendezvous."

"That, basically, is our plan," Angela agreed, "but in
the meantime you can take a look at the pictures of the
parchment and let us know what you think about it."

"I'll need to see the relic in the flesh before I can give
you my professional opinion," Stebbins said.

Angela nodded.

"I know that, but at least looking at the pictures will
give you a good idea what to expect when we finally meet
this Arab."

But before the man from the British Museum could
do anything, Angela's laptop emitted a tone to show that
another e-mail had been received.

"It's him," she said. "He wants to see me in fifty minutes, and he's given me the address of a café."

61

Bronson stood up and turned to face Angela and George.

"Right, we only have a short time, so we need to plan quickly. This is a potentially dangerous situation that we're walking into, and I want to make sure that we have the means of getting away from it as quickly as possible. So we'll be taking the car, and ideally I'd like you two to meet this man while I stay in the vehicle, somewhere with a good view of the rendezvous position. That way, I'll be able to carry out surveillance of the whole area, and provide immediate backup and a quick way of getting out of there if anything untoward happens."

Throughout Chris's speech, George Stebbins had been squirming uncomfortably in his seat, and now he spoke, directing his concerns at Angela.

"Look, I'm not all that happy about going ahead with this. My understanding was that I simply had to examine a piece of parchment. Nothing more, nothing less. I expected to be able to do this in the comfort of my hotel room or some other sensible and civilized location. I was never told that there was a possibility that there might be violence involved."

Then he swung round to look at Bronson.

"It's easy enough for you to say it'll be safe. You won't even be at the rendezvous. You'll be sitting in the car somewhere and able to drive away at the first sign of trouble."

There was steel in Bronson's voice when he replied.

"Angela knows me very well," he said, "and she knows that there's absolutely no way I would just *drive away*, as you put it. I only suggested that I wait in the vehicle because that would enable me to provide surveillance of the entire area and react if anything happened. I'm a police officer. I'm trained in surveillance and I'm a Class One police driver, so I'm the best person to have in the car. If you'd rather we did it the other way round, and you wait in the car while Angela and I meet with Husani, that's fine by me."

"You might be happy to do that, Chris, but I'm not," Angela snapped. "The only reason George is here at all is to give his opinion of the parchment, and he can't do that if he's sitting in a car fifty yards away. Either you come to the rendezvous with me, George, or there's no point at all in you being here. The clock's ticking. If we don't leave here within the next few minutes, we're not going to make it on time. It's time to piss or get off the pot."

She paused for a moment, her glance switching between the two men.

"So what's it to be?"

Stebbins looked somewhat sheepish, then shook his head.

"I think I'll get a taxi back to my hotel," he said quietly. Then he stood up and walked out of the bar.

Bronson and Angela watched him go.

"So it's just the two of us again," Bronson said, turning back to look at Angela, "and personally I think it's better that way. Now, we need to go."

62

As Bronson had hoped, the location Anum Husani had specified was positioned on a street that offered ample parking on both sides of the road, providing plenty of places to view their meeting from. He reversed the car into the spot he'd chosen, so that he would be able to drive away immediately if the circumstances dictated.

"We're still about ten minutes early," Bronson said, "so I'll come over with you and check there are no surprises at the café itself."

There weren't as far as he could tell. The café was just a café, probably chosen by Husani because it could be approached from multiple directions. As a rendezvous position, it wasn't bad.

In his e-mail to Angela, Husani had instructed her to sit on one of the tables outside, by herself, and order a *café con leche* and a glass of water. As soon as Bronson was satisfied that there were no potential dangers lurking within the building or anywhere near it, Angela took a seat.

Before he left, Bronson sat down beside her.

"I'll be in the car, with the engine running, less than

thirty yards away from you. I'll be watching you and anyone who comes anywhere near you. If there's anything you're unhappy about or you feel uncomfortable at any time, just get up and start walking toward me. I'll pull out of the parking space immediately, and we can be gone from here in ten seconds."

Angela smiled at him.

"That sounds like the kind of briefing you'd have given when you were in the Army. Just relax, Chris, and I'm sure it will all work out well. Now go. I'll be fine."

Bronson nodded, gave her shoulder a gentle squeeze of encouragement, then walked across the road to the car.

63

Anum Husani had actually arrived at the rendezvous about ten minutes earlier, and had been waiting in a small park down the street, some distance away, watching the activity at the café through a pair of compact but powerful binoculars he had purchased that morning. He'd seen a couple—an attractive blond woman and a powerfully built, tall man with dark hair—arrive and spend a little time inside the building. Then they'd come out and the woman had sat down at a table. The man had then left her and gone to sit in a car nearby.

He had assumed from the start that there would be at least one other person with Angela Lewis, somebody to give a second opinion on the authenticity of the parchment. But then again, maybe the man was her husband: they certainly seemed to be on very friendly terms.

But whoever he was, he didn't worry Husani. What bothered him was the possibility that the killer from Cairo, or some other hired assassin, might also know about the rendezvous he had arranged. He wasn't well versed in the workings of modern technology. He used a computer as a tool to do certain things, but had little or no idea what went on in the background. He had no idea if it was possible for somebody else to intercept his e-mail messages and read them, but he vaguely knew that that method of communication was more secure than using a mobile telephone.

These thoughts ran through his head as he sat on the grass, his back against the trunk of a tree, watching what little activity there was at the café.

The time he had specified for the rendezvous arrived, and still Husani didn't move, just kept watching. About five minutes later, he saw the woman sitting at the table by herself look across the road toward the parked cars and give a slight shrug. If he needed it, that was confirmation enough. It was time.

Husani glanced round cautiously, but nobody appeared to be paying him—or the blond woman in the café—any attention. He slid the binoculars into his pocket, picked up the expensive briefcase, then stood up and began slowly walking down the street, alert to any indication of danger.

Nobody approached him as he covered the short distance to the café on the opposite side of the road. When he reached a point almost directly opposite the building, he stopped and looked in both directions, like a cautious pedestrian, before walking to the other side. He weaved his way between the tables until he reached the one where Angela was sitting.

Then he stopped.

64

Angela had seen the man walking toward the café, and had half guessed—both from his appearance and from his manner—that he was the person she was expecting. When he came to a halt beside her table, she looked up at him and smiled in a friendly manner. Then she stood up to greet him.

"Mr. Husani?" she asked, and the man nodded. "Why don't you sit down and we can talk? Can I get you a drink?"

"Thank you. Coffee, please, strong black." He seemed extremely nervous, constantly looking around and tapping his fingers against the briefcase.

They sat down as a waiter approached the table, and Angela relayed Husani's order in her best schoolgirl Spanish. The waiter nodded in a disinterested manner, turned and disappeared inside the café.

"We wait for drink, then talk. OK?" Husani said.

"Whatever you want," Angela agreed.

The waiter reappeared with a small tray on which was a small cup of black coffee, a tiny china milk jug, the contents of which steamed slightly, and two wraps of sugar.

As soon as the waiter had moved out of earshot, Angela spoke.

"My name is Angela Lewis," she began. "The e-mail that you sent to the British Museum was given to me. I sent you the reply. And now we are here at the time and at the place you chose."

She paused for a moment to ensure that she wasn't speaking too fast and that Husani had understood what she said. He looked comfortable enough, so she continued.

"The British Museum is very interested in acquiring the relic that you are offering for sale. But before we can discuss the price, obviously I will need to see it to make sure that it is genuine."

Husani nodded.

"I expect that," he said, "but object is real. That why people killed in Cairo."

For Angela, that fact was one of the most compelling arguments to support the contention that the parchment was genuine, but obviously that wouldn't be enough for the British Museum.

"I understand that, and I am sure that the relic is exactly what you claim it to be. But I will still need to look at it before I can offer to buy it from you."

Husani nodded again, cleared a space on the table and then lifted up his briefcase.

"That why I bring it with me," he said. "Parchment in this case. This very, very expensive case. Man in shop tell me it bulletproof. Steel inside it, and Kelvin."

For a moment, Angela didn't understand what he meant, what the reference was to the name she normally associated with a temperature scale, and then she twigged.

"You mean Kevlar?" she said.

"Probably, yes. Anyway, case really strong."

He reached into his jacket pocket and pulled out a small but complex-looking key, which he inserted in turn in the two locks on the side of the case. Then he clicked the catches and lifted the lid.

He turned the case slightly on the table so that Angela could see inside it. Several glossy color photographs were visible, and something else underneath them.

"You have seen pictures, yes? Pictures friend Ali sent you?"

"Yes," Angela replied. "I saw those pictures. And he was my friend too," she added.

"Good. Now this is relic."

Husani lifted the photographs out of the case and then reached into the case to remove another object that looked like a folder made of thin cardboard and designed to contain unbound leaves of paper. He placed this carefully on the table in front of Angela.

She reached out for it, opened the flap of the folder and peered inside, but didn't touch the relic that it contained. Almost as she'd expected, the sight of the parchment was disappointing. It was a rough and slightly irregular oblong of brownish cured animal skin, with here and there a handful of letters and words, some obviously written in Latin, the ink having faded to almost the same color as the parchment, and all the writing barely visible.

She wished George Stebbins had had the courage to come along to the meeting, because as she stared down at the ancient relic, she was very conscious that she was essentially unqualified to make a judgment on the object. It looked old, certainly, but that didn't mean it *was* old. Angela was very well aware that there were hundreds, perhaps even thousands, of highly competent forgers working in Cairo and elsewhere in Egypt who would be perfectly capable of producing an object of this type.

But she also knew that those forgers would not have been capable of fabricating a piece of parchment containing text that could only be read in a scientific laboratory. That was completely beyond them. And most forgers, quite understandably, produced relics on which the lettering was readable, because that was the major selling point for them. Her only real concern about the parchment was whether or not it was the same relic that Ali Mohammed had examined. At least she could do something to check that.

"May I?" she asked, gesturing toward the sheaf of photographs that Husani had lifted out of the steel-lined case.

"Of course."

She selected the picture that showed the parchment in full color, when it had been photographed under normal lighting conditions. Yes. She was quite certain that these pictures were precisely the same as those she had received. She then compared the photo to the object in the folder. Unless Husani had managed to find somebody of enormous skill who could work incredibly quickly, she knew that she was looking at precisely the same object.

Angela handed back the photograph and closed the folder containing the parchment. Husani replaced everything in the briefcase, snapping the catches closed but not turning the key in the locks, presumably in case he or Angela needed to look at either the relic or the pictures again.

"Now you make offer?" Husani asked.

And that was the question Angela had been dreading. When it came to guessing the value of something like the parchment, she really had very little idea of its proper worth. In the end, she decided she needed two things—

more time and another opinion—and that meant somehow getting George Stebbins out of his hotel room.

"It is not quite that simple," she said slowly. "I am satisfied that the parchment is genuine, but I need to show it to my colleague who is an expert before I can make you an offer."

Husani didn't look very impressed.

"There other buyers interest," he said. "Your colleague is man in car, yes? Show it him now?"

"No," Angela replied. "He is just a friend. My colleague is in a hotel near here. Can we take the parchment to him so he can see it?"

She could almost see Husani's lips forming the word "no" when she heard the sudden blare of a car horn, then the roar of an engine. She spun round to see Bronson powering the rental car out of the parking space, the front tires smoking and screaming as they scrabbled for grip.

She turned back to Husani, but the Arab had disappeared. Then she saw that he had fallen backward, out of his chair, the front of his white shirt a mass of crimson.

Angela choked back a scream. Instinctively she grabbed the steel-lined briefcase that had cost Anum Husani so much money. As she wheeled round and looked back toward the road, she saw a black-clad figure standing just a few yards away. He was staring straight at her, and looking down the barrel of a long and strangely shaped pistol.

The open space of the café was a cliché come hideously to life: there really was nowhere to run and nowhere to hide.

She heard the increasing bellow from the engine of Bronson's car, but she knew he was too far away to help

her. Then she saw a faint puff of flame from the end of
the weapon, and felt in that same instant a sudden, terrible, searing pain in her chest, and an impact that knocked
her flying.

She tumbled backward, losing her grip on the briefcase. Then the back of her head hit the concrete floor—
hard—and instantly her world went black.

65

It was the noise that she noticed first. It sounded strangely distant: an intermittent thumping and rumbling sound, and another more constant hum that rose and fell. For some time—it could have been minutes or seconds—she didn't move, just stayed as still as she could, trying to make sense of what had happened to her. But it made no sense. There seemed to be huge gaps in her memory.

She gradually became aware of a voice—a familiar voice—close to her. A voice that seemed to be saying her name.

And then, slowly, things started to fit together. She realized that she was in a car, lying crumpled across the backseat. That explained the noises she could hear. But how had she got into a car? And whose car was it?

With a rush, she remembered the café. She remembered talking to Anum Husani, remembered examining the parchment. And then her normal, lineal memory seemed to fail her, and it was as if she was seeing individual frames from a movie inside her head.

Husani no longer sitting beside her, but flat on his back on the ground, his shirt deep red in color. Grabbing the briefcase. A man dressed all in black. And then the gun. The gun he was holding. And then the man firing the gun.

She gasped with shock as she relived the moment, and struggled to sit up. As she did so, a throbbing pain pulsed through the back of her head, and she cried out involuntarily, reaching up to hold the place where it hurt.

"Angela. It's me, Chris. Don't try to move. Just lie there. Just for a few more minutes."

"What happened?" she asked, her voice weak and slurred. "Where are we?"

"Madrid. We're still in Madrid, but we won't be for long. We're going to have to move quickly, but first I need to take a look at that head of yours. You cracked it pretty hard when you fell."

"I don't remember that," Angela said, "but I do know that my head hurts."

Suddenly, the world outside the car went dark as the vehicle angled downward.

"Where are we going?"

"We're at the hotel. As soon as I've parked the car, we're going up to our room. Then I'll explain what happened."

Moments later, Bronson pulled the car to a halt.

"Can you get out by yourself?" he asked.

"Did I get in by myself?"

Bronson gave her a slight smile.

"Not exactly. I'm afraid I had to more or less chuck you in there. There wasn't time to do anything else."

Angela turned round on the seat to face the open door and, with legs that suddenly seemed to be made of rubber, crawled clumsily toward his waiting hands.

As soon as he could, Bronson seized her under the armpits and gently lifted her body out of the car. Once he was sure that she could stand, albeit leaning against the side of the vehicle, he let go of her.

"Just hang on there for a couple of seconds," he said.

Bronson glanced round the garage, but he and Angela were entirely alone there, and so far he hadn't spotted any surveillance cameras. Nevertheless, he used his own body to screen what he was doing from any possible observer. He bent forward, reached down into the passenger-side foot well and removed four objects. The first was a briefcase, and the others a mobile phone and a Beretta semi-automatic pistol with a lengthy suppressor attached to its muzzle, plus a pistol magazine. He snapped open the two catches on the leather-covered briefcase and put the phone, the magazine and the pistol, complete with the suppressor, inside it. Then he closed the briefcase and locked the car.

Holding the briefcase in his left hand, he wrapped his right arm around Angela, pulling her close to him, and then the two of them began slowly walking across the garage floor toward the two lifts.

Bronson ushered Angela inside one of the lifts and pressed the button for their floor. Less than three minutes later, he was able to lock the door of their room from the inside and watch Angela sit down gratefully on the wide double bed.

Bronson put down the briefcase and walked across to where she was sitting.

"Just lean forward very slightly," he said, "so that I can see the back of your head."

He examined the wound on the back of her scalp. It was more bruised than cut, and he didn't think it would need stitches, just a dressing and a pad, neither of which, of course, he had.

"I need to clean and dress that wound," he told her.

"Just stay here on the bed while I go and find a medical kit from somewhere. Don't open the door to anybody. I'll take the key with me."

Angela silently nodded her agreement.

Bronson descended in the lift to the ground floor. There was nobody at the reception desk, so he walked through into the bar. About half a dozen people were sitting at tables in there, drinks in front of them and, as he'd hoped, the same friendly waiter he'd spoken to before was standing behind the bar industriously wiping the countertop.

Bronson immediately walked over to him.

"Do you have a medical kit I could borrow?" he asked. "My wife's bashed her head, and I just need a dressing or something to cover it."

The man looked concerned.

"If you want," he suggested, "I can call a doctor for her. An English-speaking doctor, I mean."

Bronson shook his head. "No, it's not that bad. It's just a graze, really. I just need to clean and dress it."

"If you're sure?"

He walked to the opposite end of the bar and reached below it, and then handed Bronson a small white plastic box with a red cross on it.

"Thanks. I'll bring it back as soon as I can."

The waiter nodded.

"Take as long as you need. Just make sure she's OK."

Back in their bedroom, Bronson opened the medical kit, took out what he thought he would need, and then tenderly washed the wound on the back of Angela's head in warm water. Once he'd removed most of the dried blood from the hair around the injury, it looked a lot smaller and a lot less serious than he'd thought at first. But blows to the head, even quite minor injuries, can be dangerous. There's the possibility of concussion or, less likely, a fractured skull or damage to the blood vessels inside the brain.

"How does it look?" Angela demanded.

"It's not too bad," Bronson said truthfully. "It'll still need a small pad or something to cover it, but otherwise it's fine."

He organized a pad and, as a temporary measure, loosely tied a bandage around the back of Angela's head and around her forehead, just to keep it in place.

"Right," Angela said, "now you've done your impersonation of Florence Nightingale, why don't you tell me what the hell happened in that café?"

"What do you remember?"

"It's mostly clear in my mind up to the point when you started the car. I recall turning to look over toward you, but after that I can only remember flashes. I saw Husani lying on the floor."

Angela stopped talking and her eyes widened in a delayed-shock reaction as her brain processed the implications of what she was saying.

"He's dead, isn't he?" she said.

Bronson nodded.

"I'm afraid he is, but it's thanks to him that you're not."

"I don't know what you mean."

"Let me tell you what happened, as I saw it. As soon as I got back to the car I started the engine, so I could move immediately, and started watching you, and checking the street in both directions. I really didn't think there would be any trouble, but it just seemed like a sensible precaution."

"Which it was," Angela remarked.

"I saw Anum Husani approaching. He was difficult to miss, because he was on my side of the road, but I guessed it was him because he was carrying the briefcase. Then he crossed the road and approached you at the table, and that more or less confirmed who he was. Quite a few people walked past the café, and a couple even went in and took a table on the opposite side of the terrace to where you were sitting, but I thought they all seemed entirely innocent. And then I saw a man walking along the pavement, dressed in black. He looked like a priest. Anyway, he didn't appear to be in any way threatening, and seemed occupied talking on a mobile phone."

"The man in black." Angela shuddered. "Him, I do remember."

Bronson nodded. "He stopped walking a few yards away from the café terrace, the way people sometimes do when they're concentrating on a particular subject being talked about during a telephone call. All of that seemed perfectly normal, but then I noticed that he seemed to be looking toward the café, and possibly even staring toward your table. That rang alarm bells. Then he slid the phone into his pocket, reached inside another pocket and pulled out the gun. It all happened very quickly. It turns out you can hide a lot of stuff underneath a cassock."

Angela tried a laugh that ended up a hoarse croak.

"So what did you do?"

"I knew I couldn't run across the street and grab hold of him before he fired, so I did the next best thing. I used the car as a weapon. I sounded the horn to try to distract him, and then drove straight toward him. But I wasn't quite quick enough. He must have been a professional, because he didn't even glance in my direction. He was totally focused on completing the job, and we're just lucky that the first part of the work he did was killing Anum Husani, not you."

Bronson looked at Angela's face and saw her eyes misting.

"He seemed like a decent man," she said, her voice breaking as she spoke. "He really didn't deserve that."

"The first shot the killer fired took Husani in the middle of the chest, and he was probably dead even before he hit the ground. Then I saw him switch his aim toward you. I accelerated as hard as I could, but I was a couple of seconds too late. I saw you fall down, flat on your back."

Bronson stopped talking for a moment, and Angela could see the emotion coursing through him, his eyes glistening. She'd never seen him quite this close to tears before. She reached out and gently squeezed his hand.

"At that moment I was quite certain that you were dead, that he'd just murdered you, right in front of me. So I didn't slow the car. In fact, I accelerated even harder. He tried to jump to one side, but I caught his legs with the right front of the vehicle, and he went straight down."

"Oh, God," Angela murmured.

"I jumped out, and checked to see if he was still a threat. But I'd done a good job. It looked as if both his legs were broken, and he was unconscious. He was bleeding from his nose and ears, so he'd probably smashed his head onto the pavement. If I'm honest, at that moment I very much hoped I'd killed him. I grabbed his pistol and his mobile, then searched him quickly, but the only other thing he had on him was a spare magazine for the pistol. Then I ran over to you."

For a few seconds Bronson again visibly struggled with his own emotions; then he resumed his narrative.

"You were just lying there," he said. "I didn't know if you were still breathing, and there was some blood on the back of your head, but I couldn't see any sign of a bullet wound. Then I looked at the briefcase. There was a small hole torn in the leather, and I could see the glint of metal behind it. The bullet knocked you to the floor, but some-how it didn't make it through the case."

Angela nodded weakly.

"Husani was really proud of that case. He bought it specially. He said it's lined with Kevlar. He actually told me it was bulletproof."

"Really lucky for you that it was. As soon as I saw that, I knew that you had to be alive, so I just picked you up, put the briefcase under my arm, and ran back to the car. There were people screaming and shouting, and it was only going to be a matter of minutes before the Spanish police pitched up. I really didn't want to have to answer a lot of questions from them."

"But what about the assassin? You probably killed him."

Bronson shook his head.

"If I'd stayed, I would have been the only person in-volved in the incident who was still alive, apart from you, and I can absolutely guarantee that the very first thing the Spanish police would have done was arrest me, and pos-sibly you as well. My other worry was that whoever's try-ing to recover the parchment had obviously hacked into Husani's e-mail—and probably yours as well—and if they can do that, arranging for somebody to attack you or me in prison wouldn't greatly tax their ingenuity. The only safe thing I could do was get us—and the parchment—away from the scene as quickly as possible."

"But surely somebody will have noticed the car number?"

"Maybe, but witnesses to violent action very rarely re-member anything particularly clearly. And with any luck we'll be long gone before they get around to checking."

"So where should we go now?" Angela asked.

"We get out of Madrid, and Spain, as quickly as we can. The parchment is in that briefcase, along with the pistol and the killer's mobile phone, and there's nothing to keep us here. I won't feel safe until we're back in Britain. Possibly not even then."

"I should really tell George Stebbins what's happened," Angela said. "He could be in danger as well."

"From what I saw of your Mr. Stebbins, he seems to be quite good at taking care of himself, or at least at staying out of any kind of trouble or danger."

"I know, but I'd still feel better if I told him."

Bronson nodded. "OK. While you make the call, I'll pack our things so we can leave here as soon as possible."

But as Angela reached into her handbag for her mobile, another phone—the one Bronson had taken from the assassin—began to ring.

66

For a couple of seconds they both just stared; then Bronson walked across the bedroom, unsnapped the catches on the briefcase and took out the phone. He pressed the button to answer it and lifted the instrument to his ear.

"Yes?"

"You have something that does not belong to you, and I want it," a harsh male voice stated, the English fluent but heavily accented.

Bronson didn't reply, just listened, waiting for whatever threat or demand the unidentified caller intended to make.

"And I have something that you might not want, but which I am certain that the woman with you will want to have back."

"I've no idea what you're talking about," Bronson replied.

"The British Museum clearly did not trust Angela Lewis to complete the purchase of the relic by herself," the man continued. "That is why they sent George Stebbins out to Madrid to work with her. If she wants to see him alive and in one piece ever again, you need to do exactly what I tell you."

"Who is it?" Angela demanded.

Bronson held up his hand to indicate that she should stay quiet, then replied.

"And how do I know that he's alive now?"

There was a brief pause and then Bronson heard George Stebbins's unmistakable voice in his ear.

"Bronson, Bronson. You've got to help me." He sounded completely terrified. "You've got to get me out of here. Do whatever they say. I'll— No, please, no, don't—"

The other man's voice was audible in Bronson's ear as he issued an order.

"No, you've already broken that one. Break the one next to it."

There was a sudden confusion of sound, but dominating it all was Stebbins's voice. It rose in sheer panic and ended with a piercing scream, loud enough to make Bronson move the mobile away from his ear.

"I hope you're satisfied," the male voice said again. "If you're not, we can repeat the treatment until you are, though I'm sure Mr. Stebbins would rather we didn't. I'll call again in five minutes."

The line went dead. If there had been the slightest doubt in Bronson's mind before about the competence and ruthlessness of the people they were facing, the details provided by the anonymous caller completely dispelled it.

"Who was it?" Angela asked.

"That," he said, "was trouble. I have no idea who it was, but he knew who we were. And somehow he and his cronies have managed to get hold of George Stebbins. The noise you probably heard was Stebbins being persuaded to convince us to hand over the relic."

"Oh, dear God," Angela murmured, her face turning pale.

Bronson nodded. "If we agree to do what that man wants—"

"What does he want?" Angela asked.

"He's ringing me back in a few minutes," Bronson replied. "But I assume he'll want us to hand over the parchment. And once we've done that, he will almost certainly kill us both. George Stebbins, in my opinion, is as good as dead already."

Angela nodded slowly.

"But we can't just walk away and leave Stebbins to their mercy. There must be something we can do. Can we call the police?"

Bronson nodded.

"Of course we can. The problem is that we've got nothing we can tell them. We have no idea who these people are or where they are. All we know for certain is that somehow or other they grabbed George Stebbins, that they have a proven track record for ruthless murder, and they want the two-thousand-year-old parchment that's sitting in that briefcase over there. I don't really see what the police could do to help either us or Stebbins."

"But when this man rings you, he'll have to tell you where to go, where to deliver the parchment, surely?"

"Whatever else these people are," Robson replied, "they're not stupid. My guess is that the rendezvous will be in a public place and they'll want you to be there, not me. There'll probably be a public call box or a telephone in a bar, something like that, and you'll have to answer that to receive your next set of instructions.

"Then they'll keep you bouncing around the city until they're certain that you haven't got a couple of van loads of police in tow, and only then will they finally tell you where the exchange is due to be carried out. But it won't be an exchange. It'll be three gunshots to eliminate you, me and Stebbins, and they'll walk away with the parchment."

Angela looked torn, and shook her head slowly.

"I know that. I know that you're right, but I can't just turn my back on this. I have to be certain that we at least tried to save George. My conscience won't let me do anything else. And you've got that man's gun now, so it's not as if you're completely unarmed, is it?"

"The pistol will help, but I only have two magazines for it. There's the full magazine I took out of the assassin's pocket, and the one that is in the weapon, and I haven't checked how many rounds are left in it. We know he fired twice at the café, so if it's a fifteen-round magazine, at best we might have thirteen bullets left in it."

"Unlucky for some," Angela said, with a weak attempt at humor.

"Quite. So assuming the spare mag is full, that will give me twenty-eight rounds, but really only fifteen, because if it comes to a firefight there probably won't be enough time to change magazines. The reality is that if we do end up having to face these people, I might be able to take down two or three of them, but if there are more than that, then I'm going to find myself hopelessly outgunned. The best thing we can do, Angela—and I know you're not going to like it—is to just walk away. In fact, to drive away as fast as we can."

As the phone rang shrilly, Bronson looked at Angela for a moment, both still undecided. Then she nodded, and he picked it up again.

"Yes?" he said.

It was as if the man at the other end had heard some of his conversation with Angela.

"You don't have to worry about what will happen to you afterward," he said. "I'm sure you know that certain people have died in unfortunate circumstances over the last few days, but there were very good reasons for those events, and we wish you and Miss Lewis no harm. All we want is for the item that is rightfully ours to be returned to us undamaged, and as quickly as possible. Once we have that in our possession, then the two of you and Mr. Stebbins will be free to go."

"And you really expect me to believe that, do you?" Bronson demanded. "There's an expression in English: past performance is always the best indicator of future performance. Give me one good reason why you'd treat us any differently to the others you've killed."

The man at the other end of the line chuckled softly.

"I can't, so you'll just have to take my word for it."

"Like hell I will," Bronson snapped.

And he pressed the button to end the call.

"What are you doing?" Angela demanded. "You're going to get George killed!"

"I've been stupid," Bronson replied. "That's what's happening."

67

Bronson worked quickly. He removed the back of the phone, took out the battery and then put all the components down on the desk. Then he picked up their two carry-on bags, tossed them onto the bed and began jamming their clothes in.

"Quick, help me pack."

"Chris, what's going on?"

He paused for a moment, then zipped up one of the bags.

"That phone call didn't really make any sense, and I've only just realized why. That man wouldn't have seriously expected us to trot along and meet him and his band of killers somewhere. He would know that we'd be far more likely to just run away, get as far from Madrid as we could."

Angela looked puzzled as she pulled open a drawer, took out a pile of clothes and began packing the other bag.

"So why was he calling at all? Just to gloat or something?"

"No," Bronson said. "I think it was much simpler than that. I think he just wanted us to stay here, sitting in this hotel room, long enough for him to track us down, and if I'm right, that implies that he's got more reach than even I expected."

He pointed at the disassembled phone on the desk.

"You can pinpoint the position of any mobile phone in the world as long as it's switched on, and sometimes even if it's switched off as long as the battery is still in place and there's a tracking chip installed," he said, "but only if you have access to the service provider's equipment. All you have to do is identify the cells that are in contact with the phone, and that lets you triangulate the location of the mobile. It's more accurate in a city or other built-up area because there are more cells to cope with the volume of calls."

"So you think they've found out that we're in this hotel?"

"By now, they probably know more or less where we are," Bronson said. "The good thing is that is we're in a hotel, so even if they have identified the building, they'll still need to find out which room we're in, though that probably won't take them very long. But we must move right now."

"But what about George?" Angela asked.

"Right now, I'm afraid he's a very low priority. If we don't get out of here in one piece, we're not going be able to help him or anybody else. Our first priority has got to be to lose ourselves somewhere in Madrid. If we can manage to do that, we might just be able to help him."

But as Bronson picked up his bag and walked toward the door, somebody outside gave a brisk double knock.

"Oh, God," Angela muttered. "They've found us."

68

Bronson shook his head.

"The ungodly don't knock on doors: they kick them down."

But he still put down his bag and took out the Beretta, holding the pistol out of sight behind his back before he stepped across to the door to open it.

"I just wondered if you'd finished with the first-aid kit," the bar waiter asked, looking embarrassed when he saw Bronson's serious expression. "Or if you decided you did need a doctor to look at your wife."

"Thanks," Bronson said, "but she's fine."

"Sorry. I didn't mean to interrupt," the young man muttered.

"That's fine. Thank you for your concern, but we're leaving soon," said Bronson, "and we're in a bit of a rush." With that he thrust the first-aid kit toward the waiter, along with a twenty-euro note, and closed the door again.

A couple of minutes later he and Angela stepped cautiously out of the room and into the corridor. She was carrying the leather-covered briefcase and her bag. In front of her, Bronson had his bag in his left hand, leaving his right hand free to use the silenced pistol he'd tucked into the waistband of his trousers. He hoped it wouldn't be necessary, but he was taking no chances.

The corridor was deserted in both directions, and they walked as far as the lift without seeing or hearing anyone. The descent to the garage floor seemed to take forever, and at any moment Bronson was half expecting the lift to stop, the doors to slam open, and to be faced with any number of aggressors.

When the lift finally stopped, Bronson tensed, seeing dimly through the frosted glass what he'd been dreading: a vague bulky shape standing there and waiting for the lift to arrive.

He pushed Angela behind him, at the same time slipping the silenced Beretta pistol out of his waistband and holding it slightly behind his right leg, out of sight but ready for immediate use.

With a faint mechanical rumbling sound, the lift doors slid sideways.

The man standing there looked about fifty years old, wearing a somewhat crumpled and badly cut suit, and with a small suitcase in one hand and a newish briefcase in the other. As the lift doors opened, he took a step forward, then stopped when he saw that there were two people inside it, and moved backward with a muttered apology in Spanish, glancing from Bronson to Angela.

He didn't look threatening, but Bronson took no chances, keeping the pistol hidden but ready to fire, as he and Angela stepped out of the lift and onto the concrete floor of the garage. For a few moments, they just stood there, waiting and alert, as the man stepped into the lift and the door closed.

They both breathed heavy sighs of relief as the lift moved up and out of sight.

They bundled everything into the car as quickly as possible, then Bronson drove around the garage toward the curved exit ramp. The electrically operated door was controlled by a panel beside the ramp. Bronson stopped beside it, dropped his window and pushed the button.

As the door slowly began to rise, creaking lazily, Bronson caught the faintest sign of movement in his rearview mirror. A figure was emerging from the staircase door beside the lift. He immediately recognized the man from a moment ago. He also immediately realized that his assumption about the man being harmless had been entirely wrong. The stranger was raising a black object at arm's length, and pointing it directly at the car.

69

He had barely a second to react.

"Get down!" he shouted.

At the same moment, he lifted the clutch and powered the car up the exit ramp toward the garage door, which was still opening, agonizingly slowly.

He heard a sharp crack from behind, the unmistakable sound of a pistol shot, and the car rocked with a sudden impact. The window directly behind Bronson shattered, glittering fragments of safety glass flying everywhere inside the car, and the window beside Angela exploded outward as the bullet passed through that as well.

Angela screamed in terror at the sudden noise and the shock of the flying glass. The car was gathering speed as it progressed up the ramp toward the door, the front tires smoking and howling as they scrabbled for grip under full acceleration in first gear, Bronson keeping the accelerator flat to the floor. The vehicle was weaving slightly from side to side as well, but all he cared about was covering the ground as quickly as possible.

Another shot rang out, the bullet missing the car, slamming into the right-hand wall of the ramp behind them and ricocheting away somewhere. Bronson guessed they had already moved partly out of sight. For the gunman to get a clear shot at them, he would have to run across the garage from the lift and stairwell to the foot of the ramp itself, and fire up it. That was the only advantage they had, but he guessed that the man would already be moving into position. Within seconds, he would be able to pepper the back of the car with bullets.

The opening door of the garage loomed ever closer, the bottom of the metal frame moving up vertically in front of the car. It didn't look to Bronson as if there was enough clearance for him to drive underneath it, and he daren't hit it, in case it stopped the vehicle dead.

At the very last moment, as the nose of the car powered under the slowly opening door, Bronson shifted his right foot from the accelerator to the brake and pushed hard. The nose of the car dipped as the pads hit the discs, the deceleration fierce. Hitting the brakes compressed the suspension, effectively lowering the overall height of the vehicle for that brief split second.

Bronson and Angela were thrown forward against the restraint of the seat belts. There was a grating sound from the car's roof as the rear section scraped underneath the bottom of the door. Bronson felt the tug as the impact slowed them still further, but then they were under and clear. Again he mashed his foot onto the accelerator, and the car leapt up the last few yards of the garage ramp and out of the building into the brilliant sunshine of the Madrid late afternoon.

Bronson sensed rather than heard another gunshot as the man behind them finally reached the bend in the ramp and fired at them once more. He had no idea where the bullet went, but he was certain it didn't hit the car. Even an expert will find it difficult to hit a target, especially a moving target, at a distance of much more than about twenty-five yards.

The moment the vehicle cleared the ramp, Bronson swung the wheel hard to the right, tugged on the handbrake to slide the rear of the car sideways, tires squealing on the tarmac, then continued to accelerate.

Beside him, Angela eased herself upright, her hands clutching at the dashboard and the passenger door, and peered around her, eyes wide with shock.

"It was that man, wasn't it?" she demanded. "From the lift?"

Bronson nodded.

"It was. Now we can see what we're up against. No discussion, no negotiation. As soon as he was sure who we were, he simply pulled out a gun and started shooting."

"Thank God we got away."

The road was quiet, and within a few seconds they were traveling at well over seventy kilometers an hour, getting as far away from the hotel as they could.

Every second or two Bronson's eyes flicked to the rearview mirrors. And then he saw what he'd hoped not to. A white saloon car pulled out of a parking bay and stopped briefly in the middle of the road. Then a figure ran out of the hotel garage and climbed into the passenger seat. The moment the door closed, the car began accelerating, clearly following the vehicle Bronson and Angela were in. The gunman in the hotel had had a backup man. And now they were both following.

"Shit! We're not out of the woods yet," Bronson said. "They're following us. It's that white saloon car. We need to lose them, and quickly. But I don't know these streets. You've got to get us out of this one."

70

With the rush of adrenaline, Angela recovered rapidly from the shock of being fired at. She opened the glove box and fished out a map of Madrid plus Bronson's satnav.

"I'm on it!" she said as she plugged in the satnav and riffled through the pages of the map.

"Right, make sure we don't go anywhere too busy."

Bronson had no doubt that both men in the car behind them would be armed, and if he was forced to stop the car, they could outflank him and approach him from two sides at the same time. They absolutely needed to keep moving.

The satnav finally got satellite lock, and Angela was able to see exactly where they were. She looked away for a few moments to study the map she was holding, then jabbed her finger at it.

"Got it," she said. "Take the next turning on the right, then right again."

"Done," Bronson replied.

Bronson sped round the corner, then drove up to the junction halfway down it just as the lights were turning red. He quickly checked for other traffic before spinning the wheel hard to the right and powering down the street, followed by the blasting of horns. He doubted very much if the red light would hold up the pursuing car for very long, but the crossing traffic might.

"Where now?" he asked.

"Keep going straight. You pass two junctions on your right, and then take the third."

As they passed the first junction, in his rearview mirror he saw a white car make the turn at the crossroads. At that distance, he couldn't be sure that it was the one containing the gunman, but his instinct told him that it was.

"They're still behind us," he said. "About three hundred yards back."

As they sped toward the second junction, a car pulled out from it, directly in front of them. Bronson twitched the wheel to the left and overtook it, giving the driver a blast on his horn as he did so.

Angela looked down at the map, then pointed.

"That's the junction. Turn right here."

Bronson eased off the accelerator for barely half a second and stabbed at the brakes as he checked that the road ahead was clear. Then he turned the wheel, accelerating the car again.

The road was wide, cars parked haphazardly on both sides. Half a dozen vehicles were heading toward him on the opposite side of the road.

"Where to next?" Bronson asked, his tone clipped. "A right turn is better than a left, so I don't have to cross oncoming traffic."

"Don't worry. I do possess a little intelligence," Angela replied. "So we'll go for Plan B, which is the same as Plan A, but only turning right. If you can, take the next right."

The tires protested audibly as Bronson accelerated hard right.

"You still know where we are?" he asked.

"You just drive, and leave the navigating to me."

Bronson would have laughed if he hadn't had to concentrate. Angela was always good in a crisis, and the blow she'd taken to the back of her head now didn't seem to be troubling her at all.

Angela directed him from one junction to the next, the traffic lessening noticeably the farther they drove from the center of Madrid.

Bronson had been checking his mirrors constantly, and the white car had been getting progressively farther and farther back as he'd tried to keep up the fastest speed he could possibly achieve on the roads of the capital city. Yet at the last minute it kept reappearing. But there was one simple trick he could use that would almost guarantee to shake off the pursuit. He just needed to find the right road for it.

71

"Where are you going now?" Angela asked, as Bronson turned off down the next street on the right.

"Just watch," Bronson said. "I'm following a different road sign."

About fifty yards down the street was a large blue sign with a white letter "P" in it, and without hesitation he swung the car into the wide opening directly below it. He stopped at the barrier at the entrance to the garage, took a ticket from the machine, and then drove inside as soon as the barrier lifted. There were plenty of vacant parking spaces, and he stopped the car on the second-floor level.

"Right," Bronson said, switching off the engine. "We'll sit here for a few minutes. Those guys were probably at least one or two minutes behind us, and with any luck we did manage to lose them. But even if we didn't, and they saw us heading this way, they'll probably shoot right past here and keep looking for this car out on the streets. What we need to do now is get hold of another vehicle."

Angela looked around at the dozen or so cars parked on that level of the garage.

"You mean steal one?"

"Nothing so dramatic. What I had in mind was just hiring one."

Angela nodded slowly.

"And then what? Can we just drive to the airport and get on to a flight to London? What about George?"

"We daren't risk trying to fly out of Spain now. We know the kind of connections and reach these people have. If I was trying to find us, about the first thing I'd do would be to organize a watch on all our credit card transactions plus red-flag our passports."

"Can they do that?"

Bronson nodded.

"Probably. The only way they could have got an assassin to the café where you met Anum Husani, at the time the meeting took place, would be if they had hacked into his e-mail. You didn't arrange the rendezvous on the telephone, and there was no other source for that piece of information. Hacking—or even tracking—e-mails is legally and technically very difficult. It needs either access to something like the Echelon global surveillance system or the assistance of some pretty senior guy in whichever Internet service provider supplied Husani's e-mail facilities."

"And they must have tracked that assassin's mobile phone as well," Angela reminded him. "Otherwise they couldn't have known we were in that hotel."

"You're quite right. And if they can do that kind of thing, it's not too big a stretch to assume that they will also have people working within the banking system who could put a watch on credit card transactions."

"But then the moment you rent a car, they'll know about us as well, won't they?" Angela protested.

"Yes . . . but all the credit card transaction will show is that we've hired a car. It will take quite some time for them to get to the car hire company and find out exactly what vehicle we've hired, and by the time they do that we'll be miles away. With a plane, we'd have to wait until we could get on one, and then go through security, where they could have people working for them. We're much more likely to get away with it in a hire car."

"So where are we going to drive to?"

"London," Bronson said. "If we keep clear of the autoroutes and pick places to stay where the car can be parked off the road and out of sight, we should be safe. And there's another reason as well. I think we could do something to help George."

Angela looked at him, puzzled by his sudden change of heart.

"But how can you do that?" she asked.

"We can play them at their own game. But first we have to find a hotel."

72

The backstreet hotel Bronson had picked was not exactly the Ritz, but it did have one thing that he needed: a free Wi-Fi system.

"We have something else that might help us," Bronson explained. "The mobile phone I took off that assassin."

"How does having possession of that man's mobile help?"

"Even if you try to delete almost all the personal data from a mobile phone, the unit still holds an enormous amount of information. If you've got access to the right kind of computer program, you can read SMS messages, inspect the call register, look at images loaded onto the phone, and a whole lot of other stuff."

"And you have software like that?" Angela asked. "Programs you can use to hack into a mobile?"

"No," Bronson replied, "but luckily, I know a man who does, and he isn't particularly bothered about the legal implications. I need to call Billy the Kid."

Angela chuckled when she heard the name.

"And he lives around here somewhere, does he? Conveniently on hand?"

"Of course not. He lives in a small, cramped and incredibly grubby basement flat in Tooting."

Angela regarded him with suspicion.

"So he's a hacker, this Billy the Kid person. How exactly do you know him?"

"I met him through an operation I was involved in. He was in the wrong place at the wrong time, or at least that's what he said. We couldn't make anything stick, and my guess is that he wasn't involved. Anyway, I interviewed him a couple of times and we kind of hit it off. After we let him go I kept in touch. I found that having somebody I could call on who was a *real* computer expert, not the half-trained idiots who staff the IT sections of most police stations, was really useful."

"And is he just a kid?"

Bronson nodded. "He looks about eighteen, long hair, granny glasses and grunge clothing, but he must be in his late twenties, I suppose. And he lives and breathes computers."

"OK," Angela said, "it sounds as if he might be able to help with this, but how the hell are you going to give him access to the phone?"

"Let me show you."

73

Once Bronson's laptop had loaded, he quickly clicked on the Skype icon, found a number labeled "BTK," and clicked "Call Phone." As soon as the system began dialling, he picked up his dual-function mouse-phone—a cheap gadget he'd used before and found much more reliable than the speakers and built-in microphone on his laptop—and held it up to his ear.

The one thing he knew was that Billy would answer his call, because his mobile phone was virtually a component part of his body. He never went anywhere, not even, Bronson suspected, to the shower—assuming he took one—without taking the phone with him. His call was answered in under three seconds.

"Yup?"

"Billy, it's Chris Bronson, and I need a favor."

There was a chuckle from the other end.

"Long time no see, man. How's it hanging? I know you only call me when you need help, so what's wrong? Your laptop exploded or Windows 7 crashed?"

"Oddly enough, no," Bronson replied. "Look, I don't

want to go into too much detail, but I need you to take a look at a mobile phone for me."

"No problemo. Drop it round next time you're passing and I'll check it out."

"It's not that easy. I'm in Spain at the moment, and the phone belongs to a suspected criminal. The problem is that I'm not working here officially, so I can't get the phone examined by the Spanish police. Is there any way you can do it remotely?"

There was a short pause while the man at the other end considered the options.

"Coupla questions, then. What's the connector on the phone?"

"A mini USB, the same as mine, and I've got the lead with me," Bronson said.

"No problem. It'll just look like an external hard drive. OK. You still got that remote access program I gave you? TeamViewer?"

"Yes. Do you want me to run it right now?"

"In a sec. I'll talk you through it, step by step, 'cause I know you're not too bright at this kind of thing."

"Thanks a lot," Bronson said.

"OK," Billy went on, no hint of humor in his voice, "the first thing is, you need to take out the SIM card."

"But surely the SIM card holds all the data?"

Billy chuckled again.

"Wow, you really are out of date, aren't you? These days, about all the SIM card usually holds is the phone number. Modern mobiles have big internal memories. They have to, because of all the crap people load onto them: e-mails, photographs, cached Web pages, games and all the rest. If there's anything useful on this phone you want me to take a look at, it'll be inside it. So, take out the SIM card, put the battery back in for now, and then plug it in to your laptop."

Bronson did so.

"When you've done that, run the TeamViewer program and I'll do the same at this end. Then we'll see what we can find out."

Within about two minutes, Bronson was able to see the pointer on his laptop apparently moving of its own volition, as Billy took remote control of his machine. Then things started happening quickly, as various windows opened and closed and different images and lists of information popped up and then almost as quickly vanished. Billy, in the meantime, was silent, presumably because he was concentrating.

"All righty," he said finally. "There's good news and bad news, I guess. First, you need to take real good care of Angela Lewis, if that's who that pretty blond woman is. There are several pictures of her on that phone, and she's mentioned by name in a couple of e-mails as well. My Spanish isn't that good, but what they're saying seems to be simple enough. She's supposed to die. And the man who owned the phone, who called himself Jordi, was supposed to find something, some relic, and hand it over to the man who sent the e-mails. And his name, before you ask, is Pere, no surname, so it's probably just the name he's using for this particular operation."

Bronson nodded, a pointless gesture, as he realized immediately.

"Any information about where the handover of the relic was supposed to take place?"

"No," Billy replied. "The last e-mail just tells the man whose phone we're looking at to call when the job is complete, and then Pere will tell him where the rendezvous is to hand over the cash. Seems to have been quite an expensive job. One of the earlier e-mails quoted fifty grand, euros not pounds, as long as the relic was recovered. And that's another good reason for you to take care of Angela. Like the advert says, she's worth it."

It was Bronson's turn to smile at that.

"You don't need to tell me that, Billy. I already know she's worth it."

Bronson glanced at Angela as he said the last sentence, and she looked back at him with a puzzled expression on her face.

"Tell you later," Bronson mouthed, covering the microphone, then turned his attention back to what Billy was saying.

"Listen, there's a whole bunch of data on this phone. Easiest thing is if I just pull the whole lot off it and copy it onto your hard drive. That OK with you?"

"That'd be great, Billy. Thanks a lot."

"I'll expect a more tangible show of appreciation for my services when you get back to London, my friend. Gonna charge you for an hour of my time, and you're getting away lightly with that."

"You can make it two hours, Billy, and I'll buy you a drink as well. I really appreciate what you've done for me."

"Deal. OK, I'll create a new folder on your hard drive, and I'll just call it 'Mobile.' You'll find everything in that."

The line went quiet and then, a couple of minutes later, Billy spoke again.

"Right, that's done it. Do you want me to delete the data from the phone? Be an idea if you're planning on using it yourself. I can put it back to pretty much the way it was when the guy bought it, and I could change the language to English as well, if you'd like."

While Billy had been effecting the data transfer, Bronson had been wondering if he could extract any more useful information from the mobile.

"No, just leave the phone as it is, Billy. It might be more useful to me to have the information still recorded on it. One other thing. You said that the guy in charge, the one who was pulling Jordi's strings, was called Pere. I'd quite like to find out where he is, because he's got something—or rather someone—that I want. Is there any way you can work out where he's been operating from?"

"Ah, now, that, my friend, is pretty serious hacking. I'll have to identify which local provider his phone is registered with, and then work my way inside the system to trace which cells it's been in contact with."

"I didn't ask *how* you'd do it, Billy," Bronson said. "I just asked if you *could* do it."

"Of course I can. But before I even start, Chris, you do know that this is completely illegal? You and I could both end up in the slammer if anybody finds out about it. You sure you want me to do this?"

"Going to jail is the least of my worries right now. Listen, I believe that this man Pere has probably kidnapped a colleague of Angela's, who was out here in Madrid, and they're almost certainly going to kill him unless we manage to find him first. This man called me on the phone that you've been looking at just over three hours ago, and if you can find out where he was when he made that call, that would be great."

"Right, this is your funeral, and if some guy from the thin blue line comes knocking on my door, I've never met you and I've never heard of you, OK?"

"OK."

"Make sure you leave your laptop on and I'll call you as soon as I get anything."

74

Angela had only heard Bronson's half of the conversation, but she'd been looking at the screen of his laptop throughout, and had a pretty good idea what was going on.

"I saw a couple of pictures of me," she said, pointing at the phone, which was still connected to the USB port on Bronson's laptop. "I presume those were on that mobile?"

"They were," he confirmed, "along with some details of the contract taken out on you here in Spain. Dead, you were worth fifty thousand euros, providing the killer could recover the parchment as well. Your value seems to be increasing."

"It's not really a laughing matter, Chris," Angela said.

"It isn't, and I'm not," Bronson said. "However, I think what's interesting is that the increased fee means the opposition are getting more desperate to recover that parchment."

Angela nodded.

"So what do we do now?" she asked.

"For the moment, nothing. I've asked Billy to try to find out where the call was made from when I heard Stebbins on the line. If he can do it, that's probably where we'll find him, alive or dead."

Angela shuddered.

"Do you really think they've killed him?"

"I don't know," Bronson replied. "I'm hoping they might be keeping him on ice, because they must know that he's now the only bargaining counter they have left. The one hope they have of finding us—or rather of finding you and the parchment—is if we try to rescue Stebbins."

"But if they are holding him alive somewhere, in a warehouse or house or somewhere, how the hell can we rescue him? There could be half a dozen or more armed men waiting there, just hoping that we'll show up."

"Right now," Bronson said, "I haven't the slightest idea."

75

With nothing much else they could do but wait, they ordered room service and then lay side by side on the double bed, talking through the events of the day one more time and planning their next move.

After half an hour of what quickly felt like pointless speculation, Bronson asked if he could see the parchment, the cause of all the trouble they were in. They spent a few minutes looking at the ancient relic—which was actually a remarkably dull sight, just a piece of thick dark brown leather upon which a few letters or partial words could be seen—and studying the photographs of the object that had been taken by Ali Mohammed back in Cairo what felt like weeks ago.

"Well, it certainly doesn't look like much," Bronson remarked.

"Nor did the Dead Sea Scrolls or the Nag Hammadi codices," she replied. "It's what it says, and what the text actually means in today's world, which is important. And until I get this relic back to the museum and subject it to a proper analysis, I won't know exactly what event it's describing."

The screen on Bronson's laptop suddenly changed, the screensaver vanishing as a Skype call came in.

"At last," Bronson said. "That must be Billy."

Bronson answered the call, and asked if the youthful hacker had found out anything useful.

"I managed to pull some data, yes," Billy replied, "but it wasn't easy. I had to run the hacking software through a bunch of proxies so nobody would be able to trace it back to me, and that slowed everything down. The good news is that if any of the Spanish security people decide to run a back-trace to try to find me, the trail will stop in Vienna. I thought that was kind of appropriate, Vienna being full of spies during the Cold War."

Billy chuckled at his own joke for a moment, then got down to the business at hand.

"Right," he said, "the phone number you asked me to investigate, the one that seems to belong to this guy Pere. The records only start from a few days ago, and he's used it quite a bit, and from a bunch of different places in Madrid, so I guess he's been out and about, probably looking for the two of you."

"That makes sense," Bronson replied.

"You gave me a time, or a rough time anyway, when you wanted me to nail down his location, and that's one of the places where he seems to spend quite a bit of time. I can't be absolutely specific about where that is. It's not anywhere near the center of Madrid, so there are fewer masts to use for triangulation. But I've been able to pinpoint the spot to within about thirty meters."

"That's brilliant, Billy. I'm ready to copy if you can read the location to me."

"With all this technology at your disposal," Billy scoffed, "you're still using a paper and pencil? I've already sent the location to you. You'll find it in your 'My Documents' folder on your hard drive. I've called the file 'Bad Guy.' If you want my guess, I think it's probably a warehouse or an office on some kind of industrial estate, because of its position. It's called Paracuellos de Jarama, and it lies pretty much halfway between the Barajas International Airport and the Torrejón Airport, and they're both out to the northeast of Madrid."

"That's excellent work, Billy," Bronson said. "I'll make sure I see you as soon as I get back to England to settle up with you."

"You just do what you've got to do out there, my friend. I'm in no hurry. Oh, and the last time I ran the check through the system, the guy you're looking for—or at least his mobile—was still at that location."

76

"So what do we do now?" Angela asked. "Have you had any good ideas?"

Bronson didn't reply for a few moments, just stared at the map of Madrid.

"Right now, Angela, I don't know what's a good idea and what isn't. But I do know that striking early is generally a good tactic. Think about it from the other side of the problem for a moment. The people who are trying to kill you and recover the parchment absolutely know that they've got us on the run. OK, there was a bit of a fiasco as far as they were concerned at the café. Unfortunately for them, I was there as well. But that didn't really even slow them down. They tracked us to our hotel and sent along another hit man to finish off the job. We were lucky, because we'd already left the room and were on our way to the car when he identified us."

He paused for a moment and glanced at Angela.

"Given all that's happened today, I'm prepared to bet that the bad guys are still out combing the streets of Madrid looking for us, and they'll be doing their best to make sure that we can't leave the city. They'll have a watch in place inside both the airports, and at the main railway station, and they'll be looking out for the first sign that we're on the move. In other words, they'll be doing whatever they can to lock the city down tight, and they seem to have the resources necessary to achieve that."

"So you mean that if we try to go anywhere, they'll find us?" Angela asked.

But Bronson shook his head.

"Not necessarily. My guess is that they'll be expecting us to try to leave town. But they don't know about Billy the Kid, and what he managed to do with a wireless network, a laptop computer, a handful of programs and some pretty dammed awesome hacking skills. They won't have any idea that we know where they are. And even if they did have the slightest inkling of that, I think the last thing they would expect us to do is take the game to them."

"Attack is the best form of defense?"

"Exactly. I think we should get out to this location that Billy managed to identify for us"—Bronson tapped the map for emphasis—"and see what we can do there. At the very least," he finished, "that'll be the last place in Madrid where they'll be looking for us."

Angela glanced at her watch.

"Just one question," she said. "How do we get out there?"

"I'm not sure *we* should be going anywhere. I'd far rather you stayed in the hotel. They can't possibly have found out that we're staying here, so you'd be safe."

Angela shook her head.

"I'll make this really simple for you," she said. "If you're going out, then so am I. There's no way I could just sit here in this hotel room waiting for a knock on the door, hoping it's you and dreading that it isn't. And if you don't come back, then what the hell would I do? No, if we're going to do this, we're going to do it together, whether you like it or not."

Sometimes wisdom lies in recognizing a fait accompli when you see one. Bronson knew that Angela was one of the most determined people he had ever met. And, in truth, in many ways he would rather that she was with him—in previous sticky situations she'd always proved a competent partner.

"OK, if that's what you want," Bronson said.

"It is. So how do we get out there? Use the hire car?"

"We're not going anywhere near that car. If we drive around in that, there's a good chance we'll be spotted by one of the bad guys out looking for us, or maybe even stopped by the police, because that car's missing two windows and there's a gouge in the roof where I scraped it when we drove out of the hotel garage. We'll have to hire another one."

"Right then," Angela said. "Let's go. What about the parchment and our stuff?"

Bronson glanced round the room.

"I think we have to leave it here. There's no paper trail linking us to this hotel or this room, so it should be safe enough. And we'll need to come back here afterward."

Bronson spent a couple of minutes using a cheap multitool he'd bought at Madrid airport to remove the plastic side panel from the bath, and then Angela slid the metal-lined briefcase into the space this revealed. Bronson replaced the panel and then fiddled about with some oversized paperclips he took from his computer case, bending them into different shapes.

"And they are?" Angela asked, as he slid them into his pocket.

"Door keys, of a sort. Just some rudimentary lock-picks in case they're not obliging enough to have left a door open for me."

Finally, he took out the Beretta pistol. It was the M92 model, the end of the barrel threaded to take a GemTech Trinity suppressor, in nine-millimeter Luger. Bronson checked the magazine.

"Definitely a professional," he murmured.

"What?"

Bronson showed her the magazine.

"This holds fifteen rounds," he said, "and the man who shot at you fired twice, but there are fourteen bullets left. That means he fully loaded the magazine, then chambered the first round, took out the magazine and placed another round in it. So he had one round in the breech and ready to fire, and a full magazine in the butt. That's the mark of a professional. You were very lucky."

Angela gave a shiver.

"You don't have to remind me," she said. "I can still see that man in my mind's eye."

Bronson slid the magazine into the pistol, pulled back the slide and released it, to load the first round, then removed the magazine and placed it in his pocket. Then he inserted the full magazine, giving him a maximum of sixteen shots. The suppressor made the weapon far too bulky to be concealed, so Bronson removed it and slipped it into another pocket on his jacket. He tucked the pistol into the waistband of his trousers, made sure that it was invisible under his jacket, and then glanced across at Angela.

"Right," he said, then echoed her statement of a few minutes earlier. "Let's go."

77

Finding a cab wasn't difficult, even that late in the evening, and less than five minutes after they'd stepped through the front door of the hotel, they were sitting in the back of a rather battered Mercedes and heading toward the international airport.

When they arrived, Bronson paid the fare and then led Angela toward the arrivals hall. He was reasonably certain that any watchers would be covering departures, expecting that he and Angela would be trying to leave the city. As he'd expected, there were large groups of people milling around on the pavement outside the building, perhaps waiting for friends to pick them up, or just deciding whether to take a taxi or bus.

"I'll be as quick as I can," Bronson said. "There are plenty of people around here, so just try to merge in with the crowds, and you'll be safe enough."

He kissed her lightly on the lips, then stepped to one side, strode across the pavement and disappeared inside the building.

Angela knew that what Bronson had said made sense. Of all the places in Madrid that they could have gone to avoid pursuit, the arrivals terminal at the international airport was one of the least likely. And he was right about the crowds. Granted, most of the women of about her age who were outside the building had the black hair and tanned complexions that were characteristic of Spanish nationals, and with her pale skin and blond hair she stood out to some extent. But there were enough girls and young women with fair hair in the crowds for her to feel relatively inconspicuous. And she only needed to be there for about ten minutes or so, she hoped, before Bronson would reappear and then they could leave.

It was actually closer to fifteen minutes before he walked out of the building and beckoned to her to follow him. The two of them followed the directions that Bronson had been given, and made their way to the parking area reserved for vehicles belonging to the car hire companies operating at the airport.

"It should be somewhere in this row here," Bronson said, depressing the button on the remote control.

He was rewarded by flashing indicator lights on a Renault Mégane a few yards away, and stepped over to it, opening up the passenger door for Angela to get in. Then he sat down in the driver's seat and familiarized himself with the controls before taking his satnav from his pocket and attaching it to the windscreen in front of him. When Billy had sent the information to Bronson's computer, he'd supplied the recorded position of the mobile phone in latitude and longitude, and as soon as the unit was logged on to the navigation satellites, he input the precise location. By the time he'd started the engine, the satnav had already calculated the route.

"You're not going to just drive straight there, are you?" Angela asked, buckling her seat belt.

"No." Bronson was studying their destination on the

small screen of the satnav. "Depending on how accurate the triangulation was for that mobile phone," he said, "it looks as if the place we need to get to is a part of this industrial estate. It's called the Polígono Industrial Los Planetas. So what we'll do is get over there and drive past the building that is closest to the coordinates Billy sent me. Once we've checked the area and identified the most likely location, then we'll work out a plan of campaign and decide the best thing to do."

He put the car into reverse, backed out of the parking slot and drove away. It wasn't a long drive, and within just a few minutes they were heading down a road that appeared to be recently constructed.

"I think that must be it," Bronson said, gesturing toward a large building, presumably a kind of warehouse, the only building within a large plot. Three cars were parked outside, and a light was burning in the window beside the entrance door on the right of the building. Most of the rest of the frontage was occupied by two large roller-shutter doors, which obviously allowed large vehicles to enter the building for loading or unloading.

It looked as if the industrial estate hadn't been quite as popular as the builders had probably hoped, because there were vacant lots on both sides of the road he had just turned into, each displaying a for-sale sign.

He carried on to the T-junction at the end, and then again turned right, his route taking him behind the building that Billy the Kid had identified. Time spent on reconnoitering, as Bronson knew only too well from his days in the Army, and to a lesser extent in the police force, was never, ever wasted. Unfortunately, there wasn't very much in the way of cover in the area behind the warehouse, no convenient stands of trees or even collections of shrubs or bushes that could be used to conceal his vehicle.

But there was a building occupying part of the adjacent lot. This structure was surrounded by a high wire fence, the small car park protected by a tall gate, which looked as if it was controlled electrically. An attempt had been made to impose some sort of order on the grounds inside the fence, but it all looked a little sad and unkempt. The sign above the building, giving an estate agent's name and telephone number in large and hopeful letters, said it all.

The street on the opposite side of the building was, Bronson realized, ideal. The vehicle would be on the road, ready to be driven away, only about fifty yards from his objective, but completely out of sight.

"This will do nicely," he said, pulling the car to a halt beside the wire fence surrounding the structure. Then he turned to look at Angela.

"So what's the plan?" she asked.

"For the moment, you stay here. Sit in the driving seat, keep the keys in the ignition ready to go, and the doors locked. Open all the windows about six inches so you can hear what's happening outside. If anybody apart from me comes anywhere near the car, just start it and go. Turn left onto the road in front of you, then take a right at the T-junction. According to the satnav, just beyond that there's a biggish roundabout. Take the first exit, and park somewhere along that road, so I'll know where to find you. If anyone you don't like the look of comes anywhere near the car when you get over there, drive away and come back to the same spot ten minutes later."

"Got it," Angela said. "And while I'm driving around this area trying to avoid the bad guys, what exactly will you be doing?"

"I'm just going to take a look around, that's all. Watch the building for a few minutes, check where all the doors are located, that kind of thing. When I've done that, we can decide what our next move is going to be."

Angela nodded.

"Just make sure that's all you do," she said. "Don't try some kind of one-man assault on the building."

"Trust me, Angela. When have I ever let you down?"

"Frequently," she replied, giving him a quick smile.

Bronson leaned across the car and kissed her, and in moments he'd vanished into the gloom of the late evening.

78

As soon as he had gone, Angela climbed nimbly into the driver's seat, turned on the ignition to lower the electric windows, as Bronson had asked her to do, and locked all the doors. Then all she could do was wait. And hope.

She realized that there was a good chance they were wasting their time. It was quite possible that George Stebbins had already been dead for hours, and was even then lying in some anonymous ditch on the outskirts of Madrid. But her fervent hope was that Pere, which she thought was a deceptively pleasant name, would have decided to keep Stebbins alive for a while longer, just in case he could still be used as a bargaining counter. And if that was the reality of the situation, then the chances were that her colleague would be imprisoned somewhere in the building that was now just out of sight.

Her thoughts wandered, as she thought about what might be happening to poor old George. She would never forgive herself if he got harmed because of her. She played out several increasingly terrifying scenarios in her head, then jumped as Bronson reappeared beside the car.

Angela unlocked the doors to let him climb into the passenger seat.

"What did you see?" she asked.

"It looks like a small warehouse," he said. "There are two large roller-shutter doors at the front, which are down and locked. I can see padlocks securing them to brackets on the ground, and they're probably bolted on the inside as well. Then there's the door we saw at the front of the building, where the light was, and there's a side door as well, about halfway down the right-hand side of the building. Both of those could be possible entry points. As well as the light showing at the front of the building, there's also what looks like an office at the back with lights on, so it's reasonable to assume that somebody—more likely at least three people, bearing in mind the three cars parked outside—are in there."

"And your plan is?"

Bronson shrugged.

"The same one I always have, I suppose. I'll play it by ear."

"Which means what, exactly?"

"We both go across toward the building and find a suitable place where you can keep watch. I'm going to wait for a while, in the hope that somebody comes out. If they don't, then I'll have to try breaking in somehow. What happens then, I have no idea, but at least I'll be carrying the Beretta. And like I said, I'll have the element of surprise."

"And I wait out here? Is that the idea?" Angela demanded.

"Yes," Bronson replied, "because you're the only backup that I've got."

He reached into his pocket and took out the mobile phone he had removed from the body of the assassin.

He'd replaced the SIM card in its slot, but the battery and back of the phone were still not in place. He handed all three pieces of the mobile to Angela.

"Only fit it all back together if it's quite obvious that I'm in real trouble—shots fired, that kind of thing—and as soon as it's working, dial 112. That's the Pan European emergency number. When you've told them what's going on, don't end the call, just leave the line open so they can triangulate its location. As soon as you hear the sound of sirens approaching, drive away, whether I've come back or not."

Angela didn't look happy, but she nodded anyway. Moments later they climbed out of the car, closing and locking the doors as quietly as possible.

The two of them crept slowly around the back of the building that separated them from their objective, keeping close to the fence. There was no other cover they could use, but there were no windows in the side of the structure that they were approaching, and there were no streetlights near to them.

"What about cameras?" Angela whispered.

"As far as I can tell," Bronson replied, just as quietly, "there are only two, both on the front of the building. One covers the pedestrian doorway and the other the main loading gate."

"But as soon as you approach the building, the cameras will detect you," Angela pointed out.

Bronson nodded.

"I know, but there's nothing I can do about that. I'll just have to work fast. And in any case, once I'm inside the building, anybody in there will know about it, surveillance cameras or not."

He glanced around as they approached the end of the

wire fence, and motioned Angela toward a slight dip in the ground.

"If you lie here," he said, "you'll have a good view of the other building, and hopefully nobody should be able to see you."

Angela crouched down slowly, wincing as a couple of stones dug into her knees.

"Whatever you do," she said, looking up at him, "just be careful out there."

Bronson grinned at her.

"You're starting to sound like an actor in a bad American cop show," he said. "Don't worry. I'll take care. And I'm really glad I've got you watching my back."

Without another word, Bronson walked away, his rubber-soled shoes virtually silent on the tarmac.

79

Bronson had already looked all around the building, doing his initial reconnoitre. As far as he could tell, both cameras were focused on comparatively small areas, in the immediate vicinity of each doorway. There were no cameras covering the parking area in front of the structure. Or, if there were, he hadn't seen them.

Two of the cars he had observed earlier were parked directly in front of the larger of the two doors, while the third vehicle was farther away, over to one side. He could watch from there and be hidden from view, but still be close enough to the building to react quickly to intercept anybody who came out.

He moved toward the car as fast as he could to minimize his exposure to any potential watchers inside the building, and then ducked down behind it, crouching in the shadows.

For about five minutes, he concentrated all his attention on the building in front of him and the area immediately around it, just in case anybody inside had seen his fast but stealthy approach. But he saw nobody, and no indication of any imminent threat.

Despite what he'd said to Angela, he was worried about the two cameras. If it came to breaking in, he thought he would probably be able to open the door with his collection of homemade picks. But trying to do that while being watched by the unblinking eye of a closed-circuit television camera was a very different situation. If it came to that, his best option might be to rely on speed and violence rather than stealth, to smash the lock with a round or two of nine-millimeter Parabellum ammunition.

The problem with that scenario, of course, was that if the occupants were also armed, he'd probably find himself facing two or more men carrying pistols the moment he entered the building. And that didn't sound like a particularly good idea.

He was also keenly aware that there was no certainty that George Stebbins was actually inside the premises and, even if he was there, that he was alive. He could be embarking on a fool's errand.

A sudden metallic sound from in front of him interrupted his reverie. He crouched lower behind the car and peered cautiously around the front of the vehicle. As he watched, the pedestrian door in the front of the building swung open and a figure stepped out and walked briskly across to one of the parked cars. The hazard flashers on the vehicle pulsed twice as he approached. He walked over to the back of the car and opened the boot.

Bronson knew immediately that this was the best chance he was likely to get.

80

The moment the boot lid sprang up, hiding the man from his view, Bronson emerged from his hiding place and sprinted toward the parked car.

The man obviously heard his approach—he would have had to have been deaf not to have heard him—and stepped out from behind the car immediately.

But it made no difference. Bronson was running hard, the pistol clutched in his right hand, and at the moment the man emerged into view, he was on him. Bronson crashed into him, smashing his shoulder into the man's chest and knocking him backward onto the tarmac surface of the parking area.

His opponent was down, but not out, and Bronson couldn't take any chances. He slammed the butt of the Beretta M92 into the side of the man's head. Instantly, the figure went limp as unconsciousness claimed him.

Bronson stood up and looked all around, just in case someone else had followed the man out of the building, but there was nobody in sight, and the pedestrian door was still standing wide-open.

Quickly, he bent down and searched the unconscious

man. Any doubt he might have had that the man was an innocent employee of a blameless company was quickly dispelled when he discovered the leather shoulder holster he was wearing, and the Glock 17 that was tucked into it, plus two spare magazines, both fully charged. Getting it off the man was awkward because he was a deadweight, but inside a couple of minutes Bronson was able to pull the holster over his shoulders, attaching its base loop to his own belt and shrugging on his jacket over the top of it. He checked the Glock was loaded, with a round in the chamber, and then replaced it in the holster.

He looked into the boot of the car and saw a couple of cardboard boxes inside it, the tops undone. One man carrying a cardboard box, Bronson realized, probably looks very similar to any other man carrying a cardboard box.

He leaned forward, picked up one of the boxes and turned it upside down. A number of anonymous brown-wrapped packages cascaded down from it into the boot. He pushed the boot lid closed, placed the box on the roof of the car, then reached down and dragged the unconscious man alongside the vehicle so that he would be completely hidden from the view of anybody looking out of the building.

Then he picked up the cardboard box, holding it in his left hand, supporting its underside with his right forearm, which meant that the bulk of the empty box completely concealed the Beretta pistol he was holding in his right hand.

He took a final glance around, then strode confidently across the parking area to the pedestrian door.

81

As he reached the camera's field of vision, Bronson lifted the cardboard box up high so that it obscured his face, strode quickly forward to cover the last few feet, and stepped inside the warehouse.

He altered his grip on the empty cardboard box so that he was holding it solely with his left hand, and held the pistol in his right hand behind it, ready for instant use. But the room he was standing in—a small square space occupied by a couple of desks and chairs—was devoid of human presence. At the back of the room he could see another door standing open and leading to a short passageway that was illuminated by a single fluorescent tube on the ceiling, which obviously ran down one side of the building.

Bronson strode across the room and glanced up the passageway, but neither saw nor heard anybody. About halfway down the passage was a door on the left-hand side bearing the universally recognizable symbol of a male and female figure separated by a vertical line. He checked it anyway, just to make sure that nobody was taking a toilet break.

At the end of the passage a flight of steps ascended to the next level. Still holding the box in front of him—if his basic disguise worked, then whoever was waiting on the upper floor of the building would be expecting to see a man carrying a box—Bronson climbed up the staircase.

At the top he paused for a moment and looked in both directions. There was another lavatory almost opposite the top of the staircase, and a couple of offices down the passageway to his left, but both doors were open, and no lights were burning, so he discounted them. To his right was another and slightly longer passageway, again lit by a fluorescent light, and at the end of that a door stood partially ajar, illuminated by lights from inside the room.

If George Stebbins was anywhere inside the building, that office or room was where Bronson expected to find him.

But as Bronson began to head down the passageway toward the door, it was suddenly flung open and a figure appeared there and shouted something at him in high-speed Spanish. Bronson didn't understand more than a fraction of what the man was saying. But having delivered his tirade, the man stepped back into the room. It seemed that Bronson hadn't—at least up to that point—been recognized as a threat.

He continued down the passage toward the door, clicking off the safety catch of the Beretta M92 in his right hand as he approached the end. But he'd only taken two or three steps when something hard jabbed him in the back.

Somebody had appeared behind him completely soundlessly. And whoever it was had a loaded pistol in his hand.

82

Bronson knew that in a situation like this, speed was everything.

He reacted instantly, dropping the cardboard box to the ground in front of him and spinning to his left as quickly as he could, slamming his left arm down and backward to knock away the weapon that his unseen assailant was carrying.

As the side of Bronson's hand smashed into the assailant's arm, the man's weapon discharged, the noise deafening in the confined space. The bullet plowed into the concrete floor of the corridor before ricocheting away somewhere down the passageway. Bronson was determined that the man would not be able to fire a second time.

He continued to turn, forcing the man's gun hand away from his body and at the same time bringing his own right hand, the solid lump of the Beretta pistol giving it extra weight, on a collision course with his attacker's left ear.

Less than a second after Bronson had felt the barrel of the pistol jammed into the small of his back, it was all over. The moment the butt of the Beretta crashed into the man's head, he collapsed in a heap on the floor, instantly knocked unconscious.

But that, of course, was only the start of Bronson's problems. The sound of the gunshot would obviously have alerted everybody else in the building. He had just seconds.

He reached down with his left hand and grabbed the automatic pistol that the man lying on the floor had dropped, then took a couple of steps forward before easing himself into the doorway of a room on the left-hand side of the passage. For a few seconds, he waited, the Beretta held steady in his right hand, the muzzle aimed squarely at the open door.

But nothing moved. There was no sound from inside the office, no indication that anybody had even noticed what had happened in the corridor.

That left only two possibilities. Either the man who'd attacked him and the man he'd seen at the end of the passage were one and the same person, which he didn't think was possible, or there was another way out of the room at the end, a fire escape perhaps, and the other man had already left the building.

Then a third possibility occurred to him, and he quickly moved two steps back into the office and dropped flat on the floor. Under a second later, two shots rang out, the bullets tearing jagged holes through the thin partition walls precisely where he'd been standing. Because in that instant he'd noticed the closed-circuit TV camera positioned above the office door at the end of the corridor, the lens pointing directly at him. The man or men in the other room didn't need to actually look down the passage: they could watch him on the building's internal security system.

He'd have to do something about that, and quickly.

The gunman wouldn't know whether or not either of

the two shots had hit him, because Bronson had moved out of sight of the CCTV camera, but the moment he stepped out of the office his position would be obvious. He had to destroy the camera, and try not to get shot in the process.

He didn't risk standing up, instead opening the office door wide and lying on his stomach on the floor, presenting the smallest possible target to the unseen gunman. He crawled slowly toward the open doorway. The moment he could see the side of the camera, he took careful aim with the Beretta, eased out another few inches and squeezed the trigger twice.

The pistol bucked in his hand, and he immediately rolled back inside the office. He thought at least one of the bullets had hit the camera, but he obviously needed to find out for sure.

He slid across the floor once more and risked a quick glance down the passage. The camera was still in place, bolted high on the wall at the far end of the corridor, but one side had been blown off completely, and wires dangled from the jagged opening.

The opposition had lost their biggest advantage. Again there was complete silence.

Four more shots rang through the building, two double-taps, which suggested that the gunman knew his business, the bullets driving more holes through the partition walls at about waist height, the copper-jacketed slugs passing well above Bronson, who was still lying on the floor.

Speed seemed to be more important than stealth at that stage. He stood up, stepped out of the office in which he'd taken refuge and trotted as quickly and as quietly as he could down the passageway, tucking away the Glock he'd taken from the unconscious man who was still lying motionless a few feet behind him.

At the door to the office he stopped, ducked down and snatched a quick glance into the room, registering the scene there in an instant. He immediately took two quick paces backward. It was just as well that he did so.

Two bullets ripped through the wall just a few inches in front of Bronson, who ducked down, then raised his own weapon, aimed it through the hole that the gunman had just blasted and fired twice. The man might now have moved, but it was worth a try.

There was a yell of pain from inside the office, followed almost immediately by a clattering sound and a heavy thump, and then the unmistakable noise of a body collapsing to the floor.

He stepped forward again and took another quick look.

The man he'd seen in those few microseconds was sprawled on the floor, lying on his back, a dark stain spreading across the front of his shirt.

But that wasn't what concerned Bronson at that moment. His attention was drawn to the far end of the large room, where a figure sat slumped in an upright chair, his ankles secured to the legs with plastic cable ties and his arms twisted behind his body. Even though the bound man's head was hanging down, obscuring his features, Bronson was quite certain he was looking at George Stebbins.

Freeing him—assuming he was still alive—would be the work of a few seconds, but right then he knew there was no guarantee that either he or Stebbins would be able to leave the room alive.

Because crouching right behind the bound man was another figure, a pistol resting on Stebbins's shoulder, the muzzle touching his ear and the man's finger caressing the trigger.

83

No part of the man's body was clearly visible from behind Stebbins. Bronson knew he couldn't shoot until the other man moved.

"I have to admit that we didn't expect to see you here, Bronson—you are Bronson, I presume?" the man said in fluent but accented English. "I admire the fact that you managed to track me down. How did you do it, by the way?"

Bronson kept his pistol pointing toward Stebbins, waiting for the opportunity to fire the shot that would end the stalemate. But the other man was taking great care to ensure that he was completely shielded by the body of the bound man.

"I got somebody to hack into the mobile phone records and trace your location. It wasn't that difficult, Pere. I'm assuming that's who you are. Why didn't you shoot me when I walked into this room?"

The other man smiled.

"You're right. I could have killed you a couple of minutes ago, but I don't want you dead, Bronson—at least, not yet. First, we want the relic. Hand that over and you can take this man away with you, and the two of you and your wife can fly home as soon as you can book seats on a plane. You've proved to be resourceful, and I'm prepared to ignore my most specific orders to bury you both. You've already caused me quite enough trouble."

He gestured toward the still shape lying on the floor on the opposite side of the office.

"Who gave you those orders?" Bronson asked.

"It's a business arrangement. The organization I work for has been retained by the people who own the relic. It was stolen from them decades ago, and they want their property back. I'm sure that by now you've guessed who they are."

"I have a good enough idea," Bronson said. "But what exactly does the text on that parchment say which is so dangerous to Christianity?"

The other man shook his head.

"I have no idea," he replied. "The instructions I was given included a photograph of the parchment so I could be sure that we had identified and recovered the correct relic, but not what was written on it. Don't you know what it says?"

"No. The writing is too faded and indistinct to read it all."

Pere gave what looked like a shrug.

"It's not important, at least not to me. To me this is just a job. But you can walk away from here if you do what you're told. You have to realize that you have absolutely no chance of getting away with that parchment. My organization is simply too powerful and too widespread for that to happen, with adequate resources in every nation in Europe. My group of people here in Madrid is only a small part of the forces we've mobilized against you, and even if by some miracle you did manage to get out of here in one piece, there are others waiting to hunt you down."

"So who are you?" Bronson demanded. "The Mafia?"

"No. We never make the headlines like that organization, but we're bigger and more deadly," Pere replied. "Now, the choice is yours. As I just said, if you give me the relic you can walk away. I'll tell my contact in England that you handed over the parchment in a public place somewhere and I was unable to eliminate you and your wife. Once the relic is back in Rome, where it should be, the two of you will at least have a chance of living normal lives, because there'll be no proof that the parchment ever even existed. Any photographs you've taken can be dismissed as clumsy forgeries if you were stupid enough to try to publicize them."

The man shifted position very slightly, but still Bronson didn't have a clear shot at him.

"This is the endgame, Bronson, and it's your move. Agree to hand over the relic right now or George Stebbins will die and I'll make sure you and Angela Lewis are hunted down and killed within days. So what's it to be?"

As far as Bronson could see, there was only one option open to him.

"You can have the relic," he said. "Too many people have died already over that scruffy piece of old parchment. It's in my pocket. You can have it now."

The man crouching behind Stebbins didn't move, but Bronson guessed he was smiling.

"I thought you'd see sense," the man replied. "Now, drop that pistol onto the floor and kick it away from you. Then you can put the relic on the desk behind you and just walk away. And don't try anything stupid, or I'll shoot you down where you stand."

Bronson nodded, bent his knees and carefully lowered

the Beretta to the floor, then kicked it a couple of feet over to his right, his movements stiff and controlled.

"The parchment?" Pere said. "Where is it?"

"My right-hand-side jacket pocket," Bronson replied.

"Good." Pere's smile grew broader. "Now I know where to shoot you without damaging the relic."

Bronson knew that either his gamble was going to pay off or he was going to die. As far as he could see there were no other possible outcomes.

And as those thoughts coursed through his mind, Pere swung the pistol round to point directly at him rather that at George Stebbins's head.

"I said you were clever, Bronson," he snapped, "but actually you're a bigger fool than I took you for. Why on earth did you think I would let you walk out of here alive?"

And that was the gamble. It all depended on what the Spaniard did next.

Pere slowly straightened up from behind the bound man and stretched out his right arm, still smiling as he aimed his weapon directly at Bronson, relishing the moment.

"I understood that you'd had a spell as an officer in the British Army, and that you're now a police officer. I'm frankly surprised that you learned so little in your training for either organization."

Bronson raised his hands in a gesture of surrender.

"What are you talking about?" he asked.

"The first rule of close-quarters combat. You never, ever give up your weapon, no matter what the odds or the circumstances. I thought you would have known that. You certainly should have done."

"I do know that," Bronson agreed, "but in any combat situation you have to make a judgment as to whether whatever rules you've been taught really apply. And I decided that they didn't, because I needed you to make a mistake, which you have done."

"I don't think so. You're unarmed, and I have both a pistol and a hostage. I'm going to live, and you're going to die."

Bronson nodded, and tensed his body.

"In fact, that's two mistakes you've made," he said.

84

A puzzled frown appeared on Pere's face.

"What mistakes?" the Spaniard demanded.

"First, you're standing up."

Bronson had known that he'd never be able to get the pistol out of his shoulder holster before the Spaniard shot him down. But before he'd entered the room he'd decided to give himself an ace in the hole. He'd buttoned the neck of his shirt, and then tucked the second Glock, barrel downward, into the top of the garment behind his head. Since then he'd been careful to move slowly so as not to dislodge it.

Now, with his arms raised, his right hand was a bare six inches from the butt of the weapon.

Pulling the trigger of a pistol fires the weapon immediately, and nobody can outrun a bullet. But the brain still takes a finite time to send the message to the finger to tell it to squeeze the trigger, and that was what Bronson was counting on.

With a movement so fast that Pere had no time to react, Bronson slid his right hand behind his head, seized the Glock pistol and swung it forward and downward, squeezing the trigger twice as he did so.

The first bullet slammed into the Spaniard's right shoulder, spinning him round and immediately making him drop his weapon, but it was the second one that did the real damage, tearing into the left side of the man's chest and knocking him backward. He was dead before his body hit the floor.

"And your second mistake," Bronson muttered, "was assuming that I was unarmed."

Once he'd checked the whole of the top floor and ensured there was no further danger, Bronson approached George Stebbins. He had assumed that the man was out cold, but in fact he wasn't, just rendered immobile by the plastic cable ties that secured him to the chair and made speechless by a gag taped over his mouth. He was also plainly terrified, a fact attested to by the spreading damp patch on his trousers where he had wet himself, and in a lot of pain, with three of the fingers on his left hand bent and broken out of shape.

But at that moment, even as Bronson reached into his pocket to take out a knife to cut Stebbins free, he heard the unmistakable sound of approaching sirens, and realized he had no time left. Angela must have blown the whistle.

"Can you hear me, George?" he asked urgently.

The bound man raised his head to look at his savior and nodded, his eyes imploring.

"The police are on their way," Bronson told him, "so I'm leaving you here. When they free you, tell them you were kidnapped by this gang and then there was a violent argument which ended up with two of the men shooting each other. Have you got that?"

Stebbins nodded, looking thoroughly upset and confused at what was happening to him.

"Right," Bronson said, and set to work to try to create the scenario he had just outlined.

He took a handkerchief from his pocket and did what he could to rub his fingerprints from the trigger and handle of the Glock he'd just used to shoot Pere, then stepped across the room and placed the gun in the hand of the first man he'd shot, closing his fingers around it. He picked up the pistol lying beside that body, then strode across to Pere, retrieved his weapon as well, and then repeated the cleaning operation on the Beretta automatic he'd been carrying when he'd walked into the room and placed that pistol in Pere's right hand.

It was the best he could do in the circumstances. At the very least he had now positioned the weapons in the appropriate places, and the forensic examination of the scene that would surely follow would show that the bullets that had killed the men had come from the correct pistols. Bronson frankly doubted that any halfway intelligent police officer would be satisfied that that was what had actually happened, but he had no time left to do any more, as the increasing volume of the approaching sirens confirmed.

He took one final glance around the office, checked both bodies to remove the spare magazines they were carrying, and made sure he hadn't forgotten anything. Then he ran down the passageway, quickly searched the unconscious man still lying there and retrieved another two Glock magazines from his body, then made his way swiftly down the stairs and out of the building.

85

Outside, the noise of the sirens was very much louder, and he knew that Angela would already have driven away from the scene, so he ran in the opposite direction, covering as much distance as he could before the first of the police cars arrived.

There was another industrial building about two hundred yards away, and he ducked around the back of it just as the beams of the headlights on the leading police car swept across it. Bronson stopped for a few seconds and looked back, checking that he hadn't been seen.

Once he was certain that nobody was heading in his direction, he crossed the road and began making his way between the various industrial units dotted about the estate until he reached the other road where he had asked Angela to wait for him. Almost as soon as he stepped onto the pavement, he saw the rental car parked precisely where he had expected to find it.

Less than a minute later, he pulled open the passenger door and dropped into the seat beside her.

The moment he sat down, Angela grabbed and held him for a long moment.

"I was terrified," she said, a catch in her voice. "I heard the shots and I was sure I was never going to see you again. So I called the police and then drove here as soon as I heard the sirens. What happened? Was George there?"

Bronson nodded.

"He was, and he still is," he replied. "He was tied to a chair, but as far as I could see he was unharmed apart from two or three broken fingers."

"The bastards," Angela muttered. "Why didn't you bring him with you?"

"I didn't have time to cut him free, and in any case he'll need medical treatment for his hand. And there's another reason. I left two dead men inside that building and another one with a really bad headache. I explained to George what he should tell the police, and I'm hoping that will satisfy them that nobody else was involved in there, at least in the short term."

All the time he'd been talking, Bronson had been keeping a careful watch out of the car windows, just in case any of the police officers decided they needed to widen their search of the local area. He didn't think it was likely to happen imminently, because he guessed they'd have their hands full at the crime scene. Once more cars and officers had arrived, they'd have enough manpower to cover the whole area, but Bronson intended to be long gone before that happened.

"You killed two men?" Angela asked, her voice barely more than a hoarse whisper.

Bronson shrugged, mentally reliving the sequence of events.

"It was self-defense," he said, "and I only just got away with it. If I'd been just a little bit slower, I'd be lying dead on the floor of that office back there, and George would probably be looking down the barrel of a pistol as well. I really had no choice."

Angela didn't reply, and Bronson held her gaze for a moment, then looked ahead, through the windscreen.

"We can talk about it later, but now we really must move," he said. "Are you OK to drive?"

Angela nodded, looking upset but resolute.

As they drove past the end of the road where the warehouse was located, they both glanced to their left. The flashing red and blue lights of the police vehicle were casting kaleidoscope patterns across the front of the building, but nobody was visible outside it. Bronson guessed that the police were still trying to make sense of the scene inside the office and, hopefully, summoning medical assistance for George Stebbins.

As if in answer to his silent thought, as they drove out of the industrial estate and turned back toward the center of Madrid, an ambulance screamed past in the opposite direction, siren blaring and roof lights pulsing.

"With any luck they'll pump George full of painkillers before they splint and bind his fingers, and he probably won't be in any fit state to answer questions coherently for a few hours. I just hope he remembers not to mention you, and especially not to mention me."

Then another thought struck him, and he glanced over at Angela, who was concentrating on driving as quickly as the traffic would allow.

"What happened to that man I flattened outside the building?" Bronson asked. "The one who came out and obligingly left the door open for me?"

Angela glanced at him, then turned her attention back to the road.

"He stood up a couple of minutes after you'd gone inside. He looked pretty groggy, and kept on holding the side of his head while he looked around him. But then the shooting started inside the building and that certainly got his attention. He reached inside his jacket, but I guess you'd already taken his gun because he obviously didn't find what he was looking for. He took a few steps over toward the building, then seemed to think better of it. He walked back to the car, got into it and then drove away. It was about then that I put the battery back in the phone and called the police."

Bronson nodded.

"One minor mystery solved, I suppose."

"So now that George is in good hands," Angela asked, "can we go home?"

"I bloody hope so. I just have no idea how."

86

Angela looked quickly across at Bronson as the car sped along the city streets.

"But if all of the gang are dead, then surely that's the end of it? We can just drive to the airport, buy a couple of tickets and fly back to London?"

"I don't think it's going to be anything like that easy," Bronson replied slowly. "There were only three people inside that warehouse, four if you include the man I tackled in the car park. Pere said they were only a small proportion of the people looking for us. They'll certainly be covering the airport and the railway stations. About the only way we're going to be able to get back to England in one piece is if we drive there. Trying to find one car in the vast network of roads that cover France should be almost impossible, as long as we stay off the autoroutes."

"That's a hell of a long way to drive. Are you sure there's no other way we can travel?"

Bronson shook his head.

"None that I can think of. If they don't find us in Madrid, they'll widen the search and start checking the

Atlantic ports like Santander, and probably station men at all the other airports anywhere near here, and on both sides of the border up to the north of us. They'll be covering Barcelona, Gerona, Reus, Lourdes, Toulouse and Carcassonne, places like that."

"That would be a huge manpower commitment," Angela objected. "Do you really think these people believe that old parchment is important enough to justify that?"

"I'm afraid I do," Bronson replied. "The man who seemed to be in charge inside the warehouse did explain something to me. Up till now, you and I have probably both had our own ideas about who, or what organization, is coordinating these people. I think we've both been fairly certain that the parchment was probably originally the property of the Catholic Church. Pere pretty much confirmed that, by mentioning Rome and also the fact that the relic had been stolen from them, years ago. But the people who are looking for it aren't members of the clergy, which I suppose is something of a relief. According to Pere, his organization has been retained by the Vatican to recover the parchment, and he was adamant that we would be hunted down and killed. He told me that we're facing one of the biggest and most dedicated organizations on the planet, and one of the most ruthless."

"You sound like you're talking about the Mafia," Angela said.

Bronson laughed shortly.

"No, not quite, though there have been links between the Vatican and the Mafia for decades. But if I'm right the people who are looking for us have probably got just as wide a reach as the Cosa Nostra. We're facing a group with followers in every country, who've proved time and time again that they're both extremely ruthless and very competent, who've committed murder on countless occasions and, in nineteen seventy-eight, very probably extended their lethal reach into the heart of the Vatican itself and killed Pope John Paul I."

87

"You have just got to be kidding me," Angela said, glancing across at Bronson to see the expression on his face. "I thought he died of a heart attack?"

"I wish I was. Nothing about the death of John Paul made sense. He was young, for a pope, fit and healthy, and had no serious medical problems. Ultimately everybody dies of a heart attack because sooner or later it stops beating. What we don't know is *why* his heart stopped beating, because there was no autopsy. But we do know that the day before his body was discovered, he had announced his intention to cleanse the Vatican of the influence of members of a so-called Masonic lodge named *Propaganda Due*, or P2."

"I remember," Angela said. "Roberto Calvi and Blackfriars Bridge."

"Exactly."

"But I thought it was disbanded after all that controversy over the Banco Ambrosiano?"

"So did I, but the official view must be wrong. I think it just went underground."

"So it's not the Vatican that is sending out teams of trained assassins to hunt us down? It's this P2?"

Bronson nodded. "That's what I think. I believe that the sheer existence of that parchment—or more accurately the text that is written on it—poses such a threat to the entire Christian religion that the Church will do anything, and I do mean anything, to destroy it. That's why they've handed over the job to P2, which would have no scruples at all about killing us or anybody else. After all, if they're prepared to act inside the Vatican itself and assassinate the Pope, murdering us wouldn't give them a moment's pause."

Angela drew the rental car to a stop at a red traffic light on an almost deserted street somewhere near the center of Madrid, and looked across at him.

"You're serious, aren't you? But we still don't know for sure if the parchment is real, what date it is, or what the text says."

"Well," Bronson said, "it was made pretty clear by Pere that the Roman Catholic Church has no doubts whatsoever about its authenticity, because it was stolen from the Vatican in the first place. Presumably they ran whatever test or tests they needed to do some years ago. I asked Pere what secret the text was describing, and he said he didn't know, and I'm inclined to believe him."

He paused and glanced over at Angela as she accelerated away from the junction.

"Absolutely the only thing we can be sure of," Bronson continued, "is that whatever's written on that old piece of parchment has the capability to do very serious damage to the Christian religion. The secret has to be something so fundamental that it would prove without doubt that the entire Christian religion was founded upon a lie. And that's the reason why we can't just buy an airline ticket or turn up at a railway station. If we're going to survive this, we have to keep the lowest profile we possibly can. And we have to get back to Britain."

"You're right," agreed Angela. "If we can get back to London and authenticate the relic, we can publish the information. Once it's in the public domain there won't be anything else they can do, and hopefully they'll leave us alone."

Bronson didn't respond for a short while, but then he nodded.

"I suppose that makes sense," he conceded.

"My worry," Angela went on, "is that if the parchment passes whatever tests we subject it to and we do go ahead and publish what we've found, these people might still try and kill us out of revenge."

"You could be right," Bronson said, "and our best defense against that happening will be to organize the maximum possible publicity and ensure that our names are splashed across every newspaper and magazine in the country. That way, if they do make an attempt on our lives, whatever credibility the Catholic Church has left would be completely destroyed. It's not much, but I still think doing that would be our best form of protection."

Angela snorted in derision.

"So what you're saying is that our best option is to let ourselves be murdered because that would embarrass the Vatican! I should have walked away from this right at the beginning," Angela muttered. "I wish I'd done what Ali said, and forgotten all about the parchment as soon as he told me about the murder in Cairo."

Bronson shook his head.

"From what we've seen of these people, you would still have been a target, simply because you knew about it. And we're not dead yet."

88

"That doesn't exactly fill me with confidence," Angela muttered. "So what now?"

Bronson was silent for a minute, trying to decide on their next move. He could think of only one thing they could do at that precise moment.

"Right. Quite apart from anything else, I'm tired and I'm sure you must be as well. We'll both function a lot better if we had a decent night's sleep, and that will also give us time to work out the best route we can take up through France."

"So you are quite sure that the hotel will be safe?"

"We paid cash, and we weren't followed to the building, so I don't see how anybody can know we're there. But we'll park the car a few streets away in a multistory and walk the last part. And if I see anything I don't like," Bronson added, patting his jacket pockets, "I'm now more or less a walking arsenal, so I should be able to handle any members of the opposition who have by some miracle found out where we are."

Thirty minutes later, they were in their room back at the hotel, Angela taking a shower while Bronson sipped a gin and tonic he'd prepared from the somewhat limited supplies in the minibar, and studied a map of France that also included northern Spain. He still wasn't entirely sure how comprehensive the surveillance of Madrid would be, but he thought it was certainly possible that P2 might be able to obtain access to the traffic cameras that covered much of the city. But just being able to see the surveillance footage would still leave them with an enormous amount of data to sift through.

More specifically, they would be searching for the car he'd rented at the airport. And there was something he could do about that. Before they set off the next morning, he had every intention of swapping their number plates with those from some other car. That would make the job of identifying the vehicle, far less following it, infinitely more difficult.

A few moments later, Angela emerged from the bathroom in a faint cloud of steam, a towel tied around her head like a turban and another wrapped around her slim body, and Bronson handed her the second gin and tonic he had prepared.

"There's no lemon and no ice, I'm afraid."

Angela took the plastic beaker from him.

"Right now," she said, "I don't care about ice or lemon. What I need is alcohol, the stronger the better."

As they prepared themselves for sleep, or at least rest, Angela received an e-mail.

"What is it?" Bronson asked.

"It's an e-mail from a laboratory in England," she replied, "attaching some kind of test results."

She was silent for a few moments as she scanned the message, then nodded.

"I see what it is now. Ali Mohammed must have asked for carbon-14 testing to be done on a small piece of the parchment, without telling anyone. This is the test re-sults, and he must have asked for them to be expedited, because that's a really quick turnaround."

"But why have they sent them to you?"

"They haven't," Angela replied, "or not directly, any-way. I'm just copied in, but it's been sent to Ali himself. Because I mentioned to him that the British Museum might be interested in buying the relic, I suppose he asked the laboratory to copy the results directly to me."

Bronson stood up and walked across to peer over An-gela's shoulder at the computer screen.

"So how old is it?" he asked.

"Just a minute. I need to open up the attachment."

Bronson found himself looking at some kind of a graph, and below it a table containing a large number of figures. It meant nothing to him, but Angela appeared unfazed by it, running a finger down the table as she checked the data displayed in it.

"I suppose that's good news," she said, "or perhaps bad news, depending upon your point of view. According to the radiocarbon analysis, the relic dates from AD 25, and that figure is accurate to plus or minus roughly seventy-five years—the dating can't be much more accu-rate than that—and so the parchment had to have been prepared between 50 BC and AD 100, which is pretty much the timescale I've been assuming, because of the reference to Yusef, to Joseph. If it is authentic, then that would have to be approximately the period it dates from, round about the beginning of the first millennium."

Despite the fact that he was bone-weary and had the re-assuring warmth of Angela's body lying right next to him, sleep eluded Bronson for several hours. Every time he closed his eyes, one part of his brain persistently replayed the events in the warehouse. He heard the shots, saw the blood and watched the bodies fall to the floor, time after time. Killing another human being was never an easy thing to live with, and the feeling of guilt and revulsion was almost overwhelming, despite his certainty that what he'd done was the only possible course of action he could have taken.

He finally fell into a shallow sleep at around four in the morning, but still tossed and turned restlessly for what was left of the hours of darkness.

89

Early the next morning, Bronson stepped out of the hotel and made his way to the car park where he'd left the Renault late the previous night. En route he made a brief stop at a small hardware shop, where he bought a cheap and basic tool kit. In the car park, he took the lift to the top floor and then started making his way down to the level where he'd left the Mégane, walking around each floor as he did so. Most of the vehicles parked there were shiny, meaning that they were probably in regular, possibly daily, use, but there were a handful bearing a layer of dust, which suggested they'd been parked some time before and not touched since. But on the fifth floor he spotted one car actually covered with a dust sheet, and when he took a look underneath it he guessed that car hadn't moved in months.

He checked to make sure there were no surveillance cameras that could record what he was doing, then knelt down beside the car and snapped open his tool kit. Inside five minutes he'd removed both of the number plates. Fifteen minutes after that he was able to get back into the lift and leave the multistory car park, the new number plates already attached to the front and back of the Renault.

Angela was waiting for him in the hotel room.

"Any problems?" she asked.

"Good news and bad news, I'm afraid," he said. "The good news is we have a temporary disguise for our car. The bad news is there's almost no traffic on the streets, and I don't think we can leave until it's a bit busier, and we will be less conspicuous. I think we'll need to give it a couple of hours."

"Well, I can't just sit here and do nothing," Angela replied. "I'm going to work on my translation of the parchment. If I can translate just a little bit more, that might give us another clue as to its authenticity. Like every other language, Latin evolved over time, and it's possible that if the parchment is actually some kind of forgery, I might be able to detect that from the words used or the sentence forms."

"Good idea," Bronson said, then gestured toward his overnight bag.

"And as I now seem to be the owner of three unlicensed Glock 17 pistols and a handful of loaded magazines, I'm going to clean those three weapons, just in case. Once I've done that, I plan to do a bit of Internet research. From what Pere said, the parchment was stolen from the Vatican a long time ago. That must have made the papers, at least in Italy, so I'm going to see if I can find some record of it."

While Angela worked on the specialized photographs of the parchment, Bronson sat on the side of the bed, a hand towel from the bathroom beside him, and carefully stripped each of the Glocks in turn, cleaning and reloading them.

When he'd finished, he replaced one of the Glocks in the shoulder holster he had put on under his jacket, wrapped the other two weapons in one of the shirts he'd already worn and tucked away the bundle in his overnight bag. The loaded magazines he distributed around various pockets, where they would be readily to hand if trouble started anywhere down the line.

Then he opened his laptop, and was quiet for a while as he did various searches.

"Oddly enough," he began, breaking the silence, "it looks as if the Vatican's been a target of thieves for quite some time. This very first result here is about a robbery that took place in nineteen hundred when thieves stole 350,000 lire from a room in the building, aided and abetted by some minor Vatican official."

Bronson laughed shortly as he read something else.

"What is it?" Angela asked.

"It's just rather sweet. Apparently in previous cases thieves had been forced to return whatever goods or money they had stolen, and then they were forcibly expelled through the 'bronze door,' the principal entrance to the Vatican. In one case a clerk who worked for the Papal Secretary of State stole about 280,000 francs, but wasn't able to return the stolen money, presumably because he'd already spent it. He was condemned by an ecclesiastical tribunal to undergo eight days of spiritual exercises, which would encourage him to repent his sins, and was then given his job back. I don't somehow think they'd do that today."

"Not a chance," Angela agreed.

"There was another theft in nineteen thirty-seven, and even an attempted armed robbery—thieves with guns, no less—who tried to steal the entire Vatican payroll in nineteen eighty-six. The place seems to be a hotbed of crime.

Here's another one. A couple of thieves riding motor-scooters got away with about £150,000 just before Christmas in nineteen eighty-eight. It sounds like they had accurate inside information because they identified a Vatican car in the traffic near St. Peter's Square, blocked it in with one scooter while the other man smashed a window on the vehicle, grabbed the briefcase containing the money, and they both got away on the second scooter."

"All very amusing, but that's not the kind of thing we're looking for," Angela said. "If that parchment was stolen from the Vatican, then it was either an inside job or a break-in by thieves who were looking for relics, and maybe even stealing them to order."

"But surely almost anything stolen from the Vatican would be easy enough to identify," Bronson objected. "I'm sure they must keep detailed records of pretty much everything they have in the archives. So if something was being stolen to order, whoever organized the theft would never be able to sell it."

Angela shook her head.

"For some collectors, the idea of selling any of the items they own never even occurs to them. For people like that, possession is all that matters.

"If this parchment was taken out of the Vatican, it was probably one of a number of items stolen; otherwise the robbery really wouldn't make much sense. According to one of Ali's e-mails, this relic turned up in a metal box in the wall or floor of a building being demolished in Cairo. If it had been taken by a collector, he certainly wouldn't have done that with it. He would have wanted the parchment to be displayed somewhere, in some room in his house, and probably in a specially designed case to ensure the right light, temperature and humidity to preserve it.

Because of where the relic was found, my guess is that it was picked up with a number of other items during a robbery.

"The thieves probably tried to find a buyer for it, but a grubby old bit of parchment with illegible writing on it is not the kind of thing that most collectors will be interested in purchasing. After a while, they probably gave up, locked it away in the steel box and cemented it into a wall or hid it under the floorboards so that no one would find it, and then forgot about it."

Bronson was still scanning the results of his Internet search while he listened to Angela.

"That makes sense," he said, "and it's just possible that I know when the robbery took place."

90

While Bronson and Angela were waiting until the right time to leave, a meeting of a very different type was taking place only a couple of miles away in a large and secluded house on the eastern outskirts of Madrid.

Four people were discussing the situation, though only three of them were physically present in the room. The fourth man—Antonio Morini—was sitting on a bench at the edge of a park in Rome, his mobile phone pressed to his ear and his face pale and drawn. The news that he had received just moments earlier had been even worse than he had expected, and for the first time since the Vatican's Internet monitoring system had alerted him to the problem, he was seriously considering telling the Englishman to shut down the whole operation and just walk away, to let events run their natural course, despite the likely consequences.

"Tell me exactly what happened," Morini instructed, in English. He and the men sitting in the house in Madrid had established that as their common language.

"We were in a very strong position," the Spaniard—who was using the name Tobí—replied, his voice cold and bitter. "We had traced the two of them to their hotel, and very nearly ended the matter there, but they slipped away and we lost them in the city traffic. We'd already found and seized the third man who'd flown out from London, the specialist in ancient documents, and we were using him as bait to try to pin down the other two people in a location that we could control and where we could recover the relic. Unfortunately, this man Bronson is more resourceful than we expected, and somehow he managed to identify the building where we were holding the other man. He got inside, killed two of my men and knocked out two others, one of whom is still in hospital with severe concussion. The other one is here with me now, and listening to our conversation."

"Did he tell you what happened?"

Morini barely even noticed that "Tobí" was ignoring the rules about not giving names and other details in their conversation.

"No," Tobí replied, "he was outside the building when he was attacked, and all he remembers is being knocked to the ground by this man, who then hit him on the head with a weapon, possibly a pistol. By the time he regained consciousness, Bronson was already in the building and the police were on their way. We had assumed that he had called them just before he entered, but I have a contact in the local Guardia Civil who told me that the call was actually made by a woman. Presumably Lewis was with him, outside and watching the building."

"And what about the third man, the man from London? What happened to him?"

"He was still in the building when the police arrived, and he's now in hospital, too, recovering. Some of the methods we used to interrogate him were quite—what shall we say?—robust."

"I don't need to know about that," Morini said quickly.

"I will tell you one other thing: I will make this Bronson pay. One of the men he killed was my brother."

"I don't want this turning into a personal vendetta. The most important thing is still the recovery of the relic."

Tobí gave a short and entirely mirthless laugh.

"What you want, monsignor, and what I now want are not necessarily the same thing," he said. "If there's any possibility of us getting the relic back, then we will. But right now, this is personal. We are going to find Bronson and Lewis, and then I'm going to make sure that both of them wish they'd never been born."

Even through the earpiece of his mobile phone, Morini could feel the ice-cold determination in the man's voice.

Moments later, Tobí ended the call and looked across his desk at the two men who had been waiting silently there, listening to the conversation.

"Do we have any idea where those two are now?" he asked.

"No," Santos, the man Bronson had tackled in the warehouse car park, replied. "We know Bronson hired a car at the airport here, and all of our watchers have been given details of the vehicle as well as the photographs and descriptions of Bronson and Lewis, but there has been no sighting of them so far. They might have gone to ground in Madrid, in some small hotel maybe, or they might have driven away from the city altogether. If they have left the city by car, the net will have to be so big that they might easily slip through it. We simply don't have the manpower to cover every road all the time."

Tobí stood up and walked across to one wall of his

study, where an old map of the Iberian Peninsula was displayed. For a few seconds, he just looked at it, trying to decide the best course of action. How would he get out of Madrid if he were in Bronson's shoes, guessing at the forces that would be ranged against him?

He looked at the image of Madrid, and the surrounding areas, assessing whether or not the two fugitives would risk trying to board an aircraft or a train. If they purchased an airline ticket, one of his contacts in the immigration service would know. Their two passports had already been red-flagged, and he had positioned surveillance teams at the Madrid airports and train stations.

But somehow he doubted they would use either route. From what little he knew about Bronson, he guessed that the man would want to keep his options open, and that suggested that there was only one possible way he would be considering getting out of Spain.

Tobí tapped the glass covering the map a couple of times, then turned back to face the two men sitting opposite him.

91

"Listen to this," Bronson said. "I've just found something in a paper called the *Lodi News-Sentinel*.

"There's a pretty full report here of a robbery that took place in the Vatican. The publication date of the paper was 27 November 1965, and the robbery took place in the early hours of the previous Friday morning. And if I'm reading this correctly, it does look very much like a tailored robbery, because they could have taken a whole bunch of things but they didn't, just four specific items."

"Which were . . . ?" Angela said.

"They took two historic manuscripts and two important relics of the Roman Catholic Church. According to Vatican officials, the manuscripts were priceless, and the two relics were worth about half a million dollars, so we must be talking about several million dollars at today's value."

"Typical of a newspaper to concentrate on the price of the objects, not what they were," Angela commented.

"Actually, it does go on to explain what was taken, and also how the robbery was carried out," Bronson said.

"First of all, the two relics. One of them was a facsimile of a crown that belonged to Hungary's national hero, St. Stephen, made of gold. This report said it was made in the early part of the twentieth century and was a gift from the Catholics of Hungary to Pope Pius X."

Bronson paused for a moment as he read the next section of the article.

"But it looks as if the original is still around," he went on. "According to this other Web site, the genuine crown was smuggled out of Hungary sometime after the end of the Second World War to the United States, and it was secreted in America, in Fort Knox, no less, by a group of Hungarian exiles who wanted to protect it against any claims from the Communist government which had taken power in Hungary. It was only returned to that country in nineteen seventy-eight."

"So what was the other relic?"

"That's a wee bit gruesome," Bronson said. "It was a small box, decorated with copper and ceramics, which contained a message to Congress. It was being carried by the president of Ecuador, Garcia Moreno, when he was assassinated outside the cathedral in Quito in August 1875. Apparently the paper the message was written on was stained with Moreno's blood. I think the Vatican was being a bit optimistic with its valuations if it reckoned that a piece of bloodstained paper and a fake crown were worth half a million dollars back in nineteen sixty-five."

Bronson looked back at the scan of the newspaper article on the screen of his laptop.

"The other stuff might be a bit more valuable, though whether it qualifies as being 'priceless' is another matter altogether, and you know more about this kind of thing than I do. Anyway, the most valuable item stolen was an original copy of a thing called *Canonziere* by a fourteenth-century poet named Francesco Petrarch. According to this, it was his most outstanding work and contains several sonnets, madrigals and ballads, and was written on sheets of parchment, a lot of it by Petrarch himself."

"Now that would be worth a lot," Angela said, nodding, "but I don't know about 'priceless.' You said there were four items stolen, so what was the last one?"

"That was another collection of parchment sheets. Altogether there were 152 of them, containing a number of poems by a man named Torquato Tasso, a Roman poet. But not ancient Roman—he lived in the sixteenth century. The sheets contained copies of his poems, some of them in his own handwriting, and other versions of his work written by other people but corrected by him."

"He wrote 'Jerusalem Liberated,' if I remember rightly," Angela said.

Bronson was still looking at the scan of the page of newsprint.

"Now this is interesting as well," he said. "It looks as if you were right about the items being stolen to order. The Italian police thought the same thing. They said that it would be almost impossible for any of the items to be sold, except to a collector who already knew they were going to be stolen. They believed that it was a well-organized international gang that had carried out the robbery, because they obviously had a very detailed knowledge of the Vatican and knew exactly where to find these items. What's also interesting is that they left behind stuff that was even more valuable than what they took. Apparently the display cases in the area they broke into also contained manuscripts by people like St. Thomas Aquinas, Michelangelo and Martin Luther, and even a love letter written by Henry VIII.

"After the theft was discovered, the Italian police alerted

forces around the world, because they doubted if any collector in Italy would be able to afford to purchase the items. They haven't actually said it specifically in this article, but the implication is fairly clear. It looks as if they thought the most likely destination for the stolen goods was America. Maybe some wealthy collector there had decided that he needed these items to complete his collection and didn't much care how he got them."

He opened up another Web page and read a part of the contents.

"Now hang on a minute, because this is where it gets really weird," he said. "On the very day that the thefts were discovered, the two manuscripts and the replica crown were discovered in a field just outside Rome. According to this, two men were seen behaving suspiciously in a car, and then one of them threw a case into the field, where it was picked up by the gardener of a nearby villa. When it was opened, the crown and manuscripts were inside it. That really doesn't make any sense."

Angela nodded, and a slight smile crossed her face.

"Actually," she said, "it does to me. I'd lay you money that the real targets of the thieves were the manuscripts, because some collector had arranged for a couple of really good forgeries to be made, and by organizing the burglary he could swap them for the real thing, with nobody being any the wiser. He arranged to steal the originals, and then to return the fakes. That's really cheeky, but it does make sense."

"But surely the Vatican would know they were forgeries?"

"Not necessarily. Don't forget, we're not talking about a collector with just a handful of items, each of which he would know intimately. The Vatican holds tens of thousands, maybe millions, of treasures of different types. Nobody there could possibly be certain whether or not the objects they got back were the same as those that had been taken, as long as the copies were good enough, because nobody would know them that well. And I doubt if they'd have wanted to call in an outside expert to verify their authenticity, just in case they *were* forgeries. Better by far to rationalize the sequence of events to suggest that the burglars were so overcome by sorrow or whatever at what they'd done that they decided to hand back the spoils. The Catholic Church is very good at rationalizing things that don't make sense, and they've had a lot of practice at it."

"OK, I see what you mean. But if the two manuscripts were stolen to order, why did the thieves also take the replica crown and the other box of bits?"

"I don't know," Angela said with a shrug. "Maybe just as a smokescreen, so that the Vatican wouldn't look too closely at the manuscripts when they got them back, because it would be much easier to verify that the crown was the real thing. The real replica, I mean."

She paused for a moment, her gaze distant and unfocused.

"Here's a thought," she went on. "I'm just wondering if a few years before the robbery took place some official at the Vatican didn't quite know what to do with this relic, this sheet of parchment that we've now got our hands on, and needed somewhere secure to hide it."

"I don't follow what you mean," Bronson said.

"Think about it for a minute. We're saying that this parchment contains a really damaging, explosive secret that the Roman Catholic Church would do absolutely anything not to have revealed. But they can't really destroy it, because they know it's an important ancient relic. So they've got to keep it somewhere, somewhere safe.

Storing it in the Vatican Archives probably wouldn't work, because a lot of scholars and experts in ancient documents have access to them, and they couldn't risk somebody like that finding the relic. They could have kept it in a safe somewhere, I suppose, but again any safe would be an obvious target for thieves, or even for some thieving Vatican official who happened to know the combination and decided to make a few quid on the side. Some of those reports you told me about earlier involved a corrupt official or somebody else inside the Vatican who either carried out the theft or helped those people who did the job, so the men who live and work inside the Holy See aren't what you might call paragons of virtue, obviously.

"No, I think they could well have decided that their best option was to hide the parchment more or less in plain sight. I think that when the thieves picked up the Tasso manuscript, there weren't 152 sheets there, but 153. After all, it was in a locked display case and so wouldn't have been accessible to a researcher, and I doubt if anybody was going to bother periodically checking the exact number of sheets in the case. This also fits in with what we know happened to the parchment later on. The thieves must have delivered the items they'd been told to steal, and this one odd sheet that was clearly nothing to do with Tasso or Petrarch was then discovered. The man who'd hired them probably wouldn't want it so, as we said earlier, they most likely tried to flog it themselves, but when they had no takers they simply locked it in the box, hid it and then forgot about it."

"Yes," Bronson agreed. "And years later, when the house in Cairo was being demolished, out pops the box. But I've no idea how the Vatican managed to find out that the manuscript had surfaced again. But however they did it, what they found was a worst-case scenario. The manuscript was in the possession of an Egyptian antique dealer who was almost certainly going to sell it to the highest bidder, and that was something that the Vatican couldn't permit. Everything that's happened since then has been a direct result of whatever research Husani or the first market trader—Kassim, was it?—did once they'd got their hands on the parchment. Something or someone must have alerted the Vatican, which immediately took steps to try to recover the relic and incidentally eliminate anyone who knew anything about it."

He looked over at Angela again.

"We still don't have any idea what the text says and we should hit the road pretty soon," he reminded her. "Unless you've got somewhere with the translation, that is."

Angela shook her head.

"Not really," she replied. "It's too disjointed. There are too many sentences where either the verb or the subject—or sometimes both—is invisible. The only thing I can say for certain is that whatever event is being described is not actually about Joseph himself, though I've seen his name written on it in two places and he's obviously involved somehow. It's actually about somebody else, but right now I've no idea who it is, or what's really going on, except that it could possibly be a trial."

"A trial? You mean like in a court of law?" Bronson asked.

Angela shrugged. "I don't know. It's just that some of the expressions sound like the kind of thing you might hear during a trial. But who's on trial, and for what offense, I have no idea."

92

For a few minutes after he'd ended the phone call to the man in Madrid, Morini did nothing, just sat on the bench with the phone in his hand, staring down at it as if the slim fusion of metal and plastic and silica could somehow provide the answers that he sought. But his mind was racing.

The body count was rising. Two people dead in Cairo, then the market trader Husani gunned down in Madrid, and now two more men—and he didn't even know their names, he realized at that moment—also shot to death. That made five so far and, from what Tobí had told him on the telephone, the Spaniard was utterly determined to add the names of Christopher Bronson and Angela Lewis to that tally. And still they were no closer to recovering the relic than they had been at the very start of the operation.

In fact, they were probably a good deal further away, because Bronson and Lewis would definitely now be very well aware of what was going on and would be on their guard. And this Bronson man didn't seem to be scared of taking the fight to them.

Morini had no idea what forces or numbers of men Tobí would be able to deploy in an attempt to track down Bronson and Angela Lewis, but he did know that Spain was a very big country with a vast road network, and he guessed that trying to locate those two people, even if details of their car were known to all the watchers, would actually be a very difficult task. And if they did manage to elude their pursuers in Spain, and somehow made it into France, it would be even harder—the French road system was even more complex and convoluted than that in Spain.

Morini knew he would have to make yet another telephone call to the Englishman, to update him on the utter failure of the actions his colleagues had taken in Spain— the other man had made it very clear that he needed to be kept fully informed at all times. But was it now time to call a halt to the operation? If Bronson and Lewis somehow managed to get out of Spain, would it be better to just let them go? That was one consideration, and yet the threat posed by the ancient text on the parchment was as potent as ever, and the consequences of the secret it held becoming known simply terrified Morini.

For several minutes, Morini tossed the arguments backward and forward in his head, and then decided to do nothing. He would wait to hear from the Spaniard again and, with any luck, the next telephone call he received might well bring him the news that he sought: that the troublesome pair from England had been eliminated and the parchment recovered.

That night he would, he knew, yet again pray for guidance, for some kind of confirmation that the events he'd set in train were justified in the eyes of the god he thought he still worshipped.

93

"So who was this Jerod of Cana?"

They were sitting in the hotel room discussing a few of the words that Angela had managed to translate.

"He might have been a lawyer of some sort," she replied, "if this is a record of a trial or legal proceeding, or maybe just a minor official. He probably spoke Greek because Judea had been Hellenized for some time and that language was spoken there almost as commonly as Hebrew. And he also spoke at least some Aramaic as well, because according to this sentence on the parchment he describes Yusef—Joseph—as a *naggar*."

"And that means what?"

"It's a loanword from Aramaic that has two different but related meanings. The literal translation would be a 'craftsman,' but it also had a metaphorical interpretation as a scholar or a learned man, which I suppose is another way of looking at a craftsman—somebody who works with words rather than wood, say. And that's interesting, because I had expected to find the word *teknon* being used instead. That's not Aramaic. It's a Greek word that also means a craftsman or a technician, a man who worked in metal or wood, and it was almost certainly the root of the modern English word 'technician.' But the point is that it has no other meaning."

"I don't see the significance."

"It's very simple. Forget the parchment for a minute and think back to what you were told when you were at school, during your religious instruction classes, or whatever they were called. What job was Jesus Christ supposed to have followed?"

"He was a carpenter, of course. Everybody knows that."

Angela nodded. "Of course everybody knows that," she replied. "And actually everybody's got it wrong. When you go back to the oldest known sources, to the original Aramaic, it's quite clear that whoever translated the word *naggar* assumed that the correct meaning was the literal one, that Jesus was a craftsman of some kind, a carpenter or metalworker, and more importantly so was his father.

"But actually it's almost certain that that was a mistranslation, and the word they should have used was the metaphorical meaning, a 'scholar.' Quite apart from anything else, at one point Jesus was supposed to have begun teaching in the synagogue, and there is no possible way that any carpenter would have been permitted to do that. But a scholar would actually have been expected to carry out this kind of duty, and nobody would have thought it unusual in any way."

Bronson shook his head.

"I still don't see why that's important."

"It's important," Angela said, "because it possibly shows that the parchment is contemporary with whatever event it's describing, and not something written much later. In particular, because the carpenter story became established quite quickly, it would be far more likely for a later writer to describe him as a *teknon*, using the Greek word, rather than the Aramaic *naggar*. It's not proof positive, of course, but it does suggest—at least to me—that the parchment is most probably an authentic and contemporary record of something. We just don't know what."

94

Bronson drove the Renault, bearing the stolen number plates, through the streets of Madrid, constantly checking his mirrors and all around for potential problems. So far so good. As he had hoped, their hotel seemed to have been safe.

By ten thirty they were clear of the city—most of the traffic heading in the opposite direction, back into Madrid—and steadily heading northwest in the general direction of Valladolid. That wasn't the ideal route, bearing in mind their ultimate destination, but Bronson had guessed that the majority of the surveillance would be concentrated on the obvious routes out of the city, either due north toward Burgos and Santander where the overnight ferry to Britain docked or northeast toward Saragossa and on to the French border. Well before he reached Valladolid, he would swing northeast and head toward France, staying off the *autopistas*.

The farther they got from Madrid, the lighter the traffic became, and Bronson was able to maintain a reasonably high speed, although he was careful to keep within the limits. The last thing he wanted, with three unlicensed pistols about his person, was to be stopped by a member of the Guardia Civil for an offense as mundane as speeding.

He'd seen nothing to give him the slightest cause for concern up until that moment, so when he saw a sign for Segovia he took it without hesitation, because the sooner they started driving toward the French border the better.

"Where are we heading now?" Angela asked.

"Pau," Bronson replied. "It's just north of the border and the Pyrenees. Even sticking to the minor roads we should be able to get there by late this afternoon."

They stopped for petrol shortly after they'd made the turn toward Segovia. Bronson wanted to make sure they had plenty of fuel for the crossing of the Pyrenees, and adequate petrol in reserve, just in case at any point they had to make a run for it.

He was very aware that crossing the Pyrenees and later the English Channel would probably be the two most dangerous parts of the journey. There were very few roads linking France and Spain across the mountains, and putting a team of men on each one wouldn't involve an enormous expenditure of manpower. And the opposition would need an even smaller number of people to cover both the Channel Tunnel terminal and the handful of ferry ports on the French side.

They could lose themselves in the byways of France without any difficulty—Bronson knew that. But first they had to get across the border. The main problem was that the major roads, or *autopistas*, that would allow them to travel quickly, also had barriers at each exit. These were obvious places where a watch could be kept for them, and where he would have nowhere to go if the opposition suddenly appeared in front of him.

But he had another idea. A car is a lethal weapon: over a ton of metal moving at sixty miles per hour takes a lot of stopping. He'd checked the maps very carefully before they'd set out, and he'd been pleased to find that there was at least one fast road across the mountains that didn't have any barriers, due to a strange quirk in Spanish road-building practices.

"So where are you planning on crossing the mountains?" Angela asked, as though she was reading his mind.

"We're taking the E-7, which is an *autovia*. They look pretty much the same as *autopistas*, and are usually dual carriageways, but traffic like bicycles and tractors and stuff is allowed to use them. Once we get on that road, I can wind the speed up quite a bit and cross the border into France as quickly as possible without having to stop."

"I see what you mean," Angela said, looking down again at the road atlas on her lap. "That road is marked slightly differently. Do you think we'll have a clear run through?"

Bronson glanced across at her and shook his head.

"I genuinely don't know. It all depends on how many men they have available to watch the roads over the mountains. And there are a lot of other factors, a lot of unknowns, as well. They might have access to helicopters, or possibly some of the members of P2 might actually be serving as police officers or forest rangers, that kind of thing. But it's our best chance."

95

The *autovia* ran fairly straight once it had left a small development called Villanua, and a short distance farther on, positioned at the top of a small hill that offered an excellent view both up and down the road, a young Spaniard who called himself "Juan" had been positioned with very specific instructions, a two-way radio and a set of powerful binoculars. Every time a car appeared on the gentle bend in the road where the *autovia* emerged from Villanua, he'd focused the binoculars on it.

He'd been lying in that same spot for a little over seven hours, and had been told that he was to stay there until it was too dark to see the occupants of any of the passing traffic. He'd also been told that there was a bonus in it for him if he managed to identify the vehicle his people were looking for.

As another car came into view, he tensed, focusing the eyeglasses on it, concentrating on the occupants. The people who had given him his orders were well aware that their quarry might have changed the number plates, or even the car. Privately, he had assumed he was just wasting his time and that the man and woman in question would be taking another route out of Spain. But it looked as if he'd been wrong about that. It was immediately apparent that there were two people in the vehicle, a large dark-haired man behind the wheel and a pretty blond woman sitting in the front passenger seat.

Juan glanced down at the ground beside him, where he had a large A4-sized color photograph of the woman they were looking for, then looked back through the binoculars. It was them.

The moment he was certain, he picked up the two-way radio lying beside him and keyed the transmit button.

"*Miguel, soy Juan.*"

For a few moments, there was no reply, and he imagined the man at the other end of the radio link, a couple of miles farther up the valley, being almost startled by the hithertosilent radio suddenly bursting into life. Then a deep voice, speaking heavily accented Spanish, sounded from the earpiece.

"*Si. Dígame.* What is it?"

"I'm looking at them, right now. They're in a silver-gray Renault Mégane, the same car as before, but the number plates have obviously been changed."

When Miguel replied, his voice was tinged with excitement.

"Are you sure? Completely certain?"

"Yes. I've got a photograph of the woman. It's definitely her."

"Right," Miguel snapped. "And they're heading toward me? Give me the new registration number."

As the target vehicle passed in front of the hill where Juan was lying, he read the number into the radio microphone.

"Leave the next bit to me," Miguel said. "But make your way up here as quickly as you can. You know what to do when you get to the scene."

"Understood."

Juan slid the binoculars into the case, picked up the remains of his scratch meal and stuffed everything into a bulky rucksack. He slung the straps over his shoulders and started jogging quickly down the slope to where he'd parked his old Suzuki jeep, at the side of the rough track that ran almost parallel to the *autovia*. He would be on the road behind the two fugitives in less than two minutes.

As he ran down the hill, he smiled slightly. The bonus was his.

96

Miguel had chosen his position with some care. He knew that there were no major junctions on the *autovia* to the north of Villanua until the road reached Canfranc-Estaciòn. There it split, the E-7 *autovia* running through the Túnel de Somport while the mountain road continued north, winding back and forth along the sides of the valleys until it finally rejoined the E-7 at Les Forges d'Abel, a few miles north of the French border. He had no doubt that if the two fugitives decided to try to leave Spain that way, they would take the tunnel. And that meant he had to stop them before they reached the entrance and vanished from sight into the solid stone safety of the mountain.

He knew it wouldn't be easy. He'd had to choose a vantage point that was inevitably a compromise. He'd needed to be sufficiently far away from the road so that he would have a clear view of his approaching target and have time to take his shot, but close enough so that he would be reasonably certain of hitting it.

He had also wanted a long enough stretch in front of him so that if somehow he missed with the first round, he would have sufficient time to work the bolt on his favorite long-distance weapon, a Remington 700 BDL chambered for the powerful .270 Winchester round, and take his shot before the car moved out of sight. He needed at least two or three hundred yards' distance.

Hitting a stationary target at that range, with that weapon, would not be difficult. But hitting a moving target, especially a car that could well be traveling at over one hundred kilometers an hour, was more complicated. He would have to factor in the bullet's flight time, and aim his rifle not at where the target was, but at where it was going to be when the bullet arrived.

As soon as he ended his brief radio conversation with Juan, Miguel put the radio to one side. Then he lay down flat on the ground, getting as comfortable as possible, picked up the Remington, wound the leather strap around his left arm, formed a tripod with his two elbows, and stared down the valley through the powerful Schmidt & Bender 5-25 x 36 telescopic sight. At the same time he worked the bolt of the Remington to chamber the first round from the magazine, then checked that the safety catch was off.

Away to his right, three articulated lorries were moving slowly up the hill in the right-hand carriageway of the three-lane road, directly toward him, the elevated exhaust pipes belching black smoke into the clear mountain air. Behind them, a few cars were traveling much more quickly, making easier work of the incline.

Miguel focused on each one in turn. A white van was in the right-hand lane, traveling quite quickly, but with a line of three cars approaching in the center lane to overtake it. Behind the van was another light-colored car, the driver presumably waiting his turn before pulling out to go past the van.

Miguel quickly checked the overtaking vehicles, but

none of them fitted the description of the car he was looking for, so he moved the barrel of the rifle microscopically
until he could see the car boxed in behind the van.

He gave a sharp intake of breath as he recognized the
Renault badge and glimpsed the first part of the registration number on the plate below it. The make, model and
color were correct, and when he moved his head slightly
so that he could see the note he'd made during Juan's
call, he confirmed the number as well.

He looked again through the telescopic sight, lifting
his field of view slightly to look at the occupants as a final
check: a dark-haired man behind the wheel, a blond woman
sitting beside him. He couldn't make out their features,
but he had no doubt that Juan had identified them correctly.

Now all he had to do was pick his moment.

His orders had been unambiguous. The two Britons
were not to make it out of Spain. Ideally he was supposed
to just stop the car so that they could be taken alive to
allow Tobí to enjoy himself with them. If that wasn't
possible—and as far as he could see it wasn't an option
because of the speed of the vehicle—then their deaths
were to appear to be an accident. In either case, their
luggage was to be removed and handed over to Tobí as
soon as possible.

Making it look like an accident meant he couldn't simply drive a bullet through the man's chest. But at the
speed that the car was traveling, blowing out one of the
front tires would probably do the trick. The driver would
lose control and the car would hit the barrier on the
right-hand side and with any luck somersault over it and
hit the rough ground on the east side of the *autovia*. If
he was really lucky, it might even end up in the river at
the bottom of the valley.

All Miguel needed was a single clear shot at the front of the Renault, and it looked as if his opportunity was coming. The last of the three overtaking cars was now almost parallel with the target, and as soon as that vehicle moved clear, Miguel would take his shot.

He concentrated on the view through the telescopic sight, tracking the target as he estimated the approximate range to that point on the road, and calculated how much lead distance he would need to allow. In his peripheral vision, he saw another car beginning to approach from the south, but disregarded it. It was too far away to interfere with his shot.

The overtaking car moved clear, and for the first time since it had come into view, he could see all of the Renault clearly. As he had expected, as soon as the driver had the opportunity, he indicated left and began accelerating to pull out and overtake the van.

Miguel focused, allowed just a fraction more of an angle off to allow for the bullet's flight time, and then squeezed the trigger.

97

"It's a pretty road, this," Angela said, as Bronson began easing to the left to overtake the white van that they'd been following. "It's just a shame there's so much traffic on it."

Bronson nodded and glanced in his mirror. Almost immediately, he depressed the brake pedal to slow down the car and moved back into the right-hand lane.

"What's wrong?" Angela asked.

"Nothing," Bronson replied. "But there's a Porsche 911 with Barcelona plates coming up fast from behind us, and I'd rather he was in front. The English community in Catalonia call the locals 'Barceloonies,' I gather, because of the way most of them drive."

Then everything happened very quickly.

There was a loud bang from the white van Bronson had been planning on overtaking, and the entire rear of the vehicle lurched over to the left as the back tire blew. There was a squeal of brakes from behind them as the driver of the Porsche 911 saw the unexpected shape of the van suddenly starting to fill the lane he was driving along. Bronson reacted instantly, steering the Renault over to the right, toward the hard shoulder and out of any danger.

The van driver hit his brakes as well, and steered the vehicle back into the right-hand lane and then over onto the hard shoulder. The driver of the Porsche gave a short blast on his horn, and, as Bronson waved, he accelerated past the disabled van. Then Bronson pulled out again, the car quickly picking up speed.

On the hill on the opposite side of the *autovia*, Miguel cursed and worked the bolt of the Remington to chamber another round. The unexpected action of the Renault driver in pulling back after he'd started to overtake had meant he'd hit the tire on the wrong vehicle.

But that shouldn't matter. There was another straight stretch of road in front of the Renault, and now that the Porsche had almost vanished from sight, there were no other vehicles around to spoil his next shot.

Again, he tracked the front of the car through his telescopic sight, waiting for the vehicle's speed to build up enough to make the "accident" he had planned look like a viable outcome.

"Oh, shit," Bronson muttered, as he accelerated past the white van, which had now come to a stop on the hard shoulder. The left-hand door had opened and the driver was climbing out to inspect the damage, damage that was also obvious to Bronson. The bullet hole through the rear wheel arch was impossible to miss, and he knew that the jagged hole hadn't been there just seconds before.

"What?"

"We've got problems. That wasn't just a blowout on that tire. There's a sniper somewhere on that hill over to our left, and I'm guessing we're his target. Now he's got a clear shot at us and there's nowhere we can go."

Angela stared at him.

"Dear God," she murmured. "What are we going to do?"

"Hold on and hope for the best," Bronson snapped.

Bronson hit the brakes hard, dropping the speed of the car dramatically, then floored the accelerator pedal again.

"What are you doing?" Angela asked, her voice high with tension.

"If I keep going at a steady speed, that'll make us an easy target. If I'm erratic, he won't know how much lead to allow."

He braked again, and at the moment he did so there was a crack from directly in front of the car, and a small spray of disturbed tarmac rose into the air as a bullet impacted with the road surface a short distance over to their right.

Immediately Bronson accelerated hard.

"That was another bullet," he said.

He braked again, and swerved from side to side, swinging the car into the center lane before diving back over toward the hard shoulder and accelerating.

In his concealed perch on the hillside to the west of the *autovia*, Miguel cursed again as he watched the Renault saloon dance and jiggle around through the magnified optics of his telescopic sight. Obviously the driver had realized what was going on, and was doing his best to make the car as difficult a target as possible. And he was, the Spaniard had to concede, making a pretty good job of it.

One of the most difficult shots for any sniper is a fast-moving target crossing at right angles to the line of fire, and the degree of difficulty is enormously magnified if that target isn't moving at a steady speed.

Miguel picked his moment and fired again, but even as he squeezed the trigger he knew the bullet would miss, because again the car braked unexpectedly. He worked the bolt again, chambering the last cartridge from the four-round magazine, and adjusted his aim once more.

As the weaving Renault loomed in his telescopic sight again, Miguel came to a decision. His chances of hitting one of the tires while the driver was actively trying to avoid proceeding at anything approaching a steady speed were almost nil. It was time to forget about the "accident" scenario and simply take out the two occupants of the car. His people would just have to sort out the resulting mess as best they could.

He shifted his aim, lifting the barrel of the rifle slightly so that the graticule of his telescopic sight was pointing directly at the middle of the driver's side window, and at the shadowy figure behind the glass. Miguel allowed what he thought was the right lead, and squeezed the trigger.

And that shot, he knew, was a good one.

98

Bronson braked heavily, still continuing his erratic evasive action. As he did so, there was a loud bang. The car shuddered as the bullet from the sniper's rifle ripped into the thin metal of the bonnet and plowed its way out through the right front wing.

Angela squealed in fear and clutched at Bronson's right arm as she saw the metal tear open just inches in front of the windscreen.

"Are you OK?" Bronson asked anxiously, glancing at her as he again started to weave and accelerate.

"Yes. Yes, I'm fine. God, he's going to get us!"

Bronson checked the instruments, in case the bullet had ruptured a hydraulic line or torn apart a section of the electrical system, but saw no abnormal readings.

He braked firmly, then accelerated again, keeping his foot hard down on the pedal, and swung the car over to the left, almost into the southbound left-hand lane of the road and drove straight toward the oncoming traffic.

"What are you doing now?" Angela demanded, stifling a gasp, her eyes wide and staring as a maroon-colored saloon car swept past them in the opposite direction, the driver's hand pressed firmly on the horn.

"Trying to save our lives," Bronson said. "Hang on."

He braked hard again, twitched the steering wheel to the right, and then accelerated as hard as he could.

Miguel knew that his last shot had hit the car, but he didn't know where. He'd been expecting to see the side window shatter, but that hadn't happened. It was possible the bullet had dropped farther than he'd expected, but the car was continuing with undiminished speed, so presumably the round hadn't hit the engine or any other vital component. He still had to stop it, somehow.

Miguel shook another four rounds out of the box of ammunition on the ground beside him, fed all of them into the magazine as quickly as he could, loaded the first cartridge and immediately brought the rifle back to the aim. In under half a second, the now familiar shape of the Renault saloon filled his telescopic sight and again he concentrated on nothing but the sight picture.

And now, it looked as if the driver was trying to rely just on speed to get away from the ambush, because the car seemed to be accelerating steadily, no sign of braking or even weaving.

Miguel smiled slightly. That, he knew, was definitely a big mistake. He didn't care how fast the car was traveling; there was no way it could outrun a bullet from his rifle. He allowed a little more lead to account for the increased speed of the target, took a breath, released about half of it to still his breathing, checked the sight picture once more and squeezed the trigger.

Then the nose of the Renault dipped again under braking, but Miguel knew the driver had reacted too late.

99

Bronson transferred his foot from the brake to the accelerator pedal, slammed the gear lever into third, and continued to drive the car as fast as he possibly could. He'd seen their possible salvation.

"I thought you needed to brake and weave," Angela asked, a tremor in her voice. "Why are you going so fast?"

Bronson kept both hands on the steering wheel, and gestured with his chin.

"To get alongside them," he replied, "as quickly as possible. He won't be able to shoot through them."

Angela stared through the windscreen as realization dawned.

"And I never even saw them coming," she said.

Miguel recoiled involuntarily from the rifle. Something totally unexpected had just happened. He'd been expecting to see the impact of the bullet on the driver's door—he had no doubt that that last shot would end the matter—but instead his sight picture had suddenly filled with a flat white object moving across his field of vision with a blur of speed.

He looked up, away from the telescopic sight and realized in that instant precisely why the driver of the car had been traveling so fast and with minimal evasion. Heading south, down the western side of the *autovia*, was a long line of articulated lorries, a rolling bulletproof shield that would protect the target vehicle until it was almost certainly out of range. With the trucks doing perhaps seventy to eighty kilometers an hour downhill and heading south, and with the car on the other side of the *autovia* heading north at—probably—by now well over 120 kilometers an hour, Miguel knew he had no chance of hitting it in the split-second gaps when the car might be fleetingly visible to him.

For a moment, he wondered where his last bullet had hit, but in a few moments it became perfectly obvious. The driver of the leading truck switched on his hazard warning lights and began braking the vehicle to a halt on the hard shoulder just off the carriageway. Miguel swung his rifle around so that he could take a look at it through the telescopic sight, and the hole in the right-hand side of the truck's engine compartment was immediately obvious. His shot had been good, he knew that, but in that fraction of a second before it should have hit the Renault saloon, the lorry had simply driven into the bullet's path.

Miguel didn't hesitate. As soon as the driver of the truck saw the bullet hole, he would know exactly what had happened and would immediately call the police. It would take them time to get there, but he needed to be long gone from the hillside before that happened. The car was by now out of range and invulnerable. Cursing, he unloaded the rifle and slipped it into the carrying case, picked up the ammunition and all of the spent cartridges that had been ejected from the weapon, and made his way as quickly as he could off the hill.

He'd have to make the call straightaway. Now it would all depend on what forces they would have time to mobilize against this man and woman in France. But that wasn't his problem.

100

The posted speed limit at the entrance to the Somport Tunnel was 80 kilometers per hour. As Bronson turned on the headlamps and swung the Renault around the gentle left-hand curve that led into the tunnel entrance, the car was traveling at almost double that, well over 140 kilometers an hour. He applied the brakes and the Renault immediately began to slow.

"Are we safe now?" Angela asked.

"I hope so," Bronson replied. "This tunnel crosses the mountains and comes out north of the Pyrenees. We should be out before they can get people there. Unless there's someone posted there already . . ."

A little under six minutes after Bronson had driven the Renault into the southern end of the tunnel, they drove out into bright late-afternoon sunshine in France with a total lack of drama or excitement. Nobody shot at them, and no cars followed them, a situation that continued all the way down the valley until they reached Oloron-Sainte-Marie, where Bronson finally began to feel safe.

"They won't find us now," he said, "unless we're really

unlucky. There are just too many roads that we could take—there's no possible way they can cover every one."

"So what now?" Angela asked. "Do you want to stop somewhere here?"

Bronson shook his head.

"Not yet," he replied. "We'll drive on for a while and get to the north of Pau and Tarbes, deep into the countryside. Then we'll find a small hotel and stop for the night. These days, you don't have to show a passport or any form of identification at French hotels, and we'll pay cash, so as long as the car isn't visible from the road we should be safe enough."

About two hours later, Bronson drove into a layby just outside Cadours and did what he could to conceal the damage the sniper's bullet had done to the car, knocking the twisted metal more or less back into shape and smearing mud over it.

Then they drove on, continuing northeast into the countryside, finally finding a room in a quiet *chambre d'hôte* not far from Carmaux. It was approached by a long drive, and not even the house was visible from the road.

The room was a large double with a tiny balcony facing west, and they enjoyed the luxury of sitting on it to watch the last rays of the sun sink below the horizon while they ate the baguette and blue cheese Bronson had bought in a garage en route. It wasn't a gourmet dinner by any standard, but it tasted as good as anything either of them had ever eaten before.

Then they fell into bed together and made love with the kind of desperation that only comes when both parties realize that it might be for the very last time.

101

Early that evening, Antonio Morini again left the Vatican, his mobile phone in one pocket of his civilian jacket. He had followed his usual timetable earlier that afternoon and sat in a café for half an hour, waiting and hoping for a call from Tobí in Madrid, but had heard nothing.

When he'd finally tried calling the Spaniard's mobile, the system told him that it was unavailable. That in itself could have been encouraging, because it might mean that they'd found and stopped Bronson and Lewis in some remote area of the Pyrenees. On the other hand, it could also mean that Tobí had nothing to report, and had turned off his phone to avoid having to talk to him. Or it could mean something much worse . . .

And that was why the Italian had decided to make one further call, later in the day than his timetable dictated, to try to find out what was going on.

This time, Tobí answered almost immediately, but what he had to report was exactly what Morini hadn't wanted to hear.

"They're in France," the Spaniard said immediately once they were connected. "I'd positioned a team on the road to stop them close to the border, but they were lucky and got through. My shooter is certain he hit the car, but he obviously didn't do enough damage to stop it."

Morini felt sick to his stomach. Another failure. "Where did they cross the border?"

"North of a place called Jaca. The closest city in France to that location is Pau. But to save you asking the question, I have no idea where they might be now. From Pau there are *autoroutes* and fast roads going north, east and west and they could easily have reached Toulouse or Bordeaux within an hour or so of crossing the border, or taken some of the minor roads and lost themselves in the depths of the French countryside. I hope you have some surveillance teams in place already in France, because if you haven't I think the only way you'll be able to catch up with these people now is to intercept them when they try to cross the Channel."

"We were relying on you and your men to stop them," Morini said tightly, his anger and irritation showing.

"We did our best," Tobí replied, "and we very nearly had them. They just got lucky." He paused for a moment, then continued. "When you do catch up with these two, let me take care of Bronson. You owe me that much."

"You had your chance and you failed."

"Somebody is going to pay for that, so if I can't get to Bronson, I promise I'll get to you instead."

"Don't even think about it," Morini snapped, "and do not contact me again," he finished, and ended the call.

And then he knew he had no option. He had to call the Englishman.

As always, his call was answered in a matter of seconds, and he quickly relayed what the Spaniard had told him, finishing with the unwelcome news that the fugitives were now somewhere in France, and almost certainly safe from detection, at least until they tried to cross the Channel.

The Englishman's voice was cold and hard when he replied.

"I will ensure that suitable retribution follows this fiasco," he snapped. "Now, we know they're in France. I will alert three of our operatives there and then you can call each in turn with my orders. Even we don't have the manpower to cover France, but it will be a different matter when they try to cross the Channel. And if they do manage to get across to England, I have another plan. Anything else?"

"Only that your man in Spain threatened me if he wasn't allowed to take care of the male fugitive. Apparently one of the casualties in Madrid was his brother."

The Englishman snorted.

"I'll handle that," he said, and ended the call.

Within half an hour, Morini had received the text and made the calls, passing on the orders he'd been given. He'd received assurances from each of the three French members of P2 that surveillance operations would be put in place to cover all modes of transport leaving France.

Morini finished by talking to the P2 man in Paris, François.

"The one thing you haven't told me is what you want to happen to these two people if and when we manage to find them," François said.

Morini didn't hesitate this time.

"They are expendable. But the most important thing is the relic. That must either be recovered and handed to me or utterly destroyed, with proof. There are no acceptable alternatives."

François appeared unsurprised at the Italian's instructions.

"That's very clear, but you must also be aware that the price will be higher because of the greater risks involved."

Morini hadn't expected that question, but there was really only one possible answer.

"The budget is effectively unlimited, as long as you succeed."

102

Breakfast was exactly what they needed—a choice of strong coffee or hot chocolate, croissants and a couple of small *pains aux raisins*, fruit and yogurt—and they cleared the lot. Bronson paid the bill in cash, and they were back on the road by just before eight in the morning.

After traveling slowly for four hours on minor roads, weaving through village after village, they stopped for lunch: another selection of sandwiches purchased in a cafeteria attached to a small service area, washed down by moderately suspect coffee.

"God knows what this service station food is doing to my complexion," Angela muttered as she swallowed the last of her chicken sandwich. "I'd kill for a nice crisp salad. I'll be really glad to get home. I can tell you that. How are we going to get across the Channel?"

"Probably a ferry. The danger with the Tunnel is that it's an entirely closed environment. If we're spotted when we drive onto the train, or even when we're waiting to embark in the car park, there's nowhere for us to go. At least on a ferry I'll have room to maneuver. The problem is that the Channel is a choke point, just like the Pyrenees, but even more restricted. And we have to cross it and get back to Britain, somehow."

"I did have one idea that I thought might work," Angela said.

"Let's hear it."

"As I see it, the trick really is to convince anybody who's following us that we'll be in one particular place at a certain time, while we're actually somewhere else."

She glanced at Bronson, who nodded slowly, lifting an eyebrow.

"So here's an idea. Later on today, when we're north of Rouen, say, why don't you ring up the ferry company on your mobile and use one of your credit cards to book a particular crossing for this evening. If you're right and these people are able to track our credit card transactions, that will tell them precisely when we'll be arriving at Calais, and so that's where they'll turn up to intercept us. In the meantime, suppose we don't go to Calais or Dunkirk or any other port, but instead head for Le Touquet.

"And what's there?"

"An airfield," she continued, "and it's a popular destination for private flyers taking day trips from Kent. A friend of a friend of mine—his accountant, actually— quite often flies down there for lunch in his own aircraft. If we turn up there this afternoon with some sob story about needing to get back to Britain as quickly as possible, I think we might find somebody with a couple of spare seats in his Cessna or whatever. And if we can't talk our way onto a private aircraft, there's a regular daily service to Le Touquet, operated from Lydd Airport in Britain, so we could buy seats on one of those aircraft as our last resort. Anyway, that's what I thought."

Bronson was silent for a moment, looking for flaws in her proposal. Then he glanced across at her.

"That's a bloody good idea," he said.

By five o'clock that afternoon they were on a back road near Abbeville, and the satnav was steadily counting off the kilometers to go to the Côte d'Opale Airport at Le Touquet.

Bronson hadn't been quite sure what to expect. Some small airfields he'd visited in the past had been little more than rights of way in a plowed field, but Le Touquet had a proper tarmac runway, taxiways, hard-standings and even a control tower. And there were a lot of light aircraft parked on those hard-standings, most with registration numbers beginning with "F"—meaning they were of French registry—but quite a lot with a "G" for Great Britain. The terminal building wasn't all that big, but it was certainly busy, and Bronson and Angela heard a mix of accents and languages as they moved around inside.

Bronson had suggested that Angela waited in the car outside while he tried to thumb a lift from some home-going Brit, but she'd pointed out very sweetly that most private pilots were men and she was far more likely to be able to persuade one of them to accept a couple of passengers than he was, as a bulky, menacing and hairy-arsed middle-aged man—a description he wasn't entirely happy with—so they had both gone inside the building, Bronson weighed down with their bags. Angela quickly homed in on a couple of likely men, standing talking together on one side of the lounge. They were unmistakably English, casually but expensively dressed and probably in their late thirties.

"I'll try them first," she said. "Try not to get into any trouble while I'm away."

"Trouble? Me?"

Bronson watched as Angela made her way over to the two men and held a brief conversation with them. After a minute or so, she turned and walked back to him.

"They can't help," she said, "because they only arrived a short while ago and they're staying in the area overnight. But they did suggest that another friend might be able to do something. He should be landing anytime now with a couple of passengers who are also overnighting in Le Touquet, and they're pretty certain he'll be going back empty. They gave me the registration number of his aircraft—I think they said it was a four-seat Piper PA28 Cherokee—and his name, Gary Burnside."

"That sounds ideal," Bronson said. "I'll get you a drink while we wait. Nonalcoholic, just in case."

"Just in case what?" Angela's normally cheerful disposition was almost restored, probably because nobody had shot at her so far that day.

103

François was beside his desk in his house in Saint-Cyr-l'École, just west of Versailles, looking down at a map of northern France. As he stood there trying to anticipate every possible move his targets might make, he received a telephone call that was entirely unexpected.

"It's me," the voice said, and François immediately recognized the man as a contact he had in the banking system.

"You have something for me?"

"I thought you might like to know that a short time ago a person named C. Bronson bought a ticket on the 19:55 Calais-to-Dover ferry using a credit card in that name. I checked the transaction, and the booking was made by phone, from a British-registered mobile. The registered address of the cardholder is in Tunbridge Wells in Kent, and that ties in with the information you gave me earlier. It's almost certainly him."

François was surprised by the news, to say the least.

"Thank you," he said. "Let me know if you hear anything else."

He put the mobile down on his desk and stared again

at the map. The more he thought about the information he'd just been given, the more suspicious he was about what it meant. As far as he could tell, there was no good reason why the fugitives would need to prebook a ferry ticket.

He should his head. The only reason why the man he was looking for should have purchased a ticket in advance was because he had devised some other means of crossing the Channel, and the one place he wouldn't be was at the Calais ferry port at five minutes to eight that evening.

He would have to look very carefully at all the other possible routes over to England. The Eurostar terminal in Paris was covered by his men. His eyes roamed down the ports, all of which he knew were already under surveillance. Another possibility, he supposed, was that they might try going to a fishing port or marina and hire a boat and captain to take them across the Channel. But that seemed unlikely, unless they offered a huge sum for such an illegal smuggling operation, or were *really* persuasive, the kind of persuasion, in short, likely to be backed up by a couple of firearms. That was just about possible, perhaps, but the Channel had blanket radar coverage, and he was quite sure that if any unauthorized vessel made the journey between the French and the British coastlines, it would probably be intercepted long before it reached port on the English side.

The more he looked, the more certain François became that the purchase of the ferry ticket was simply a ruse, something to distract him and his men from working out what was actually going on. He ran his eyes down the almost straight coastline shown on the map from Outreau down to Le Crotoy, where the coast of the country bent gently around to the west. And as he scanned the names and symbols on the map, one tiny mark almost leapt out at him, and he suddenly realized what he'd been missing. He'd covered the ports, and the railway stations and the airports, but there was another way that the two fugitives could leave France that had not until that moment occurred to him.

Immediately, he snatched up his mobile phone and dialed a number from memory. The moment the call was answered, he issued his instructions.

104

They didn't have long to wait. Only about fifteen minutes after Bronson had bought a couple of cups of coffee at the bar, a Piper landed smoothly on the runway and taxied across to the hard-standing close to the terminal building. Angela looked through the window at the aircraft, checking the registration as the pilot turned off the engine.

"That's it," she said. "Keep your eye on him when he comes in, and then I'll see if I can work my magic on him."

Three figures, two men and a woman, emerged from the aircraft, one of the male figures with a bulky carry-on bag in each hand, the woman carrying a slim handbag and wearing an attitude, and the other man holding a clipboard. It wasn't difficult to work out the dynamics of the trio. Inside the terminal, the man carrying the bags escorted the woman through the building and they walked through to the other side to where a taxi was waiting. The pilot completed whatever paperwork he had to do at one of the desks manned by officials, and then strode over to the bar and ordered a coffee.

The moment he was settled at a table, Angela squeezed Bronson's hand and then walked over to him.

A couple of minutes after she'd introduced herself and sat down beside him, she beckoned to Bronson, who walked over to the table and joined them.

"This is Gary Burnside," she said, "and this is my husband, Chris. Gary," she went on, turning to face Bronson, "has kindly agreed that we can hop a ride with him back to England, for the remarkably modest sum of one hundred pounds."

"Each, that is, and it'll be cash, please," Burnside emphasized, looking Bronson slowly up and down.

Bronson nodded.

"That shouldn't be a problem, though some of it might have to be in euros, if that's OK with you."

"Anything negotiable suits me, squire. And I gather you're in a bit of a hurry, so as soon as I've put myself on the outside of this cup of hot brown, we'll kick the tires, light the fires and get going."

"You're ex-military, aren't you?" Bronson asked.

"How did you know?"

"I was in the army," Bronson said, "and I've only ever heard people in the military refer to coffee as 'hot brown.' And 'kick the tires' sounds like an RAF expression."

"It is. 'Kick the tires, light the fires, check in on Guard, last one airborne's a sissy' is the full unexpurgated version. But you're right. I did a short-service commission in the Crabs, went through Cranwell, learned to fly a Hawk and then had a slight difference of opinion with my lords and masters, which is why I'm now tooling around the sky in a red and white Piper, offering lifts to people I don't know."

"Well, we're both very grateful, and we are in a hurry, that's true."

Burnside drank the last of his coffee and stood up.

"Then let's get moving," he said, and led the way toward the doors.

"Do you need to file a flight plan or anything?" Bronson asked.

"Yes, but I've already filed for both legs, because you have to give four hours' notice of the return journey, which is irritating for such a short trip," he replied. "I do this flight on a regular basis, ferrying people backward and forward, and I'd only planned to be here at Le Touquet for about fifteen minutes."

"But you were planning on flying back empty," Angela pointed out. "Will it be a problem having us in the aircraft as well?"

"Only if you want it to be," Burnside replied, "and if we tell them. I've never been met by any British Customs officers when I've landed after one of these trips, and if we keep quiet about the fact that you're in the aircraft, the chances are nobody will ever find out. The Frogs aren't bothered, and probably won't even notice you climbing into the aircraft. I'll just bend the rules slightly. Unless, that is, you're especially keen to answer a lot of stupid questions from a man in a peaked cap and take the risk of a full-body cavity search?"

Bronson grinned at him.

"I think we can probably forgo that particular pleasure," he said.

Within twenty minutes, Burnside had taxied the Piper to the end of the runway, paused to allow another aircraft to land, then obtained takeoff clearance from the local controller in the tower, swung the Cherokee onto the runway and pushed the throttle fully forward.

The ribbon of tarmac unrolled surprisingly quickly in

front of them, and within a matter of seconds, he was able to ease back on the control column and lift the aircraft into the air. Burnside continued the climb to a west-bound semicircular flight level, then leaned back in his seat, his eyes never still as his gaze swept across the controls and instruments, then the view outside the cockpit, and then repeated the same sequence again.

Bronson and Angela were sitting in the seats behind the pilot. They'd tried as far as possible to remain out of sight.

"It's very noisy," Angela almost shouted.

Burnside half turned in his seat and smiled at her.

"An inevitable consequence of sitting about three feet away from an unsilenced engine running at almost full power, my dear," he said. "It's when it all goes quiet up here that you need to start worrying."

"I completely forgot to ask you," Bronson said. "Where will we be landing?"

"My home base is Redhill Aerodrome. That's only a couple miles or so outside Reigate. You can pick up a taxi easily enough and there are plenty of railway stations if you need to go further."

"Excellent. That should do us nicely."

As the Piper had taxied away from the hard-standing, a French-registered car drove quickly down the approach road to the Le Touquet airfield and stopped in the car park outside with a brief squeal of its tires. The driver got out and scanned the other vehicles that were parked there, clearly looking for one car in particular.

After a few moments, a grim smile appeared on his face, and he strode across the car park to where a Renault Mégane was standing. He took a small piece of card out of his pocket and compared the registration number of the vehicle in front of him with the details he had written down several hours earlier. Immediately, he took out his mobile phone and dialed a number, and while he was waiting for the call to be answered he looked all around the car, noting the track of the bullet that began in the bonnet in front of the passenger's seat and ended with a jagged tear in the right-hand front wing.

"I'm at Le Touquet now," he said, as he turned and walked steadily toward the terminal building. "The car is in the parking area here. I've checked the number and it's the same as we were told by our friends in Spain, and there's a bullet hole just in front of the windscreen, passenger side. What do you want me to do?"

His steps slowed as he listened to the instructions he was being given, and he came to a complete halt a few moments later.

"Done," he said, and ended the call.

Inside the terminal, the man checked every single person, looking for anyone who resembled the descriptions he had been given. It was soon obvious that his quarry was nowhere in the building, so they must have already left. But no matter. There was still a second part to the plan.

He strode across to the other side of the room, stopped a man wearing light blue trousers, a short-sleeved white shirt and a badge that identified him as a local official. The searcher produced his own documentation and asked a couple of questions, with the result that less than five minutes later he was studying the ATC logbook, which recorded details of all takeoffs and landings and, more importantly, listed the destination airfields of every plane that had taken off from Le Touquet.

Three minutes after that, he had the information he needed, though he wasn't certain there was enough time left to do much with it. The records showed that the two fugitives could have been passengers on any one of six aircraft, and they were landing at four different airfields in Britain, probably too many to cover at such short notice.

But as he left the air-conditioned interior of the terminal building, he was already passing the information up the line by text message.

105

"Thank God for that," Angela muttered as Gary Burnside set the parking brake and switched off the engine of the Piper, and they watched the propeller spin somewhat jerkily to a stop.

It had been an uneventful, if bumpy, flight from Le Touquet, and there had been an intermittent crosswind at Redhill, so the landing had also been somewhat bouncy. Angela really hadn't enjoyed it at all. But now they were down on the ground again, and back in England, and for that Angela was supremely grateful.

The three of them climbed out of the aircraft and walked over to the terminal building, where they were completely ignored by everybody, and Burnside led them through to the main entrance, where two taxis were parked outside.

"There you go, my friend," Burnside said. "Not a Customs officer in sight, only a couple of licensed bandits in taxis. England awaits you, as indeed do I, or at least I await a certain amount of folding money, as we agreed."

Bronson handed over the slim wad of notes that he had prepared.

"There's one hundred in sterling and another hundred and fifty euros, which means you've made a bit on the deal. Have a drink on us. We really owe you, probably more than you'll ever know."

Burnside slid the money smoothly into his trouser pocket and nodded his thanks.

"I really didn't believe the inventive story your good lady span for me, but I thought she seemed like a decent person, and you're not so bad yourself. One word of warning, though. I know the weather's quite warm at the moment, but if I were you I'd try and make sure that you keep your jacket buttoned up. In that leather shoulder holster under your left armpit is what looks suspiciously like a Glock 17, and carrying one of those around this green and pleasant land is strictly forbidden. As in: 'do not collect two hundred pounds and go straight to jail' kind of forbidden. So take care."

Bronson nodded, smiling ruefully.

"It's a long story," he said, "and you really don't need to hear it, but thanks again."

After Burnside had walked away, Bronson paused, looking pensive.

"What's wrong?" Angela asked.

"We're here, but I'm not sure we're going to have it that easy. I don't want to climb into a taxi out there only to find that the driver is a hit man from P2 waiting for us with a sawn-off shotgun."

"You really think they could know we're here?"

"I have no idea, but we've come so far I really don't want to take any chances."

Bronson turned away and strode across to a general notice board. Pinned along the edges of the board were a number of business cards from companies offering various services, including taxis. He picked one of the cards at random, took out his mobile, dialed the number and held a short conversation.

"The car'll be driving down Kings Mill Lane in about five minutes," he said, ending the call. "We'll go out of the other entrance, just in case."

Moments later, they slipped out of the building, behind the waiting taxis, and made their way through the car park. Nobody appeared to be taking any notice of them, but they still moved cautiously, trying to keep out of sight.

They'd almost reached the road when they heard the sound of a car, accelerating hard, approaching the aerodrome and getting closer by the second.

"Our taxi?" Angela suggested.

"Probably not," Bronson replied. "This way."

106

Bronson quickly led her behind a white van that offered a place of concealment and also a vantage point from which they could see the entrance to the terminal, and the two taxis still waiting outside.

A dark-colored saloon car swept into the aerodrome, tires chirping as the driver took the corner at speed, and slammed to a halt behind the second taxi. Two men got out and ran inside the building.

"Walk quickly, but don't run," Bronson said, as he and Angela headed in the opposite direction.

"Bad guys?" Angela asked.

"Definitely."

They'd barely left the premises when they saw a taxi coming around the bend, heading toward them.

"That's our ride, I hope," Bronson said, glancing at the business card he was still holding to confirm the name of the firm.

Seconds later, they were sitting in the backseat as the driver headed toward Tunbridge Wells, Bronson checking behind them for any signs of pursuit.

When they reached Bronson's hometown, he directed

the driver to drop them near the center, not beside his house. As soon as the taxi had gone, he and Angela walked a couple of hundred yards to the nearest cab rank, waited until the first two taxis had pulled away, and then sat down in the third vehicle. That, Bronson hoped, would end any possible pursuit.

About half an hour later the second taxi pulled up outside a hotel on the southern outskirts of Sevenoaks and they climbed out. They picked a double on the first floor at the back of the building, near the rear fire escape.

"We could have gone to your place," Angela said, "or don't you think that would have been safe?"

"I don't think we can take any chances, not until we've published this thing. Look, let's go down to the restaurant and see what they've got on offer, because I'm really quite hungry. Then we can decide our next move— somehow we have to get you and the parchment up to London and into the museum, get the relic authenticated and translated, and go public."

"And then we just let the Vatican and the Roman Catholic Church face the consequences," Angela finished for him.

107

Antonio Morini's feelings of desperation and guilt were growing more acute with every passing minute. He had hoped that, with the resources at the disposal of the French P2 organization, the two people he was chasing would finally have been identified and stopped while on French soil, but yet again they had done the unexpected and outsmarted their pursuers. And so, once again, he picked up the phone to dial the British mobile number.

When Morini ended the call, the Englishman put his mobile down on the desk in his study with exaggerated care, a white-hot anger burning inside him. Ever since he'd taken over the leadership of P2, he'd done his best to weed out the dross, to ensure that every member pulled his weight and acted promptly and efficiently in the best interests of the organization. But clearly, given what had happened in both Spain and France, he hadn't done enough. Heads, he had already decided, would definitely roll because of this shameful failure, and where P2 was concerned that was not a figure of speech.

In the meantime, the ball was now in his court, because the two fugitives were on his home turf and the responsibility for stopping them lay firmly and unequivocally on his shoulders. A fact that pleased him rather more than he'd expected.

Bronson and Lewis now had very little choice about what to do next. Lewis would have to decipher the text, and then they would probably go public with the results. And because of that, he knew exactly where to find them.

For the first time since Morini's initial call, he felt absolutely confident of success. And as a bonus, he would now have the chance to prove, once and for all, why he was the rightful leader of P2.

108

The British Museum was only a short distance down Great Russell Street, and once inside the building Angela led the way straight up to her office, where she followed her usual routine and set about grinding some Blue Mountain beans for her morning coffee.

"While this is brewing," she said, "I'll take the parchment to one of our specialist laboratories here and see what they can do with it. The coffee machine is right in front of you, there's a comfortable chair over by that bookcase, and I can see that there's a novel sticking out of your jacket pocket, so you can just relax until I get back."

"Sounds like a deal to me," Bronson said, and retired to the chair as instructed.

About twenty minutes later there was a knock on the door, which then opened, and closed again almost immediately, whoever was outside presuming that Angela's office was empty.

It was over two hours before Angela finally returned, pushing open the door and walking across to her desk, a cardboard folder in her hand.

"I hope that's fresh coffee," she said, glancing at the filter machine.

"It certainly is," Bronson confirmed. "I made it about ten minutes ago. Any luck?"

"Yes, definitely. I won't bore you with the technicalities of it, unlike the man in the laboratory where I've just spent the last one hundred and twenty tediously endless minutes. Suffice it to say that almost all the text showed up using a thing called multispectral imaging, where we could irradiate the parchment using a number of different wavelengths of light. We fed the results into our state-of-the-art digital image processing program, which analyzed what we've got and then spat it out to an ultra high-resolution laser printer."

"And that's without the technicalities, is it?"

"Yes," Angela replied firmly. "That really is the short, short version. Trust me on that."

"So have you got everything you need now?"

"Just about, yes. The only thing I haven't got is the complete translation of the text, which is what I'm going to do right now."

"And what then?" Bronson asked.

"Then, in order to go public with this, I'll have to write a short report about how the parchment came to be in my possession, then pass that up the line here in the museum with a request that a statement should be issued describing the relic and what the text says. If that's approved, then I'll have to work up a fully detailed report that will need to be checked and peer-reviewed, and then published in the appropriate professional journals. After that, we'll need to set up a display here in the museum which will house the parchment and all the information relating to it."

"So it won't be a fast process, then?"

"Nothing moves quickly in the world of academe, my friend. But what we will be able to do once I've written the report is ask the public relations people here to issue a press release outlining what we found and what we believe is the significance of the relic. And that, hopefully, will be enough to get us out of the firing line. Now just sit there and be quiet while I do the translation."

Angela took a number of photographs out of the folder and stared down at them through a magnifying lens, the pictures illuminated by two powerful shadow-free lights. Then she picked up the radiocarbon dating report that Ali had arranged to be sent to her and studied that for a couple of minutes, before going back to the parchment.

"I know you told me not to talk," Bronson said, "but you look puzzled. Is there anything wrong?"

"Hmm, there is one thing that's bothering me."

"Which is?"

"The language. There's a kind of signature block at the end of the parchment that identifies the author as a centurion, a fighting man. He would have been trained in the art of war, in battle tactics and swordsmanship and hand-to-hand combat, but he wouldn't have been trained to write in classical Latin. In those days, in the first century AD, the common man would have spoken and written—if they could write at all, which is by no means certain—a language called *sermo vulgaris*, or vulgar Latin. But the text on the parchment is more like classical Latin, which is a bit of a surprise."

"You don't mean that after all we've been through with that relic you think it's a forgery?"

Angela shook her head. "No, I don't. It's possible that the centurion was far better educated than most men in his position. Or, alternatively and this is perhaps even more likely, maybe the centurion didn't write it, but simply signed it, and had the text written by a professional scribe. In which case it's more than likely that classical Latin would have been used."

"Forget the signature block. What about the text itself? Does it contain some dreadful secret about Joseph?"

"Just a minute." Angela looked troubled, and was silent as she read through it again, scribbling as she went.

"No, not about Joseph," she said slowly, almost sadly. "He actually comes out of this incredibly well. And Jesus isn't involved either, except peripherally. No, this document is a bit of a surprise, because it's all about Mary."

109

"This parchment provides the first, and as far as I know the only, written account of one crucial event. If its authenticity can be established, then the most important single event that the Church has claimed as absolutely true over the centuries—and which is the cornerstone of its faith—will be proven to be wholly and completely untrue. A blatant lie, in fact."

Bronson looked somewhat skeptical.

"We've been here before, Angela. Remember the tomb of the liars?"

"I know, and I do remember. But this—this is different. You can argue about the actual status of St. Peter and St. Paul all day, but at the end of it you have to acknowledge that both of them were only bit-part players, people—if either of them ever actually existed, of course—who came along after the event. This is much more fundamental than that. This goes straight to the very heart of Christianity, and to the Catholic branch, in particular."

There was a brief double tap on the door, and then it swung open.

"You're back then? Have a good time?"

Angela looked up at her visitor and nodded.

"Hello, Charles," she said. "Yes, we're back and no, it wasn't particularly enjoyable. Have you heard from George Stebbins? Oh, sorry," she added, gesturing toward the easy chair as the man stepped fully into the room. "This is my husband—or former husband, I suppose I should say, Christopher Bronson. Chris, this is Charles Westman. He's a specialist in ancient weapons."

Westman nodded to Bronson and took another couple of steps forward.

"I think the museum received a somewhat garbled message from a hospital in Madrid," he replied. "I hear Stebbins had some kind of an accident over there."

Bronson laughed shortly.

"I suppose the word 'accident' does more or less cover it," he said.

"So what did happen?" Westman asked.

Bronson shook his head.

"I didn't get to know Mr. Stebbins very well, but I got the feeling that he would probably far rather tell you himself, in glorious high-definition color with all the lurid details, when he finally gets back."

Westman smiled briefly at Bronson and then turned his attention back to Angela.

"You left in an awful hurry," he said, "and I gather from the rumors running around this building that you were after some kind of an important ancient relic. Is it true? Did you get it?"

"We did get it," Angela said, "against all the odds. And this time, we really were up against it. We've been chased and shot at across most of Europe, and we were very lucky to get back here in one piece, with the relic."

"And is that it, that sheet of old parchment?"

Angela nodded.

"Yes, and as far as I can tell it's probably the real thing, though I was a bit bothered by the language that was used on it. I was expecting vulgar Latin and I got classical Latin, but with hindsight I think I can more or less understand why that was the case. And we've even got a radiocarbon date that ties up pretty well with what we found out about it."

"But what is it?" Westman asked, a faint hint of exasperation in his voice. "All you've told me is that you've got some Latin text written on a bit of parchment."

"For God's sake, Angela," Bronson interjected, "tell the man what it is before he explodes."

"Just winding you up a little, Charles—just like you do to me when you're in the mood." Angela pointed down at the piece of parchment on the desk in front of her, the photograph next to it that she'd used for the translation still illuminated by the two bright lights.

"What we're looking at here is a legal document, written by—or at the very least signed by—a centurion of the Roman Regiment *Cohors I Sagittariorum*. It's an account of the trial, a sort of impromptu field court-martial, of an archer named Tiberius Iulius Abdes Pantera, who was accused of the alleged rape and impregnation of a woman, shortly after the destruction of a town named Tzippori.

"I know that period isn't really your field, Charles, but in those days Roman soldiers accused of crimes were normally tried by their peers, and that appears to have been what happened in this case. According to the text on the parchment, the archer Pantera was accused by a man named Jerod of Cana, though he wasn't the plaintiff. The account doesn't identify exactly who or what Jerod was, but from the context I think it's fairly clear that he was either a lawyer of some sort or possibly just an educated man who spoke multiple languages, which he would have

needed to represent an Aramaic- or Greek-speaking Jew
in a tribunal conducted entirely in Latin."

"'Greek-speaking'?" Westman asked, a puzzled expression on his face. "Why would a first-century resident
of Judea have spoken Greek?"

Bronson glanced at him, but didn't speak.

"That's easy," Angela replied. "That area had been
Hellenized for some time. Anyway, Jerod of Cana presented his case on behalf of the plaintiff, a man named
Yusef bar Heli, claiming rape against the woman to whom
he was betrothed. I assume that Yusef didn't speak Latin,
which was why he was being represented by Jerod. Yusef
bar Heli is listed on the parchment as being a *naggar*, a
loaned Aramaic word meaning a craftsman, but which I
think was used here to indicate that he was actually a
scholar or a learned man, which was an alternative translation of the word."

Angela glanced at her handwritten translation of the
Latin, then continued.

"Anyway, Jerod presented his case against the archer,
surrounded by a group of soldiers from the legion who
would act as the jury in the case and, if necessary, as the
executioners. Even in those days rape was a very serious
offense under both Roman and Jewish law, and anyone
convicted of it was quite likely to be sentenced to death.

"On the other side of the coin, in the heat of battle,
rape and sexual assault were frequently used by members
of the legions as tools for subduing a conquered population, and in that context it was not only accepted but
often actually encouraged. The reason why this particular
case was brought at all was that it hadn't occurred during
the Roman attack on Tzippori, in 4 BC, but a few days
later. And there were two other factors as well. First, the
victim wasn't really a woman. She was a girl just barely in

her teens, a virtual child who had been betrothed to Yusef bar Heli. The second factor was that she was now pregnant.

"The other point about this, I suppose," Angela continued, "is that it was never going to be a fair trial. Pantera was almost certainly guilty of the rape charge and at any other time, and in any other place it is likely that he would have been convicted. But he was acquitted, because every Roman soldier watching those proceedings knew perfectly well that next time it might be him standing in the circle awaiting his fate, and for that reason alone hardly any of these trials-by-peers ever opted for a guilty verdict.

"Pantera claimed in his defense that he had indeed had carnal relations with the girl in question, but stated that she had lain with him willingly, and not once but on many occasions. According to the record, he even produced witnesses, soldiers from the legion, who supported his claim, so the result was never in any real doubt.

"At the end of the trial, the soldiers overwhelmingly voted 'not guilty,' and Pantera walked free. The centurion signed the report of the trial and I imagine it was sent off to Rome along with all the other bits of routine correspondence that were generated by the army of occupation in Judea."

Again Angela paused in her recital and glanced down once more at the old and discolored parchment in front of her.

"I have no idea what happened to the parchment after that. The most likely scenario is that it was filed away somewhere in Rome, and eventually, along with thousands of other ancient relics of various sorts, it came into the possession of the Vatican. At some point, somebody in the Holy See must have looked at it and realized its significance, and no doubt they hid it away in a place that they considered to be safe. But at some time within the last century, and most likely, Chris and I think, in nineteen sixty-five, a pair of thieves broke into the Vatican and carried out a burglary to order. They grabbed the items they had been told to steal, and we believe that the parchment was hidden in or under one of these two objects."

"So you mean it was stolen from the Vatican, but by accident?" Westman asked.

"Yes, that seems most likely. The parchment then vanished from sight, probably because the thieves didn't know what they had. It didn't surface until a few days ago in Cairo, when a local antique dealer got hold of it. We're not sure exactly what happened after that, but somehow the Vatican, or perhaps some other group of people within the Roman Catholic Church, learned that the relic had been found again and began taking immediate steps both to recover it and to eliminate anyone with any significant knowledge of it."

"That's all very interesting, Angela, but all you've done is describe the trial of a Roman archer who was accused of rape. Why would anybody, two thousand years after the event, care in the slightest about this?"

"You didn't pick up the reference, then?" she replied, looking at Westman. "The name Yusef bar Heli doesn't mean anything to you?"

He shook his head.

"According to some other accounts," Angela said, "he was also known as Yusef ben Yacob or Yusef bar Yacob. I also didn't mention the name of the victim, the young girl who was raped by Pantera. According to the parchment, her name was Maryam, but it's come down to us through history just as 'Mary,' just as we now know Yusef bar Heli simply as 'Joseph.' And their firstborn son, fathered not by Joseph but by Tiberius Iulius Abdes Pantera in an act of sheer unremitting evil and violence and lust, they named Yeshuah.

"Normally, that would be translated as 'Joshua,' but today almost everybody in the world knows that man not as 'Yeshuah bar Yusef,' or even as 'Joshua,' but as Jesus Christ."

110

When Angela finished speaking there was a long silence in the office, almost as if the words she had used and the names she had said had imposed a kind of stillness and gravity on that moment.

Bronson broke the silence first. "How did you know that Angela was referring to the country in the first century AD, Charles?"

Westman half turned to look at Bronson, who was still sitting in the chair beside the closed door.

"I know quite a lot of things," he replied, then turned his attention back to Angela. "And you believe all that, do you?" he asked.

"The story of the possible rape of Mary by a Roman archer has been around for a long time, for a lot longer, in fact, than some of the Gospels. The problem is that it's just been a story, with no documentary evidence or independent sources to back it up. At least, until now. As far as I can tell from my examination of this parchment, it's the real thing. It appears to be an entirely authentic contemporary account of the trial of the man who fathered Jesus. A fetus which today would probably have been legally aborted in most Western countries due to the violence of its conception.

"This proves beyond doubt that there was no immaculate conception, and no virgin birth. Instead there was a brutal assault by a heavily armed man against a defenseless child. And what I find particularly appalling about this, almost as appalling as the crime that is being described on this parchment, is the undeniable fact that the Vatican has known about this for decades, possibly centuries, yet chosen to cover it up. And what's more, when there was a chance that the text of this parchment would be made public, the Mother Church of Christianity sent a bunch of hired killers to recover the relic and to cover their traces by eliminating all those people who had knowledge of this object."

Westman nodded.

"I quite agree with you," he said. "That is simply appalling. Could I take a closer look at the parchment?"

"Of course," Angela said, and slid her chair slightly to one side so that Westman could stand beside her and see the relic clearly.

The ancient weapons specialist bent forward slightly and peered down at the parchment. Then he straightened up and glanced across at Bronson.

"I really must congratulate you," he said. "Your deductions and conclusions have been remarkable, quite remarkable. In fact, as far as I can tell from what you've said, you've only got one thing wrong in the entire story."

"And what's that?" Angela asked, puzzled.

Westman shook his head and reached into his jacket pocket.

"The Vatican didn't send hired killers after you, as you suggested, though of course it's true that the entire operation was initiated from Rome. Please remain seated and absolutely still, Bronson," Westman went on, drawing out a long knife with a dark and mottled blade, which he rested against the delicate white skin of Angela's throat.

"This blade of this dagger was forged from Damascus steel in a crucible in Persia in the middle of the eighteenth century," he went on, his previously gentle voice now edged with steel. "It is quite literally as sharp as a razor, and if my hand so much as twitches, your lady friend will be dead in less than a minute. And hers will not be the first life that this blade has taken in my hands."

111

Angela's eyes were wide with shock and terror as she looked helplessly across the room at Bronson, Westman's hand wrapped across her mouth to stop her crying out. She reached up and seized Westman's knife-hand, trying to push it away, but his grip was like iron, the muscles of his arm tensed and rigid.

"Now," Westman said, staring at Bronson, "as I was saying, it wasn't the Vatican who sent people after you in Spain and France. It was another organization that you may have heard of: P2, or *Propaganda Due*, a lodge that I have served all of my adult life, and that it is now my privilege to head. This is not the first time that the Church has called upon my services through P2, and I doubt that it will be the last."

The change in the man was extraordinary. The mild-mannered academic had vanished, and Westman's entire demeanor, even the way he was standing, seemed to ooze a sense of menace that was almost palpable. It was, Bronson realized belatedly, an extremely effective disguise. Who would suspect that a bumbling museum specialist would also be the head of an international criminal organization?

"You haven't made a very good job of it this time, have you?" Bronson snapped.

"There was nothing wrong with my plan, Bronson. You just got lucky, that was all, and some of my people didn't do as well as they should have. Every organization has trouble with its staff, even P2. Don't worry. As soon as I've finished here I'll be taking steps to ensure that those who failed me did so for the very last time."

"What do you want?"

"Now that," Westman replied, "is a very good question. The ideal solution would have been for the nineteen sixty-five robbery at the Vatican—you were right about that—not to have taken place, in which case the parchment would never again have seen the light of day. Unfortunately, as we don't own a time machine, we will have to improvise. Obviously I will have to destroy this relic, and all the other evidence that you've so cleverly collected. Once it's been reduced to ashes, that will ensure that it can never do any harm."

"You're quite happy, are you then, to acknowledge that Christianity is a sham, nothing more than a distorted superstition with no more credibility than witchcraft or devil worship?"

"That doesn't bother me at all. As far as I'm concerned, every religion is just a form of organized superstition. But look at it this way, because it might help ease your sense of injustice before you die. If you destroy the basis of Christianity, which this relic could do, hundreds of millions of people will lose their faith overnight. The results would be utterly catastrophic, affecting the population of virtually every country in the world. There would be enormous civil unrest, and there could very easily be hundreds of thousands, even millions, of deaths as a direct result.

"So I'm very much afraid that the two of you will suffer a couple of unfortunate accidents. I think probably you're going to have an argument, during the course of which you, Bronson, will punch Angela and she will fall badly and break her neck. In a fit of remorse, you will then take your own life by cutting your throat. All very sad, I'm afraid, but just one of those things."

Westman pulled Angela up to her feet, the pressure of the blade on her throat irresistible, and moved her round from behind her desk. He kept her body directly in front of him, using her as a shield. Then he stopped in the middle of the office and looked at Bronson.

"I'll destroy the parchment last, of course, at my leisure, which means it's now time to arrange your untimely demise."

As he spoke, Westman switched the dagger to his left hand, his movements slick and practiced, keeping the edge of the blade just millimeters from Angela's throat the entire time. Then he reached into his jacket pocket and took out a small revolver, which he aimed at Bronson.

"I gather from my colleagues in Spain that you may well be carrying a pistol, Bronson, so kindly stand up slowly, remove it from whatever holster or pocket you have it in, and drop it on the floor in front of you."

Bronson got slowly to his feet and stood in front of the easy chair, but he made no move to reach for his weapon.

"Take out your pistol and do it now," Westman ordered sharply.

Bronson opened the left side of his jacket to reveal the shoulder holster with the Glock 17 nestling in it.

"Hold your coat open with your right hand, and take out the weapon with your left hand, finger and thumb only."

With Angela a bare fraction of an inch away from death, Bronson knew he had absolutely no choice. But he made one last appeal to the man's reason.

"You don't have to do this, Westman. As far as I'm concerned, you can destroy the parchment but simply let us go. That way you get rid of all the proof, and nobody gets hurt."

"If only things were as easy as that. I know it's a cliché, but the two of you really do know too much for me to allow you to live. Now drop that pistol on the floor and kick it over toward me."

Bronson eased the weapon out of the holster and dropped it onto the floor of the room. Then he kicked the pistol, which slid well out of his reach, over toward Westman.

"Good. I'm pleased to see that you can follow simple instructions, because I will have another one for you in a minute or two."

Westman relaxed slightly now that he had disarmed Bronson, and appeared to consider the situation.

"I hadn't actually expected you to be here this morning, Bronson, and your presence in this room does make things a little more awkward for me. I had hoped I could have arranged Angela's accident, taken the parchment and the other stuff and just slipped quietly away. I suppose the real question is how much you love her. Do you, for example, love her enough to cut your own throat? If you do, and if you do that right now, then I promise you that she won't suffer when I kill her."

"Are you out of your mind?" Bronson demanded.

"Not at all. It's a very simple matter. You're going to die—be in no doubt about that—but I'd rather not shoot you because of the noise. Angela Lewis here is also going to die. The only thing in doubt is how. If you do as I tell you, you'll suffer a sharp pain in your throat as the knife cuts into your neck, but if you do it properly and sever the carotid artery, you'll be dead inside a minute, so you won't have to suffer for long.

"Angela, on the other hand, could take a very long time to die. I've wanted to bed her for the last couple of years, but for some reason you've always been in the background, like some kind of a looming threat, and she's never responded to my advances. But now, in these circumstances, I don't think she's in a position to refuse. And I'd probably enjoy it just as much, maybe even more. So I'm offering you a choice. Kill yourself now, and I give you my word that I won't do that. I'll just break her neck, that's all."

Bronson stared at the man, scarcely able to believe what he was hearing. Then he glanced at Angela's face, and as he did so she gave a quick but deliberate wink.

Then she spoke for the first time since Westman had grabbed her, her voice laced with fear and panic.

"Chris, please. God knows what he'll do to me if you don't agree. If you love me, really love me, do this one last thing for me."

Bronson stared at her, an expression of disbelief on his face. He wasn't sure what she had in mind, but he knew she must be planning something.

"I give you my word that she won't suffer," Westman said again. "That's a promise."

Bronson shook his head and closed his eyes briefly. He just hoped Angela knew what she was doing. Then he looked back at Westman and nodded.

"Give me the knife," he snapped.

"I thought you'd see reason," Westman said. "You must be very proud of him, Angela."

He brought the revolver up to Angela's shoulder, so

that the muzzle rested against the right-hand side of her head; then he moved the knife away from her throat and tossed it gently across the room toward Bronson.

And at that moment, as Westman's attention was directed toward Bronson, Angela moved. She whirled around to her right, hitting out at Westman's right arm with the blade of her forearm, instantly knocking the pistol to one side.

"Now, Chris," she shouted.

But Bronson was already in motion. Because as well as the pistol in the shoulder holster, he also had a second Glock tucked into the waistband of his trousers in the small of his back. As Angela moved rapidly away from Westman, ducking down and away from him, diving for cover, he reached behind him and smoothly drew the weapon.

Angela's sudden and unexpected action had taken Westman by surprise, but he was reacting quickly, bringing his revolver around to bear on Bronson again, his finger tightening on the trigger as he did so.

Westman fired first, but his pistol still wasn't accurately aimed, and the bullet slammed into the wall of the office about eighteen inches from where Bronson was standing.

Bronson took the extra tenth of a second to make absolutely sure that the muzzle of the Glock was aimed directly at Westman's center of mass. And then he squeezed the trigger, twice, the heavy crack of the larger nine-millimeter cartridge much louder than Westman's small-caliber revolver.

He didn't need a third shot. Both of his bullets had slammed into Westman's torso, the first just below his rib cage, the second a few inches higher.

For the briefest of instants, the other man stayed on his feet, his pistol dropping to the floor from nerveless fingers.

"That wasn't supposed to happen," he murmured.

Then he tumbled backward, collapsing on the floor in an untidy heap. He gave one deep and pain-filled moan, and then stopped breathing. ·

"Quickly," Angela snapped, scooping up Bronson's discarded Glock and the dagger with the Damascus steel blade. "This place will be swarming with people in minutes. Give me your shoulder holster and his revolver."

In a few moments, Angela had placed the holster and all the weapons apart from the Glock Bronson had fired at the bottom of a cardboard box, and emptied another box of potsherds on top of it. Then she almost ran to the door and wrenched it open.

"I'll hide these in the laboratory," she said. "Get his fingerprints on that pistol."

"I've always said she's good in an emergency," Bronson murmured to himself, and bent down beside the dead man.

He wiped the outside of the pistol, placed it firmly in Westman's limp right hand and did his best to transfer his fingerprints onto the weapon. Then he grabbed it around the slide, as if he'd been struggling for possession of it, and then held it in a firing position and dropped it near the dead body. And that was pretty much all he could do.

As he straightened up, Angela stepped back into the room. Behind her Bronson could already hear the sound of running footsteps, getting closer.

Angela stepped behind her desk, stuck her tongue between her teeth and then slapped herself twice across the cheek, hard, before slumping back in her chair. A thin trickle of blood emerged from one corner of her mouth.

"You went to the loo," she said. "When you came back, Westman was attacking me and you grabbed him to pull him off me. He pulled out the pistol, the two of you struggled, and the gun went off."

"Twice?" Bronson asked, raising his eyebrows.

"Maybe it's got a hair trigger or something. I don't know. Guns are your thing. Think of a good reason."

Moments later, the door burst open and a burly security guard stood framed in the opening, a two-way radio in his hand. He took one glance into the office and spoke urgently into the radio.

"We'll need an ambulance and you better call the police as well," he added as he noticed the pistol lying on the floor. "Are you all right, miss?" he asked, seeing the blood trickling from Angela's mouth.

And then it seemed as if the whole world arrived in the office, and the rest of the day passed in a blur of questions and uniforms and still more questions.

112

In the train on the way back to Sevenoaks, Bronson and Angela sat in the half-empty carriage in virtual silence, both still shell-shocked by the events of that day. As the train accelerated away from Orpington, Angela stirred herself.

"What can we do, Chris?" she asked. "I've known Charles Westman for years. He was the last person I would ever have suspected of being involved with any organization more dangerous than the local Rotary Club. And he turns out to be the head of a group that rivals the Mafia for its ruthlessness. If you can't trust somebody like him, who the hell can we trust?"

"I know. It seems completely unbelievable."

"So what can we do?" she asked again. "I don't want to spend the rest of my life jumping at shadows, but we could end up doing that if we make this public."

"I suppose it all depends on how important the truth is," Bronson said. "I know your opinion of the parchment, but so far nobody else knows what you've found. That does provide us with a couple of options."

"What options?" Angela asked, a puzzled frown on her face.

"Well, you might not like it, but I did have one idea."

113

Antonio Morini sat in his office at the Vatican and read again the Italian translation of a short report he had just been sent. It had been released by the British Museum in London and had been headlined "Early Second Century Forgery Discovered." He'd read the text three times in Italian and had found the original English version on the Internet and had read that twice as well, and he still wasn't sure what to make of it.

Could it be possible that the parchment that had caused so much consternation in the corridors of the Vatican when it had been stolen in 1965 had actually been a forgery all the time? Techniques for examining ancient documents had improved out of all recognition over the previous half century. It was, he supposed, at least possible that what had been believed by the Vatican's scholars to be a contemporary description of a trial held two thousand years ago could actually be shown using modern methods to be nothing of the sort. That was one possibility, and there was no real reason to doubt it. The second option was that the parchment was precisely what the Vatican had believed it to be all along, but for some reason the people who had it in their possession had decided to publicly renounce the truth and go along with the idea of it being a second-century fake.

And in fact, he suddenly realized, it really didn't matter which version of the truth was actually the truth. The Vatican and Christianity were off the hook, so to speak. If anyone in the future examined the parchment again and came to the conclusion that it was the genuine article, then they would have an uphill struggle to prove their case against the authoritative analysis that would be provided by the British Museum when the full report on the relic was released in a month or two.

Morini leaned back in his chair and breathed a sigh of relief. Finally, he could lock away the protocols in the safe and return to his normal duties. Hopefully he could forget the terrible doubts that had been plaguing him over the last few days. Shove them to the back of his mind and pretend they had never existed.

The Englishman hadn't answered his phone for the last two days, and Morini hadn't known quite what to make of that. He'd try one last time, to discuss the report that had just been released. He would need to call him off the hunt, because any other deaths now could open up the entire thing all over again.

He changed into his usual civilian clothes and left the Vatican City. He would, he thought, treat himself to an ice cream today, now that the operation had finally been terminated. It would make a pleasant change to wander the streets of Rome in a carefree manner, as opposed to the nervous tension that had been his constant companion for the previous week or so.

He headed toward his normal café, but as he turned almost the last corner, and walked down the tiny alleyway adjacent to the café, he was suddenly aware of a man approaching him quickly from behind, and he turned to see who it was.

The moment he did so, the stranger, a heavily built man with a dark complexion and black hair, slammed into him and knocked him to the ground, driving the breath from his body.

"I warned you," the stranger growled. "If you didn't give me Bronson, I told you I'd come after you."

A flash of mortal terror coursed through Morini's body as he realized who the man was.

"You don't understand," Morini said, his voice laced with terror. "I need to—"

"It's too late for that now, monsignor, far too late."

The Spaniard leaned down—it almost looked as though he was helping the old man up—and with a single powerful blow drove the knife that he had concealed under his jacket deep into the Italian's body, thrusting up under the rib cage and seeking out the vital organs of the upper torso. The tip of the blade ruptured Morini's heart, and almost immediately the Italian moved no more.

"Debt paid in full," Tobí murmured, then stood up, straightened his jacket and walked away without a backward glance.

AUTHOR'S NOTE

This book is of course a novel, which means that it's fiction. But as with all the books in this series, I always try to build my fiction on the solid ground of established fact.

Vatican Robbery

The daring robbery that took place at the end of November 1965 happened exactly as I described it in this book, and my account is based upon contemporary police reports and newspaper stories about the event. Obviously, I invented the profession of the two thieves, but because of the route they used to enter the Vatican it is almost certain that they were either acrobats or at the very least had extensive climbing experience.

They took only the four items that I claim they stole, a somewhat peculiar selection of treasures in view of the priceless relics that surrounded them when they effected their entrance to the building, and it is also a proven fact that in less than twenty-four hours three of these treasures—the replica crown and the two collections of literary manuscripts—had been returned in precisely the manner I described.

I have no idea whether or not the manuscripts that were returned to the Vatican were the originals, but in my opinion the only sensible explanation for this event is that it was a robbery to order, to allow a wealthy collector to get his hands on the genuine manuscripts. At the time, the Italian police were convinced that this was the most likely motive for the theft, and made statements to the press to this effect.

And I think it is at the very least a strong possibility that the two manuscript collections that were recovered were actually very good forgeries. Common sense suggests that nobody would plot or plan such a daring robbery, which was undetected until long after the thieves had left the Vatican City, only to hand back the three most valuable objects stolen that very same day. I have not been able to find out if the two manuscript collections are currently on display anywhere in the Vatican, or if they are locked away somewhere, out of the sight of anyone who might be able to raise doubts about their authenticity, but my money's on the latter.

Parchment

The background information that I supplied about ancient parchment and ink, and modern methods and techniques for making such ancient texts readable is accurate, if somewhat simplified for the purposes of the narrative.

Propaganda Due, P2

Again, the historical information in the book about the P2 lodge is accurate, including the details of the death of the banker Roberto Calvi, whose body was found hanging under Blackfriars Bridge in London.

One aspect of his death that has never really been explored is the possible significance of this location, the "Black Friars" being a direct reference to members of the Dominican order, who were specifically charged by the Vatican with investigating heresy. In short, with conducting the Inquisitions: the Dominicans were essentially the Pope's personal torturers.

It could be argued that Calvi had betrayed the Vatican through his machinations at the Banco Ambrosiano, and possibly hanging his body underneath a bridge named after the Dominican order was a not very subtle way of suggesting that he had died as a heretic, killed on the orders of the Pope like so many thousands of other heretics over the centuries.

The death of Pope John Paul I was entirely unexpected and in all sorts of ways highly suspicious, not least because it occurred within twenty-four hours of his announcing his decision to remove Archbishop Marcinkus and the other members of P2 from the Vatican Bank. Whilst there is no proof that he was murdered, it is fairly clear that he was unable to trust at least some of the people around him, and they may have felt that they owed a higher allegiance to the P2 lodge than they did to the Pope himself.

If this were the case, and of course now it is mere conjecture, then his supposed death from natural causes begins to look even less likely to be based in fact, and the idea of a deliberate act of murder increasingly plausible. But because the Vatican will never permit the autopsy of a Pope's body, there is almost no chance that we will ever find out for sure precisely what happened on the night of 28 September 1978.

Codex S

The monitoring system employed by the Vatican to monitor Internet searching, and which I named Codex S, is a figment of my imagination. But that doesn't mean that the Vatican doesn't actually have some system that works in a similar fashion.

The Pantera Rape

In the prologue I make oblique references to the rape of Mary, and this idea forms the core of the story. It is indeed possible, as I suggested, that the Roman Emperor Constantine—as the first emperor ever to embrace the new religion—might well have been troubled by the influence of a second-century Greek philosopher named Celsus. He wrote a comprehensive attack on Christianity called *The True Word*, which contained a detailed account of this alleged rape. His work has not survived, but it was later criticized in detail by Origen, who first stated each of the arguments advanced by Celsus, and then attempted to refute them, thus providing a largely complete copy of the earlier work.

Later writers have criticized the claim made by Celsus that the father of the man later known as Jesus Christ was a Roman archer, citing the lack of any historical evidence for this assertion. Interestingly, no writers have ever attempted to rebuke the idea of a virgin birth for the same reason—the complete lack of evidence—despite the manifest biological impossibility of such an event ever occurring. Whilst it is an extremely unpleasant idea to suggest that the founder of Christianity was the product of a violent rape, this actually makes far more sense than the alternative explanation that is claimed by the Church.

In fact, the story about Mary being impregnated in a rape by a Roman archer has been around for longer than most of the Gospels. The tale of course suffers from precisely the same problem as the Gospels, in that there is not a single shred of proof that the rape ever took place, or indeed that the Gospels themselves are anything more than works of fiction.

This is one of the most fundamental problems about Christianity: there are simply no independent sources that support any of the statements and claims made by the Catholic Church through the ages.

Ultimately, belief in God or belief in Jesus—or belief in anything else that cannot be proven—is simply a matter of faith, not a matter of fact.

Read on for an excerpt
from James Becker's

THE FIRST APOSTLE

Available from Signet.

SPRING, AD 67

Jotapata, Judea

In the center of the group of silent watching men, the naked Jew was struggling violently, but it was never going to make a difference. One burly Roman soldier knelt on each arm, pinning it to the rough wooden beam—the *patibulum*—and another was holding his legs firmly.

General Vespasian watched, as he watched all the crucifixions. As far as he knew, this Jew hadn't committed any specific offense against the Roman Empire, but he had long ago lost patience with the defenders of Jotapata, and routinely executed any of them his army managed to capture.

The soldier holding the Jew's left arm eased the pressure slightly, just enough to allow another man to bind the victim's wrist with thick cloth. The Romans were experts at this method of execution—they'd had considerable practice—and knew that the fabric would help stanch the flow of blood from the wounds. Crucifixion was intended to be slow, painful and public, and the last thing they wanted was for the condemned man to bleed to death in a matter of hours.

Normally, victims of crucifixion were flogged first, but Vespasian's men had neither the time nor the inclination to bother. In any case, they knew the Jews lasted longer on the cross if they weren't flogged, and that helped reinforce the general's uncompromising message to the besieged town, little more than an arrow-shot distant.

The binding complete, they forced the Jew's arm back onto the *patibulum,* the wood rough and stained with old blood. A centurion approached with a hammer and nails. The nails were about eight inches long, thick, with large flat hea 's, and specially made for the purpose. Like the crosses, tney had been reused many times.

"Hold him still," he barked, and bent to the task.

The Jew went rigid when he felt the point of the nail touch his wrist, then screamed as the centurion smashed the hammer down. The blow was strong and sure, and the nail ripped straight through his arm and embedded itself deep in the wood. Compounding the agony of the injury, the nail severed the median nerve, causing continuous and intense pain along the man's entire limb.

Blood spurted from the wound, splashing onto the ground around the *patibulum.* Some four inches of the nail still protruded above the now blood-sodden cloth wrapped around the Jew's wrist, but two more blows from the hammer drove it home. Once the flat head of the nail was hard up against the cloth and compressing the limb against the wood, the blood flow diminished noticeably.

The Jew screamed his agony as each blow landed, then lost control of his bladder. The trickle of urine onto the dusty ground caused a couple of the watching soldiers to smile, but most ignored it. Like Vespasian, they were tired—the Romans had been fighting the inhabitants of Judea off and on for more than a hundred years—and in the last twelve months they'd all seen too much death and suffering to view another crucifixion as much more than a temporary diversion.

It had been hard fighting, and the battles far from one-sided. Just ten months earlier, the entire Roman garrison in Jerusalem had surrendered to the Jews and had immediately been lynched. From that moment on, full-scale war had been inevitable and the fighting bitter. Now the Romans were in Judea in full force. Vespasian commanded the fifth legion—*Fretensis*—and the tenth—*Macedonica*—while his son Titus had recently arrived with the fifteenth—*Apollinaris*—and the army also included auxiliary troops and cavalry units.

The soldier released the victim's arm and stood back as the centurion walked around and knelt beside the man's right arm. The Jew was going nowhere now, though his screams were loud and his struggles even more violent. Once the right wrist had been properly bound with fabric, the centurion expertly drove home the second nail and stood back.

The vertical section of the T-shaped Tau cross—the *stipes*—was a permanent fixture in the Roman camp. Each of the legions—the three camps were side by side on a slight rise overlooking the town—had erected fifty of them in clear view of Jotapata. Most were already in use, almost equal numbers of living and dead bodies hanging from them.

Following the centurion's orders, four Roman soldiers picked up the *patibulum* between them and carried the heavy wooden beam, dragging the condemned Jew, his screams louder still, over the rocky ground and across to the upright. Wide steps had already been placed at either side of the *stipes* and, with barely a pause in their stride, the tour soldiers climbed up and hoisted the *patibulum* onto the top of the post, slotting it onto the prepared peg.

The moment the Jew's feet left the ground and his nailed arms took the full weight of his body, both of his shoulder joints dislocated. His feet sought for a perch—something, anything—to relieve the incredible agony coursing through his arms. In seconds, his right heel landed on a block of wood attached to the *stipes* about five feet below the top, and he rested both feet on it and pushed upward to relieve the strain on his arms. Which was, of course, exactly why the Romans had placed it there. The moment he straightened his legs, the Jew felt rough hands adjusting the position of his feet, turning them sideways and holding his calves together. Seconds later another nail was driven through both heels with a single blow, pinning his legs to the cross.

Vespasian looked at the dying man, struggling pointlessly like a trapped insect, his cries already weakening. He turned away, shading his eyes against the setting sun. The Jew would be dead in two days, three at the most. The crucifixion over, the soldiers began dispersing, returning to the camp and their duties.

Every Roman military camp was identical in design: a square grid of open "roads," their names the same in every camp, that divided the different sections, the whole surrounded by a ditch and palisade, and with separate tents inside for men and officers. The *Fretensis* legion's camp was in the center of the three and Vespasian's personal tent lay, as the commanding general's always did, at the head of the *Via Principalis*—the main thoroughfare, directly in front of the camp headquarters.

The Tau crosses had been erected in a defiant line that stretched across the fronts of all three camps, a constant reminder to the defenders of Jotapata of the fate that awaited them if they were captured.

Vespasian acknowledged the salutes of the sentries as he walked back through the palisade. He was a soldier's soldier. He led from the front, celebrating his army's triumphs and mourning their retreats alongside his men. He'd started from nothing—his father had been a minor customs official and small-time moneylender—but he'd

risen to command legions in Britain and Germany. Igno-
miniously retired by Nero after he fell asleep during one
of the Emperor's interminable musical performances, it
was a measure of the seriousness of the situation in Judea
that he'd been called back to active service to take personal charge of suppressing the revolt.

He was more worried than he liked to admit about the
campaign. His first success—an easy victory at Gadara—
might almost have been a fluke because, despite the best
efforts of his soldiers, the small band of defenders of
Jotapata showed no signs of surrendering, despite being
hopelessly outnumbered. And the town was hardly stra-
tegically crucial. Once he'd captured it, he knew they'd
have to move on to liberate the Mediterranean ports, all
potentially much harder targets.

It was going to be a long and bitter struggle, and at
fifty Vespasian was already an old man. He would rather
have been almost anywhere else in the Empire, but Nero
was holding his youngest son, Domitian, as a hostage,
and had given him no choice but to command the campaign.

Just before he reached his tent, he saw a centurion
approaching. The man's red tunic, greaves or shin protec-
tors, *lorica hamata*—chain-mail armor—and silvered hel-
met with its transverse crest made him easily identifiable
among the regular soldiers, who wore white tunics and
lorica segmenta—plate armor. He was leading a small
group of legionaries and escorting another prisoner, his
arms bound behind him.

The centurion stopped a respectful ten feet from Vespasian and saluted. "The Jew from Cilicia, sir, as you ordered."

Vespasian nodded his approval, and gestured toward
his tent. "Bring him." He stood to one side as the sol-

diers hustled the man inside and pushed him onto a wooden stool. The flickering light of the oil lamps showed him to be elderly, tall and thin, with a high forehead, receding hairline and a straggly beard.

The tent was large—almost as big as those normally occupied by eight legionaries—with separate sleeping quarters. Vespasian removed the brooch that secured his *lacerna,* the purple cloak that identified him as a general, tossed the garment aside and sat down wearily.

"Why am I here?" the prisoner demanded.

"You're here," Vespasian replied, dismissing the escort with a flick of his wrist, "because I so ordered it. Your instructions from Rome were perfectly clear. Why have you failed to obey them?"

The man shook his head. "I have done precisely what the Emperor demanded."

"You have not," Vespasian snapped. "Otherwise I would not be stuck here in this miserable country trying to stamp out yet another rebellion."

"I am not responsible for that. I have carried out my orders to the best of my ability. All this"—the prisoner gestured with his head to include Jotapata— "is not of my doing."

"The Emperor does not agree, and neither do I. He believes you should have done more, far more. He has issued explicit orders to me, orders that include your execution."

For the first time a look of fear passed across the old man's face. "My execution? But I've done everything he asked. Nobody could have done more. I've traveled this world and established communities wherever I could. The fools believed me—they still believe me. Everywhere you look the myth is taking hold."

Vespasian shook his head. "It's not enough. This rebellion is sapping Rome's strength and the Emperor blames you. For that you are to die."

"By crucifixion? Like the fisherman?" the prisoner asked, suddenly conscious of the moans of the dying men nailed to the Tau crosses beyond the encampment.

"No. As a Roman citizen you will at least be spared that. You will be taken back to Rome under escort—by men I can ill afford to lose—and there you will be put to the sword."

"When?"

"You leave at dawn. But before you die, the Emperor has one final order for you."

Vespasian moved to the table and picked up two diptychs—wooden tablets with the inside surfaces covered in wax and joined with wire along one side as a rudimentary hinge. Both had numerous holes—*foramina*—pierced around the outer edges through which triple-thickness *linum* had been passed, thread that was then secured with a seal bearing the likeness of Nero. This prevented the tablets being opened without breaking the seal, and was common practice with legal documents to guard against forgeries. Each had a short note in ink on the front to indicate what the text comprised, and both had been personally entrusted to Vespasian by Nero before the general left Rome. The old man had seen them many times before.

Vespasian pointed to a small scroll on the table and told the prisoner what Nero expected him to write.

"And if I refuse?" the prisoner asked.

"Then I have instructions that you are not to be sent to Rome," Vespasian said, with a smile that didn't reach his eyes. "I'm sure we can find a vacant *stipes* you can occupy here for a few days."

*   *   *

AD 67–69

Rome, Italy

The Neronian Gardens, situated at the foot of what are now known as the Vatican Hills, were one of Nero's favored locations for exacting savage revenge on the group of people he saw as the principal enemies of Rome—the early Christians. He blamed them for starting the Great Fire that almost destroyed the city in AD 64, and since then he'd done his best to rid Rome and the Empire of what he called the Jewish "vermin."

His methods were excessive. The *lucky* ones were crucified or torn to pieces by dogs or wild animals in the Circus Maximus. Those he wanted really to suffer were coated in wax, impaled on stakes placed around his palace and later set on fire. This was Nero's idea of a joke. The Christians claimed to be the "light of the world," so he used them to light his way.

But Roman law forbade the crucifixion or torture of Roman citizens, and that rule, at least, the Emperor was forced to obey. And so, on a sunny morning at the end of June, Nero and his entourage watched as a swordsman worked his way steadily down a line of bound and kneeling men and women, beheading each one with a single stroke of his blade. The elderly man was the second to last and, as specifically instructed by Nero, the executioner slashed at his neck three times before his head finally tumbled free.

Nero's fury at the failure of his agent extended even beyond the man's painful death, and his body was unceremoniously tossed into a cart and driven miles out of Rome, to be dumped in a small cave, the entrance then sealed by rocks. The cave was already occupied by the remains of another man, another thorn in the Emperor's side, who had suffered crucifixion of an unusual sort three years earlier, at the very start of the Neronian Persecution.

The two diptychs and the small scroll had been handed to Nero as soon as the centurion and his Jewish prisoner arrived in Rome, but for some months the Emperor couldn't decide what to do with them. Rome was struggling to contain the Jewish revolt, and Nero was afraid that if he made their contents public he would make the situation even worse.

But the documents—the scroll essentially a confession by the Jew of something infinitely worse than treason, and the contents of the diptychs providing unarguable supporting evidence—were clearly valuable, even explosive, and he took immense care to keep them safe. He had an exact copy made of the scroll: on the original, he personally inscribed an explanation of its contents and purpose, authenticated by his imperial seal. The two diptychs were secreted with the bodies in the hidden cave, and the original scroll in a secure chest in a locked chamber in one of his palaces, but the copy he kept close to him, secured in an earthenware pot just in case he had to reveal its contents urgently.

Then events overtook him. In AD 68, chaos and civil war came to Rome. Nero was declared a traitor by the Senate, fled the city and committed suicide. He was succeeded by Galba, who was swiftly murdered by Otho. Vitellius emerged to challenge him, and defeated the new Emperor in battle: Otho, like Nero before him, fell upon his sword.

But Otho's supporters hadn't given up. They looked around for another candidate and settled on Vespasian. When word of events in Rome eventually reached him, the elderly general left the war in Judea in the more than capable hands of his son Titus and traveled to Italy, defeating Vitellius's array on the way. Vitellius was killed as Vespasian's troops secured the city. On 21 December AD 69, Vespasian was formally recognized by the Senate as the new Emperor, and peace was finally restored.

And in the confusion and chaos of the short but bitter Roman civil war, a locked wooden chest and an unremarkable earthenware pot, each containing a small papyrus scroll, simply disappeared.

About the Author

James Becker spent more than twenty years in the Royal Navy's Fleet Air arm and served during the Falklands War. Throughout his military career he was involved in covert operations and numerous classified projects. He is an accomplished combat pistol shot and has an abiding interest in ancient and medieval history. His previous novels, *The First Apostle, The Moses Stone, The Messiah Secret, The Nosferatu Scroll* and *Echo of the Reich* also feature Chris Bronson and Angela Lewis.

ALSO AVAILABLE FROM
NATIONAL BESTSELLING AUTHOR

James Becker

ECHO OF
THE REICH

Berlin, 1936: African-American Jesse Owens wins four gold
medals in the Olympic Games. Hitler refuses to place the
medals around Owens's neck and vows to develop a means
of wiping "inferior" races from the earth.

London, 2012: Chris Bronson is ordered to infiltrate a group
of anarchists who plan to disrupt the Olympics. But he's
convinced that there's something even more sinister at play—
and soon finds himself immersed in a decades old secret and a
deadly revenge plot that he must stop before it's too late…

DON'T MISS
The Nosferatu Scroll
The Messiah Secret
The Moses Stone
The First Apostle

**Available wherever books are sold or at
penguin.com**